White Dog Fell from the Sky

Eleanor Morse has taught in adult education programmes, in prisons and in university systems, both in Maine and in southern Africa. She currently works as an adjunct faculty member with Spalding University's MFA writing programme in Louisville, Kentucky. She lives on Peaks Island, Maine.

White Dog Fell from the Sky

ELEANOR MORSE

FIG TREE
an imprint of
PENGUIN BOOKS

FIG TREE

Published by the Penguin Group
Penguin Books Ltd, 80 Strand, London WC2R ORL, England
Penguin Group (USA) Inc., 375 Hudson Street, New York, New York 10014, USA
Penguin Group (Canada), 90 Eglinton Avenue East, Suite 700, Toronto, Ontario, Canada M4P 2Y3
(a division of Pearson Penguin Canada Inc.)
Penguin Ireland, 25 St Stephen's Green, Dublin 2, Ireland (a division of Penguin Books Ltd)
Penguin Group (Australia), 707 Collins Street, Melbourne, Victoria 3008, Australia
(a division of Pearson Australia Group Pty Ltd)
Penguin Books India Pvt Ltd, 11 Community Centre,
Panchsheel Park, New Delhi – 110 017, India
Penguin Group (NZ), 67 Apollo Drive, Rosedale, Auckland 0632, New Zealand
(a division of Pearson New Zealand Ltd)
Penguin Books (South Africa) (Pty) Ltd, Block D, Rosebank Office Park,
181 Jan Smuts Avenue, Parktown North, Gauteng 2193, South Africa

Penguin Books Ltd, Registered Offices: 80 Strand, London WC2R ORL, England

www.penguin.com

First published in the United States of America by Viking Penguin,
a member of Penguin Group (USA) Inc. 2013
First published in Great Britain by Fig Tree 2013
001

Printed in Great Britain by Clays Ltd, St Ives plc

A CIP catalogue record for this book is available from the British Library

ISBN: 978-0-241-14565-4

www.greenpenguin.co.uk

Penguin Books is committed to a sustainable
future for our business, our readers and our planet.
This book is made from Forest Stewardship
Council™ certified paper.

ALWAYS LEARNING   **PEARSON**

for Catherine & Alan

I have walked through many lives,
some of them my own,
and I am not who I was . . .

—Stanley Kunitz, "The Layers"

White Dog Fell from the Sky

1

The hearse pulled onto a scrubby track, traveled several hundred feet, and stopped. The passenger door opened, followed by the driver's door. Two men stepped out. They walked to the rear door, and together the men slid out a coffin and laid it carefully on the ground. They returned to the car, struggled with something inside, and dragged out a limp body. It was so covered with road dust, its face was gone.

The driver splashed a bucket of water over it, nudged it with a toe. Rivulets ran down the side of one cheek, water etching through dust to walnut-colored skin.

"He's late, no more in this world," the passenger said.

The eyelids fluttered, and the driver said, "See, you are wrong." They stood a moment and watched the man on the ground. Then they loaded the coffin back into the hearse and fled. There would be trouble when the man came to. Or if he didn't, there would also be trouble.

The sun was risen above the first line of scrub when Isaac opened an eye. The light hurt. The hearse was gone, and with it the small cardboard suitcase his brother Nthusi had given him. A wind blew close to the ground, kicking up a fine dust, covering over the tracks. The dust would cover him too, he thought without interest, if he lay there long enough.

A thin white dog sat next to him, like a ghost. It frightened him when he turned his head and saw her. He was not expecting a dog, especially not a dog of that sort. Normally he would have chased a strange dog away. But there was no strength in his body. He could only lie on the ground. I am already dead, he thought, and this is my companion. When you die, you are given a brother or a sister for your journey, and this creature is white so it can be seen in the land of the dead. The white dog's nose pointed away from him. From time to time, her eyes looked sideways in his direction and looked away. Her ears were back, her paws folded one over the other. She was a stately dog, a proper-acting dog.

A cigarette wrapper tumbled across the ground, stopped a moment, and blew on. A cream soda can lay under a stunted acacia, its orange label faded almost to white. Seeing those things, he thought, I am not dead. You would not be finding trash in the realm of the dead.

He heard a voice nearby, a woman calling to a child, scolding. He sat up. No part of his body was unbruised. Which country was he in? Had he made it over the border?

He called to the woman, but she didn't appear to hear him. She stood with a child near a makeshift dwelling made of cardboard, propped up with a couple of wooden posts, with a roof of rusted iron and blue plastic sheeting. She gripped her child tight around his upper arm, and with the other hand splashed water from a large coffee tin. Her boy struggled and broke free, running so fast that tiny droplets of water fell out behind him. "Moemedi!" she cried.

"*Dumela, mma,*" Isaac said in greeting, getting to his feet and wobbling toward her.

She eyed him. Clouds of dust rose as he struck his pants with his hands. "Where am I? Which country am I in?"

She didn't answer.

He stood silently, and then said, "Please, *mma,* am I in Botswana?"

"*Ee, rra.*" Yes, sir.

His palm traveled down the length of his face, as though opening a curtain. His eyes filled with relief and with the fear of the kilometers between him and his mother and brothers and sisters and all he'd known and understood and embraced and finally escaped.

The woman must have seen the boy inside the man, lost like a young goat in the desert. "Where is your mother?" she asked.

"Pretoria."

"Your father?"

"Johannesburg."

"What are you doing here?"

He was unable to speak.

"Do you want tea?"

"*Ee, mma.*" He took a step toward her and fell backward onto the dog. As he was going down, his eye caught the soda can in the bushes. The sky had been blue, the dog white, but now the dog was blue and the sky white.

"You are drunk."

"No, *mma,* I've had nothing to drink."

"My husband is a jealous man. You cannot stay here," she said. Her body was already bent, even though her boy was young, running, running with his friends among thorns and discarded tin cans. She disappeared into the cardboard shack while Isaac sat on the ground with the white dog. Long ago before he'd gone to school, he remembered his mother telling him that there were oceans on Earth. She said that the water was so big, you could not see to the land on the other side. She'd heard that the water threads connected to the moon, so when the moon grew larger, the waters also grew larger, like an older brother sharing food with a younger brother. But she didn't know where the big water came from and went back to. Maybe to the center of the Earth, she told him, where it can't be seen, flowing underneath. His head felt like that water, with the moon pulling on it, the waters going back and forth.

The woman came back out of her house, with a tin mug. She brought a small stool for him to sit on. He stretched out his hand respectfully, right one reaching, left touching the right elbow. He bowed his head in thanks.

She sat on a rock near him and studied his face. "Where are you going?"

"I don't know."

"Are you hungry?"

"*Ee, mma.*"

She rose again and came back with a bowl of sorghum porridge. She poured reconstituted powdered milk on it and gave him a spoon. "Who hurt you?" she asked.

"No one."

"Why are you not telling the truth?"

"The journey hurt me. No one person. I traveled out of South Africa in a compartment under a casket."

"Surely not. But I did see a large car travel up that track. I saw the men pull you out and throw you on the ground. When you spoke to me, I thought if I do not speak, if I pretend I don't see it, that thing will return to the dead."

He smiled.

"You did not have money for the train?"

"The train was not possible." His friend Kopano passed in front of his eyes. Two men, wearing the uniform of the South African Defense Force, walking toward a van, no hurry. The train disgorging steam beside the platform. The conductor: *Get your dirty kaffir hands off.*

It did not matter whether she believed him or not. Now, the problem was not the journey that brought him here, but where to sleep tonight and the night after. In the darkness, it is said that you must hold on to one another by the robe. But where was the robe? He would need to leave here. He would thank this woman and be gone.

"What is this place called?" he asked the woman. Makeshift dwellings stretched as far as you could see.

"Naledi."

From what can you not make a house? Oil drums, grass, mud, sheets of torn plastic, tires, wooden vegetable crates, banged-up doors ripped from cars and trucks. Each place was called home by someone, maybe ten people, sleeping side by side on the floor, crawling out in daylight, when the sun is drying the blades of short grass that the goats have not yet eaten, drying the leaves of the acacia trees with its heat. For a few moments only, this Naledi would be wreathed in morning mist. Would he be here tomorrow to see it? He put his hand out without thinking and touched the fur of the dog.

"When did you come here?" he asked the woman.

"It doesn't matter when I came. The government says they are going to knock down all the houses."

"What will you do then?"

"*Ga ke itse.*" She shrugged. I don't know. "They'll bring the bulldozers and knock the houses down, and then the people will come back
and build the houses again." She looked as though he should know
these things. He watched her as she disappeared around the other side
of the house.

Outside Pretoria, where he'd lived, the police came after the sun had
set. You could hear people crying that they were coming. In the darkness they ran. They jumped over fences and disappeared into the night.
There were no maps for where they went. They rose from their beds
and climbed out their windows, and each moment was a place they
didn't know and had never been. With the sound of the police vans,
thousands departed under the rags of darkness. His mother didn't have
legal papers. She barricaded the door and hid under the bed and told
the children to be as still as stones. But the baby cried and the police
knocked the door down and they put his mother in prison for seventeen days. When she was gone, there was no food except grass and stolen mealie meal. Their stomachs heaved and sorrowed with emptiness.
The bitter heart eats its owner, his mother said when she returned. He
didn't know whether she was telling him that her heart had been eaten,
or that he must be careful not to let himself be eaten. After that, she
sent her young children, all but the baby, to live with her mother in the
place the whites called the homeland, which was nobody's homeland,
only a desolate place no one else wanted. His mother had to stay in
Pretoria, where there was work for her. She'd told Isaac, as the second
oldest, that he was not to cry for her, but sometimes when she was
gone and the wind had blown across the empty ground and drowned
the sounds of the night, he couldn't help the feelings that rose in his
throat and spilled out of his eyes.

He wanted to tell the woman in the cardboard house these things,
but he couldn't; his silence was the silence of an old lion that's been left
behind. And then he thought, no one has left you behind. You are the
one who's left everyone behind.

The woman returned, and he told her, "*Ke batla tiro.*" I must find work.

"Do you know English?"

"Enough." He didn't tell her he'd finished four years of university back home and started medical school. What was the point? He had no papers, no one would believe he had anything to offer but the strength of his back.

"Then you must go into the town and ask for gardening work at each house. Do you know how to say this in English?"

"I can say it."

"But they won't hire you," she said. "You are too dirty. Take off your shirt and give it to me." She went around the side of her house and poured water out of a five-gallon oil can into the coffee tin she'd used when she'd tried to wash her boy.

Isaac felt light-headed from the sweet tea and porridge. He couldn't see properly. He went to push up his glasses, but he found now that they were lost, probably in the bottom of the compartment under the casket. A single crease of worry marked the skin between his eyes, as though a thumbnail had carved it. He ran his hands over what remained of his hair, which, in his doubt and fear about leaving, he'd shaved, as though the straight razor moving over his head had been a holiness, the marking of an end, a kind of benediction. He was a solidly built man, eyes a deep well of intelligence, eyebrows like a bush. His ears were at a slight angle from his head, as though curious. His bottom lip was full, his top lip not. In his face was a kindness mixed with a certain ferocity.

The woman slapped Isaac's shirt against a rock, dipped it in the coffee can and slapped it again. She must have been pretty once. Her breasts were large and her bottom was firm. He thought her husband was a lucky man. She was a brightness in this place called Naledi.

He stood shakily and went around the back of the house to relieve himself. The white dog followed and stood by his side. High above his head, a black-shouldered kite circled. The bird did a great arc in the sky, turning its head with small jerks. Isaac peed into the hot dirt. His head felt wooly, his thoughts scraped down to bone.

When he returned, his shirt was draped over a post, and the woman had disappeared.

He went back and sat on the stool, and she crept up behind him and poured the shirt water over his head. He leapt up in anger, and then his anger trickled down his breast and onto his belly as laughter. The woman fetched more water and told him to wash. She gave him a stick to brush his teeth, and when he'd finished he smiled into her face, and she smiled too, and then she looked away and banged the coffee tin with the heel of her hand and yelled for her son. But the boy was gone, running wild over the goat paths with his friends.

"*Leina la gago ke mang?*" he asked her.

"Luscious Moatlhaping," she said. "That is my name." She didn't ask his.

"When it dries," she said, pointing her chin at his shirt, "you will go." But he couldn't think about that yet, could hardly keep his chin from falling onto his chest.

He lay down in the sun and dreamt troubled dreams, of pursuit, of open veldt that gave no cover or shelter. When he woke, sweating and confused, there was no sign of the woman, only the dog keeping watch. His head hurt. The wind had blown his shirt off the post. As he put it on, he faintly smelled the woman. It gave him strength. He wanted to give her something before he left, but he had nothing. In the suitcase, his brother had packed three shirts, a pair of pants, *mhago* for the journey—oranges and sweet biscuits. The undertaker who transported the dead would be eating the food and wearing his brother's shirts.

His feet were unsteady when he set out. From a distance came the sound of shebeen music. He pictured cartons of Chibuku strewn about, the taste of sorghum beer, raw and sour with the haste of brewing, old men with red eyes. The music grew louder. He felt someone following him, turned around, and there was the white dog, trotting behind, just close enough to keep him in sight.

"*Tsamaya!*" he said, flinging his arms in the air. The dog cowered and crouched down.

"*Tsamaya!*" he yelled again. Go away! He stooped down and pre-tended to pick up a rock, and she slunk away, looking over her shoulder. He set forth again, but when he turned, there she was, trotting the same distance behind him.

The shebeen was close now. Then he saw them: sitting on their rickety *kgotla* chairs in the shade of an acacia were the same sorts of old men he'd seen a hundred times at home in South Africa.

"*Dumelang, borra,*" he greeted them. They stared suspiciously. "*Lo tsogile jang?*" How are you?

"*Re tsogile,*" said the oldest, continuing the greeting.

He pulled up a three-legged stool and sat a little distance from a man with grizzled salt and pepper stubble on his chin. On the radio, a new group was singing, a woman wailing. Her voice sounded like the yelping of a wild dog. So much animal. You'd want to know that woman. You'd also want to keep your distance.

"Which way to town?"

"Go that way," said the oldest man. "Follow the path, and there is the road. Northward is the town." He waited for Isaac to say where he came from and where he was going but was met with silence. The less people knew about where he'd come from, the safer for everyone. Isaac rose to his feet, thanked them, and was gone.

The path was strewn with goat droppings and cans. Behind him, the music grew fainter. He heard a rumble in the distance, and as he emerged from the bush he was enveloped in the dust of a three-ton truck traveling south in the direction of Lobatse, sliding through the sand like a wounded beast. With every step, he shed parts of himself—friends he'd never see again, debts of kindness he'd never repay, empty hopes, his biochemistry notebook, his anatomy and physiology book as thick as a fist. He was surprised how fast that life was dropping from him. He thought how soon he'd be unable to imagine himself walking on the streets that had been his home, how even the memories would fade to ghosts and then to nothing. He wanted to chase after them, but he would be running backward.

The future was blank. Only two days ago, it had been inhabited with obligations and dreams, by soft-eyed Boitumelo, by his mother, and by Moses and his other brothers and sisters; it had been pointing the way to sweetness like a honey badger running toward a hive. He pictured his little brother Moses sitting on the ground, his hands fashioning a car from bits of tin can and wire he'd found here and there. You hold the future for others, not only for yourself.

His mind swirled, became confused, remembered things he didn't want to remember. Back home, a few months before he left, he'd walked out one late afternoon to buy a half loaf of bread, and he'd seen a crowd catch a middle-aged man suspected of complicity with the South African Defense Force. They took that man, and they beat him with sticks and tire irons; they kicked him in the belly, and when he was unable to stand, they sat him in the middle of the road, forced a tire over his head, drenched it with gasoline, and lit it. There was nothing to do but turn away.

The sun was becoming hotter now. The path scrubbed along beside the main road, a road for feet. A group of men were coming his way, kicking up sand. He sensed trouble, but there was no time to get out of their way. He walked slowly to one side to let them by, dropping his eyes. He saw two large, flat feet pass by, then smaller dark feet in flip-flops. The third set of feet, wearing black leather shoes without socks, stopped in front of him.

"What the hell are you doing here?"

Isaac pushed past.

"Stop!" said the voice.

He broke into a run, but the hunger made his legs sluggish. He tried to push his body forward but it refused, and then he felt his shirt pulled backward.

"Isaac Muthethe!"

No one knew him here, he knew no one. How did the police get his name? He chopped at the hand holding him.

"What the fuck," said a voice, half laughing.

He turned to find Amen, an old classmate from secondary school.

"I thought you were the police."

"You beggar," Amen laughed, "do we look like police?" He picked up Isaac's hand and held it. "This is my friend," he said to the others.

Isaac looked into Amen's face, which had changed, hardened. He'd had no idea he was here and suspected he was doing ANC work. He'd grown a beard, a scraggly "O" around his mouth which crept from his chin to his ears, partly covering a dimple in his right cheek—a feature that had made him look mock-innocent in school but now looked mistaken.

"Kopano is dead," Isaac said. "I was beside him when they killed him. It's no longer safe to stay back home."

"I didn't know."

They walked a few steps. "So you will avenge his death."

Isaac stopped. "What does that mean to avenge a death—kill once, twice, three times more? Where does it end?"

Amen's eyes were set wide, one looking left while the other looked straight ahead so that it was impossible to escape his gaze.

"I'm saving my own life, that's all."

"If you're saying you're a coward, Isaac Muthethe, you're not the Isaac I once knew. Where are you staying?"

"I have no place."

"Where did you stay last night?"

"I was over the border last night."

"Come to my house. I have a wife now. And a little girl. Also with us are three comrades, and another woman and her child. What's one more?" He looked at the white dog. "Did you bring this one with you?"

"No." The dog moved back a few paces and hunched beside a bush. The word "comrades" meant that it was true: Amen was working with MK, the military wing of the ANC. Botswana was the staging area for violent acts against the South African Defense Force across the border. It was not work he himself could do. Not because he was afraid to die. Was that true? Maybe he couldn't spare his own precious life for something bigger. Why else had he fled? "Yes, I'll come with you," said Isaac. Later, he'd look back and see that this moment led to another that led all the way down a road he'd never meant to travel.

"First we must see someone," said Amen.

The group walked back into the twisted paths of Naledi. Again, the white dog trailed at a distance. The music of the shebeen grew louder again. The same men still sat under the tree.

Beyond the packed dirt where the old men drank, Amen took a path to the right. After five minutes, they turned left, and then right, and then right again. Then down a smaller path, a single rut, finally stopping in front of a door—really a piece of rubber from a truck bed that was tacked over an opening. "Wait here," said Amen to Isaac while the rest went inside.

Isaac sat in the dust, looking in the direction of Kgale Hill. There was talk, low in the throats of the men inside, and the sound of one man speaking, first contemptuously, then pleading. It seemed he owed them something. His voice reminded Isaac of the way people back home implored a policeman: a voice stripped of its manhood, a faltering don't-hurt-me sound, an eating-dirt, empty ragman voice. He thought about lifting the piece of rubber to see what was happening. And then the sounds grew worse. If it had been one man to one man . . . but that wasn't what it was. *Meno a diphiri.* The teeth of hyenas.

The dog whined.

"*O a lwala,*" he told her. He's sick, that man in there. "Soon he'll be better . . ." A fist or shoe bore down. The man groaned. He'd heard that Botswana was a peace-loving country, that you could sleep safely in your bed at night. Now things had gone quiet, and he felt afraid.

The rubber door trembled. "Pah!" said Amen, slapping out. "He shat his pants!"

Isaac turned away. That meant he was alive, he supposed. The others moved away from the door.

He looked at Amen. "What did you do it for?"

"He was one of us, and he tried to turn his back."

"So what will happen?"

Amen spat and started down the path. "He'll go home," he said over his shoulder.

"And be arrested," Isaac said.

"Maybe not, it doesn't matter."

"It does matter," said Isaac. "You won't live to be thirty if you keep using your fists."

Amen stopped and turned to face him. "This isn't what I choose either, understand? But you like what's happening back home? You like it? Then go back there, man. Ha! Go back and enjoy the life they've carved out for you. Live in a little rotting box. Scuttle out onto the street like a cockroach."

I'll stay with him for a few days, Isaac thought. Only a few days.

2

Kagiso was cooking when they reached the house. "My wife," said Amen. She smiled shyly, bent her knees a little, and clasped her two hands together. When she looked up, her mouth was open in a wide smile, as though she were saying WAH! Her face was still girlish, her mouth plump, her teeth very white. She wore a light cotton dress made from navy blue material and a scarf tied over her head, knotted behind her neck. As she stirred beans over a fire, straight-legged, bent at the waist, thumping the sides of a three-legged pot with a big wooden spoon, the breeze stirred her dress. The moment filled him with desire, not just the smell of beans and goat trotters coming from the pot, but also—Isaac had to look away—the smooth skin at the back of her legs, the hair curling out from under her scarf at the nape of her neck.

Amen gestured for Isaac to sit down on the stoop. At first he said nothing, then, "What happened?"

"What do you mean?"

"To Kopano. I want to know the whole story. And what you're doing here." One did not trifle with Amen, not years ago when he was thirteen or fourteen back in school, less so now. His wide-set eyes were intense, passionate, but something else was there too—an ancient injury living side by side with an easy arrogance. Menace, the child of this union.

Isaac felt like a bird falling from the sky, sinking into sand. He wanted just to sit in the waning sunlight and watch Kagiso stirring the pot. He was tired, too sad to speak. He saw himself on that day, standing in the clear winter sun on the train platform next to his friend.

"Kopano and I were waiting for a train to Pretoria," he said. "We had a month's holiday from medical school. Kopano was going home. I was going to see my mother. And then to see my granny and my younger brothers and sister in Bophuthatswana."

He remembered on that day the white butterflies were migrating. Isaac had never asked anyone where they came from or where they were going. He doubted whether anyone in the world knew. While they waited, Kopano talked about someone he'd met, a man who was head of the Black People's Convention. Kopano's voice rose and fell in the sunshine while Isaac watched the blizzard of butterflies, hundreds of thousands pouring northward, delicate white wings beating the air, going places he'd never go. Every now and then, one would glide close enough for him to see the brown veins and the brown tips of the wings, the color of a marula nut.

He felt the beat of the train in his feet before he saw it. Then it appeared in the distance, its homely black engine engulfed in steam, the goods and passenger cars trailing behind. A glint of metal on the front of the locomotive flashed in the sun.

"We watched the train as it came toward us."

The white butterflies lifted higher into the air, and the rumbling of the wheels filled Isaac's body. Kopano looked upward, his eyes following the still wings gliding on air currents. His face, normally fervent and weighed down with responsibility, relaxed and lifted. He may even have smiled.

"Two white men, wearing the uniform of the South African Defense Force, seized Kopano and threw him into the path of the train." The men seemed to hesitate, as though deciding what to do with Isaac. Then they turned, walked down the platform in no particular hurry, and climbed into a police van.

"Did you try to stop them?" asked Amen.

"They came out of nowhere."

"Afterward?"

"No." People who saw what happened moved away. They hurried into second- and third-class train carriages; women held their babies close.

Isaac found a conductor on the platform. He would not tell Amen what happened next. He'd never tell anyone. To his shame, he went down on his knees, holding the conductor's pant cuff. *Please, baas, please help, I beg of you. My friend is under the train.*

Get your dirty kaffir hands off me. The conductor glanced at the tracks. *Your friend should have been more careful.*

He was pushed. You saw it. It was no accident.

The conductor kicked out with his shoe. *I tell you, boy, get away.* The train departed, and what was left of Kopano lay between the tracks.

Sitting in the afternoon sun now, safe in another country, Isaac closed his eyes and found nothing between him and it: the sound of the train receding, thunder in his ears, Kopano's body dragged down the track, blood sprayed onto dirt and gravel. And the horror of a small gray mouse running between the rails looking for food.

"I walked to the hospital. I got them to fetch the body. I caught the next train to Pretoria, and I told Kopano's mother and his grandmother. I told you already, I'm here to save my hide."

He rose and went behind Amen's house, his head bowed, unable to bear the thought of Kopano's mother. She'd been expecting her son. She'd cooked all day. Her hair was newly plaited. He imagined her sitting in the shade, a neighbor braiding her hair, smoothing it with her hands, their low voices, her joy.

Isaac sat on his haunches and looked at nothing. The heat was stifling.

Growing up, he'd thought of himself as ordinary, the second of six children. But others thought differently. He was "the smart one," encouraged to remain in school. His mother had once told him, "Each person on Earth carries with them their own pouch. That person brings it wherever they go, carried in their hand. Your pouch never empties, only fills and fills. What's on the bottom remains on the bottom and is covered over in time. You are given things to care for. You are given things that are difficult to understand."

In his pouch were his mother's white employers in Pretoria who had no children of their own. They'd singled him out, paid his school fees, given him books, paid for him to go to university. After he'd graduated, Hendrik and Hester Pretorius said, Keep going. He applied to the University of Natal Medical School, Non-White Section, and was accepted. Until Kopano, his pouch had been filled only with good fortune.

Stephen Biko, the antiapartheid activist, had attended the same medical school as Isaac and Kopano. If it hadn't been for Biko, Isaac wouldn't have been at Kopano's side when he was killed, and he wouldn't now be in Botswana. But the legacy of Biko shamed him into joining the South African Students Organization. He hadn't wanted to go where there was trouble, but he attended one illegal meeting with his friend, and then another, until it was unthinkable to stay away.

On September, 12, 1977, not long after Kopano's murder, Biko died in detention in the Eastern Cape province. Colonel Pieter Goosen, the commanding officer of the Security Branch in Port Elizabeth, suggested that Mr. Biko might have fallen on the floor during a scuffle and bumped his head. The postmortem examination showed five lesions to the brain, a scalp wound, a cut on his upper lip, abrasions and bruising around the ribs. After the "scuffle," Mr. Biko was shackled and handcuffed, left naked for a couple of days, and finally driven twelve hours in a semiconscious state to Pretoria, where he died from a brain hemorrhage.

Blacks were not allowed to travel to King William's Town where Biko's funeral was held. Although Isaac hadn't been there, he'd read what Desmond Tutu had said before the crowd of fifteen thousand: "The powers of injustice, of oppression, of exploitation, have done their worst, and they have lost. They have lost because they are immoral and wrong, and our God ... is a God of justice and liberation and goodness." The Reverend Tutu was a man worthy of respect, but Isaac could not agree with him. If our God is a God of justice and liberation and goodness, why does He not intervene?

Isaac and his oldest brother Nthusi mourned on the streets of Pretoria with thousands of others. *Amandla!* the crowd shouted. *Ngawethu! Power! The power is ours!* During the gathering, Isaac told Nthusi in a low voice that the police had killed his friend, and that it was likely they would find him next. He couldn't bear to look at his brother. When he finally glanced in his direction, he saw disbelief and rage. Nthusi's face said, *You. The one who carried hope for our family.*

"Why aren't you in hiding?"

Isaac repeated the words of Biko: *You are either alive and proud or you are dead, and when you are dead, you can't care anyway.*

"You're a fool," Nthusi said. "Look what happened to Biko. And to Mohapi, hanged in his cell. And Mazwembe. And Fenuel Mogatusi, suffocated. And Mosala, beaten to death. And Wellington Tshazibane, hanged in his cell. And George Botha, pushed six floors down a stairwell. And Mathews Mabelane, pushed out of a tenth-floor window . . ."

"Stop."

"They'll beat you until you have no brains. You might not care for yourself, but if something happened to you, it would kill our mother." An upwelling of anger caused Nthusi to lurch to one side, away from Isaac.

They walked along in silence, people all around them.

Finally, under his breath, Nthusi said, "You must go."

"Where?"

"North. To Botswana."

They walked back home in a sea of angry, sorrowing people—Zulu, Xhosa, Tswana, Sotho. The crowd walked slowly, a girl in a yellow dress holding her sister's hand, young men shaking their fists, a grandmother in a faded blue head scarf, all singing.

Nkosi sikelel' iAfrika
Maluphakamis'upondo lwayo
Yizwa imithandazo yethu
Nkosi sikelela, thina lusapholwayo

Nthusi had a friend who knew an undertaker who traveled back and forth across the northern border. This man had a special compartment fitted under his hearse for smuggling yellow margarine out of Botswana into South Africa, in defiance of the dairy farmers who wanted to keep margarine white so it couldn't be sold as butter. Every so often, this undertaker smuggled people in the other direction, into Botswana.

On the following Sunday, Isaac embraced his brother and asked him to say good-bye to his mother, to Boitumelo, to his granny, and his other brothers and sisters. He pushed the tears down into the leather shoes his brother had given him off his feet. He climbed into the hearse and lay down in the cavity. He was not a big man, but his body was jammed into the compartment, unable to move. Over the top, the undertaker and his cousin slid a mahogany coffin containing the body of a Botswana government official who'd died unexpectedly in Pretoria.

The hearse rattled north. The compartment smelled of metal and oil—and he preferred not to think of what else. He braced his mind the way a wildebeest braces its body against a sandstorm. His family came to his mind one by one, first his mother, then Moses, Lulu, Tshepiso, his youngest brother, and Lesedi, his baby sister. Then Kopano. Not his friend, no. Bloody shreds of matter without indwelling. No recognizable head. An arm beside the tracks. A shoe in the dirt. He heard his own voice pleading with the conductor, calling him *baas*, master, a word he swore never to use. *Please, baas, please help, I beg of you.*

Your friend should have been more careful.

Not if he lived to be a hundred would he forget. And that conductor wouldn't forget either. In some part of his crocodile brain, he'd remember the day his train crushed a black man.

The compartment under the coffin seemed to grow smaller. He imagined a jagged rock puncturing the casing of the metal container that held him. His body couldn't be far from the road.

After a time, the hearse slowed, the talking between the men in the front seat stopped, and he knew they were approaching the border. His heart beat into his ears; behind his closed eyelids, his skin prickled. He stopped breathing, listened, took a shallow breath, stopped, listened. A man outside was walking around the car. Then the vehicle was rolling again.

What had been a rough asphalt road became dust and deep corrugations. Isaac fought the instinct to burst out and upward, but he would have disturbed the dead, something more unthinkable than dying himself. Between Lobatse and Gaborone, he lay in a fetal position, slamming into the metal floor. He thought he wouldn't survive the beating. Then he thought he'd suffocate. He coughed and spat and finally lay still.

Isaac felt the weight and pull of Amen's passion on the other side of the house, the way he'd be dragged into it if he didn't resist. He moved away from the wall he'd been leaning against. His brother's shoes were made of hard brown leather, too small for his feet. Already, blisters were biting his heels and the tops of his toes. Meanwhile, his brother would be walking around in the flimsy sneakers he'd left behind in exchange. A dove flew onto the roof, and he looked into the sky. You survived, he told himself. Maybe it's a good thing; maybe it's not. His granny always said, *Don't worry about your own well-being. Worry about the well-being of people with less than you. If God breaks your leg, He'll teach you how to limp.* Nthusi's shoes would teach him that.

Amen and Kagiso and Isaac and the others sat outside and watched the loud red sun slip down. The dust in the air created a haze that settled over the dying day. Their voices sounded thin. *Pula e kae?* asked Lucky, one of the comrades. Where is the rain? *Ee, pula e kae?* said Khumo, another comrade. Already it was April with the chances of rain nearly gone until next year. Khumo's wife, Kefilwe, hummed and rocked their two-year-old child. Her eyes squinted against the sun, perspiration beading her forehead, up where the soft hair met her face. She looked sallow-skinned, spent. Where is the rain? Where? Like a song, an incantation to whoever made the clouds.

  When Isaac's plate was empty, Kagiso filled it again, and then once more. "You eat like a hyena who's lost his kill to vultures," she said. He laughed. When he'd finished at last, she spooned what little remained onto the ground for the white dog. Then, with her legs stretched out in front of her, she held her baby, Ontibile, in her lap and pulled out her breast. The child nursed hungrily, her hand kneading and slapping at the breast. When Kagiso changed breasts, Ontibile looked into her mother's eyes, held the nipple with her teeth, and smiled as milk spilled from the corner of her mouth. When the sky darkened and the baby's eyes closed, Kagiso gestured for Isaac to follow her inside.

The house was a heat sink. Inside, a door connected one room to a second. Kagiso had hung magazine pages on the wall: a Lil-lets tampon ad with a black woman smiling, a child holding a McVitie's digestive biscuit and looking up at his mother.

While Amen held forth outside, Kagiso spread out two mats on the floor, one for her and Amen and their baby and one for Isaac on the other side of the room. He lay down, and strangeness overtook him. He didn't belong here. These were not his people. The child's sleeping breath took him back to his brother Moses, who had tangled around him in sleep all the years before Isaac had left for university. His youngest brother, Tshepiso, had slept near them like a solitary old ostrich, sometimes on the mat, sometimes on the floor.

Night deepened. Amen came in and lay beside Kagiso.

Isaac dreamt he was standing on a stretch of ground towering over a vast pit. His father's tiny figure labored far below. Hundreds of black men worked with picks around him. From one side, a small stream flowed into the pit. As Isaac watched, the stream widened, and water poured in. Men swarmed toward it, trying to stop the onrush. There seemed to be no path out of the hole. Still, his father stood. Just stupidly, as though someone had told him to stay in one place until he died.

Then Isaac was in a rattletrap truck with his uncle, his father's brother. They were hungry, and his uncle swerved this way and that, trying to run down a guinea fowl. The birds flew up, flew up, and still they could not pin one under a tire.

He woke. The night was very dark. A low, hot wind blew. He saw his father again: a loose slung bravado inside a ruined body. After Isaac had been born, his father had worked for many years in the mines. When he finally returned home, the babies began again. When money ran out, his father had returned to the mines and sent money each month. After a time, the money stopped coming. His mother had tried to get in touch with the mine to find out whether he was dead or alive, but her letters went unanswered. She thought he'd abandoned them. She wanted Isaac to share her anger, but the anger was in her heart, not his. He missed his father, the way he missed his mother now.

Differently from how he missed Boitumelo, her fragrant mouth, her warm breath against his neck. He'd told Nthusi to tell her he was gone for good, not to wait for him. They would have been married. Her hip bone jutted out like the rump of an eland. Her black eyes. Her teeth nipped his flesh, here, here. Now she'd marry someone else.

He woke again when the dogs of Naledi began to bark. Farther out, beyond the place where people were sleeping, he heard the wild dogs answering. The sound made a circle of wildness, enfolding and holding the world of people, like the darkness that surrounds the light of a lamp. It felt safe to him. The dogs were speaking to each other, passing their dog words between them. Outside, the white dog made a low noise in her throat.

3

Close to dawn, he felt a tugging at his shirt and opened his eyes. Ontibile had crawled toward him, half asleep, and lay down next to him. On the other side of the room, Amen's arm was thrown carelessly over Kagiso, his face vulnerable, his fists open, not remembering what they'd done to the man behind the rubber door.

Isaac got up quietly and sat on a rock outside the house. Ontibile followed him, laid her head against his lap and sucked her thumb. His palm touched the curve of her back and rested there. The white dog stood and wagged her tail uncertainly and sat down with her nose against Isaac's foot. Her coat was dull, and every one of her ribs stuck out. "I have nothing for you," Isaac said, "you must go find someone else."

Today, he needed to search for a job.

But people would ask where he was from, and it would be unsafe to tell them. He wished that his great grandfather were sitting here beside him. He would have known how to proceed. He'd known *monna mogolo*, the old man, only a few weeks, but he counted him as one of the wisest people he'd ever met. *Monna mogolo* was short, light-skinned, and had many wrinkles. He laughed easily, and his eyes crinkled shut with good humor. To protect his head from the rays of the sun, he wore an old Easter bonnet, the veil in tatters, the hat squashed almost flat.

Isaac hadn't left his side for the three weeks he'd visited. Great grandfather preferred to sleep outdoors. It was August, and the nights were cool and the moon full bright. The Hunger Moon, the old man had called it, the one before the rains. When the rains came, if they came, the moon would turn the color of an ostrich egg, he said—no, even whiter, like the white of a cattle egret's feathers.

During his mother's time and his mother's mother's time, *monna mogolo* said, his people's lands were taken by white men who hunted animals for sport and left the meat of the kudu and springbok to rot in the sun. Those people chased ostrich from their horses until the great birds could run no more and dropped to the ground. They laid claim to the water holes, muddying them with the hooves of their sheep and cows until you could no longer see the faces of ancestors in the clear water. His people were pushed into smaller and smaller spaces, and when they had no game to hunt, they began to hunt the white man's cattle on the nights when the moon was a sliver and the Earth was dark. They destroyed the fences and took the cattle. White men pursued them, killed some, seized others and put them in prison in Cape Town. Many in prison died from grief, locked away from their wives and children. Great grandfather had gone to that prison, and his son was taken away while he was there and put in a school where he was made to forget his own language. When you forget your own words, he said, you are like a tree without roots, a son with no father.

He told Isaac other things. He said there are two places on the body which other men read like a map. One is at the throat and one is at the solar plexus. He put his knuckle-heavy hand on Isaac's head. If you hold your head high and expose your throat and chest to danger, this says to others, *I am not afraid*. But if you are sunken-chested and hang your head like an old mule, people will know you are weak and fearful and they will slip in behind your weakness. This was what *monna mogolo* taught him, to carry himself like a proud, fearless man.

After his great grandfather went away, Isaac waited for him to return. One morning he woke with a strange tapping in his chest, like the beak of a bird tapping from the inside. He rose and said to his mother, "*Monna mogolo* is dead."

"Why do you say such a thing?" she said.

He went to school, he came back home, he ate porridge that night. The next day, he went to school, and when he returned home, his mother said, "My brother has told me our grandfather is dead."

Ontibile shifted in Isaac's lap and opened her eyes onto his face. A warm wind brushed his cheek, and mist rose from the dawn-damp earth. The moon was setting on one side of the sky as the sun was rising on the other side, huge and fiery red like a drunkard's eye. The white dog stretched her paws in front of her and got to her feet. The sun rose into the lowest branches of the trees, beating its slow steady beat. An uneasiness lay over the house.

His impulse was to leave now—walk out and find his way to town, but still he sat. A plane flew over. Ontibile got up and toddled behind the house. The dog followed her and then came back and sat near Isaac. Soon after, Amen came and sat on the threshold next to him. "*Ontibile o kae?*" he asked.

"She went around that side."

"Why did you not watch her? . . . *Tla kwano!*" he yelled. Soon after, she wobbled back and went inside.

Isaac picked up a small stick and twirled it between his palms. The sun was hotter now. The tin roof began to pop, expanding with the heat. Two doves called from a roof next door, the sound of death in their throats.

Isaac and Amen were quiet next to each other, listening to the sounds of the day waking. At last Amen spoke. "Do you remember my sister?"

"I never met her."

"She died on the sixteenth of June, in the Soweto uprising. My only sister. I quit school and joined the MK, *Umkhonto we Sizwe.* They gave me training in Angola. Six months the first time."

"I'm sorry about your sister. I didn't know."

"I received training in pistol shooting, hand grenades, the AK-47, explosives, and land mines. And also the building of secret cells, which Murphy Morobe and I have carried out in Soweto. Now, for these last nine months, I am in Botswana, participating in certain necessary raids back home. I am not at liberty to say more. But I can tell you that without work such as this, apartheid will never end." He paused. "You are a smart one," he said. "You would rise fast."

"It is not my way," said Isaac, standing.

"She was my only sister," Amen said again. "She did no one any harm. She was only asking to speak her own language in school. When the police shot her, she lived only a few hours. If I'd been beside her, perhaps I would have taken the bullet for her."

"Is that what you wish?"

"I would never wish to die."

Along the road, many people were walking, most of them in one direction. Isaac passed a young woman who was strong and handsome. A baby slept on her back, cinched close with a muslin wrap, then a plaid blanket wrapped over the woman's breasts and around her waist. Her hands were busy knitting. "*Dumela, mma,*" he said. "*A go khakala kwa motsing?*" Is it far to town?

"*Nnyaa, rra,*" she said.

She carried a sack, draped over one elbow, which he offered to carry for her. She slid it off and handed it to him. They walked together in silence, connected by a string of green knitting yarn.

"Where are you from?" she asked.

"From South Africa." And then he remembered it was not safe to say this.

"My brother works in the mines," she said.

"My father too, if he's alive." They walked along without speaking. "I'm looking for work," he said.

"Are you a good worker, or lazy?"

He laughed. "Do you think I would say lazy if I'm looking for work?"

She smiled, the same smile her baby had, sleeping against her back. Her fingers went very fast, knitting. "Is this your dog?"

"No, *mma,* she is only following me."

"Maybe she will find you work." She laughed. "Do you know how to garden?"

"No."

"When they ask, you mustn't say no. Say you've worked in many gardens. Do you have a letter of reference?"

"No."

"Then you must tell them that you have lost the letters, but you are a very good worker, very dependable. But even so, you will not get the job."

"Why not?"

"*Aiyee!* Too many people looking. Everywhere, looking looking."

"Where do you work?"

"In the Old Village. But the new village is better. I will tell you one thing: on Lippe's Loop, a gardener was sacked yesterday."

"Lippe's Loop, where is that?"

She pointed.

They walked along in silence again until he felt a tug on the bag. The woman said good-bye, turned toward a narrow path, and paused. "Go that way, up beyond a distance. At the third house on Lippe's Loop, you must ask." He stood at the side of the road and watched the baby's head bob gently against her mother's back.

As he set out, he felt a kind of happiness. The white dog walked by his left heel. He passed a house where a woman swept a threshold with a bundle of grass tied together. Her legs were straight and her bottom stuck out. Two goats walked, single file, into the bush. The sun shone bright and brighter.

You can't ever know what the next hour will bring, he thought. It can bring happiness or sadness, life or death. Hadn't this been true ever since he was born? Perhaps the police would come and take your mother away. Perhaps white people would offer to pay your school fees. Perhaps a spark from the cookstove would ignite the cardboard covering a window and your aunt's house would burn. Perhaps your brother would fall and cut his foot or your father's sister would die from tuberculosis. All these things had happened, but you couldn't know them beforehand.

He thought of Nthusi, how when he was young he'd heard about the Flying Wallendas who traveled all over the world, stretching ropes from the top of one high building to another, between one bank of the river and the other, over waterfalls and chasms. His brother had stitched together a place in his mind that let him fly over the tops of trees, across the world with a suitcase full of tightropes and bright, sparkly costumes. One day he found a rope, or stole one, and stretched it from the bumper of a rusted-out car to the hands of Isaac—all the trees had been cut down for firewood. "Hold it tight," he said, but when Nthusi tried to climb onto the rope with his bare feet, he dragged Isaac across the dirt. Then it was Isaac and his sister Lulu holding one end, pulled across the dirt toward the car bumper, then Moses and Tshepiso, with their feet braced in the sand, and Nthusi trying to get up on the rope. They held him, but he fell and fell. And then Isaac tried and he fell, and his sister Lulu tumbled onto the ground before she even tried because her laughter made her eyes close.

Before Isaac left, his brother told him that Karl Wallenda, the greatest tightrope walker in the world, had fallen to his death. It had happened in March, several months before. The rope had been stretched between two hotels in Puerto Rico. A high wind blew, and Karl Wallenda's wife begged him to wait, but he said no, he'd be all right, not to worry. When he got out between the two buildings, a gust hit him and at first it looked as though he'd regain his balance, but then he fell. He fell and fell, and the Earth that we call sweet became his executioner.

When Nthusi told Isaac that Wallenda had died, the light vanished from his brother's eyes and turned dead as ash, as though the suitcase that lived in his head had fallen with Karl Wallenda. And when Nthusi said good-bye to Isaac, it was as though Nthusi knew now that he'd never go anywhere, that he'd forever be the oldest son who cared for his mother—the one to comfort her, the one who'd do his best to earn enough money to send the little ones to school when he was too large and ignorant to ever go himself. Nthusi's eyes became dark smudges of light, like smoke that rises from a fire that hasn't enough wood.

Of all the members of his family, Nthusi's heart was the bravest. But in the case of his brother, it would have been better not to have been born for all the joy that his life would bring him. What was God thinking, to punish his brother like that? Sometimes it felt that He didn't think at all, that humans—especially black ones—were his playthings. It seemed that white people were the ones who believed in divine justice. That was because long ago, they'd come with their guns and greed and taken what they wanted. They'd long since forgotten what they'd done, and now they thought the land had always been theirs.

The bitter heart eats its owner. It was necessary to forget certain things but not his brother who gave him his own leather shoes for the journey. He walked along, listening to the way the soles of his brother's shoes thumped the sand softly, like guinea fowls landing in dust. Someday, he'd do something for Nthusi, ten times over. But that time was not now, maybe not for many years.

A man was approaching from the opposite direction, carrying a sack of sugar over his shoulder. Isaac crossed the road and waited. "Excuse me, *rra,*" he said, "where is Lippe's Loop?"

"I don't know," the man said, walking on.

He passed several more streets. The trees were gone. Everywhere, the houses looked the same. White with blue trim. He wondered who lived in them. He'd never been inside houses like these. From outside they looked strongly built. But the trouble was, they were so much the same, you could be drunk and walk into your neighbor's house and never know the difference until you lay down with his wife.

The white dog was limping, and he stopped and lifted her paw. There was blood, but he couldn't see what caused it. He spit on his thumb and rubbed the spit over the pad. She leaped away from him. "White Dog," he said, "come here." And then he realized what he'd done: when you name an animal, she becomes yours forever. He went down on his haunches and looked at her. "You're unfortunate to have ever chosen me," he said. "I have nothing to give you." She returned to his side. He took her paw again, and she held very still, shaking. A thorn was lodged deep. He talked to her and told her that it would hurt to pull it out. He tried to grasp the thorn but it broke. He pinched and squeezed and brought it to the surface while the dog stood patiently, her eyes pained. The thorn was from the tree that grabs you and won't let go. Now, it had the pad of her paw, but finally—*out!* She danced and leapt off her four feet in gladness.

When he wasn't expecting it, he found Lippe's Loop and turned down the road. It was an empty road, without people. The woman said the third house, but there were three houses on the right and three on the left. He chose right. A dog came barking up to a gate, a Doberman who could rip your throat out. White Dog sat at a distance, her ears pointed, hackles raised. Isaac tried talking to the barking dog. "Please, *rra,* let me pass. I need a job." But the dog barked furiously and leapt at the fence.

A servant woman came out. "What do you want?"

"*Ke batla tiro.*"

"There is no work."

He turned and crossed the road. There was another gate, but no dog. He told White Dog to wait, entered the gate with his head down, and closed it behind him

"*Koko?*" he called, rapping on the door.

A white woman came out of the house. She had a blue dress and short white hair and an expression of distaste on her face.

I'm not a thief, he wanted to tell her. "I'm looking for work," he said.

"I have no work," she said.

He pointed next door. "In this house, do they have work?"

"I don't know. You have to ask yourself." She turned her back on him and went into her house. He went out the gate and closed it behind him. White Dog was waiting. The Doberman barked crazily.

He tried next door. "*Koko?*" He waited. And then he saw a gardener slopping water out of a hose onto hard-packed earth and moved on. At the next house, he knocked again. No one came, but he felt eyes looking at him from behind shiny, blank windows. Those eyes made the back of his neck prickle, and even though a lilac-breasted roller flew over his head in a flash of brilliant blue wings and turquoise head, he only half saw it.

When he finished walking Lippe's Loop, he left that street and went down the next one that said "loop." He could see the pattern—there were loops and a cul-de-sac in between. On this street, there was also nothing. Shame sat heavy on his head, that he should need to beg like this. He turned back to the main road. Everywhere, it was the same. The people living on the other side of the walls, with their courtyards spilling bougainvillea—red, fuchsia, white, purple—their servants hanging their sheets and pillowcases and shirts on the line, their gardeners laboring in the sun, what did those people know? Had they ever seen a police dog go after a child? Seen their mother dragged off to jail? He began to feel anger at the peace he found here and the complacency of the blue sky and quiet roads, the watchdogs that made sure nothing would change. It was peaceful, yes, but what was the measure of this peace? It seemed that just under the surface was a familiar order—a few people owned everything. Aristotle said that it was unbecoming for a young man to utter maxims. But how could you resist Aristotle's maxims? In a democracy, Aristotle said, the poor will have more power than the rich because there are more of them, and the will of the majority is supreme. In time, Aristotle's wisdom would be borne out. It was necessary to believe this. Otherwise, where was the hope?

He called White Dog and went back toward the main road and down another cul-de-sac with houses on either side. They looked unused. You wouldn't want to enter them. The earth was scuffed and swept clean as concrete. Flowers were planted in tight little formations. He knew why people got rid of everything green. They were frightened of snakes. They wanted the ground clear so they could see a black mamba from a long way off.

He knocked on gates all day, eighty, a hundred, he lost count. At last, he turned toward Naledi. White Dog trailed, her tail down, ears back, as though she'd heard each "no" and needed to lie down and put her head between her paws. A truck passed on the road heading north, and a cloud of dust fell over their heads. Isaac left the road and sat on his haunches in the bush near where a footpath branched three ways. Flies buzzed around a pile of goat droppings. A Toyota truck passed on the road, and then a Peugeot. "What shall we do?" he asked White Dog. Small pouches of fatigue bagged under her eyes. She wagged her tail at the tip. Neither of them had had food or water all day.

When he reached Amen's house, the sun had nearly set. He poured water for White Dog and drank from a tin cup. Khumo, Amen, and Lucky were away. Kagiso said they were working.

"When will they be back?"

"I don't know," she said, her face sorrowing.

"Where have they gone?"

"This also I don't know."

She dished up a plate of mealie meal and beans and gave Ontibile her breast while Isaac ate. When he'd finished half the plate, he gave the rest to White Dog. Music from the neighborhood shebeen floated through the air. A bat flitted here and there after mosquitoes. In the waning light, Kagiso's nipples were erect and plump with milk. As Ontibile began to nurse, a small pool of darkness widened across Kagiso's dress as her other breast leaked in sympathy.

She seemed very unhappy. "Are you frightened?" he asked softly.

"Of course. One day he won't return, and then what will I do?"

You will marry me, he thought, and I'll be Ontibile's father. "I don't know," he said. The sky was almost completely dark now, and night was beginning: the sound of barking dogs, the relief of shadow, the earth giving off its faint moisture. "Where were you born?" he asked.

"Here in Botswana."

"You have family in Gaborone?"

"In Mochudi. Sometimes I think of going back to them . . . But please," she said hurriedly, "you won't tell him."

"No." You are very beautiful, he thought. Her face was meant for joy.

"Did you find a job?" she asked.

"There was nothing."

"Tomorrow maybe you will find something."

"Perhaps."

"If you pray, then you will have more luck."

"I don't pray for myself."

"Then I will pray for you."

He smiled at her. She was like a child. He was touched that she'd do this for him. He believed in something larger than himself, but there was no evidence to point to someone or something listening to a man with brown leather shoes and a sweaty shirt. He didn't find this unusual or disturbing. Why should he be noticed when there were so many others to notice? It was like the dry blades of grass at his feet. Every blade was different, reaching for the sky in its own humble way, but from a goat's perspective, they were all the same: something to eat.

"What was he like back then?" she asked, only her eyes and mouth visible in the darkness.

"Amen?"

"Yes, when you knew him in school."

"Pretty much the same." Brash, overbearing, reckless was what came to mind. "He was good at sports. Sometimes he pushed people around. He told funny stories, played tricks on people. He was someone you noticed."

"Did you like him?"

"Not very much, no."

"Why?"

"We were different." He saw himself back then, shy with others, a serious student. Serious in all things. He had to be. He knew this by the time he was eight years old.

"Yes, I see." Her body was swaying, rocking Ontibile. "Sometimes he pushes me around too. But I don't mind. I'm different from you."

How could she not mind? One day, she'd have a mind of her own, but now, she was young. She rose with Ontibile and went inside. White Dog sat down, groaning a little, and rested her cheek against his foot. The skin of her forehead was wrinkled; her cheek was also wrinkled where it pressed against him. He wished again that he could call upon *monna mogolo* and ask him what to do. He owed part of his being to this old man who'd given him love for the stars and the moon and the trees and the wide silent sky and the summer thunder, who made him proud to be a human being with the same blood in his veins. His great grandfather was what some people call a Bushman, but he thought this was not as respectful as calling him one of the San people. Back then, he didn't know what his grandfather's kind were called, or care. He only learned later, when his mother taught him a few words of the click language, the language stolen from his son while the old man was in prison. He didn't know how his mother had learned those words, only that they were precious to him now. His mother said that all the peoples on Earth come from the first San people. There was no one alive who did not have their beginnings in Africa. For thousands and thousands of years, the San people lived in the Kalahari, where they gathered food and hunted. What would the world be like now if it were peopled by them rather than the ones who'd stolen their land, killed their wildlife, stolen away their children and wives, and made them into slaves?

He thought, if they were like his great grandfather, there would be laughter falling from the sky. These days, people live in the world as though they are precious vessels, separate, each holding something that must be guarded. But his grandfather taught him something different. We are doorways, openings into something greater than ourselves, something that we don't understand and will never understand. We have nothing precious in and of ourselves. We are only precious in that we are part of something that is too big to know.

4

Before the sun was up, he was out of the house. He did not want to be seen, or to speak to Kagiso that morning. He took a little water and gave some to White Dog, who trotted beside him, her tail held high; then they were down the path and out onto the road. He could feel the heat at the back of his neck like a beast stalking him, its hot breath coming closer. His heart felt sad, his bones tired, but it was his duty, he said to the morning, not to give in to those things, not to dishonor the freedom he'd been given. The pain inside Nthusi's shoes reminded him with every step that he was here because of his brother.

He didn't know where those shoes would take him, but when he came to the place where the woman with the green knitting yarn had continued straight, he followed the way she had gone, toward the Old Village.

Although it was early, the road was already full of people. He passed women with tins of water sloshing on their heads, others with heaps of firewood piled high. Two school girls with scrubbed knees and blue uniforms, a man wheeling a single tire down the road, hand over hand. One half of a car, attached to wheels, pulled by a donkey and driven by an old man. A teenaged boy carrying a sack of sugar slung over one shoulder. A small girl with an even smaller child clinging to her back, legs wrapped around her hips.

When he had a job, he would buy paper and a pen, an envelope and a stamp and tell his mother that all was well. But these days, all was not well, and he wouldn't write to her, not yet. His old life felt farther away than the moon: his family's faith in him, the chemistry lab with its gouged wooden tables, his cell biology teacher, who walked with his wide feet splayed, his tie stained, his mind brilliant. The heat had already begun to travel off the pavement through the soles of his shoes. Where was the Old Village? A Toyota pickup truck came by, followed by a three-ton Chevy with people hanging out of the back. At last, he came to a small grocery store on a corner. He knew what would be on the shelves: oranges, a half sheet of newspaper folded around a half loaf of brown bread, chips, sweet bananas, Coca-Cola. Everything a person could want.

Boitumelo was to have been his wife. They were going to have four or five children. At work, he would have cured the sick, delivered babies, put his younger brothers and sisters through school. What you expect, though, is not what will be. When you're a baby, moving down the birth canal into the world, about to take your first breath, a young animal eager for life, you don't know that you'll come out into a dimly lit dwelling into the arms of a midwife, a woman with shriveled breasts and tired shoulders who's brought thousands like you into the world. You don't know that there's black and there's white, and you've arrived on the wrong side of the fence, boy.

He stood outside the store for several minutes, watching people come and go. Africans and Europeans were using the same door, and when he looked inside, a white woman at the counter was waiting on a black African man. It stunned him. Outside, someone had discarded the *Botswana Daily News*. It had been trampled upon, but it was still legible. He sat under a tree, cross-legged, and read the caption of a picture on the front page. "The Minister of State for Foreign Affairs, Archie Mogwe, greets the U.S. Ambassador, Donald Norland, on arrival in Gaborone." The two men were shaking hands. Another article began: "Water alight? Unbelievable, but villagers at Keng, some 125 kilometers west of Kanye, are convinced that they have witnessed a case of burning water and look on the incident as a sure case of 'super-witchcraft.'"

Inside the paper was a picture of a handsome man standing next to a white woman. To his astonishment, Isaac read that this man was the president of Botswana, His Excellency, Sir Seretse Khama, standing next to his wife, Lady Khama. They were holding a pair of scissors together, cutting a wide ribbon, presiding at the opening of an agricultural fair. Sir Seretse Khama had a large head, a black mustache, and a regal bearing. His wife was rather plain looking with a strong, kind face. She was pale and wore a small white hat. He'd heard a rumor of this marriage back home, but he'd dismissed it as an impossibility. Nowhere could a black man marry a white woman, surely. But here it was, the two of them, their hands touching. He folded the paper carefully and put it in his pocket to study later. He felt dazed and disoriented. Not only Sir Seretse Khama and his European wife, but a newspaper full of the news of African people.

The trees grew larger down here in the Old Village. Vines spread over shaded patios. The servants' quarters were larger, with stoops to sit on. Chickens scratched in a yard. He turned down a small road, where three huge jacaranda trees grew beside an old colonial-style house with whitewashed walls and a wraparound porch. An odd noise, like an untuned radio, came from the rear of the house. He walked farther down the road to see what the noise was. Birds babbled in vine-shaded cages that hung from the back and side of the house and from the shade trees. Bee eaters in blues and yellows and greens sat in cages, parrots behind bars shrieked into the trees, parakeets twittered next to their mates. It was a carnival of birds, an amazement, although truth be told, it was sad to see them in cages. What is a bird if it can't fly? It might as well be a cockroach.

A gardener toiled in the yard, and Isaac walked on. Three houses farther up the road he asked for work and was turned away. At a fourth house, he was met by a barking Alsatian. White Dog put her tail down and slunk off to the side of the road. There was no fence or gate around the yard, and he saw no gardener. He put his hand out to the barking dog, thinking, she'll either bite it or sniff it. She did neither. He walked past her into the yard, wondering whether she was one of those stink-pot dogs who make you think they're your friend and then bite you on the ass. He wouldn't turn around. He'd make her think he wasn't scared, even though a little animal scurried up and down his backbone, yelping in fear. Alsatians had always spooked him.

A white woman came out of the house. She was dressed as though she was going to work.

"I am looking for gardening work, madam."

"Have you any experience?"

"Yes, madam." It was the truth, if it was life she was asking about.

"Do you have references?"

"No, madam. A thief took my suitcase on the train, but in any case, I am an excellent worker."

"Your English is not bad. You're from South Africa, aren't you?"

He nodded.

"Are you here illegally?"

He thought it best not to answer.

"Well, I don't mind either way. Our gardener left this past week—his mother took sick in Francistown. I'll give you a try and pay you in food today. If you do well, you can come back tomorrow."

"Thank you, madam."

She led the way to the side of the house. "I'd like a bed of flowers here."

"Marigolds?" It was the only flower name he knew in English.

"Not marigolds. There are already too many marigolds in the world. I don't know what kind yet."

"Yes, madam, thank you."

She handed him a spade, and he set to work. White Dog sat solemnly near the road, her paws crossed. Isaac dug, squaring the corners of the garden carefully, turning over the dirt and breaking up the clods with his hands, sifting it through his fingers so the smallest seed could survive. He worked steadily, not stopping for anything. When he finished, he paused. The woman came out, as though she'd been watching him.

"Why did you make it square?" she asked.

"I thought this is the way you would like it." White people were always making square corners.

"Don't think about what I like. Think about what's beautiful. Straight lines look like a cemetery."

"Yes, madam."

"Please don't call me madam. Have you eaten today?"

"No, *mma*."

"What do you like?"

"I beg your pardon?"

"What do you like to eat?"

To be asked such a question. "I like meat," he said quickly, then thought he might have sounded too bold.

She didn't look bothered. "I'll ask Itumeleng to bring you meat at noon when we have it. Have you met her?"

"No, madam."

"She's here every day. If you have questions when I'm at work, you can ask her. Give this bed some curves and then please put water on the trees in the back. They're new, and need watering every day."

"Yes, madam."

"Please don't call me that. When you call me madam, I feel like I'm a hundred years old."

He smiled and then grew serious. "What must I call you?"

"Call me Alice."

"Madam, I cannot."

"Well, then." She shrugged helplessly. "Don't call me anything."

5

When she'd first come here, Alice found that there were no basements in Botswana. Life was lived in the god-eye of light so bright, it felt as though you could hold your hand up to the sun and look through it to bone. How huge the sky was, broken by nothing. Birds flew into it and disappeared, like stones in water.

Lying in bed in the heat next to her sleeping husband, she wondered whether this was what had happened to the child she'd hoped to conceive. Would a baby be daunted to come into this world of interminable blue sky, heat that scoured your brains clean? The sky had been blue for months, unbroken by the smallest cloud. Some days she felt her throat wanting to scream, to break the flatness of that blue.

Within the past several weeks, she'd wondered whether the emptiness of her womb had to do with not loving Lawrence deeply enough. She blamed herself, and then she blamed Lawrence. She'd not expected to have to work so hard at love; it had become a kind of hard labor. The word that came to her when she thought of her husband was "hidden." She couldn't tell whether his emotional vagueness was something peculiar to him with her, or whether he'd be this way with anyone.

They'd been in Botswana a year and a half now, brought here from the States because of Lawrence's job. Alice had begun looking for work immediately and found a position with the Ministry of Local Government and Lands, working on land-use policy connected to the San people. She knew she was damn lucky; it would have taken her ten years to be qualified for a similar job back home. But she didn't feel lucky. She felt like crying. And she blamed herself for that too. Look around you, she told herself. So you never have a baby. Make a different life.

Lawrence stirred next to her. Because it was summer, they began work every day at seven and finished at five, with a big chunk out of the middle for napping. She touched him on the shoulder and then shook him gently. "It's time."

"You don't need to tell me."

"I thought you were asleep."

"I wasn't."

"Why are you grumpy?"

"Who said I *was*?"

They got out of opposite sides of the bed, dressed, and drove back to work together in her truck. His Toyota was being repaired. Before she let him out at the Ministry of Finance and Development Planning, he said he needed to work late that night, not to wait for him. "How will you get home?"

"I'll find a ride."

"And if you don't?"

"I'll walk."

"You could call me."

"Alice, stop."

"What?"

"Just don't."

6

It took Isaac three quarters of an hour to walk to the Old Village, White Dog at his heels. She who must not be called madam was outdoors when he arrived. "I need to go," she said. "I'm late for work. Please water the trees, and make a plan for the garden. As you can see, it's not had much attention. Could you make a garden plan, something different from the usual? Do you understand?"

"*Ee, mma.*" Why did white people always have to ask, *Do you understand?*

"Walk around the village," she said. "Or take the bicycle at the back of the house. Look at other gardens, and tell me what you think would work well. We'll pay you thirty rand a month. And my husband doesn't like water to be wasted. He's traveling for the next ten days."

And then she was off, backing her truck down the driveway. Suddenly she stopped and rolled down the window. "Is this your dog out here?"

"Yes, *mma.*"

"Is it a him or a her?"

"A her, madam."

"They should be all right then. I don't mind her as long as she doesn't fight with Daphne. I think things will work out fine. I'm glad you came back."

Why *wouldn't* he come back? He waved until she was out of sight.

This madam was the tallest white woman he'd ever seen. She had big bones, like a man's bones, and although her face was young, her hair was already becoming gray. She pulled it back from her face with a clip, but it fell back into her eyes. It was halfway between African and European hair, but an African woman would not have it falling everywhere. Her eyes were gray like her hair, and large, with a little blue in them. Her nose was not quite straight, as though it had at one time been broken. In the middle of her chin was a tiny valley. She was not an unpleasing looking person, but he didn't really trust her. Why didn't she tell him what she wanted? She was the one paying him. Something different from the usual? He didn't know what the usual looked like. He felt for a moment that he had not been born to be someone's gardener, and then he stopped and told himself that this thought was nothing more than arrogance. He was no better than the next man, and you can find happiness in any kind of work. But the thought returned, and with it the dream in which his father had labored in a vast pit. The waters rose and still his father stood as though he'd been told to stand still until he died. Would he too stand still until he died? For as long as he could remember, he'd felt that you were given one small, precious life, not to be squandered.

"*Tla kwano.*" Come. White Dog followed him into the yard, looking for the Alsatian, her hackles raised like a small brush fire. It wasn't long before Daphne discovered her cowering beside the house. She and Daphne circled and sniffed each other under the tail, and White Dog flopped down with her paws in the air, her mouth turned up in what looked like a smile. Isaac turned his back and disappeared. Leave them alone and let them work things out in their dog way.

He weeded and watered the new citrus trees, and then he went to the door of the house and called out for Itumeleng. She poked her head out. At first her face looked almost innocent, but look a little longer, and you saw something sassy in her eyes. A little girl clung to her skirts.

"I'm going out," he said. "Madam has asked me to look at some other gardens and come up with a plan."

"I'm not your wife," she said. "You don't need to tell me where you're going."

He laughed. "You wouldn't like me for a husband?"

She wrinkled her nose. "I have one child already. What would I do with another?" She turned to go back inside and stopped. "So she hired you?"

"*Ee, mma.*"

"Even though you know nothing about gardens?"

"How do you know?"

"The way you are digging yesterday. Like the spade is your master." She laughed. "And your hands are soft."

"Is this your child?" The little girl had her mother's dark, snapping eyes.

"What? You think it's madam's? Where are you from?"

"South Africa."

"What are you doing here?"

"Working."

"Most people find work there, not here." She thought she knew why he was here, he could see it in her eyes. "Are you with the ANC?"

"*Nnyaa, mma.*"

"So . . . if you're going, you better go," she said.

She reminded him of one of his aunties on his father's side, a saucy tongue in her head, hard to love but easy to like from a distance. He called White Dog out to the road. A neighbor dog slavered and barked and threw himself at a chain link fence. White Dog followed close behind. They hadn't reached the main road before Isaac remembered that she hadn't had any water. He retraced his steps past the barking dog and went back into the yard, turned the hose on, and cupped his hands to make a small bowl.

"You're back," said Itumeleng out the window. She gave him a square gallon tin for White Dog, who drank and drank. Isaac held the hose out and drank his fill too and then remembered that she who must not be called madam had said not to waste water. It was running all over the ground, gouging out a little stream bed. He shut off the faucet and scuffed out the evidence with Nthusi's shoe. Itumeleng came back out with two slices of bread. He ate one and gave the other to White Dog.

Setting out once more, he crossed the road and came out onto a footpath. He walked a bit, stepping around goat droppings, until he approached a widening in the path where he sat on his haunches. From this place, he could study how things grew. There were no straight lines anywhere. The footpath curved around rocks. The trees and shrubs and grasses grew up where a seed had fallen. So, this was the first principle: fling seed out of your hand and let it land where it will. And mix things up, large and small, rocks and plants. And don't make things too tidy. You want the crested barbet and the mourning dove to feel at home, the weaver bird to make its nest in a tree. The birds need grass and sticks and a certain untidiness. They don't want everything perfect, like a woman with cornrows and no hairs out of place. You feel with a very neat woman, if you touch her, she'll shatter. He called White Dog and went back toward the road, searching out the garden where he'd heard the birds singing in cages. He lingered at the gate, peering in, listening to the circus of sounds. A parrot with a blue neck cackled to its mate. Tiny little birds flew around inside the cages, chirping to one another. Inside the garden was a large sunken space, deep earth and shade, looking like coolness itself, surrounded by orange, lemon, and grapefruit trees and banana trees with long scarves of waving leaves. The sides of the sunken garden were lined with flat rocks, and in between the rocks were desert plants—blue green, dusty blue, some of them flowering, and a cluster of huge aloes with stalks. At the bottom were flagstones with creeping plants between them, and a small table and two upholstered chairs, facing into a syringa tree.

An old African with a crooked back, wearing a tattered safari suit, bent over a patch of flowers on the near side of the sunken garden. "*Dumela, rra!*" called Isaac.

The man turned and greeted him back. His hair was short and mostly gray. The knuckles of his hands were knobbed. His face was filled with calm, as though he'd seen many things and was tired now.

"I was studying to see how you've made the garden."

The man moved toward Isaac on legs that looked painful, took off a battered hat, and held it in his hand. He looked at Isaac suspiciously. "You're not from here, are you?"

"No," said Isaac.

The old man stuck the long tip of his little fingernail in his ear. He looked at his feet and said, "Sit," offering Isaac a piece of ground. They were quiet together, then unexpectedly the old man said, "Never trust a woman." Isaac could not have agreed less. He would trust his mother, his granny, or Boitumelo with his life, any one of them.

It seemed that the old man did not plan to elaborate, but after some time he went on. "I am telling you how I came to make this garden. I once loved a woman, a beautiful woman. We were happy. I thought myself the luckiest man in the world. But when our son was born, she grew restless. She neglected the cooking, she refused to wash our clothes. She gave our child to other people to watch. In those days, I was collecting firewood and peddling it from a donkey cart. One day, I came home and found her in bed with my best friend. This was a man I knew before I could walk and talk. At first I didn't believe what my eyes told me. I walked away into the bush.

"But I realized my eyes had spoken the truth. That night, I sharpened a knife on a stone and killed him. And then I put the knife down in plain sight and sent a boy to call the police. I thought of killing my wife too, but I was not able to raise my hand against her. I was held at Lobatse and transferred to Gaborone where I stayed many years.

"At first I made furniture in the prison. Then they put me in the garden, growing vegetables. In time I became the head gardener. When I came out of prison, I was an old man. That is how I came here, and that is why I tell you, never trust a woman."

Out of respect, Isaac didn't argue.

"These people hired me when I came out of prison," the old man continued. "They are good people, especially the madam. And no one else will have me now."

"Why is that?"

"*Ke a lwala.*" I am ill.

"*U lwala fa kae?*"

"*Go botlkoko makgwafo.*" The lungs. That is where I'm sick.

"You thought to make the garden this way yourself?"

"*Ee, rra.*"

"I'd like to make something like this."

"Why not? Take your time. Don't hurry. When you finish, come

back, and I'll give you some things to plant." He leaned over a succu-
lent and said, "If you cut here, put it in the ground, it will grow."

"Thank you, *rra*."

"I have a child as I told you," the old man said, "but I wouldn't know
him if he walked down that road."

"I have a father working in the mines outside Johannesburg, if
he's alive. Perhaps I would not know him now, either. You can drop a
city into the hole where he works. One man is so small, he disappears.
I saw this place only once. Small men die for big men. They live in a
prison just as surely as you were in prison."

"*O botlhale thata.*"

"No, *rra*, I am not wise. But I can tell you I don't want to be in
prison, my own or someone else's."

They spent several hours in the garden while the owners of the
house were out, the old man showing him plants, telling him their
names, the season when they bloomed, how long the blooms lasted,
how delicate or robust they were. "This is protea. Gladiolus. Zinnia.
Zinnia is a flower you can depend upon."

With White Dog trailing, Isaac returned to the house and watered
the garden again. That evening, walking back to Amen's house, he
swam in the names of plants: syringa, ranunculus, spider gerbera, calla
lilies, Christ thorn, lion's ear, Schlecter's geranium, white breath of
heaven.

Amen was still gone, and Kagiso was crying. "He goes away for a
long time and comes back without speaking. Last September," she said,
"he was one of the men to assassinate Leonard Nkosi, one of our own
people."

"Did he tell you this?"

"No. But I know it. I heard about Nkosi being killed. And I saw
with my own eyes. When Amen returned, he was a different man. He
was no longer a man I knew. But I still love him, that's the truth. Can
you love and hate at the same time?" She was looking at him as though
his words would seal her fate.

"If you say you do, you do. When all this is over, the two of you can
live in peace."

"It will never be over, and he will never be at peace. He has fire in his brains."

He understood why a woman could love Amen. He didn't get drunk and sit in the shade of a tree all day. He'd mastered fear. He knew what his life was being lived for.

"And now, God protect him," Kagiso whispered.

That night in the darkness, she thrashed and called out in her sleep. Isaac went to her and held her hand. He had no words that would both tell the truth and bring comfort, so he remained quiet. She couldn't know in the dark, but his desire rose in him as he squatted beside her. You are a weak man, he told himself as he stumbled out of the house into the night. He sat on the threshold for many minutes cooling his blood while White Dog kept him company. In the light of a nearly full moon, her eyes seemed to see another world. He didn't know who or what she was, but in this half light, he could imagine the dark sky tearing open and White Dog falling to Earth, getting to her feet, and sniffing its strangeness. She was not like other creatures. There was a patience in her that only wise beings possess.

In the morning, he left before Kagiso was awake, shaking off the broken night behind him. The sun was just rising, and only a few people were out. He wanted to have one more look at the sunken garden before he proposed the idea to she who must not be called madam. White Dog trotted on ahead. She sat a moment to squat and then rejoined him. Suddenly the sweetness of the day hit him on his head. You big stupid, he thought. While you're running around in your brain, all the time the sun only wishes to wake you to its beauty.

His stomach felt hollow with hunger once more, but he thought that soon his body would step beyond hunger and his stomach's cravings would end for a time. He passed the store on the corner and turned up the small road leading to the sunken garden. The birds in the cages were waking. Isaac crept into the garden. He wanted to stand in the bottom of the hole to see how deep it was, to see the stones at the bottom. He hurried down the steps and called softly to White Dog, but she wouldn't follow him. At the bottom, he sat down on one of the chairs to see how it felt, resting below the surface of the earth. If you could start each day like this, your head would be large and cool and your worries would be over.

He closed his eyes and stretched out in the chair.

"What the bloody hell do you think you're doing?" The voice came from above and behind.

He jumped up. The man was ruddy-complexioned, leaning over the hole.

"It's my mistake, surely," said Isaac scrambling up the steps past the man, head down. He ran hard and stopped only when he'd reached the main road. White Dog was already ahead of him. "I could have explained," he said aloud. He would have told that man how beautiful the garden was, how he'd meant no harm. His heart roared from the encounter. He thought, you are a fool. If he'd had a mind to take you to the police, you would have been returned to South Africa. From there, it would have been a short walk to your grave.

The land was broken up like a shattered mirror. A man like that could say what was his, and no one could argue. Every person alive thinks they are the center of the universe, that they are everything, when in fact each of us is less than nothing. A crested barbet flew to the top of an old thorn tree, its red feathers flashing, trilling metallically, like a sentry.

7

Alice found Isaac outside the door at quarter past six that morning. He was sitting next to his dog with his back propped up against the half dead tree that held the nest of the crested barbet. "Do you know what time it is?" she asked.

"No, *mma*."

"It's very early. Are you in trouble?"

"No, *mma*."

"You have a place to go at night?"

"*Ee.*"

"Far from here?"

"In Naledi."

"How long does it take you to walk?"

"I don't know, madam . . . *mma*."

"We have a bicycle we're not using. Why don't you ride it back and forth? It would be easier, wouldn't it?"

"Yes, but what if something should happen to it?"

"Nothing will happen to it."

"*Ke a leboga, mma*," he thanked her. "I have an idea for the garden. Shall I tell you now?"

He began to talk, striding behind the house. "Here," he said, "I will clear the ground so that the new fruit trees will have more light. Soon— maybe by next year or the year after—they will give you oranges and lemons and *nartjes*. And here I will plant a white bougainvillea to stretch up into the syringa trees so when the trees are not flowering, the bougainvillea will bring light to the darkest part of the garden. Here," he said, "I will plant coral creeper. The flowers have no smell but they are such a beautiful color, they will make your heart sing. And here," he skirted a hole, "I will block this opening and find the exit, so you need not fear snakes any longer. And there is another hole over there."

"Those are snake holes?"

"*Ee*. I haven't seen them. But never come out here in the darkness, *mma*, without a flashlight. If you get a cat, they will rid the garden of small snakes."

"My husband is allergic to cats."

"The cat can live outside."

"Cats hunt snakes?"

"Yes, madam . . . *Not* madam. You are *not* madam." He smiled. "They hunt the young snakes and kill them before they grow large."

He walked to the rear of the house, about three paces in front of her. "With your permission, I wish to leave the aloes, even though they are untidy. The birds have made several nests. See? Here and here? These aloes have been growing for many years. They are keeping history." He was thinking that the new part of Gaborone had no history, only bull-dozers and more houses every day. "It is good for people to remember what Africa once was . . ."

"Before Europeans turned up?"

"I didn't mean that. Most especially I did not mean to say it to you."

"Let me tell you something, Isaac. If you offend me, I'll tell you. And if I offend you, you can tell me."

He was quiet a moment. His eyes went still as stones. *Never*, his face said.

She glanced at him and thought, Why *would* he trust me? "Never mind."

"I beg your pardon, *mma*?" She didn't answer.

He led the way to the barren side of the house, where the almost dead tree stood. "The crested barbets live here. With your permission, I will trim the dead parts here and here and put animal manure around the base. Perhaps it will grow stronger."

She wanted to say, "Do whatever you like." She knew nothing

about supervising. The very idea of a gardener was appalling. Why should she be a madam and he be asking her permission every time he turned around?

"Here," he said, "I would like to dig a large hole, at least two meters down."

"A hole?"

"A sunken garden where you and your husband can sit." He moved about ten feet away, and made an oval with his arms. "At the bottom will be flat rocks. On the sides, bigger rocks and many plants. Sometimes they will bloom, sometimes they will be quiet, with just their leaves. And I'll plant trees all around. There are rocks near the dam if you can drive me there."

"And the plants?"

"An old man will give some to me."

"It's a lot of work."

"Yes. You would pay me the same whether I do a lot or a little work. If I just wander around and splash a little water here and there, the day will go by so slowly, I'll fall asleep under a tree, and you'll fire me."

She laughed. He was a handsome man with an open, intelligent face. She wondered what his story was, whether she'd ever know. "Have you eaten anything today?"

"No, I have not."

"How do you plan to work without eating? I'll ask Itumeleng to give you porridge in the mornings. And food for your dog. And you don't need to work tomorrow or Sunday."

"I wish to work all seven days."

"I'll pay you the same amount."

"You cannot pay me for the days I'm not working." He was quiet a moment, looking at the ground. "If I work seven days a week, I earn thirty rand a month. If I work five days a week, I will earn twenty-three rand a month."

"How do you figure that?"

"Five over seven is equal to the unknown divided by thirty. Therefore, seven times the unknown equals one-fifty. One-fifty divided by seven equals a little less than twenty-three rand." He stopped, realizing he'd said too much.

"You never worked in a garden before, did you?"

He hesitated. "No, *mma*."

"How far did you go in school?"

"I completed university. Before I came here, I was in fact in my first year of medical school."

"Why didn't you tell me?"

"If I had told you, you would not have hired me. I have no papers. I came with nothing. Only the clothes on my back. You are angry?"

"No."

"It was necessary to leave for political reasons."

"You don't need to say anything more. I don't need to know. I don't want to know."

"Thank you, *mma*. I will come Saturdays to water the trees. Two days is too long for them to go without water."

"Well, then, Sunday and Tuesdays are holidays. You will have two days off each week, and you'll be paid thirty rand for five days."

"Yes, madam."

"And don't come on Tuesday. And please don't call me madam."

He smiled, put both hands together, and bowed slightly. "I understand, *mma*."

"Can I ask you how old you are?"

"Twenty-seven years old, madam. I worked three years before I attended university. My mother's employers helped me go to university and then medical school. I was very lucky."

Lucky? How could he say such a thing?

He went to the faucet and turned on the hose.

8

Lawrence returned home from Swaneng the following week-end. When he stepped from the truck, he kissed Alice's cheek, not her mouth. It was impossible for her to know whether the coolness between them these days was temporary or permanent. Since coming to Botswana, certainties eluded her.

Daphne had recently gone into heat. Lying on the cool cement of the kitchen floor, she panted happily, leaking blood. The male dogs were gathering outside the window for the third night in a row. When darkness fell, they would moan and fight and howl while the Siren paced restlessly.

Lawrence and Alice got ready for bed and climbed in. Their good-night kiss felt like two blind animals bumping into each other in the dark. A small whimper rose to Alice's lips, the kind of cry Daphne made to the dogs on the other side of the wall. Lawrence felt miles away, as though his heart were buried down a mine shaft. She wanted to shake him, tell him to wake up. She could almost hate him when he was like this. Outside, she could hear the dogs at it, circling the house, cracking the bones of their desire, woofling and digging, the smaller ones jumping up and down on their hind legs. Alice found it creepy imagining them out there, a gang of sex-starved ruffians under the Southern Cross, vying for young Daphne in her first blooming.

Lawrence had promised Daphne's former owners, who'd returned to Scotland, that she'd be bred with Peter Ashton's dog, who had an equally good Alsatian pedigree. Alice would never have made a promise like that. She didn't trust all that hyperbreeding. She liked mutts.

They were better adjusted, and their names were better. Daphne. How pretentious, but that was the name she'd come with. Alice lay in the dark imagining Peter Ashton watching with satisfaction and interest while his dog did it to their dog. Peter Ashton's dog will never have her, she thought.

Lawrence was awake. He was the only man she'd ever known who could curse without making a sound. She'd once thought of his silent cursing as a kind of sweetness in him, a resignation in the face of forces more powerful than himself, but on this particular night she felt something vicious brewing. He got out of bed, his displeasure subtle and potent, and clattered around in the bathroom filling a metal bucket at the tub.

She slid her feet out of bed and onto the waxed concrete floor. Lawrence looked at her and sloshed toward the door with the bucket. "I didn't want this damned dog in the first place," he said.

"You *did* want her. Stop rewriting history. *I* was the one who didn't want her, if you'll take the trouble to remember." She followed him out the door and pulled it tight behind her. The garden was dark as a black hat. She thought of the snakes Isaac had warned her against, and Lawrence's bare feet. Go ahead and bite him, she thought.

Lawrence threw the water and bucket at the largest gang of marauders. A bearded, low-slung dog was standing on a stone making humping motions. In a fury, Lawrence picked up the bearded dog and heaved him, hard, toward the street. The dog yelped through the air and landed.

"What are you doing?" she yelled.

"He's on our property."

"So why not get a gun and shoot the whole lot then?" She turned and walked back to the house. Minutes later, the gang was back, Daphne sobbing, her nose pressed hard against the screen of the kitchen window. Alice slammed the window shut.

9

Some days, Alice talked to the emptiness in her womb as though it were an unfurnished room. Talking had never come easily with Lawrence. What formed in her mouth were the words, *Which of us is flawed?* Their eyes no longer met. Sex was sweaty and unappealing. Unlike some people who love to bury their heads in damp armpits, the thought of sticking to Lawrence in this heat was revolting.

It was Saturday afternoon, and Alice found herself talking to Lillian Gordon over the side fence. Lillian was wearing a turquoise two-piece lounge suit, her ears overstretched by a pair of heavy gold earrings. The two women stood in the wispy shade of a wild thorn that grew on Alice's side of the fence. "When's the baby coming?" Lillian asked.

"Never," said Alice. "I can't get pregnant."

"My first miscarriage was in Kampala, Uganda," Lillian said. She'd been five months along, she said, twenty-three years old. Her husband was out of town, and she began to bleed. She was afraid to go to the hospital, afraid to drive through the streets of a strange, volatile city. She'd nearly died. The next miscarriage was in Namibia. After that, she'd had at least one miscarriage a year, fourteen in all, until she was all used up. The babies grew to about four months, and then her uterus tipped them out. Her babies were buried all over the continent of Africa. Her voice was matter of fact. It didn't change even when she said they would have survived if she'd been near a major hospital in London. Lillian Gordon was not the sort of woman who dispensed or received hugs, but Alice reached through the fence and touched her hand. She told her that she and Lawrence had decided that they didn't really want children. It wasn't true, but it was what she'd begun to say to herself, and it was better than crying all over the place.

"We've been asked to a dinner party at the Lunquists'," she told Lillian.

"Tonight?"

"In an hour."

She didn't want to go. The only reason to say yes was knowing that she'd hear Hasse Lunquist play the piano. He was a sweet-tempered man who'd had his piano shipped out, courtesy of the Swedish government. He worked for Radio Botswana. His wife, Erika, worked in Lawrence's section at the Ministry of Finance and Development Planning.

Alice went inside to get ready. Lawrence was just stepping out of the shower looking happy and rosy. "Your turn," he said. Daphne was asleep on the floor, gathering energy for the night.

"How long do dogs stay in heat?" Alice asked.

"Three weeks," he said, but she could tell from the way he hesitated that he'd just made this up. She didn't remember Lawrence ever saying, "I don't know."

"Why don't you just say you don't know when you don't? It's okay not to know."

"I told you the answer. I don't know why that doesn't satisfy you."

She walked into the bathroom and stepped out of her clothes. The water trickled over her body. She imagined it sizzling with the heat in her. And then she thought of Lillian's uterus. Fourteen times it had turned and poured her babies out, small worlds disappearing.

Once upon a time, Lawrence had told her that she had a beautiful body. Well proportioned, he called it, as though she were a horse. At thirty-one, her body was still young, but next year it would be less young. By then, all the auburn would be gone from her hair, replaced by gray. I'm young, she thought. I'm still young. I could still make milk, given a chance. I could make a baby if things were right between us. On the surface, it looked fine, but it wasn't. She thought of the old aloes in the garden, their thick, elephantine gray-green whorls, the brown stalks reaching for the sky. Keeping history, Isaac had said.

But history didn't matter to Lawrence. Layers—of time, or meaning—made him nervous. He didn't talk about his childhood, about his mother or father, or his mother's mother or father's father, or any of the rest of his family. He had hordes of relatives, young, old, ancient. He didn't mention his own history, or theirs. If he and Alice had a child, he wouldn't care about the child's history. He'd trim down memory as short as he kept his hair. He was a handsome, energetic man who each weekday morning took a shower, pulled on his safari suit, pulled up his kneesocks, shined his shoes, worked hard, came home for lunch, went back and worked hard, came home for dinner, ran at sunset to keep his body trim, invited people over who would help his career, went to bed, woke up, took a shower, and pulled on another safari suit.

This was not a reason for leaving someone. He was kind. He didn't beat her. She couldn't remember the last time he'd raised his voice. He didn't look at her, but how many people did look at the person they lived with? She stood in the shower until she heard Lawrence, the water-usage monitor, tell her to turn the water off. She let it run awhile longer.

When she came out, he was sitting on the bed in his olive green safari suit, wearing kneesocks a darker shade of green. He'd bought this suit after they came out to Botswana, over the border in Mafeking at an Afrikaans department store. "You look quite the colonial," she told him. She felt overheated and mean-spirited and couldn't stop herself. She didn't want him to touch her, not then, not later that night, not ever.

At the Lunquists that night was another couple. Judith and Stephen. Canadians. And a single man named Hal, a Brit, bald, wisps of hair above his ears, dark blue eyes. They were agriculture people. It was a relief to get away from the economists. Hal talked about trying to teach agriculture demonstrators new seeding practices. People in Botswana traditionally broadcast seed across the soil, and now the Department of Agriculture wanted farmers to plant seed in rows for higher yields. "The problem," he said, "is that no one wants to change."

"What makes people change?" asked Judith.

They were all drinking gin and tonics. Frosty glasses, heat pouring off their hands.

"Nothing," said Erika Lunquist without energy. Small beads of perspiration clung to her brow, near her hairline. Her hair was dark, her back ramrod straight, her eyes a glacial blue. "People don't change. They just keep doing what's familiar over and over." The room grew silent. She was talking about something other than broadcast seeding.

"I don't agree," said Stephen.

"It's true," said Judith. "People always go back to what they know. Give them one drought year, and they'll be already saying this new method doesn't work."

"So what are we doing here?" asked Lawrence.

"I don't know. What are we doing here, darling?" Erika asked Hasse, but there was no darling in her voice. It seemed as though they must have been fighting before everyone had come.

Their children were out in the garden. Out the window, Alice saw one turn and head toward the house, and the other two follow. They were barefoot, and they ran fiercely, elbowing each other out of the way. As the kitchen door banged shut behind them, Erika jumped. They came into the room: strange, wild children with pale eyes, like humans raised by wolves. Their feet were dusty, and their white-blond hair was tangled and thatched.

"Go into the kitchen," Erika said to them. "Your supper's there."

"What about pudding?" asked the oldest, jumping up and down on one foot backward out of the room.

"Listen to them," Erika said. "They sound like English boys." But they didn't.

During a lull after they'd left, Judith said, "Apropos of nothing, a disturbing thing happened to us two days ago. Our dog came home with a stomach wound."

"An abrasion," said her husband.

"Worse than an abrasion," Judith said. "A dirty wound. Gravelly. His front paws too. Do Batswana generally dislike dogs?"

Alice looked at Lawrence. "What kind of dog?" she asked.

"A miniature schnauzer. With a cute little beard. We've kept him in the last two nights."

"Where do you live?" asked Lawrence.

"A little way up from the Old Village."

"That accounts for it then," said Lawrence.

"For what?"

"For the fact that your dog hasn't been in our yard the last two nights, making an ungodly racket, attempting to hump our dog." He was holding his glass tautly and looked explosive.

"How do you know it was our dog?"

"I threw him out of the yard. These things happen when dogs are allowed to run loose and a man is deprived of sleep." He laughed a little, a laugh of self-forgiveness, but no one joined in.

"You *threw* him?" said Judith.

"He didn't seem to understand he wasn't welcome."

"You injured him," said Stephen.

"You didn't know what he was up to?" Lawrence asked.

Just apologize, Alice thought. All you need to do is apologize.

"No," said Judith. "We just thought he was out sniffing around."

A wash of laughter snorted out of Alice. It wasn't funny. And then she was crying. She excused herself and went through the kitchen toward the bathroom. The boys were sitting at the table stuffing themselves with pudding. She went into the bathroom and shut the door. She splashed water on her cheeks, dried her face on a towel, and thought of walking home. She fled into the garden and stood under a banana tree, its big fronds waving like clown hands, beating in the hot wind. All he'd needed to do was say, *I'm sorry, I lost my head*. But would he ever do such a thing? Lawrence was never wrong. Never, ever. It was tiring living with a man who was never wrong. *I don't even like you,* she said to him under her breath. It shocked her a little.

Politeness got the better of her, and she returned. There was an awkward silence when she walked into the room. They were already sitting down at the table, the Lunquists' servant, Neo, passing dishes of food. Neither Judith nor her husband would look at Lawrence. Stephen studied his meat, cut it into small bites, and put each piece carefully into his mouth as though it might detonate. They were like people on a life raft, afraid to tip. The heat was undiminished.

Out of the corner of her eye, Alice saw the Lunquists' cat dash under Hasse's chair. It was a large black animal with long white whiskers, formidable, as wild-looking as their children. She took little notice of it until the crunching began. She looked down and saw that the cat had brought in a green lizard, which struggled in its claws. The lizard's tail lay a few inches from it. "Hasse," Alice whispered.

"What?"

She pointed.

"Oh, that. He seems to prefer eating when we do." Crunch went the head.

Judith and Stephen talked dispiritedly about tours of duty they'd experienced elsewhere in Africa. Hal, who'd been sitting quietly, mentioned his mother's visit, which was just over. He said that she'd found everyone in Botswana so friendly. Hal was as uncontroversial as a pan of warm milk. Alice could imagine him as a little boy, hopeful, anxious to please, outgunned by overbearing elders, stripped of his longings. Someone at work had told Alice that Hal and his mother had been invited to lunch at the house of an anthropologist who lived outside Lobatse. His mother had needed to use the outhouse during the visit. There'd been a rumbling of tin as she wedged her way in, and then the whole thing had fallen on its side. Hal would never tell this story. He would only try his best not to think about it.

After the Swedish cake and granadillas and coffee, Alice asked Hasse to play for them, assuming they'd all come listen, but she was the only one who followed him into the other room.

"What do you want to hear?" he asked, lifting the heavy lid of the grand piano and propping it open.

"A lizard-gobbling tune."

"That sickened you."

"Yes."

"Well I'll play something to soothe your nerves, shall I?" He sat on the bench and began the second movement of Beethoven's *Pathétique*.

The music was deeply reassuring, settled into itself, melancholy tinged with hope. The melody repeated itself an octave higher. Hasse lingered over this note, that one. He played beautifully, but Alice felt something aloof in it, some part kept in reserve, uncommitted. He had dark brown hair, a cleft in his chin, and intelligent-looking, heavily lidded eyes framed by round, rimless glasses. His mouth was the most expressive part of him, both lips full, a little amused—by himself? by the world? by Beethoven? He looked as though he'd play with a woman like that cat with the lizard. He leaned away from the keyboard and closed his eyes, then slowed down before beginning the more agitated middle section. He hesitated, opened his eyes, and stopped playing.

"What's wrong?"

He looked at her. "Your husband is sleeping with my wife."

She heard a sound inside her, like something falling.

A mixture of emotion played over his face: sadness, resignation, and a small touch of pity or triumph—was she imagining it?—that he was in control of this information and Alice was not. "You didn't know?"

"No. I don't believe you."

"Observe."

She thought about it a moment. "How long?"

"It began several months ago."

"How did you find out?"

"She told me." He didn't say Erika. He seemed unable to utter her name.

He started the adagio again, played a few measures, and stopped. "I'm sorry," he said. "Maybe I shouldn't have told you."

She shook her head. It could have meant yes or no.

"Why in god's name did you ask us to dinner?"

"*She* asked, not me."

"What for?"

"For appearances. For everything on the surface to look normal."

Some bitter sound came from her.

"And you?" he said. "What will you do?" He stood up, came to her side, and put a hand on her shoulder. She closed her eyes, leaned into him a little. His hand was broad, music lingering in it.

"I don't know." The hurt and rage hadn't come yet, just the burning shame.

"I've always liked your eyes," he said. "Beautiful gray eyes. Would you like to meet sometime?"

She snapped to. "No," she said.

"Perhaps I could make you happy."

"I'm not looking for that." Yes, she said to herself. Play me the way you play Beethoven. "I need to go," she said.

They returned to the dining room, and a familiar-looking man wearing a moss green safari suit sat with his chair pushed back at an angle. The man had quietly festive eyes. "I'm ready to go," she said to him. She watched what he did as they said good-bye, where his eyes went. She saw them slide gently under the cerulean blue sleeveless blouse of Erika Lunquist and heard a voice inside her say, This is what grownups do.

10

Marriages survive such things. Hundreds of thousands, millions do, she told herself. Putting his arms around her in bed, Lawrence said that they'd be stronger for this. He seemed more animated, more present than he'd been in months. "Will we?" she asked. Wretchedness—what's too much to bear? And then the idea of "stronger" caught hold for a moment, the spidery feet of a bird closing around a branch. Yes, perhaps they'd be better off, perhaps this would dislodge some torpor in them, cause something to flare into life. They were still sleeping in the same bed. He said that it was possible to be happily married and continue like this indefinitely. She didn't ask him not to see Erika. It felt as though it was his business, not hers.

He said gently, "I'm not stopping you, you know."

"Stopping me from what? Leaving?"

"No. I love you."

She didn't believe him. "What? What do you love?"

He looked into her face, his eyes searching the contours. "I love the gap between your teeth," he said. "I love your hair." He went to touch it.

Without thinking, she tilted her head away. Those weren't things to love—hair, teeth. She wasn't even responsible for them. "Is that it?"

"No," he said. "Of course not." They fell silent. Once she'd loved his face, the penetrating aqua eyes, shyness in their depths, the scar under the left one that he'd gotten as a boy, running pell-mell into the branch of a tree. She'd loved his mouth. She'd loved his bashful uncommunicativeness, how she'd had to tease words out of him, the way he neglected his socks until the holes grew so large, three toes came through. She'd loved his old-fashioned sense of honor, at least she did when she believed he possessed it. Now, she didn't know who he was.

He began again. "What I mean is I'm not stopping you from seeing someone yourself—if you wanted to."

"I don't need your permission," she said coldly. "It's already been offered, and I turned it down."

"Who was it?"

She wouldn't tell him. What she found unforgivable was the way his eyes dilated with excitement when she threw out that piece of information. How dare he? She picked up her pillow and moved into the spare room. She hunted around for sheets and dragged them out of the closet. When she lay down on the bed, the sheet felt cool for a moment, and then it turned hot. Out the window was a remote sliver of light, a wedge of new moon shining in all its blank indifference.

She heard Lawrence get up, and then the sound of truck wheels crunching over gravel. She was stunned, humiliated. Until now, she'd told herself, okay. This is normal, this is modern. But now, sobs erupted that couldn't be stopped.

The dogs were waiting for Daphne. Alice got out of bed and found her lying on the kitchen floor, exhausted, her head on her paws. She'd gotten out during the dinner party at Erika and Hasse's. She looked up but didn't raise her head; her eyes looked bleary. The pack outside seemed to be thinning. Alice asked, "Are you pregnant?" Daphne lifted her chin and put it down again.

She pictured the perspiration near Erika's hairline, her bone white skin and dark hair. Lawrence touching her. There was a ferocity in that woman, wolf-mother. Lawrence never had a chance. She was playing with him for her own reasons, she didn't really want him, but he didn't know that yet. A wave of protectiveness washed over her, metamorphosing to rage. "Bastard," she said as she climbed back into the guestroom bed, the word bouncing off the white wall.

11

Five days a week Isaac worked at the sunken garden, hardly stopping to eat. He came early in the morning and worked late. His tools were a pick and shovel and a wheelbarrow, which he used to bring dirt out from the floor of the garden to the mounded lip. Every hour, he moved great piles of earth. Alice worried he'd get sunstroke and told him not to work so hard. She didn't know what drove him. All she knew was that he couldn't go back home, and he had no future she could see.

It was a late Friday afternoon. Isaac had dug down six or eight feet. The hole was already ten feet long and six feet wide. She'd agreed to go out the following day and buy some small trees with him to plant on the perimeter of the hole. She was inside with the doors and windows shut against the hot wind. Suddenly, his voice was at the door facing the garden. "Something has happened, *mma*. I have broken the water pipe with the pickax." Behind him, water geysered skyward.

"Don't worry," she said. "It looks bad, but it'll be okay."

He jumped down in the hole and turned in circles. Alice ran inside to call the water people. For once, the phone was working, a kind of miracle. She came back out and told Isaac that the people would soon be coming.

She tried to stuff an old nightgown into the pipe and was holding it there with the handle of a rake when the water blew past the nightgown and shot back skyward. She climbed out of the hole. "Well, *that* sure didn't work." Daphne paddled around at the bottom of the hole in the mud while water erupted above her head.

A pickup truck drove into the driveway. At first she thought it was the water people, but then she saw that the driver was Peter Ashton, and beside him, Lawrence. In the back of the truck was Peter's Alsatian dog, chained to the bar behind the rear window, straining toward Daphne.

"Isaac hit the water main," Alice said to Lawrence. "What's that dog doing here?"

"It's the one the Moretons recommended."

"You're going to set him loose on her?"

"I wouldn't put it like that."

"The two of you were just going to stand here and watch him screw her?"

"They're dogs, Alice. This is what dogs do."

"Get him out of here!" she yelled. "Get your goddamn dog out of here, Peter Ashton, or I'll take him out with a rake!"

"For god's sake, Alice, get control of yourself!" said Lawrence.

"I'm in control of myself. Get that dog out of here."

Lawrence turned and climbed into Peter's truck, and the two of them drove away.

"I'm very sorry, *mma*," Isaac said. "I wasn't thinking."

"It's all right. It could have happened to anyone. The water people will be coming soon."

He looked toward the geyser. "I must go, madam. I'm very sorry to cause you trouble. I hope you understand why I cannot stay."

She didn't understand, not then, but she said yes, of course, go if you need to.

She fed Daphne and shut her in the kitchen. A government truck pulled into the yard, and three men got out, two whites and a Motswana. The Motswana clicked his tongue. "Oh shame," he said. One of the Europeans said it would take them some time to get the water shut off and the pipe mended and suggested she might like to sleep elsewhere that night. There'd be no water at least until the following day, maybe several days. She left a note for Lawrence, telling him that there was no telling when the water would be back on, that she'd be staying with the Gordons for a few days. She ended with, "I can't see you right now. Please drop a note in the mailbox if you won't be here, and I'll feed Daphne."

She walked next door with her pillow and a few clothes in a paper bag. She was covered with mud. "What a mess you are," Lillian said, peering out the door at her.

"Isaac punctured the water main with a pickax. The men are over there fixing it. There won't be any water, probably for a few days. Can I come in?"

"Stay as long as you like. Gerald's away. You better take off your shoes, and I'd say a bath is in order." She dug out a blue towel and pointed her toward the bathroom. Alice turned on the faucet. The walls were a shouting shade of blue. The sink, bathtub, and toilet, all blue.

The bathroom reminded her of Lillian's last dinner party, when she'd served Jell-O eggs on a bed of lettuce for one of the courses. To make them, she'd blown out real eggs, sealed one end of each shell, and filled them with different colors of Jell-O. When they'd set, she'd peeled them painstakingly. Like the bathroom, they were absurd, a kind of parody of a dinner party. The guests had been impressed, at least they said they were, and Alice had watched Lillian watching them, one eyebrow cocked.

The tub filled, and she sank into the water, which instantly turned brown. Had she just left Lawrence for good? She didn't know.

At the moment, she had to admit she didn't care where he spent the night, and she wouldn't care if he didn't come back. Something had snapped, seeing him there with Peter Ashton's dog straining after Daphne, the two men ready to set him loose. She couldn't put a finger on why it had bothered her so. It had to do with Daphne not having a choice. At least with the neighborhood ruffians, there was a kind of natural selection. But to will it, to set it up . . . Alice plunged under the water, rinsed her hair, let out the muddy water, and filled the tub again. Lillian had dozens of lotions arrayed on shelves. The shampoo was creamy and smelled of peaches. She lay back and breathed. Her body had not felt her own since the night at the Lunquists'. She'd felt defensive, under siege, sad, unlovely. A gray hair stuck to her belly and she went underwater and floated it away.

Lillian was in the kitchen when she came out. "I never cook when Gerald's away," she said.

"What do you eat?"

"Whatever I feel like. Mayonnaise out of a jar. Canned sardines."

Alice laughed. "Yuck."

"But tonight, I thought we'd have this." She set a plate of toast on the table, and two boiled eggs upright in egg cups. "Speaking of food, how was your dinner the other night?"

"The Lunquists? It was a disaster."

"I've always hated dinner parties."

"I thought you liked entertaining."

Lillian huffed out of the side of her mouth. "So what happened?"

"It turns out Lawrence has been sleeping with the hostess. Her husband told me that night."

"Ah, not a fun evening."

While Alice talked, Lillian whacked off the top of her egg with a knife, sprinkled salt, and dug in with a small spoon. Between bites, she broke off bits of toast and ate them. Alice loved watching her eat; she got such immense pleasure from the simplest food. Her profile was a fallen glory, her breasts sagging. Her face was a ruin, wrinkled to lizard skin by years of African sun. She took a sip of tea and looked at Alice. "So, what will you do?"

"Leave him?" asked Alice in a small voice.

"Is this the first time?"

"Yes."

"Does he love her?"

"He's infatuated."

"People get over it. No one's perfect," Lillian said. "He seems decent enough."

No one's perfect, Alice said in her head, rolling it around like a marble. She felt as though she were seeing the world through Lillian's glaze of disappointment and compromise and something harder to define. Not resignation, not joy. If the feeling were a color, it would be gray green, the color of moss on the north side of large trees, the thing that endures, that softens edges.

Next door, the house was dark. She went home to check on Daphne, and shut the door firmly against marauding dogs.

She and Lawrence met a couple of days later over the back fence. The water had drained halfway out of the hole. Five orioles called, *weela-weeoo, weela-weeoo,* as though they'd flown into paradise. Lawrence was wearing the shorts of his safari suit and a T-shirt with a smear of tooth-paste down the front. "I'm finished with her," he said. "I told her last night it was over. I never loved her. You know that, don't you, Alice? I was obsessed, I can't explain it."

How did she know he wasn't still obsessed?

"It was like a drug," he said hanging onto the fence like a criminal. "I didn't want it, well I did. Yes, I did very much, the way you'd want a cup of coffee after not having one for three days. No, stronger than that, much stronger. Do you hate me?"

She considered his question. His hair was rumpled and needed to be washed. "No. But I don't trust you, and I don't trust that it's over."

"It's over. I swear it. I miss you. Will you come home?"

She studied him a moment and smiled at him for the first time in weeks. "No, I don't think so."

"Well if you don't hate me, do you like me?" He touched her finger through the fence.

"That's not really the question."

"What *is*?"

"We didn't make a nest for ourselves. It's dry sticks. We couldn't make a baby." Her eyes filled.

"Do you want to go home, I mean *home* home?"

"No."

Their fingertips touched once more, and she returned to Lillian's house. It was quiet inside, and the white-walled rooms were cool and peace filled. A faint smell of veldt rose from the grass rugs. Martha, the Gordons' servant, was in the kitchen humming a song, pulling it from low down. Alice saw the back of her, the motion of her arm whipping something in a bowl. She walked into the guest room and sat on the bed. The orioles still called. They didn't know that the water was sinking into the earth, more each day. She looked down at her hands resting in her lap, one on top of the other.

Lillian was having a bath. "Well?" she called through the door.

"He wants us to try again. Do you think I should?"

"It has nothing to do with me," Lillian said. It was quiet behind the door as though she was thinking. "Why don't you come in?"

"In there?"

"What do I have to hide?"

Lillian was wearing a white bath turban and her face was rosy from the rising heat. Under the water, shimmering just under the surface, were stretch marks crisscrossing her belly. Hope, and hope again. "Sit down," she said. Her breasts were flattened out, draped softly to each side. Alice perched on the edge of the tub, near her feet.

"What does your heart say?" Lillian asked.

"My heart?" As though she'd never asked it anything.

Lillian slid underwater and sliced up through, her face shining with droplets. "That's all that matters. Do you want to go back or not?"

She wasn't sure.

Lillian sat up in the bath and said, "It's none of my business, but when I was your age, I thought my life was over. I'll dry off and we'll have a cup of tea, and then you can sleep on it."

The water came back on. Isaac had disappeared without a trace. Each afternoon after work, Alice drove to Naledi, parked the truck, and walked around looking for him. She went down one path then another. The place stretched out in all directions, shacks and cardboard houses as far as you could see. She was ashamed she didn't even know his last name. One day, she thought she saw him on the road. She stopped the truck, rolled down the window and shouted, "*Dumela, rra!*" A stranger turned his face to hers, and that's when she stopped her search. He'd come back, or he wouldn't.

Gradually, the mud subsided. The orioles and their sweet song disappeared.

12

Lawrence left for a ten-day work-related trip, and Alice returned home. That same night, between ten and eleven o'clock, she walked up the driveway of a house she'd promised herself never to enter again. She couldn't have explained to herself or anyone else what she was doing, or why. All she knew was that Hasse had sought her out at work and asked her. Yes, she'd said, thinking of Beethoven. Yes.

Erika was also out of town, maybe with Lawrence. She didn't know and she didn't want to know. Hasse and Erika's wolf children were in bed. Hasse was in the bath when she arrived. He asked her to come in, as Lillian had. She wasn't in the habit of watching people bathe. It felt like something better done in private, but Alice stood in the door watching his beautiful Swedish cock floating pink and innocent just below the surface of the water. His glasses were on, gently steaming.

She slipped off her shoes at the doorway. In her Cincinnati mind, she was only there to talk about the situation. In her un-Ohio mind, she knew what she was doing and what would happen. He got out of the bath and dried off. He wrapped the towel around his waist. The towel was pure white. They padded into the kitchen together, where he took two glasses and a whiskey bottle down from a shelf. He opened the refrigerator and took out a floppy plastic packet of milk, snipped off a corner, and poured the contents into a jug. "I have an ulcer," he said. "I drink my whiskey with milk. Do you want to try it?"

She nodded. Deep laughter lines played at the edge of his eyes. He must have been at least ten years older than Erika.

"Egg in yours?"

She laughed. "No."

He held her shoulders and looked into her face. "You are quite beautiful," he said. He ran the back of his finger down her cheek and over her lips, moving her hair back with the palm of his hand. He looked at her fondly, paternally. The tips of his ears were rosy from the bath. He smelled of soap. He poured whiskey into both glasses, more in his than hers, then filled them up with milk.

"*Skål!*" he said, clicking her glass.

"*Skål!*" she said back. It occurred to her that what she was doing was wrong, but it was a passing thought, unimportant.

"Come," he said, taking her hand and leading her to the bedroom. He put his hand on her shoulder at the threshold of the room. "You want this, don't you?"

She nodded, a lump in her throat like loss.

They set the drinks down on the bedside table. He undressed her slowly, appreciatively. She took off his glasses and unwrapped the towel from his waist. His cock, so indolent and pink in the bath, had woken. They climbed into bed. Somewhere, a dog was barking. A small light shone in the room, on his side of the bed. His body was square and firm, his back broad. His touch on her skin was light, as though he cared for her. There was a blue vein in the middle of his forehead under the thatch of hair. The thought came to her, I don't know this man.

He asked her which way she liked things. She didn't know what he was asking. His English was perfect, but his thinking was Swedish. His hand grazed her thigh, indicating that he'd like her on top. She felt young, self-conscious, lacking prowess.

He felt it and said in her ear, "It's all right, you can do whatever you like."

She loved him then. And what she did came from her heart, all of it, for those moments.

But it was over. And after the strokings and murmurings, they sat up with their backs to the wall and drank the whiskey and milk. He searched for his glasses, and she put them back on him. He looked like the conductor of a boys' choir. Churchy. She told him so, and he looked very slightly hurt. She'd meant no harm. She thought if they were ever together, their lives would begin to weave just like this, one small hurt, a backing down and recovery, another and another until a tapestry was woven, as complicated as any other. The euphoria of newness would last a month, two months, a year, and then they'd be caught in something of their making and beyond their making.

She felt him pulling back. Had he thought she could be something to him? They seemed to realize simultaneously that they were not destined to become each other's saviors. They'd been shot out of cannons, two hurtling objects meeting in midair. "I'll drive you home," he said.

"No, please, I want to walk. It's a beautiful night."

"I'll walk with you."

"No, I feel quite safe. Thank you, you're very sweet to offer." Her eyes told him it had been good with him, and it was over. She kissed him again and shut the door behind her softly.

There was something necessary about putting one step in front of the other in the shadows of moonlight, her flashlight searching for movement at her feet. Puff adders were the most dangerous snakes at night: sluggish in the cool of dark and unable to move out of the way. Along the road, she wondered, What just happened? Did I go there to even the score? She hoped that wasn't true. She didn't think it was. She was drawn to the music in him. He made love the way he made music: sensitively, expressively, holding more than a little in reserve. However much had been held back, though, she felt deeply grateful to him, as though she'd been seen again.

She found her mind tracing the pathways that had brought her to this road on this night—as though each step could be unraveled and retraveled—the men who'd touched her, taught her something, and left.

Michael was the first. In the spring of her junior year, they'd both quit their cross-country teams, and every day after school, he took her home to his room. He was shy, tender, perfect. For the junior talent show, he came on stage in his thick glasses and dirty white sneakers and a baggy Sherlock Holmes double-breasted raincoat. He carried his cymbals, one in each hand, his glasses glinting in the spotlights like fevers of the brain. When he clanged the cymbals together, the audience went wild. She felt in that moment that she loved him as much as it was possible to love anyone. But she was wrong. Then there was Drew with the bad reputation, and Zachary, the aesthete, and Brandon with the beautiful, sad eyes. And a while later, Lawrence.

She undressed and lay in bed, with the moon passing across the window. The lights of the Gordons' house shone across the boundary fence. She thought of Hasse, his kindness, his sweet lovemaking. And then an image of Erika and Lawrence flashed into her mind. She imagined a hotel room, and her face grew hot with shame and fury. Her heart pounded, and finally it slowed. The moon passed out of sight, and she slept.

The following day, Alice came home from work at lunchtime. Isaac was still among the missing. The house was very still, except for the trilling of the crested barbet in the tree. Daphne was asleep, visibly pregnant. Alice patted her, asked her how she was while Daphne thumped her tail against the floor and panted, too hot to stand up.

Alice sat down at the wooden table in the kitchen with a glass of water, gulped it down, and refilled the glass. She was losing weight, not because she wanted to. Her head, her whole body, was dizzy with memories. In those early days of being together with Lawrence, her love for him had been a spring colt, a shiny, shy thing. He was a man for whom words came hard, like water at the bottom of a deep well, with only one bucket to the top. She'd been patient, thinking there would be words worth waiting for.

In graduate school, they'd moved into a scantily winterized outbuilding ten miles outside of Providence, part of a no-longer-working farm. The windows rattled in the wind. In May, the lilacs dwarfed the building they lived in, dwarfed everything in sight. They were almost frightening when they bloomed, throwing their scent into the air so insanely, there was nothing to breathe that wasn't lilac.

Lawrence was in a doctoral program in economics. Alice was in anthropology. Lawrence's extended family sprawled like the lilacs. She loved them, perhaps more than she loved him. His sister, Wren, his brothers, Howard and Jeremy, his empty-headed young niece, Dahlia,

his bulky aunts and rumbling uncles, and especially a caustic great uncle who lived alone not far from them and dressed impeccably, a silk
cravat hiding his stringy old neck.

After Lawrence had successfully defended his thesis, his adviser told
him of a job in newly independent Botswana in the Ministry of Finance and Development Planning. As soon as Lawrence told Alice it
would be good for his career, she knew he'd be going. He left Providence in June and asked her to visit the following summer when she'd
be working on her thesis.

After he left, his letters were full of his work, and when she thought
back on them, not very interesting. But something in her wouldn't let
him go. It all felt promising. She went to Botswana that next summer
to visit a man she thought she might marry. From Providence to London, from London to Johannesburg. From Johannesburg, she boarded a
night train to Mafeking, and in the morning changed trains for Gaborone. When she woke somewhere between Mafeking and the border
of Botswana, a bleached and pitiless landscape stretched forth, with no
sign of human habitation. Only when the train stopped at small stations could she see that the land was peopled with children, dozens of
them, selling beads and *mopane* worms and carved wooden statues
stained with mahogany-colored shoe polish. Few people on the train
bought anything, but the children's voices were high and loud and
their hands empty of food. From a young sculptor, she bought a soapstone carving of a boy's face. The chin was long and eager, the lips full,
with small vertical cracks carved into them.

When the train arrived in Gaborone, she caught sight of Lawrence
before he saw her. He was wearing a safari suit and moved with an ease
she hadn't seen in him before. His face had filled out, and he looked
large and healthy. His straight brown hair, which had once hung in his
eyes, was combed back from his forehead.

He held her carefully by the shoulders, and they kissed each other
on the lips. The veldt had slipped into his eyes. For some reason she
thought she might have gotten the wrong person, that perhaps she was
kissing Lawrence's brother. She touched his cheek and mouth with
two fingers, like a blind woman.

She was dazed by the strangeness around her: women carrying their babies on their backs, tightly bound to them like bandages, the sound of Setswana, the train station with its tea shop, the dust that hung in the air and caught in the throat, the smell of rotting vegetables. Sights and sounds and smells poured through her. A boy gnawed on a long piece of sugar cane. A donkey stood tethered to a cart loaded with wood, its eyes clotted with flies.

Lawrence took her elbow and led her to his pickup truck. His flat was undistinguished, part of a Type I government building that adjoined another flat and another after that, with an enclosed piece of ground in back where a clothesline hung. Underneath the clothesline was baked dirt, swept clean of vegetation and surrounded by a chain-link fence. Inside, the government-issue furniture was tinted the same shoe polish color as the wooden carvings the children had been hawking on the train platform.

While Lawrence went to the bathroom, she sat at the table and took the covers off the food that Dikeledi, his servant, had cooked. Strips of beef sat sullenly in a metal bowl beside another bowl that held white rice, scooped into a sticky ball; in another were little round squashes cut into halves. On the far end of the table was some kind of tinned fruit with a pitcher of custard sauce beside it. Lawrence sat down, and they served themselves. Dikeledi was in the kitchen, and then the door shut behind her, and Alice heard her shouting to friends in the backyard.

She felt suddenly forlorn.

The beef was tough and dowsed with black pepper. She told Lawrence it was good. In those days, she didn't set out to tell lies, but the truth was often buried under politeness. In fact, the rice was without salt, the squashes watery like something that had been strangled and drowned. Lawrence held her hand after lunch and led her to the bedroom. An hour later, he was on his way back to work.

He'd taken a job as an underling in the Ministry of Finance and Development Planning and had already been promoted twice. His friends were mostly economists, and their principal topic of conversation, apart from where to get good marijuana, was development. She didn't know what they were all talking about. The word was one she'd heard before only in relation to breasts. Except for Lawrence, she was offended by these economists who talked as though Botswana had been a great emptiness before they'd arrived.

During the days he was at work, she toiled away at her thesis. It was winter in the southern hemisphere, with rainless warm days and cool nights. In the evenings, she and Lawrence read around a small electric fire. She looked up from her book at the two glowing rods and there he was. After the sun went down, the stillness in him was different from his daytime self. Occasionally they stepped outside to the little closed-in area by the clothesline and looked at the Southern Cross and he put his arm around her waist and drew her close. She didn't ask what she was doing there, or what she was doing with him. His body was sturdy, like an answer. She looked into eyes that mirrored that wild, parched veldt and saw infinite space stretching before them that she mistook for their life together.

Lawrence and she shared a single bed, which encouraged feats of athleticism; they each slept half on and half off the mattress, like cheetahs. They woke in the cool of the night and made love, sometimes three or four times. They were young, and it cost them nothing. She remembered the dark, rushing desire in her ears, the furious fumbling out of sheets into each other's arms.

Some days, Alice tried to speak with Dikeledi, but they knew only a few words of the other's language. She felt awkward being waited upon and found herself smiling too much, dropping things, over-thanking. Dikeledi was short of stature and tireless; her movements were like humming—unconscious, tuneful, at peace. Her skin was dark, coffee-colored, and her eyes forceful. Her bottom lip was full and her mouth good-humored. She lived behind the flat, in the small tin-roofed servants' quarters, and on Sundays, she put on a red polka dot dress and a white hat shaped like a pancake and walked to the Seventh-Day Adventist Church in the old part of Gaborone.

A few times, Alice went across the road to escape the flat, but what was out there frightened her—the blind blue sky and unrelenting sun. Thorns, tinier than the smallest hooked claws of a cat, waited under dusty leaves. They caught in her hair and plucked at her sleeves like beggars.

By the end of the summer, Lawrence and she were engaged. What did she know? Nothing. Yogi Berra once said, "If you come to a fork in the road, take it."

13

After the water explosion, Isaac ran into the bush, afraid that the police would find him and deport him. Toward nightfall, he crept out and walked back to Amen's house. He knew the gardening job was finished. One of the first things he'd been told was, "My husband does not like water to be wasted." It was a misfortune that her husband should have come home and seen the water shooting into the sky. And there she was, shouting at her husband and his friend when the person she should have been shouting at was himself.

He did not respect people who ran away, and now he'd done it twice—once from his country, and once from his job. Fleeing was like lying: you do it once, and you'll do it again. But, he told himself, I will not do it again.

Every day now, Amen was saying, "You must go for training in Angola. You are doing nothing now. Think of the country where you were born. Your country is like your mother. You would not turn your back on your mother."

He needed to find somewhere else to live, away from Amen's badgering, but he had nowhere to go. He did not want to train with the MK, of that he was sure. And he would not turn his back on his own mother who'd given him life and breath and suckled him and taught him what was right and wrong. He had disappointed her, he could not embrace her, maybe not for many years, but he would keep her and his sisters and brothers in his heart. Several weeks ago he'd bought a pencil and paper and an envelope and posted a letter to ask her forgiveness and to tell her that he was safe in Botswana. Before he'd sent it, he

asked she who must not be called madam if he could use her post office box address. Any day now, he was expecting a return letter from
Pretoria.

After he'd stayed out of sight for ten days, he thought, I will not hide
any longer. What happens will happen. On a Saturday morning, he set
out for the Old Village to inquire about the letter and to say again that
he was sorry.

All along the road, people were making their way here and there. He
thought of the divided stairways back home, the divided bus and train
stations, the divided public toilets. All the time, all the time, you were
watching for where black people were forbidden. Heaven help you
if you set your black foot on sacred white ground. Even after you
died, you'd go to a *nie blank* cemetery: no one wanted your black ass
anywhere near a white person, even though everyone was dead. Here,
he could see no signs, not one, but the watchfulness had not died
in him.

When he came to the house in the Old Village, the great hole he'd
dug was as he'd left it. The water was gone and the mud looked like
cracked china. Some of the dirt he'd shoveled out and taken to the top
of the hole had slumped down after the water had poured over the top.
To see this hole gave him a great sense of shame. It felt to him that
White Dog even hung her head. The garden was empty of any person.
He called "*Koko?*" No sound came from inside, and just as he was at
the point of going away, Itumeleng came out of the servant's quarters.
"*Ijo!*" she said, surprised.

He greeted her, and told her he wanted to see the madam.

Itumeleng pointed next door. "She's living there once again," she
said in Setswana. "She returned here when the master was away. Now
he's back and she is gone there again."

"I see."

"So you have returned."

"*Ee, mma.*"

"I was thinking you were not going to return."

"I only came to see the madam."

"Why did you not come back?"

"Because my job is finished."

"The madam told you not to come back?"

"After what happened, I know it is finished."

"You don't know this."

"Yes, I know it."

He did not want to go to ask for her next door. He squatted by the old half dead tree, looking in that direction, then told White Dog to wait and walked into the yard next door and knocked on the door. An older woman answered. He greeted her and told her that he was looking for the madam. She did not appear to be a friendly person. Only with reluctance would she tell him that madam had gone to the prison farm for vegetables. "I will wait outside on the road," he told her.

He thought of the moment when he'd raised the pickax over his head and it had fallen on the water pipe with a crunch. More and more, his life seemed to move like this, punctuated by events that changed things forever. He remembered in secondary school, the same school where he'd met Amen, an English teacher had said that when you write, you should be sparing of exclamation points. This was good advice, not only for writing but for life itself. It was best to let commas and periods carry you. If he and Kopano had not become friends, if he had not been persuaded to go to that first meeting of the South African Students Organization, if he and Kopano had not traveled together on that particular day . . .

Her truck was coming up the road. He stood in the road and waved as she drove toward him.

"Where on earth have you been?" she asked, leaning out the window. "I'm glad to see you."

"And you, madam. I am truly sorry to have caused you trouble."

"Where have you been?" she asked again.

"I thought the police would deport me."

"That's why you left?"

"Yes, of course."

"It never occurred to me. You weren't in danger of deportation."

"You don't know this, *mma*." It came out sounding harsher than he'd meant it. "What I mean is that it is different for me than for you."

He saw something flicker over her face, a kind of sadness.

"I'm sorry for causing you trouble," he said.

"It could have happened to anyone."

"It was my responsibility, *mma,*" he said. "That's why you pay me. Please let me be sorry."

When he looked back at her, she was smiling. "I won't stop you from being sorry. I'm sorry for not understanding. Several people stopped by asking for work, but I told them we already have a gardener."

"You were speaking of me?"

"Of course I was speaking of you. After you disappeared, I went looking for you in Naledi, but I didn't know your last name."

"Isaac Nkosi Muthethe is my full name."

"Isaac Nkosi Muthethe. Now I know. Who are you staying with in Naledi?"

"I am sorry, *mma,* but I am not at liberty to say."

"I see."

"It is only for reasons of their safety."

"Why is that?"

"Please, I can't say more than this."

She nodded.

"I didn't come to plead for my job. But I wanted to ask if my mother has written."

"No, she hasn't written. Your job is still here, unless you'd rather find other work."

"I wasn't wishing for anything but this work, *mma.* However, perhaps your husband wouldn't wish to see me again. I've wasted more water than ten hippos."

She smiled. "It doesn't matter what my husband thinks. I hired you, and you are still hired." He started to thank her, but she interrupted. "This is your job until you find something more in line with your abilities. I don't want you to leave, but I hope for your sake, it won't take you long to figure out something else. I'll help however I can."

"Thank you, *mma.* I have no other plans. Perhaps someday, but not for now."

"All right then."

"There's one thing I wish to ask."

She waited.

"I wish to fill the hole."

"After all that work?"

He couldn't imagine her and her husband sitting there in the cool of shade trees, in peace. "It was not such a good idea after all, and the sight of it is painful. I'll fill it and plant vegetables."

"It's your garden, Isaac. You do what you like. Can you grow tomatoes and lettuce?"

"If there are seeds and water, they will grow."

She looked down the road. "I'm not living here at the moment. It's just my husband and Daphne." She looked as though she was going to say more, but a bicycle came by, ridden by an old man. It was wobbling, and Isaac moved out of the way. "I'll still pay you at the end of this coming week on Friday."

"You must deduct the time I did not work."

"I'll pay you as usual. Please don't argue. I'm glad you're back, Isaac Nkosi Muthethe." She started the truck suddenly and drove up the road toward the neighbor's house, and he walked back to the garden.

Starting that day, he began to fill the hole slowly, one shovelful at a time, time for sweat and humility to run down his backbone, to moisten the waistband of his pants. As he worked, he pondered his conversation with her. It shocked him that she'd come to look for him. He did not understand her. Sometimes she was like a small child, wild and clumsy and unsure. At other times, her words came out with sharp, angry edges. Then again, she might be full of kindness and wisdom. Of these three people, he was never sure who would be speaking.

At noon, her husband drove up the driveway. He walked to the hole, hands on his hips. "Quite a mess, hey?"

"*Ee, rra.*" There was something in Isaac that did not want to apologize to this man.

"What are you doing?"

"Filling in the hole, *rra*. I have told the madam I wish to plant vegetables here."

"Whatever she says." But his eyes said something else. "Well, carry on."

He didn't need to be told to carry on. He watched the man's back cross the threshold and enter the house. He was a handsome man, and aware of it. He'd seen him several times before, and always, it seemed, he preferred not to say much. That was one way to have power—to let others stumble around while you remained watchful, without words. It didn't seem that she who must not be called madam would be happy with this man.

If he had married Boitumelo, he believed they would have been happy for their whole long lives. He didn't believe, though, that his mother would ever again be happy with his father—even if his father returned. Perhaps his mother had loved him early on, but then troubles fell on their heads. They blamed each other for things beyond their control: the Pass Laws, no money, the roof falling in chunks during the heavy rains and smashing their crockery. It was a mystery why men and women loved and why they did not, a mystery he would perhaps never understand.

"She's back now," Itumeleng told him the following morning. "But they're not sleeping in the same bed. I know because of the sheets."

"*Ijo!* Don't tell me these things," Isaac said. He threw another shovelful of dirt into the hole. "You're like a chicken picking up every piece of dirt in the yard."

"You would like *mabele*?" She curtsied as though he was Sir Seretse Khama.

He smiled. "*Ee, mma.*" She brought out a bowl of porridge and poured milk into it. He sat on his heels eating while Daphne and White Dog romped around the yard, nipping at each other's backsides. Daphne's mouth was upturned as though she was laughing.

From inside, he heard them talking: the husband's hardly audible shadow-words and the madam's lighter, more musical voice. It didn't sound like fighting but it didn't sound like love, either. He didn't believe this man would beat her. Not physically. But from her face, he could see that he'd hurt her.

He finished the porridge, rinsed the metal bowl and spoon at the outside faucet, and placed them just outside the door. No one could say now that his hands were not the hands of a gardener. He rubbed them together and heard a rough, dry sound they'd never made before.

The madam and her husband got into the truck and drove off. You could see that their hearts were not beating together, the blood in their veins wanted to flow toward different oceans. He walked to the hole, picked up the spade, and threw in another shovelful of dirt.

The madam came home alone after work. She inspected the hole and told him she noticed a difference. Itumeleng had just gone into the house, having taken four sheets off the clothesline. Her little girl was sitting on the stoop at the servant's quarters. Isaac couldn't have said what caused him to look up when he did, but he suddenly dropped the spade. White Dog was down on her haunches, ready to spring at something. "Come!" he called sharply. "*Tla kwano!*" At first White Dog ignored him, then backed like a stealth soldier away from a six-foot snake. Itumeleng's daughter started to toddle from the servant's quarters toward the house. "No!" he screamed. "Stay!" She began to cry and ran back into her house.

Isaac picked up a long limb that he'd sawed from the crested barbet tree that morning, his eyes on the mamba the whole time. Its skin was silvery in the sun, like metal. The snout was square, the head coffin shaped. He didn't need to be told this was the fastest snake in the world. You get bitten. Fifteen minutes later, you're dead. It opened its mouth. Black inside. The blackest cave. When a black mamba shows the inside of its mouth to a herd of Cape buffalo, the sight is so fearsome, the animals stampede from it. Now there was a stampede in his chest, the hooves beating hard.

The snake hissed. It flattened its neck and stood up high. He threw a rock on the other side of it to make it turn.

Madam screamed for him to get away, get away! But he brought the limb down on the snake's back with all the force in him. The snake twisted and turned to strike, and he struck again, closer to the head. It was one fast muscle, a muscle that could do anything. Again and again, he brought the limb down on the writhing body until finally it twitched, jerked, and went still.

He dropped the tree limb and went into the undergrowth and was sick.

That snake had only wanted to live. When he came out, she who must not be called madam thanked him, although something else was in her face. A kind of horror.

14

The letter from his mother had taken two weeks to be delivered from Pretoria. He sat on the flat rock under the large aloes and opened the envelope. As he read, he heard his mother's voice among the trees. Her voice was a deep one, almost like a man's, with a roundness like the sound of a large gourd, a vessel for holding things. He read the words quickly, turned over the page and read the words again. And a third time. White Dog sat next to him, with her legs crossed in front of her. On the fourth time through, he wept. White Dog put her nose under his arm and pushed upward. She made a sound in her throat as though she wanted to offer comfort. When his tears were finished, he folded the letter, replaced it in the envelope, and put it in his pocket.

He remembered the last time he'd kissed his mother's cheek, softer with age every time he kissed it. This letter started the longing in him again, a longing that roared inside him the way a fire moves across the veldt, consuming grass and trees and termite hills and all the living creatures that run before it. One morning, he thought, he would wake and not care about his safety and return to his family. His mother pulled him like the Earth pulled the moon: the thought of the years and troubles piling up in her, until one day she'd be gone, with an emptiness beside her where he should have been. Someday, his sister Lulu would have breasts that would flood her with surprise. Day by day she'd become a woman, and he would not be there to protect her from harm. He'd be a stranger to her, and to Moses and Tshepiso.

On his own, he might make his way to the border, walk along the fence and find a way under or over when the moon was dim. But then what? He'd have no passbook. He'd need to walk at night and hide during the day, steal food, run from everything. Dogs would pursue him. His mind would weaken. He wouldn't know north from south, east from west. He'd have no money, no friends.

He walked around to the front of the house and was surprised to find the madam waiting for him.

"Is everything all right?" she asked.

"No, *mma*, everything is not all right. My baby sister has died from malaria." He turned away. "She was so young, she hardly knew life. Now my mother is alone."

"Where are your other brothers and sisters?"

He stopped a moment. Surely she must know. At first he didn't want to speak. His heart was angry that you can be this close to South Africa and be so blind. But then he asked himself how was she to know? Even if she went there, she wouldn't be allowed to see the things that all Africans see and know.

"Of course you must have a pass at all times," he told her, "and if you're not working, you are not permitted to live in Pretoria. My father is missing and there is no money. My mother must work in the city and send money to the children who are living with their grandmother in the homeland, which is not our homeland. The government calls it the homeland, but the land is poor, there is nothing there, the schools are poor, everything is poor and shabby."

"When did your sister die?"

"On the nineteenth of last month."

"And the rest of your family?"

"My sister Lulu and my young brothers are no longer in school because they have no shoes. My oldest brother Nthusi is now working in the mines. Soon, perhaps, there will be enough money for them to return to school."

"Your father?"

"He too was working in the mines in Johannesburg. As I told you, he is missing. Perhaps he is no longer alive. We don't know."

"I'm very sorry, Isaac. I have no words for how sorry I am."

"Thank you, *mma*. There is nothing to be done."

He watched her get into the truck and drive away, back to her work.

His mother had said nothing about herself in the letter, but he could feel her sadness. She said she did not have anger toward him. She wrote that it was better for him to be alive in Botswana than dead in South Africa. He picked up the spade and went back to work, standing at the top of the hole. With each shovelful of dirt, his anger grew, until he felt he could fill this whole hole with his fury. He felt he could hit someone's neck with a spade, break their neck the way he'd broken the neck of the snake.

His brother Nthusi now worked in a hole a hundred thousand times the size of the hole he was filling. He remembered his dream, his father standing in the bottom of an enormous pit, still standing there as the waters rose, making no effort to save himself. He imagined the hope in Nthusi's heart now dead, working in sneakers too big for his feet, laboring until his body broke.

When he walked home that night, he could hardly drag his body up the road. He knew what he would find at Amen's house. Amen was away training new recruits, and there was not enough money for food because Kagiso's mother was sick, and she had to send all her money to Mochudi for medicine. For a week, the meal at the end of the day had been mealie meal, the same food that started the day.

When he arrived, Ontibile was crying for milk. Kagiso was cooking over the fire and paying no attention to the baby, but she looked happy. Her brother had come to Gaborone from Mochudi and brought with him a bag of dried beans and the leg of a goat. Her brother had returned home, and the smell of meat was coming from the three-legged pot.

Ontibile put her arms around Isaac's neck, and he picked her up. She made little singing noises as he rubbed her back, and then her head sank onto his shoulder. Later, after they'd eaten the meat and beans, he watched Ontibile lying on her back, asleep, peaceful, her arms outstretched as though no harm would ever come to her. Ontibile. *God is watching over me.* This was a good name. If he ever had a little girl, he would call her by this name.

He went outside where the still air held the heat of the day. He walked to the water pump and brought water back in a tin and washed his face and body behind the house. Only the poor die from malaria. If his mother had not been poor, his sister would be alive. He said nothing to Kagiso. Let her enjoy her full belly and be happy for once. White Dog would not leave his side. She knew his grief, this dog who was more than a dog, this dog who had fallen from the sky.

Kagiso was asleep next to their baby when Amen returned home.

In a dream, her brother had been holding two goats, lashed together with a rope around their necks. The sky turned black and the birds flew for cover and the rains pelted down. She and her brother tried to shelter under a tree, but the rain poured from the branches, down their necks, into their shoes.

Amen climbed onto the mat beside his wife, and for a moment she didn't know what was dream and what was husband, and then her arms found their way around his neck, and she pulled him to her. She smelled the night on him and his own smell she'd recognize anywhere, even if she couldn't feel the fringe of beard pressed against her cheek and feel with her tongue his one front tooth standing behind his sweet-tasting lips. She pulled his head to her breast like a child and felt his breath go out all at once, in a great torrent of relief as though he was now free to breathe the air that surrounded both of them, as though the work he needed to do was done forever. Their child stirred on the other side of her and moved into the curve of her back.

15

Isaac had heard Amen come home in the night, but he didn't wish to see him. Before the sun rose, he left for the Old Village. On his way to work, he stopped to see the old man who'd made the sunken garden. He told him he'd dug a similar one but was now filling it in. When the old man heard the story, loud laughter poured out of him. He bent over double to catch his breath. And then he laughed again, barking and coughing.

The old man dug up a tomato plant and wrapped it in a plastic bag. His hands were old, turned on themselves sideways, as though they were asking a question.

As he left the yard, Isaac heard the old man's laughter again. He turned to wave, and the old man was gesturing for him to come back. "I have something for you," he said. He walked Isaac to the shade of a tree on the opposite side of the garden. Inside a cage were two young cats. "Do you want them? The master says I must find a home for them or else I must drown them."

"Drown them?"

"He doesn't like cats. You'd better take them."

"I don't know."

"They came into the garden last week. I've been feeding them milk. He tells me I must kill them today."

Isaac opened the door of the cage and picked up the smaller of the two by the scruff of its neck. White Dog sniffed it, and the little one hissed and arched its small back. It was very thin, the color of a lion, and had a pattern of circles on either side like targets. He peered into the cage. "What happened to their eyes?" One cat was cross-eyed, the other wall-eyed.

"I don't know," the old man said.

Isaac laughed. "*Go siame, rra,* I'll take them. Tomorrow, I'll bring back the cage."

When he returned with the cats, he was unlucky enough to meet the master.

"What's in the cage?"

"There are two cats, *rra.* To rid the garden of snakes."

"The snakes will eat them, not the other way around."

He remained silent. He had learned back home never to contradict a white man, no matter what nonsense they may utter.

"Alice!" Lawrence called toward the house. "He's got cats."

She came out. "Awhile back, I told Isaac I'd look for an outdoor cat for the snakes."

"There are two of them," said Lawrence.

She looked into the cage. "What's wrong with their eyes?"

"I think their mother had venereal disease," said Isaac.

"They look healthy enough otherwise," she said.

"Did you forget I'm allergic?" asked Lawrence.

"Darling, relax. They're outdoor cats. They're for the snakes. I told you, don't you remember? Isaac killed a black mamba."

"These cats won't stand a chance against a snake like that."

"I want to keep them anyway."

"Well, then, keep them."

"Do you like the name Mr. Magoo?"

"I don't give a damn. Call it what you want."

"They were going to be drowned today," Isaac said.

"So you had no choice," said Lawrence.

"*Ee, rra,* there was no choice."

The madam always paid him on the last Saturday of each month. Out of the thirty rand, he gave twenty to Amen and Kagiso for room and board. And each month, he saved five rand for shoes for Nthusi, putting the money under a loose chunk of concrete in the floor in Amen's house. The rest he used for food.

When he opened the envelope on that particular Saturday, he found ninety rand.

"You've given me too much, *mma*." He held out the extra money to her, but she reached forward with both hands and closed them around his. "For your two brothers and your sister, for school," she said. He stood before her, his heart pounding. Before he could gather himself, she walked quickly back inside the house.

He returned to Amen's house with the money inside his shoe, thinking about how he could best send it to his mother. After everyone was asleep, he took out enough for room and board and food for the month. The rest he placed under the chunk of concrete.

16

Twilight. An old woman was fishing in the dam, thin legs stretched down over the bank, her head bowed toward the water. Alice was there with her friend, Muriel, walking on the lip of the dam, just the two of them on that scar of earth, bulldozed like a bowl to collect water. The sun glowed red against the edge of the sky, the breath of wind still hot.

Alice and Lawrence had known Muriel in graduate school back in Providence. One of those odd quirks of fate had brought them to Botswana at the same time. When Alice had first met her, Muriel was happy in herself, happy to please anyone who crossed her path. Her hair went halfway down her back, and she was slender and willowy, her eyes magnified by large, round, rimless glasses. In the eight years since then, she had the same glasses, but her face was worn, less eager. Her husband Eric had come to Botswana as a hydraulic engineer, partly responsible for the building of this dam. Muriel was a librarian at the National Library.

Alice had asked to meet her after work.

The old woman landed a fish, popped it in a bucket, and walked down the path. Alice and Muriel stood next to each other, looking toward the dam, watching a flock of sacred ibis feed. The birds were very tall, white except for black tail feathers and black necks and heads. In the water's reflection, their legs looked twice their actual length.

"So what's going on?" asked Muriel.

"Lawrence and I are getting a divorce."

Muriel stopped in her tracks. "Oh, Allie, I can't believe it. You've always seemed perfect together."

"Not so perfect, it turned out."

"I'm really, truly sorry."

"Lawrence got involved with someone. Erika Lunquist."

"I don't know her."

"You'd probably know her if you saw her. I didn't tell you before
you went on leave. I thought it would blow over. I stayed at the Gordons' a couple of weeks, and then Lawrence and I agreed we'd try and
start over. He stopped seeing Erika, at least that's what he said.

"I can almost respect a man who's got enough passion to love two
women at once. But it turns out I'm not the sort of person who can
share. It tore me up, and I told him he had to choose. He chose to stay
married. He said it was over with Erika, that it had been more about
sex and fascination than love. Those weren't his words, but that's more
or less what he said.

"So we took up life together again. But a couple of weeks later I ran
into Hasse, Erika's husband. He asked how I'd weathered the camping
trip. 'What camping trip?'

"'The one our spouses were on together.' I thought Lawrence had
been working.

"When he got home from work, I lost it. He told me the trip had
been planned for a long time, and they'd needed to say good-bye.
Good-bye! That's all you needed to say, I told him. One word. It didn't
require four days together. He said he understood why I was upset, he
was sorry he'd hurt me, and that he'd never, ever lie to me again.

"But then it happened again. The third time, I told him it was over.
I couldn't be married to someone I couldn't trust. In fairness, I can't altogether blame him."

"*I* can," said Muriel.

"No, listen. My body didn't want him, and he knew it. Who doesn't
want to be desired? Maybe I'd have done the same thing. The point is,
the marriage was dying. And now it's dead."

The sun was half above, half under the horizon. It traveled down the
sky slowly, and then seemed to plummet. The ibis began to move

differently, their attention no longer underwater. They appeared to be listening for something, some signal. Suddenly they rose as one bird and spread across the sky in a long line. It felt like a kind of holiness, white wings dipped in black. Alice looked out over the calm, darkening waters of the dam and began to cry. She threw a rock hard toward the water, and it landed with a splash. The sky was deep purple except for a rising sliver of moon.

"Will you stay here?"

"I don't know. I'm still in our house in the Old Village. He moved out with Daphne."

"You gave him your beautiful Daphne?"

Don't, she wanted to say. "Yes, I gave him Daphne. We'd better head back."

Muriel walked in front of her, and every so often she turned around and said wise things, half of which Alice didn't hear: "You'll be happy again, you'll see."

Tears leaked out in the darkness. The path widened and soon they were walking side by side over a rutted track toward the place where they'd parked the truck. They held hands to steady each other in the dark.

Muriel started the truck and drove toward the Old Village. "You know," said Alice, "you and Eric don't have to stop liking Lawrence."

"Are you kidding? I never want to see him again."

Part of her was glad to hear those words. She never wanted to see him again, either.

At home, Muriel said good-bye, and her truck lights disappeared down the road. Alice opened a can of sardines for the cats, and Magoo purred and rubbed against her ankles. "Where's Horse?" she asked. The long-legged, cross-eyed one.

She picked up the soapstone carving of the boy's head she'd bought on that first trip here. The boy's face was innocent, hopeful, as she'd been. The soft stone was greenish gray with small scratches and dents. She held it in her hands and thought about something she'd once said to Lawrence. They were lying in bed. He turned to her, hoping to make love, and she told him she couldn't—her body felt nothing for his. It was true, but an unforgivable thing to say.

Once upon a time, she couldn't have imagined a day without him, and now she shuddered to think of his hands touching her breasts, shuddered to think how she'd taken off her clothes while his eyes traveled the geography of her nakedness.

What scrap heap in the world could hold all the loves once felt, now vanished?

She set the sculpted head back on the table, got up, brushed her teeth, and climbed into bed. The first issue of *Botswana Notes and Records* was on the bedside table. Her boss from the Ministry of Local Government and Lands had asked her to have a look at it before she completed the position paper on land use and the San people. She checked the table of contents and turned to an article about the hunting practices of the !Kung San. When a man is ready to hunt, she read, he smears a nerve toxin from the pupae of a small beetle along the upper shaft and point of an arrow, which is then wound with sinew and hardened over a fire; if he nicks himself with the poisoned arrow tip, he dies.

The San hunt in pairs. They position themselves downwind from the herd and choose an animal. The stalker moves forward while the other man watches and gives hand signals. When the stalker is within fifteen meters or so, he rises and shoots an arrow into the animal's stomach. Depending on the freshness of the poison, it can take one to three days for an animal to die. The hunters see by the spoor when the animal is weakening. A gemsbok will grow sick unto death, stagger, and fall to its knees.

She lay the article facedown on her chest. Once, she'd held a Bushman arrow in her hands. The husband/wife anthropologist couple in Lobatse had showed her the arrow. Its head was made of fencing wire, pounded flat, the shaft was made of reed, the haft about ten centimeters long. A bone joint fit into the shaft and was bound with sinew to the head. It was very light, a thing of beauty.

She'd drafted this paper about land use, knowing far too little. Because she had a degree, because she could put words down on paper, she was helping to make decisions about people's lives she knew next to nothing about. Of what possible benefit were her words to them?

She called Horse once more. Magoo, who thought it was a call to a second supper, rushed in from the garden. She went back to bed and turned the page to another article, about the great Sechele, chief of the Bakwena, who was born in the early 1800s. She read about how Sechele's father had been murdered by his half brother, Moruakgomo, a villainously ambitious man. Moruakgomo had also murdered his half-witted brother, Segokotlo, his last obstacle to power. The brothers went out in the bush together, and Moruakgomo told his simple-minded brother that they were going to pray for locusts to come so their people would not die of hunger. "Here," said Moruakgomo. "Here is where the gods live." Poor Segokotlo bent down to put his head into a fresh ant bear hole, and Moruakgomo cut off his head with a hand axe.

Power and cruelty. Cruelty and power. The same old story. She turned off the light and lay there. In the darkness, tiny soft footsteps fell on the floor, closer, closer. She knew the sound, but somehow the steps filled her with dread. Mr. Magoo jumped on the bed and stood on her stomach, his eyes staring into the dark like a haunt. "Where's Horse?" she asked. He rubbed his chin on hers and purred, his paws imprinting her throat and chest.

17

The next day, Muriel stopped by to ask how she was doing and to invite her to Thanksgiving dinner that night. "We're having a few people over. Just a spur of the moment thing."

She pictured herself there solo, wearing some brave little festive outfit, surrounded by couples. "Thanks, dearie, but I think I won't." She wanted to tell Muriel why, but it felt too wearisome to explain. Some shred of dignity she was trying to hang onto, and she'd lose it in the process of explaining.

She left work early and drove to the co-op for food. This would be the first Thanksgiving in her life that she wouldn't celebrate in some fashion. In the street, she ran into Hasse.

"What are you doing out of work so early?" Those eyes, full of irony and sparkle.

"I suddenly had an impulse to cook something resembling a Thanksgiving dinner."

"I'd invite you to join us, but I don't think you'd enjoy yourself."

"You've got that right."

"How are you?"

"I'm on my own now," she said. But he already knew. She saw it in his eyes.

"You're okay?"

"Yes," she said. "How about you?"

"I'm well enough," he said. But he wasn't, and he knew it. He'd compromised one time too many, and he'd become a compromise rather than a man. He saw that she knew this, and they parted. But not before she saw the question mark on his face.

She knew what he was asking, and she answered with a quick kiss on his cheek. "You're a wonderful man," she said. "But no."

To the right of the Presidential Hotel, an old man sat on a flattened cardboard box. His shirt was disintegrating, his pants held up by a piece of twine. He was making tin boxes out of large sheets of metal that sounded like thunder when he cut and shaped them. His hands were as twisted as trees braced against gales. Near him, a young man sitting on a blanket was selling wormy wood sculptures.

Alice headed to the co-op, where most items she had in mind wouldn't be on the shelves. She walked down the aisles, looking for canned cranberry sauce. It was a long shot. All of a sudden, there was Lawrence, standing in front of a can of peaches, studying the label. She thought of rushing for the door, but she told herself not to be a coward.

"I wouldn't buy those peaches," she said over his shoulder. "Probably been there since the Boer War."

He whirled around. His face said *I thought you'd left the country*. And then he smiled and kept smiling. He couldn't stop smiling. They talked about their work, about his mother who'd been sick.

"You probably thought I'd left by now," she said. "I have no immediate plans. How about you?" It sounded as though she thought Gaborone wasn't big enough for the two of them.

"No plans beyond the end of my contract next year," he said. "Then we'll see."

We? Then she remembered he'd always had trouble with the word "I."

He picked up the can of the peaches he'd been staring at, thought better of it, and put it back. "Good to see you. You look well." He started down the aisle and turned and took a step back toward her. "I'm sorry, Alice."

"I'm sorry too." It came out sounding as though she blamed him, not what she felt. For a millisecond, she thought of asking him for

Thanksgiving dinner, but she thought it would only make them both miserable. She watched him walk the rest of the way down the aisle and through the door and out into the sunshine. Whatever food he'd come for, he'd decided against, or forgotten.

She dropped the can of peaches into her basket. Nearby was some ancient pumpkin pie filling which she grabbed along with four cans of fish for the cats. She paid at the cash register and came out into the furnace of sun. She passed a man selling ostrich egg necklaces and bought one for her mother, and then filet mignon at the butcher, all the time replaying the words Lawrence had spoken. The heat had flattened the mall into dust. Her eyes shimmered and wobbled. Her bearings were gone, her head pounded. She felt drunk, disoriented, as raw as the meat wrapped in butcher paper.

When she noticed her friend Peter Daigle walking ahead of her, she hesitated.

"Peter!" she finally called out. He didn't hear.

"Peter!" she called again.

He turned. He was wearing a khaki-colored safari suit, one kneesock slipped down around his ankles, his bald head burned by the sun.

"What are you doing here?"

"I'm down for a couple days. Here for the big city lights."

"Where? Where are they?"

"Happy Thanksgiving," he laughed.

"Happy Thanksgiving back."

"I'm having canned herring in my hotel room," he said. ". . . unless you'd like to join me for dinner."

"Why don't you come over to my place? I'm cooking. By the way, had you heard that Lawren . . ."

"I heard from Muriel and Eric."

"He and I just ran into each other in the co-op. First time in a couple of months."

She thought his eyes said, *Yeah, and you look like crap.* "I'd love to come," he said. "What can I bring?"

"Your own handsome self."

When he arrived that evening, he kissed her on the cheek and handed her a bottle of wine. He'd changed into a shirt and pulled up his socks for the occasion. "Okay, I'll just say it and get it over with," he said. "I never thought the two of you belonged together." They walked toward the living room and paused in the wide doorway. "I don't want to trash him."

"Oh, go ahead."

"I never could imagine the two of you in bed."

She raised an eyebrow.

"You're way higher intensity than he is," he said. "He seems half asleep most of the time. And there's something a little slippery about him. I never can figure out what he's really thinking. Anyway, the single life suits you. You're looking well."

"Thanks." But he was lying. She'd aged ten years in the months since Lawrence had departed. "Want to open the wine?" They went into the kitchen, and she passed him the corkscrew and a couple of glasses. She'd cooked a stroganoff with beef, bacon, white wine, sour cream. The rice was done. She turned on the burner under the frozen peas. He stuck his nose into the stroganoff pot. "Smells great."

"Sorry it's not turkey."

"I don't even like turkey. How did we ever get stuck with that for Thanksgiving? Did you know that the Pilgrims ate swans?"

"I'm glad we don't. By the way, I have no appetizer. We'll just eat, okay?"

"Are you apologizing?"

"No. Yes." She stood over the stove, about to dish up the food, made a sudden movement, and knocked her wineglass to the floor. The glass shattered, and red wine splashed over his shoes and her bare feet.

"Don't move," he said. He put his arms around her and lifted her away from the shards and set her down. He swept up, grabbed a sponge and paper towels and mopped up. "There might still be some. You'd better get shoes."

"I'll be okay."

"That's not a pumpkin pie I see . . ."

"It is."

"You made it? I can't remember when I last had pumpkin pie." They sat down at the table. Conversation was halting, awkward. Not knowing what else to talk about, she asked how he'd come to Botswana.

"I was a religious nut," he said, smiling.

"As in converting the pagan masses?"

"More or less. I was sent out here for two years, in the grand missionary tradition, with a small band of believers." He took a gulp of wine.

"And?"

"And after two months, I thought, I don't even like these people. And this whole concept of salvation. Suddenly it made no sense. So I bailed and found a job with Shell Oil. I've been here ever since. Strange isn't it, the way things can change overnight?"

"Yes."

"So what about you?" he asked. "Have you moved on?"

She'd always thought of Peter as a bit of a galoot, but it wasn't true. He was more like a seatmate on a Greyhound bus who has kind eyes and is willing to listen. It surprised her.

"Not really. But I will in time." They finished up the first course, and she poured him coffee and gave him a slab of pie.

"So what happened?" he asked.

"I don't really know how to explain it. Everything revolved around Lawrence and his work. I became bored, inattentive. His attentions turned elsewhere . . . I guess you'd say it was mutual, although it didn't feel like it at the time."

"Well, let me say it—I never really liked the guy. It's hard to put a finger on. You'll be grateful for this someday. Great pie, by the way."

"Are you with someone, Peter?"

"No, I've tried. Both sexes. It's not going to happen in this lifetime."

"Maybe that'll change."

"I doubt it."

"I don't think I'm cut out for it either," she said. She felt no sparks with Peter, doubted that she'd ever feel that way again.

"You'll have a happy life and be better for this."

"You're sweet to say so."

"I mean it." He got up to go shortly after that. "I'm on the road early tomorrow. Can I help with the dishes?"

She thanked him and told him no. His face when he bent to kiss her good night contained a deep, wide loneliness. He thanked her, and she shut the door, thinking of something she'd read in a Philip Larkin poem she'd taken out of the library: how in everyone there sleeps a life unlived as it might be lived if one were loved.

She went to the sink and soaped up the dishes. *A life as it might be lived if one were loved.* She thought of Lawrence's pasted on smile, his eagerness to get away. And his step toward her, and his surprisingly tender, *I'm sorry, Alice.* Once upon a time, she would have said there was nothing in her life she really regretted. Now, she wouldn't say that, but what she regretted was hard to name. Not the years with Lawrence, not even the end. It was not being awake enough: being half asleep when she met him, half asleep when she read his distant letters. He'd asked so little of her, and she'd responded with half herself. His emotional vagueness, which drove her crazy, had been in her too— like a disease passed between them. Never mind what he did. She needed to account for her own half there–ness, for the deprivation and narrowness of that life with him, and the rage that followed when she woke.

A wolf spider sat on the wall by the kitchen pipes, hairy, fanged, as big as a small plate. She clapped a pot over it and slid the top on. She felt brave, capable. Out in the garden, she set the pot down, took the lid off and made a run for it. As she headed for the house, she heard a cat yowl behind her. She turned, and the ghost of Horse walked toward her on rangy, long legs. He was twice as gaunt as before. "Where the hell have you been?" Horse followed her into the kitchen, inhaled a can of sardines, and another, before settling into a rattling purr. "Where were you?" But he only purred and purred. Mr. Magoo came into the kitchen to investigate, hissed and put his back up. Then some ancient memory surfaced. His tail went up, and he dragged it under Horse's nose.

18

In the wild part of the garden behind the tall aloes, the flat rock stored its coolness in the shade of the jacaranda trees. Out here, he could think, and Itumeleng could not find him to shout her sillinesses. When he put his palm on the rock face, he felt connected to something beneath, all the way to the center of the Earth. He'd been in Botswana for seven months now. He'd had three letters from his mother and one from his mother's employer, Hendrik Pretorius. He wondered if Boitumelo were yet married. He tried not to think about her. It made him half crazy, but his mind went there like a wandering goat.

Still, it was something else he'd come to this rock to think about. This morning, as he was leaving Amen's house to go to work, he asked his friend, "Where's the bicycle?"

"I sold it," Amen said. "I needed the money."

Isaac couldn't believe his ears. "You sold it? It's not mine."

Amen had lifted his shoulders in a shrug. "A bicycle is nothing to a European. Tell her that it was stolen, and she'll buy another, and then you'll have a bicycle again."

Isaac punched him. It was the first time in his life that he'd punched another man in the face. Amen took a step back, not quite falling to the ground. He was a big man, but he didn't strike back. He'd prefer, Isaac saw, to catch him off guard. He didn't know when he'd retaliate, but it would come. Living with Amen, there would be no rest now. He'd need to be watchful, and Kagiso—he saw it in her eyes—would be watching too. He felt bad for her, the way each day another sparkle fell out of her eyes onto the ground.

It would take a year of wages to save enough for a new bicycle. He needed to find another place to live, but there was no place to go. He'd need to confess about the bicycle. He was late for work this morning, and she'd noticed he hadn't ridden it. He'd told her that he had to mend a puncture. It is said that the end of an ox is beef, at the end of a lie is grief. That lie slipped off his tongue before he could bring it back. Now he needed to decide if he must tell her that he'd lied as well as lost the bicycle. He thought he must tell her everything. If you climb a tree, you must climb down the same tree. But he would wait a few days.

He left the rock and cleared the lemon tree of weeds and checked the six chili peppers, which were in little pots, waiting to be transplanted into the garden. He gave each pot water and touched the plants. Somewhere he'd heard that plants respond to touch, even to love. She who must not be called madam had asked whether he could grow hot chili peppers. The old man had given him eight seeds in a folded paper. Six seeds had germinated, one had not. He'd kept the last seed for Kagiso to plant, but it was lost. Each of the six pepper plants now had strong green leaves. He wanted to take a leaf on his tongue to see if there was fire in it, but to take one would be to damage the small plant, so he only imagined the flames in those leaves. In three or four days, he would transplant the peppers next to the tomatoes in the garden.

With a watering can, Isaac poured water on the lettuces and spinach, filled the can, and watered each tomato plant, then went down the row of onions. The carrots were just coming up with their feathery leaves, and he watered beside them so he wouldn't drown the young carrots. He tried to make his mind like the mind of a plant. He went back to the onions and watched as their stems stirred. When they turned one way they were green, another way and they were blue gray. They rustled against one another like the sound of a man walking through long grass.

Late that afternoon the madam asked to talk to him. His heart sank. But instead of talking about the bicycle, she told him that she'd be going on a long trip, probably for two or three weeks. Would he live in the house and watch over things and feed the cats?

He asked whether Itumeleng would not be here, and she said that Itumeleng would be going home with her daughter to see her mother.

"Then I'll stay in the servant's quarters?"

"I thought you would stay in my house."

"I would rather stay in the servant's quarters."

"Wherever you stay, I'll pay you extra while I'm gone."

"I'll look after your house with pleasure, *mma,* but I don't want extra pay." It was too good to be true. Before he left for the day, he learned that Itumeleng didn't want him living in her room. She said that she'd had too many men there already, and it had brought nothing but bad fortune. Isaac laughed. He would stay in the little room near the kitchen in the main house.

She left on a Saturday. That night, White Dog slept just outside the kitchen door. For the first time in Isaac's life, there was no other breath sighing near him at night. So much stillness, it felt like the space between stars. In Pretoria, there were voices outside, radios, drunks, people arguing, singing, footsteps going by, and inside, whisperings, snorings, murmurings of sleep. Now he felt he might be the last man on Earth. He got out of bed, walked outside, and looked up the large trunk of a syringa tree, into its boughs holding the sliver of a new moon. He imagined that he could hear a low sound coming from the stars and from the great black space around them, a low deep sound: the vast engine of the universe. He had never seen the ocean, but he imagined this sound to be similar to the sound of the sea when it's rumbling, the great waves gathering and falling.

White Dog did not understand what he was doing out there in the dark. She put her head on one side and looked up to see what he was looking at. He wondered, could she hear what he was hearing? White Dog knew things from the other world, things that most dogs don't know, but perhaps it all came through her nose. Dogs are one big nose.

He left the door open to the night air to let the heat of the day out. The polished concrete floor at the entryway was cool on his feet. Through the darkness, he felt his way toward the bedroom with his hands and bumped into a wall. When he stopped, he still heard that low, deep hum. He lay in the small bedroom with his eyes open and imagined the thousands and millions of people on Earth who would never be alone the way he was alone tonight. Every sound he heard was large: the wings of a moth, the donkey boiler outside the window groaning as the water inside its tank cooled, the creak of the floor in the living room.

The room where he slept was the same size as the house he'd once shared with his mother and five brothers and sisters. In this house, there were still six more rooms, some of them much larger than this one. A screened veranda ran the length and width of the house on two sides. A small village could sleep here.

In the morning, just after dawn, he heard a sound like a mouse across the floor. He got up and walked in the direction of the noise. A crested barbet, covered in chimney soot, wooffled over the open screen at the living room window, looking for a way out. Isaac recognized it as one of two birds that sang at the top of the tree outside the kitchen door. He went back into the bedroom to put on his trousers, and when he came out, Horse had it in his jaws. The wings were flapping. He pressed his fingers outside the cat's mouth to release the jaw, and the bird flew up onto the curtain rod. He picked up Horse, put him outside, and closed the door. Back in the living room, the bird looked down from the rod.

Every day he was in the habit of speaking to this bird at the top of the tree: "Good morning, and how did you spend the night?" But this morning, he said, "I go to the trouble of putting thorns around the trunk of your tree to protect you from the cats. But now you must fall down the chimney and put yourself in the mouth of the cat? How many times do you expect to be saved?" The bird looked at him from the top of the curtain. He was very dirty and his feathers were sticking up untidily. When Isaac went to him, the bird seemed to understand he would do him no harm. Or perhaps he was too frightened from being in the jaws of a cat and could only stare. Isaac picked him up with two hands and opened the outside door. "Pshhhh! Pshhhh!" he said to

Horse, who ran under the aloes. Isaac opened his hands, and the bird stood there a moment before flying. He weighed almost nothing, and his feet felt friendly on Isaac's palm. His mate was waiting on the branch of the tree when he flew up next to her, making the alarm call *puta puta puta!*

19

Alice's hair was stiff with grit and dust, and she'd never felt happier. Only the dusty road before her existed, the bush and the sun and the bright, wide horizon. She thought of home, the large kitchen sink, the screen on the veranda where the geckos ran up and down chasing flies, Isaac pottering about in the garden, Itumeleng calling over the fence to friends. She could picture these things, but Gaborone felt a million miles away.

The group had been on the road a day and a half already, having set off from Gaborone in two government Land Rovers and a three-ton truck driven by Sam, Motsumi, and Shakespeare. The idea was for them to gather information about the interplay between livestock, wildlife herds, and the !Kung San that would enable them to draft a national policy that would protect all three. They were to talk with !Kung San leaders, visit cattle posts, view a veterinary boundary fence, take in the Tsodilo Hills, stop off in Shakawe, and return home. Everything was arranged for them—drivers, food, cook tents, cots, sleeping bags.

Representing the Ministry of Local Government and Lands were Alice and C.T., her boss. The Ministry of Agriculture had sent their new assistant permanent secretary, Arthur Haddock, who'd recently arrived in Botswana from Wisconsin, plus Ole Olsen from the Division of Veterinary Sciences, and Will Vreeland, a wildlife specialist and a friend of Alice's. A British guy who was studying !Kung San paintings in the Tsodilo Hills would be meeting them east of Maun.

She was traveling in one of the Land Rovers with her friend Will and the new assistant permanent secretary. Arthur Haddock knew how to greet people with a *dumela, mma* or *dumela, rra,* and that was about it. This must have been his first trip out, but it didn't stop him from telling Sam, the driver, how to do his job. "Aren't you even going to stop?" he asked, when a hornbill collided with the windshield.

"Very dangerous to stop, *rra.* Anyway, the bird is dead."

Thirty kilometers down the road, the vehicle got a flat tire. Mr. Haddock said that there needed to be a more systematic regulation and monitoring of government vehicles. Alice wanted to say, *Hey, buster, this isn't Milwaukee.*

Sam glanced at him. "Many thorns on the road, *rra.* You have a new tire, she goes over a thorn, and boom! Flat."

They stayed in Francistown that night and went on toward Maun the following day. Deep sand tracks made the driving treacherous. One false move and the vehicle would jump the track and they'd turn upside down. It was already December, and there'd been no rain here. Next to the track, cattle stumbled over the earth, their rib cages hollow.

By midafternoon, they'd reached Nata, two hundred kilometers west of Francistown, where they stopped to meet up with Ian Henry, the specialist in San rock paintings. They inquired after him, but no one in the village seemed to know where he'd gone. A national measles and vitamin A campaign was under way beneath a shade tree; schoolchildren in faded gold uniforms with brown collars were being dragged there for vaccinations.

"Where the hell is he?" asked Arthur Haddock.

"He probably got tired of waiting," Alice said. "We're half a day late."

Ian Henry did appear a couple of hours later, saying he'd needed to talk to a man who lived farther up the Nata River. Alice remembered then that she'd met this fellow the previous year, after he'd written a proposal for a permit to work in the Tsodilo Hills. Her first impression of him had been of someone disorganized and borderline cavalier. To that was added the word combative, after he and Arthur Haddock got into a discussion after dinner over San trance dances.

"Pagan rituals," said Haddock.

"Pagan is a pretty loaded word," said Ian. "Not that far from 'nigger.' And where do you get your information?"

"I saw a film before leaving the States."

"Ah, a film. A very dependable and rigorous source. Did you ever talk to a San healer?"

"It's obvious what's going on."

"Obvious? How?"

"I've seen that same sort of mumbo jumbo in the States."

"This is not mumbo jumbo. Healers risk their lives to cure others. When they enter a trance, they're often in excruciating pain—and they believe they may not return to the world. They do it for each other, and for their community. When was the last time you had that sort of courage?"

"I'm going to bed."

"Your mind is as closed as a cuckoo clock."

"You've had too much to drink."

"*In vino veritas.*"

"You're the kind of fellow who needs the last word, aren't you." Ian Henry was silent, and Haddock disappeared into his tent.

Alice smiled. "*Are* you?"

"I could have gone on to tell him that I'd once had the honor to enter the kind of trance I was talking about. But I didn't."

"Very restrained of you."

All three vehicles stopped midmorning by the side of the road, and Will said he'd like to take a detour to the Makgadikgadi Game Reserve to check out what was there. Haddock asked if that was part of the agenda.

"No, it's not necessary to visit the Makgadikgadi," answered Will, "but I thought we were here to learn things we didn't already know."

"Ngamiland is where we're supposed to be going," said Haddock. He turned and headed toward a Land Rover, but one of his shoes slipped on the sand. His arms windmilled, and he went down on one knee, as though praying. Alice wanted to laugh, but then she felt sorry for him. Who would wear shoes like that in the desert?

"Why don't we just split up?" said Alice's boss. "Anyone who wants to take in the Makgadikgadi can. The rest can go straight to Maun. We'll meet there." There was a small stampede toward the two vehicles not carrying Arthur Haddock. Sam got stuck with him in the truck, and the rest crammed into the Land Rovers.

As they wallowed up the sandy track in the Land Rover, Will said, "Between Nata and Gweta is mostly *mopane* forest, but off the main road . . . well, if you've never seen it, you're in for one of the most fascinating sights on Earth. These salt pans were at one time part of an ancient inland lake. There are remnants of stone age civilizations on outcroppings. If there's rain, water forms at the point where the river joins the Sowa Pan. It's a nesting place for flamingos migrating from Namibia. I've seen literally thousands of birds there."

The main road crossed a narrow finger of the northernmost edge of the Ntwetwe Pan. They turned south at Gweta. On either side lay alternating dry grasslands and *mopane* trees, opening out occasionally onto plains dotted with palms. Thirty kilometers later, Ntwetwe Pan appeared. Looking south was an eerie expanse of white salt and white sky and searing sun.

"Astronauts apparently can make out the outlines of the old lake from outer space," Will said. "From close up, you'll see where the shore was. You have to be careful crossing. This time of year, the surface looks completely dry, but the water can be just a couple of centimeters below the surface. I can't tell you how many times I've fallen through and had to spend all day digging out." His face had been sunburned over and over until his skin was burnished a deep reddish brown.

The pan was terrifying, the horizon white and fathomless, a savage, demonic, eerie place. So hot you couldn't breathe. Alice sat next to Ian. She couldn't see his face, but he was hardly breathing. One gets used to a landscape that's human in scale. There's a future because it can be seen, just over the horizon if we choose to walk there, or ride there. But there was no future or past here. The horizon was unreachable, unknowable, swallowed in white.

"I'd love to go to sleep and wake up here someday," she whispered to Ian.

They stopped partway across and got out. Ole Olsen, a big, strapping Norwegian, was in the other Land Rover. His chest was collapsed, his chin tucked down as though he'd received a blow. She went over to him. "Okay?" she asked.

"Can't get my breath," he said. "It's like we're on the bloody moon."

They drank water, climbed into the vehicles, and retraced their steps back across the pan. Close to sunset, they crossed the Kuke veterinary fence. Alice wished Haddock had been there to see the devastation. The carcasses of dozens of wildebeest were piled against the barrier. Will said they'd been trampled when their herd had run headlong into the fence while trying to migrate toward the Okavango Delta.

A few live animals grazed on scraps of grass not far from them. They tore at her heart with their homeliness and simple desire for water. Their noses were long and wide, their horns unremarkable, their beards, manes, and tails thin and scraggly. Their legs appeared too spindly to hold even a drought-ravaged body, ribs sticking through dull fur. A patient resignation clung to them, like people who've lost everything. The oxpecker birds sat on their backs and necks, picking bugs off.

Will told the group, "They depend on seasonal migrations for survival. During drought season the herbivores move toward sources of surface water. After the rains, they move back to grazing in and around the central Kalahari. Because of these fences, they've been cut off from sources of water and food, and squeezed into areas that are overgrazed by cattle. The herds die of starvation if they stay near water and die of thirst if they move to better grazing. By some estimates eight hundred thousand wildebeest died at Lake Xau in the year after the fences went up.

"The fences were meant to stop the spread of hoof-and-mouth disease in cattle, but there's no evidence that they're effective against it. Hoof-and-mouth is airborne, carried by birds and wind, so how would a fence stop it? It's a crude attempt, unfounded in research, a holocaust for wild animals. Of course this has been devastating for the !Kung San as well. As wildlife is dying, so is their food supply."

. . .

That night, they camped in a grove of baobab trees. Ian wanted to in-
troduce the group to a man he knew, one of the San people. He set out
in one of the Land Rovers across the bush to where he thought he'd
be. "It's the drought," he said when he returned to the campsite alone.
"They've moved on, I don't know where."

Ian, across the fire from Alice, had begun drinking steadily. When he
heard the maniacal, barky laugh of a hyena, he said to her, "They chew
your nose off at night, you know, if you're sleeping out in the open."

"Come on!" She was in no mood for it.

"Really, I knew a bloke camping outside Molepolole . . ."

"Get out."

"Hey, lovey," he laughed, "why don't you just lighten up, enjoy the
night?"

"I'm not your lovey."

"I didn't mean anything by it."

She looked at him, thought about how he'd sat motionless in the
face of that endless horizon earlier in the day, hardly breathing. It occurred to her that the sight had frightened him. She got up, threw a
log on the fire, and left. Walking outside the circle of light made by the
few lanterns in the tents, she leaned against the back of one of the
Land Rovers. She didn't want to be wasting her years, poised for a fight
with any man who looked at her wrong. She set out for a walk, but
once the light had vanished behind her, she stopped in her tracks.
There was no moon yet, she had no flashlight, and the darkness was to-
tal. She retreated. In the hugeness of that silence, every rustle felt like a
menace.

The next day, they came across an adolescent elephant, walking slowly
away from them, up a track beside the boundary fence. He felt along
the wire every now and then with his trunk, searching. Will had seen
him before, he said, trying to find a way through. He'd been separated
from his family by the fence. It was one of the saddest sights Alice had
ever seen.

On the south side of the Okavango, one of the Land Rovers ran out of gas. Every vehicle was fitted with an auxiliary tank, so when the primary tank ran out, the line was switched to the other tank automatically. But it turned out that the line to this second tank was blocked. The two drivers, Motsumi and Shakespeare, talked in Setswana; then Shakespeare rinsed out a plastic sugar bag and siphoned fuel out of the second tank into the bag, and poured the fuel into the working tank. He did this several times; they drove another five kilometers, and the Land Rover ran out of gas again. In a clearing surrounded by *mopane,* they finally stopped to camp.

They decided that Shakespeare would drive to Maun the next morning for a replacement line, while the rest stayed behind. Once he was in Maun, he'd let Sam and Haddock know they'd been delayed.

Within an hour, a huge dinner was ready. She sat next to Ian, chewing a mouthful of beef, tough as a buzzard. Even out here, in the middle of nowhere, the "professionals" were divided from the cooks and drivers, who sat on the far side of the fire, their backs to the dark bush. Ian, absorbed in his tin plate of meat, rice, gravy, and pumpkin, was happy as a child when he discovered that someone had thought to bring ginger biscuits for dessert. It was only when he'd downed four or five that he seemed to notice anything around him. He turned to her. "I'm sorry about last night. I was a bit cheeky."

"Never mind."

"So, what are you doing here?"

The question irritated her. She couldn't help it. Most expatriate wives came to Botswana as appendages, existing for the purpose of organizing dinner parties and entertaining their husbands' colleagues. No one expected a woman to have a brain in her head. "I could just as soon ask you the same question."

"No offense intended," he said.

"You know, you've met me before."

"I have?"

"My office gave you leave to do the research you're conducting. I guess our meeting wasn't all that memorable."

"I'm grateful for the permission granted."

She couldn't tell whether he was being ironic or not. "To answer your question," she said, "I'm helping to work out compromises between the !Kung San and the Department of Agriculture. Agriculture holds all the cards. I'm one of several people trying to even the deck."

"I wish you good luck with that. As you already know, I'm just a useless toiler. What I do will make no difference to anyone but myself."

"I don't agree."

"How would you know?"

"I read your proposal. People assume that San paintings are nothing more than primitive daubing, with the occasional brilliant rendition of a sable antelope or giraffe," she said, "worth something only because they're so old. But to bring that disappeared world back to life, to try to discover something of the people who inhabited it, what could be more important than that? It might make someone think again before they destroy a culture."

"Do you know the work of Lucy Lloyd and Wilhelm Bleek? Without Lucy, a whole language would have been lost forever."

"It's lost anyway."

"Aren't you the gloomy one."

"Not always. What got you going on all this?"

"I grew up in Manchester, one of five kids," he said. "My mum was a housewife, my dad repaired refrigerators. My dad loved books. He'd read to us at night. He wasn't big on story books. He went in more for real life. He was daft on history, on anything to do with far-off places. Once, he brought a book home on the Bushmen. I was the youngest—three of my brothers and sisters had already left home. Just me and my sister Mary still there. The book had all sorts of pictures—Bushmen sitting under rock shelves, Bushmen hunting eland, a picture of the ruins of a Christian mission. I understood, looking at that photo, that things disappear. Someday I'd be gone, my mum and dad would be gone, my sister Mary, the sitting room, the electric fire, the settee. But it wasn't me or them I was really thinking of—it was those short men crouching in the desert with their bows and poisoned arrows.

"'Where are those little men now?' I asked my father."

"'Dead.'"

"'All of them?'"

"'It was years ago those pictures were taken.'"

"'And what about the paintings on that rock?'"

"'They'll still be there, I reckon, if the rain hasn't washed them away.'"

"'Sure? You mean, if we went there, you and me and Mum and Mary, we could see them?'"

"'Your mum would never go on such a trip. But when you're dead and gone, those pictures you draw now, if someone thinks to look after 'em, it'll be as though part of you's still here.'

"That's when I caught the bug. I'd always wanted to be an artist. I had a knack for it, but compared with a real professional, I wouldn't have made the grade. Through luck and a little elbow grease, I was given a scholarship to Cambridge. Studied anthropology and fine arts and fell into this. What about you?"

Most of the group had drifted away. It was just Sam and Motsumi tending the fire. "What about me? I'm from the Midwest. My mother and I lived close to the river that borders Ohio and Kentucky, just the two of us. My father drowned when I was four. He was a cop. Apparently he was trying to arrest a man running across the Clay Wade Bailey Bridge. It was around one in the morning. He jumped over a railing after the guy and they figure he didn't realize there was a break between the road and the pedestrian walkway. In the dark, he thought he was jumping onto the walkway, but he landed in the river. The water was so cold it took three weeks for his body to surface."

Across from them, Sam pushed a large log into the center of the fire. It flared and sent sparks toward the stars. "Do you remember him?" Ian asked softly.

"Not really." Not memory, but imagining the ice floes far below, the shock when he hit, every fiber of his body broken with disbelief.

"I used to like swimming in very cold water," he said and stopped. "I'm sorry, that was a right stupid thing to say."

"It's all right. What did you like about it?"

"I guess the simple surviving of it. Mind you, I don't have a self-destructive nature. Nor did I have one then. It was something else. Heightening life, I suppose."

He was quiet a moment, looking upward. "Have you read van der Post? He talks about how every human on Earth has a longing for the vast. How does he put it? As the natural coherence of the world vanishes, there's a guilt that grows great and angry in the basement of our being. The beast wants its day. And culture wants to desensitize us to what we've lost. That's why Bushmen are all but stamped out. They're a direct threat to a 'civilized' culture that's inherently unstable. All you have to do is look at one of their paintings, and you know what we've lost. They're alive to the tiniest gesture: the way an impala turns, the way an antelope lifts its head."

"Didn't van der Post father a child with a fourteen-year-old girl who was under his care on a sea voyage?"

"I don't know. It's likely that he did. Not good form. But still, does that wipe out everything else he ever said or did? The point is, people have lost their courage. They've gone for safety. No one wants to be reminded what a tiny speck in the universe we are, but knowing that's the key to everything. We're afraid of big spaces. We herd for safety, and before you know it, you've got civilization. But in the wild, look what happens. Which animals do lions choose to prey upon? Zebra and wildebeest. Animals that travel in herds. The herd feels like safety, but it only makes us more vulnerable."

"Animals in herds *are* safer. The chances for any individual's dying is slim."

"I don't mean we need to wander around in the desert by ourselves. I mean face how ridiculously small we are. Just look at this sky. How many hundreds of billions of galaxies are we seeing, as big or bigger than our own? Freedom comes from knowing you're a dot. Smaller than a dot.

Sam and Motsumi had gone to their tent. "Listen to me pontificating," he said. "You were talking about your father."

"I'm done talking about him." She told Ian she needed to go to bed. She wasn't tired, but something between them was ratcheting up. She was scared, actually. It had been awhile since she'd talked to a man with even one idea in his head. There were men, plenty of them, better looking than Ian, without the beginning of a paunch, without the gold tooth, bottom left of center, but not who read books, and thought, and imagined, and asked questions. She had an irrational desire to start a fight, drive him away.

"Are you married?"

"Not anymore," she said.

"How long has it been?"

"Eight months."

"You fell out of love?"

"Something like that. I didn't know what I was doing."

"Who does? Who hasn't fucked up their life?"

It was an opening, but something kept her from asking how he'd fucked up his. She didn't want to know. They were quiet.

"Have you ever been to Moremi?" he asked.

"No."

"Would you like to go?"

"How far is it?"

"We could get there and back in a day. Nothing else is happening tomorrow. We'd have to ask if any of the others want to go, of course."

The "we" wasn't lost on her. "That would leave everyone else without a vehicle," she said.

"Damn it, do you want to go or not?"

"Sure I want to go."

"Well, then, we'll go." He left to talk to the others and came back saying they all wanted to stay here. How had he put it to them? A long, grueling drive? Not much to see? Somehow she knew he'd figured a way for them to be alone.

She tossed on her cot, the sound of her heartbeat in her ear. Blood pumped through chambers and echoed. Her head was pillowed on the lump of sweater she'd brought for chilly nights. The sound continued, magnified, her head filled with it. She missed rain. She wanted it to fall in torrents, for the dust to rise off the steaming earth.

She believed her parents had been deeply in love. After her father died, her mother became a ghost. Once, she'd wondered out loud whether Alice's father had jumped from the bridge on purpose. It never would have occurred to Alice if her mother hadn't said it. Growing up, she tumbled around in her mother's anger. Much of it seemed directed at her, as though she should have saved her father and hadn't. She remembered Saturdays, rain-drenched windows, rivulets forming and reforming on the glass, streaming down. A clock humming on the wall, with its click to the next second, and the next.

Her mother was protective of her and ambitious for them both, but she'd never led Alice to believe that happiness was something within her grasp. After her father died, her mother went back to school and became an English teacher.

"Why don't you date anyone, Mom?" Alice asked one night. Her mother was lovely still, with a southern European kind of elegance. Eyebrows that arched upward and fell gracefully. Her nose, long, slightly curved. Her skin, ivory and unmarked. It was her gray-green eyes, though, particularly the melancholy in them, that carried her beauty.

"I'm not putting you through that," her mother said.

"Through what?"

"A string of losers, in and out of my bed. I don't know any man I'd want to date."

"There are men around who aren't losers."

"Show me one."

Alice was reading *Jane Eyre* in a fast-track sophomore English class. "Mr. Rochester," she said.

"Mr. Rochester was a figment of Charlotte Brontë's imagination," her mother snorted. "In real life, her sisters and brothers died of TB. Then she married her father's curate and died in childbirth. Her husband was boring and selfish."

"You don't know that."

"I know the type. Someday, you'll know what I'm talking about."

Alice got off the cot and lifted the flap of the tent. The half moon was heading downward, toward a clump of baobab trees on the horizon, bare-limbed, their trunks broad and wrinkled. Somewhere in the distance was the sound of two black-backed jackals, yips rising and falling, silence. And nearer, the sound of her heartbeat in her ear.

20

The two of them left early the following morning, conspiratori-
ally, slipping out before the others had left their tents. She knew there'd
be talk, speculation about whether they'd shared a tent, but she didn't
care. The baobab trees were bathed in saffron light as the mist rose off
the great plain to their east. The engine of the Land Rover was loud,
alien in that bird-filled air. Ian started up with the headlights off and
then flicked them on after they'd left the campsite. One beam was
crooked and shone drunkenly into the scrubby limbs of trees as the vehicle labored through the sand. She'd raided the cook's tent before they
left, and she offered Ian coffee from a thermos. He waved the cup away.
"Have to pay attention or we'll turn turtle."

She poured some for herself and took a sip.

"So, we got away," he said.

"I feel a little guilty."

"Do you often feel that then?"

"No more than the next person . . . Well, maybe a bit more."

As a guinea fowl raced across the track, Ian's foot came off the accel-
erator for a moment and went back on. "Why did your marriage come
to grief?" he asked. "You don't need to say if you'd rather not."

"Lawrence lied to me about an affair. We could have withstood
that, but then he kept lying. There was something dishonest at the
core of us. He was . . . is an economist. It seemed that's all he could talk
about."

"What did you like about him?"

She looked out the window onto the tawny grass, tufted around red

earth, the occasional termite tower rising like a stalagmite. She thought
of a time when she and Lawrence had done angel stands together in
the grass, he lying on his back with his feet in the air, she balanced on
his feet, flying through the night.

"Underneath it all, he has a kind nature. Not courage, but kindness.
He's not just in this country for himself, but because he wants to help.
He believes he's making things better."

"Do you?"

"Probably not. But I'd say the same for what I'm doing. I appreciate
that it matters to him. But it's good that it's over. I see that now. I felt
half dead around him."

"I've felt that kind of dead," Ian said, glancing at her. "It's preferable
to be all the way dead."

"I don't want to be any kind of dead."

"What do you want for yourself then?" he asked.

She watched the track, and him out of the corner of her eye. His
head was large, his hair dark with streaks of gray. One side of his tor-
toiseshell glasses was mended with duct tape. Lawless eyebrows strayed
down over brown eyes. He was a bear of a man, with large hands. He
was beginning to sag here and there—the lower part of his face toward
jowls, the skin over his eyes meeting his eyelids in their downward
journey.

"What do I want for myself?" She searched out the black specks on
the horizon, trying to make out the animals. "A life that's large, not
small."

"With someone or without?" He was watching the animals too.

"It depends."

He waited for her to say more.

There were hundreds in the herd, maybe thousands, moving relent-
lessly forward. "I think they're wildebeest," she said. They were driving
along a rise, with the plain stretched beneath them. The herd formed
and re-formed, darkening the drought-swept ground. Their heads
were down, tails dangling, wind weariness in their bodies.

"Poor bastards," he said. "They don't know what's ahead of them."

She pictured the fingers of the Okavango Delta reaching into the dusty plain. You could almost smell it, miles away. There's a way around that fence, she thought, at the same time she knew there wasn't.

When she was a girl, her mother had taken her to places on weekends. An aquarium one Saturday, the Cincinnati zoo the next. A shark tank in the center of the aquarium had extra thick glass you could press your cheek against. It felt cool, and when you turned your head, it was as though you were underwater. She remembered her mother screaming as a shark came up on the other side of the glass and nosed the place where her cheek was.

What she remembered most about those outings, though, was her mother's melancholy—the collapse of a world, her daughter a single thread connecting her to what went before. A young ape in the zoo held a banana in one hand and sat close to the bars looking out. Kids came up and screamed. "Hey! Hey!" Alice stood in front of him a long time waiting for him to look in her direction. Their eyes met straight on. Then he lowered his head, peeled the banana delicately, carefully, and dropped the peel at his feet. With a single motion, he popped the whole thing into his mouth and swung away, up into the limbs of a fake tree. He dazzled her, that beautiful young ape. She'd seen the wild in him, the great forests, and for a moment she lived there too.

It was like that now.

Ian turned up a smaller track, headed northwest. The herd was to their right now, and they could see the first animals about a half kilometer from the fence. He stopped and fished a pair of binoculars out of his knapsack, then started up the vehicle again. His face looked suddenly hard. He was no longer driving in an ambling, relaxed way. She felt a kind of terror overtake her.

"Where are we going?" she asked.

"I don't want to involve you, but there's something I need to do."

It was mad being out here with a man she hardly knew, the nearest person too far to reach on foot even if she'd known where she was.

"I'm going to try to cut the fence," he said quietly. "I could go to prison for it. You could go as my accomplice. If you want, I'll leave you here under a tree and come back for you."

It only took a second to say, "I'm coming too."

They drew closer, still unable to see the wire but close enough to see the posts stretching endlessly in either direction. The first animals in the herd were already close to the fence. It was too late, she thought, even as she scrambled out of the Land Rover and Ian rummaged among the tools in the back.

He found a screwdriver, a claw hammer, a pair of vice grips, a wrench, a funnel for oil, nothing useful. He grabbed the vice grips and hammer, and they ran to the right of the area where the animals were headed. When they reached the fence, he held the wire with the vice grips and twisted the claw of the hammer around the wire, then rocked it back and forth. "Stand back in case it snaps."

The wire was thick, and the tools were useless.

He tried again. And then he tried digging around a post with a rock and the hammer, but the dirt was cement hard. The first of the wildebeest arrived at the barrier about two to three hundred meters away. Others followed. Some of the first were pushed into the fence and fell. Alice turned away. Ian watched for a few moments and turned and slammed the hammer into a fence post. It flew out of his hand, and he left it there and stalked back to the Land Rover. "Bloody hell," he muttered. "Bloody fucking hell . . ." She picked up the hammer and followed him.

She was surprised to find him in the driver's seat with tears running down his cheeks. She climbed in, and he put the vehicle in gear and drove away. They headed toward Moremi Game Reserve, their mood somber. "It's people like that cold fish," he said, "responsible for that. What has he ever learned in Milwaukee about this world? He's frightened of anything he doesn't understand. Did you hear him last night?"

"Yes, I heard him. God knows how much money he'll be in charge of dispensing."

"Or how he'll use it. If he saw what we just saw . . ."

"It wouldn't make any difference," she said. "He'd find a way to justify it."

They drove along for a while without talking.

"We're about ten kilometers away from the park," he said. "There'll be mosquitoes. You're on chloroquine, aren't you?"

"Yes." What did he think she was, an idiot?

In the park, they saw more wildebeest, waterbuck with their tawny skin and white rumps, hundreds of impala, red lechwe, zebra, giraffe browsing on trees, a family of warthogs, a saddlebilled stork. In the late afternoon, a double rainbow spread over a wide plain of yellow grass, where a small herd of sable antelope was grazing, their white cheeks and chins giving their faces a kind of delicacy, their ringed horns swept back in great curves. She thought this was the most devastatingly beautiful thing she'd ever seen.

He stood close to her, quiet, looking out. "No lions today," he said finally.

"I didn't come just for lions."

"What did you come for then?"

She turned toward him. "I've loved everything about being with you today. Even the worst of it."

They drove back toward camp slowly, taking a detour to try to find the man he'd been looking for the other night. He pulled off the track and headed overland across scrub savannah. They bounced along as the light slanted into gold. She didn't see the group of grass huts until they were nearly on top of them, built in a loose circle near a water hole. Two women sat outside, one with a baby at the breast. Several children played near a small fire. She recognized Ngwaga's name as Ian greeted the group in a language of clicks and pops.

"They say he's coming back soon," he told Alice. An old woman joined the group and looked at them curiously. Her small breasts hung flat on her chest. Her eyes were small, intelligent, distant-looking. One of the younger women offered them a cup of tea and biltong. The tea tasted like ashes, like red dust and sun.

She looked at Ian, squatting companionably near the three women. He wasn't handsome in any conventional sense, but his eyes were extremely blue. Blue enough to disarm, to take up space of their own. She guessed he was somewhere between ten and fifteen years older than she was. She hadn't bothered to ask. He offered cigarettes to the group, and they smoked together companionably as the color seeped slowly out of the sky. Ngwaga finally returned with a skin bag slung over one shoulder and embraced Ian. He was a healthy-looking man with a small white scraggle of a beard, deep horizontal lines running across his forehead, and a ready laugh. When he went to shake Alice's hand, he held out just his fingers, warm and leathery. They set out in the Land Rover, the three of them sitting side by side, making their way slowly over darkening scrub, back to the main track. At one point, Ngwaga pointed to her and laughed, nudged her leg with his skinny thigh.

"What did he say?" she asked Ian.

He didn't answer her.

"Tell me."

"That my woman has long legs like an ostrich."

She laughed. "Big feet like one too." She let the "my woman" go.

She had no idea how Ian found his way. It was night when they returned, with the others already eating dinner around the fire. "Any food left?" Ian asked.

"Goat stew," said Shakespeare. "Plenty left." He'd returned with the replacement fuel line.

She sat on the other side of the fire from Ngwaga and Ian, who passed a bottle of wine between them. The darkness took up all the space around them. The moon was a curved palm low in the sky. Alice couldn't take her eyes off Ngwaga. He sat in a circle of firelight, disturbing nothing, in harmony with fire, night, stars. He spoke with his hands, his tongue clicking as he formed words. He filled a small pipe with tobacco and lit it. When he'd had a few puffs, he turned to Ian and spoke for a while. When he'd finished, Ian nodded, grew quiet, and stared into the flames. A few minutes later, Ian crossed to the other side of the fire and sat down next to Alice.

"Okay?" she asked.

He nodded. "You?"

"Yes, what was he saying just now?"

"A story his grandfather had told him. About how the wind used to be a man. But then Wind no longer walked as he used to do, he no longer slept with his wife. He flew about. 'That is how the wind behaves,' he said. 'It flies about. It goes from place to place to place, always moving, never standing still. You are a man like that. A man who is part wind.'"

"Do you think that's true?"

"Yes."

"Does it worry you?"

"To be so entirely transparent?"

"I mean the wind part."

"I've never been otherwise. But I guess it serves as a warning."

"For me? I already knew it."

Across the fire, Sam said, "Ngwaga wants to know what happens to the spacemen who walk on the moon when the moon becomes smaller."

"What do you think happens?" Ian asked him.

"They must only take trips to the moon when the moon is full," Ian translated. "They must hurry to accomplish their work. And as it grows smaller, they must run to the side without the bite out of it. And when it's time to come back, they wait until the moon is setting, and then they jump to the Earth."

"You're not going to let him keep thinking that," said C.T.

"Why not?" asked Ian. "Why shouldn't he think that?"

"Because it's wrong."

"*You* explain it then," said Ian. "Alice and I were just going anyway."

It was not gracefully or graciously done. And part of her didn't like that he'd spoken for her. She excused herself, said good night, and left the light of the fire. She found Ian standing in the shadows, halfway to the tents.

"You're a bit of a hothead, aren't you."

"That was boorish of me," he said. "But I had to get away from that prick."

"My boss?"

"Why, do you like him?"

"I don't dislike him."

"He's a conventionally minded little man. He ought to be adding columns of figures instead of the job he's doing. Why shouldn't people believe what they want to believe about the moon?"

He peered at her in the darkness. "Are you happy?"

"Why do you ask?"

He pulled her toward him and kissed her. His mouth was soft and tasted of wine. Something in her head said, This man is a rapscallion.

She expected he'd ask to come to her tent. She had no answer for him, but she knew there was no will left in her. As though hearing this, he said, "We don't have to hurry. We have all the time in the world."

Do we? she wanted to ask.

"Don't you feel that?" he asked.

"No." She felt hot now, feverish. She took off the light jacket she was wearing and threw it over her arm. She began to cry softly.

"Shall I come to you tonight then?"

She began to shake. "No." Something had grown too full in her to be held. She could love this man, given half a chance, and it scared her silly and shattered her with happiness. She could hardly see him in that light. He moved closer and drew her body to his. She cried harder.

"What?"

"Don't worry," she said.

"What?"

"I've been pent up." She stopped abruptly and wiped her nose on her sleeve like a child. She hated to cry.

"You've been living like a Hartford housewife."

"It wasn't his fault."

"I didn't say it was. But it wasn't in your nature."

She squeezed his arm with both hands.

"I'm too old for you," he said.

"What difference does it make?"

"It makes a difference. Think about it."

"I have."

"You don't know who I am."

"I know enough."

"What do you know?"

"You're uncivilized."

"How do you know that?"

"I've been watching you."

"And I you."

"And what have you seen?"

He paused. "You're bright and brave, and you've been hurt. Your best time is early morning."

She laughed. "Your best time is when the moon rises."

They stood side by side, her head against the top of his arm.

"Well good night then," she said.

"You're going?"

"Yes." But then she didn't. They went back to the campfire and found no one there. Ian kicked up the ashes with his boot and threw on a couple of hunks of wood. A shooting star flared across the edge of her vision, and then she wasn't sure whether it was a star or a spark from the fire rising into the darkness. And there was the moon over the top of the low trees, shining with all its distant mountains and valleys. She looked at him out of the corner of her eye and saw a shaggy head, dark against the light of the fire.

"What are you thinking?" he asked.

"That you look like a beast in this light."

"Friendly or savage?"

"Midway."

The fire hit a pocket of air inside a log and exploded.

Over the following two days the group met with Bushmen leaders outside of Maun, and with a group of ranchers, all of whom managed large herds of cattle. One of Alice's jobs was documenting conversations with groups whose positions felt irreconcilable. Arthur Haddock was immovable. He'd return to Gaborone and talk with his wife of forty-five years about the primitive men he'd met who were still running after wild animals with bows and arrows.

The roads were very bad: deep sand, deeper ruts, rocks jutting up unpredictably here and there. One or another vehicle got stuck and had to be dug out. On the way to Sehitwa, the truck had a flat, then a shock absorber on one of the Land Rovers went. The temperature gauge on the second Land Rover began climbing, and after changing the tire on the truck, it spiked up to the danger zone. The three vehicles stopped. "The gauge is bad," said Shakespeare optimistically. He put his hand companionably on the hood. He filled up the radiator, and they started out again. The gauge stayed in the red zone. They stopped again. "Could be a leak somewhere," said Will.

"I say we turn around," said Haddock.

"We've got two more vehicles," Alice said. "Why would we turn around?"

Will lay down in the sand and wriggled underneath the Land Rover. He came back out. "The radiator's taken one too many rocks." He had a short conference with Shakespeare and Sam, who rummaged around in a tin box and brought out a container of pepper. They let the radiator cool down, then Shakespeare removed the radiator cap, measured out a couple of teaspoons of pepper into the palm of his hand, and threw in the grains.

They let it sit for a quarter of an hour so that the grains could settle and plug the hole, brewed tea by the side of the road, and started up the vehicles again. The gauge went down and stayed down for an hour or so, but then began climbing again. They arrived in Sehitwa close to nightfall, and Sam went looking for a mechanic. It turned out the only one around was away for the week up near the Caprivi Strip. "We can stay here and wait for the guy to get back," said Will, "we can take a chance and go on, or we can limp back to Maun. I'd say we go back. There are too few vehicles on the road if we get into trouble. The good Land Rover can follow the other."

"Trip's over," Haddock said, with something close to satisfaction.

"Trip's not over," said Alice. "That leaves one vehicle." She'd wanted to get to the Tsodilo Hills ever since coming to Botswana. She'd seen pictures of San paintings on red rocks, the strokes of their ancient brushes capturing mystery. She could picture the lonely hills, the overhanging cliffs that protected the paintings. She knew Ian had been there dozens of times, had copied each panel of drawings into a notebook, had studied them stroke by stroke.

"It's probably best to call it a day," said her boss.

She looked at the Chevy truck, its willing snout, its sturdy wheels sitting in the sand, and thought it could get her there. The moment felt like a microcosm of her whole life—near misses, giving up too soon. It made her want to scream, standing there in the heat, eyes stinging with tears she had no intention of shedding.

"Don't mind me," she said. "I'm going off to pee. Avert your eyes." She walked behind the truck, pulled down her pants and squatted. A small dribble was all there was. She pulled up her pants and stayed behind the bed of the truck and whispered, *Fuck! Fuckfuckfuck!* She was wrong about the tears, which came without her bidding. She'd understood through Ngwaga that the !Kung San were still living forces, their world existing beyond the comprehension of people like her. She felt she'd been close to perceiving that mysterious, incomprehensible world, that she would have touched it beyond Nokaneng and Gomare, in the hills rising from the plains.

21

Isaac went to the small grocery store in the Old Village to buy bread one morning, and read the news on the front page of the paper.

> South African security forces attacked two houses in a poor neighborhood of Botswana's capital, Gaborone, early today, killing seven people and wounding three. A car with South African registration plates was seen in the neighborhood of one of the houses shortly before gunfire interrupted the predawn quiet.
>
> According to government officials, two men were killed by gunfire at one site, while at the other site, two men, two women, and a child lost their lives. The incursion touched off fears of a renewal of cross-border attacks by South African forces against African National Congress guerrillas. The Botswana government has deplored the attacks against its citizens and called upon the United Nations for condemnation.

The couple who ran the store were South African, talking to a white customer when he came in. "They used loudspeakers," the wife said, "and told people to stay in their houses. The South Africans had no choice really. They have to take care of this violent fringe before they kill any more innocent people."

The white customer said, "What about the two women and the child?"

"Those women were connected to the ANC. They were connected. The child couldn't be helped."

Isaac bought a paper and went outside. A dove sat in a tree on the corner, singing her song. He didn't buy bread. He would never buy from those people again. He intended to read the rest of the story, but he knew in his knees, in his gut what had happened and where it had happened. White Dog followed him, her tail low. Isaac took her back to the house, gave her food and a bowl of water, told her to stay, and walked up the road toward town. He was not sure, but he remembered that Amen was going to teach a training course in Angola. He had not spoken ten words to him since they'd fought. Unless Kagiso was visiting her family, she'd have been there last night. Ontibile had been next to her, lying on the mat on her back with her arms outstretched and her mouth open, dreaming the dreams of a child.

He walked straight to the Princess Marina Hospital and through the front doors. The Sister in charge told him that she could not give him any information, that she was under orders not to give out names. She was a white woman, in the garb of a nun. "Are you a family member?"

He paused. "Kagiso is my sister, and Ontibile is her child."

"What is their surname?" she asked.

He hesitated, trying to remember, during which time the nun knew he was lying. "Thebe," he said.

"I'm sorry, we're doing our best for the child."

"And the mother?"

"I regret I cannot say."

"May I see the child?"

"No, sir. I don't believe you are a close family member. I'm under strict instructions."

He went away, cursing himself. He had paused in front of that nun because in his head Kagiso and Ontibile never had a surname. They were just Kagiso and Ontibile. It seemed that Ontibile might be alive. Kagiso, he didn't know. She was either at Ontibile's bedside, or she had passed from this world.

He turned around and reentered the hospital. A young Motswana

Sister met him. "Can you tell me if Kagiso Thebe is with Ontibile, her child? I am here to give her something."

"She is not with the child."

"Has she been here?"

The first Sister reappeared. "I am sorry, sir. You must leave now."

He went out into the street. The sun was so bright and strong there was no hiding from it. In his mind the train was coming for Kopano. He saw the two members of the South African Defense Force, their uniforms the color of dirt, their berets worn at an angle, as though they were saying life is a joke. He was filled with such rage and hatred he couldn't see. The road was a white hot light, like an electric wire humming. He cursed Modimo in the heavens, he cursed the country of his birth. He cursed Amen for his arrogance. His fists were in his eye sockets, his head exploding with the ruin of lives. If they have touched Kagiso or Ontibile, his voice was roaring—what, what would he not do?

He ran toward Amen's house, his body disorganized, his feet hardly working, falling down the street. People moved around him, giving him space. He felt heavy with a complicated, helpless shame. He could do nothing. Feet running, running. The sun so hot. No shadow anywhere. He plunged down the path into Naledi.

At the shebeen, he stopped. The old men were sitting under trees on *kgotla* chairs sucking their gums. Red-eyed with *Chibuku*, stubble on their chins. Loud music was playing. "*Dumelang, borra,*" he said.

"*Dumela, rra,*" one said, as though he didn't want to.

They stumbled through the rest of the greeting, asking each other how they'd gotten up that morning. Fine, fine. He stood in a pool of quiet.

"Do you know about the South African shooting last night?" he asked.

"*Ee, rra.*"

"Was anyone hurt?" It was best to be innocent, the young goat that bleats and knows nothing.

"*Ee, rra,* people were hurt. Just there." The old man pointed in the direction of Amen's house. "But you cannot go there. There are many police."

"Did you know any of the people in the house?"

"No, *rra,* we didn't know them."

Another said, "We hear that it was women and children. Family of ANC members. The South Africans fired on the house. They didn't care who was in there."

"Shame," said a younger man, wearing a skullcap.

"I have heard they have done the same in Lesotho," said the most grizzled of the old men. His shoulder was bare, his shirt ripped around a jutting bone.

"And in Angola."

"*Ehee.*" Their voices became a low music.

"Did you know the people in the house?" the man with the ripped shirt asked.

"I lived in that place," said Isaac. It shocked him that he'd told them. Tears came to his eyes. He wanted to sit on the ground at the knees of the grizzled man and be comforted. All these months he'd told no one where he lived, or with whom, and now he'd told these strangers.

The old man's rheumy eyes overflowed. He looked up at the leaves of the mosetlha tree as though to say we are alive by God's grace. "But you were not there last night."

"No."

"The angel of death had mercy on you."

"*Ee, rra.*"

Several of the old men looked at him as though he were already dead. And then one of them said, "It's not their country to do with what they please. Those bastards came over the border last night. They brought their guns into this place and killed mothers and babies."

"We need an army," said a round-faced, dark-skinned man who'd said nothing up until then. "How does the government protect its people? We need guns, we need soldiers."

"You think that would stop them?" the grizzled man said. He turned to Isaac. "If you go there," he gestured with his chin, "they will shoot you too."

Isaac said good-bye and hurried on his way. The closer he came to Amen's house, the quieter it seemed to become—like being in a lonely place, hearing footsteps approaching from behind, you don't know who is coming, and you sense it is an evil thing and the hair rises up on the back of your neck. The person uppermost in his mind was Kagiso. He pictured her that first day he met her when her eyes sang with joy. She smiled so wide, like a girl. Her dress stirred in the wind. Her neck was damp with the steam coming from the cooking pot, and little hairs curled out from beneath the scarf wrapped around her head. Walking toward Amen's house, he feared for her the way a man fears for his wife, so strongly that his ears boomed. He thought of the night when Amen was away and Kagiso called out in her sleep and he went to her and held her hand.

As he came around the last corner before the house and saw the police vehicles and a great swarming crowd of people, he could still see nothing of the house. From where he stood, he recognized a few neighbors, but there were many strangers too, people who'd come from far away. The police were shouting, "Get back, get back! Go home!" But the people were not moving. Their lips were silent, and they stood watching, solemn as a church. Isaac pushed his way into the crowd and stood in front of the door.

To the left was the wall where Kagiso had hung the magazine pages. The bullets from the guns had put a hole in the woman's smiling head and in her hand holding the box of Lil-lets tampons, and there were holes in the boy looking up at his mother and eating a McVitie's digestive biscuit. And farther into the room, splashed on the wall, were dark sprays of blood.

The police closed the door. They shouted again for the crowd to get back, get back! They pushed with their sticks turned sideways, and people moved a little, but when the police turned their backs, the crowd came forward again, a little closer than before. Next door was a woman he'd seen many times. She was filling her can with water. He pushed out of the crowd and went to this woman and greeted her softly, "Dumela, mma."

She started as though he were a ghost. "You were not there?"

"No, mma."

"You are one lucky person."

"Do you know who is alive?"

"No one, *rra,* except for one little child."

"The mother?"

"The mother is late."

"You are sure?"

"I am sure. My husband is with the police."

"Do you know which child is alive?"

"I do not know this, *rra.*" She was holding a cloth in her hands and twisting it until the cloth rose up in a knot.

He walked away. The road to the Old Village was quiet, subdued by the deaths in town. When he returned to the house, the sun was close to setting and White Dog was waiting, her tail wagging just at the tip. He leaned down and patted her. Where the smooth fur grew was a lump which he knew to be a tick. He pulled it from her and squashed it in his fingers. He washed the tick blood from his hands, drank some water from the spigot, and filled a bowl with water for White Dog. Mr. Magoo and Horse sat watching him with their slitty eyes. Inside, he fed canned sardines to them. His stomach was an empty cave that did not wish to be filled.

White Dog trailed him, and Isaac went to the quiet place in the wild part of the garden and squatted by the big aloes. The sky was light when he went there, and little by little it darkened until one and one, and ten and ten, and a thousand and a thousand million stars came out. He looked at the stars and planets and felt them ripped from their sockets by a wind hurled from the heavens. To whom would he pray? In that huge, quiet, senseless darkness, he understood that he could no longer believe in a god who let such things happen. All his life, he'd been taught to pray, but now there was no one there. When he was younger, his favorite book in the Bible was the book of Ezekiel. *Then the spirit took me up, and I heard behind me a voice of a great rushing, saying, Blessed be the glory of the Lord* ... At night, he'd believed he could hear the great rushing stars and the wings of the living creatures that touched one another and the tumult of that mighty voice. In the space between the noise of people and radios had been the great voice, the glory that could not be seen. The voice was gone now, stilled like a child who turns blue before taking his last earthly breath.

That night, he dreamt that he was traveling in a car driven by Amen. They were headed toward the border, south on the Lobatse Road. The lights of a lorry traveling in the other direction came closer and closer, and he shouted at Amen that they were on the wrong side of the road. It was already too late. Amen swerved, and Isaac woke into darkness.

Lying in bed, he remembered the money under the loose bit of concrete in the floor of Amen's house. He'd heard people say they would bulldoze the house. His eyes stared into the dark room, all the time thinking about the concrete which hid the money that would buy his brother's shoes and help the younger ones return to school.

He knew now without a doubt that it was his duty to get them out of South Africa. Those men who came over the border were true to their nature. You could live in Bophuthatswana or Pretoria or Johannesburg trying to make the best life you could, but all the while you would find white men wishing you evil. He had an idea that whatever his life was lived for, it must be lived for getting his sister and brothers away from there. One baby sister was already dead, a death that would not have happened if she had been somewhere else.

He turned on the light and put on his trousers. The darkness was close and hot. In the kitchen, he wrote a letter first to his mother and then to his mother's employers, Hendrik and Hester Pretorius. To both he said that he would like to get Lulu, his seven-year-old sister, and his two brothers, Tshepiso and Moses, out of Bophuthatswana into Botswana. He did not know how to manage this, he told them, but if they could find a way to get the children across the border, he would find a place for them to live and a way to care for them. They would go to good schools and be safe every day. He believed that his mother might agree. She never saw the children now except for a day every few months. She knew what awaited them if they stayed in South Africa. He said in the letters that he was working for a good person and that all would be well if the children could reach the border. He believed with every beat of his heart that this was the right thing to do.

He wanted also to write to Nthusi, but he did not know where to find him. When he got the money out of the floor of Amen's house, he would wait to hear from his mother and then send the money and ask her to buy shoes for Nthusi. He put his head down on the table intending only to close his eyes for a moment, but when he next opened them the sun was up, and his neck felt as though an ox had stood on it. He fed the cats and White Dog and watered the lemon and grapefruit trees and the vegetables in the garden. The flowers of the tomato plants had already set into tiny tomatoes. Each small chili pepper was reaching with small hands toward the sky.

He made *mabele* for breakfast. The last time he'd seen Kagiso, she was making porridge. Kagiso found such pleasure in food. How happy she was after her brother had given her the leg of the goat. He could imagine the smell of the meat coming from the three-legged pot, see Kagiso's legs straight as she bent from the waist, stirring the stew. He could not believe she was gone.

The sadness told his belly not to eat, that it would only make him sick. He drank some water, left the pot of *mabele* on the table for when he returned home, picked up the two letters to mail, changed to a clean shirt, and went outdoors. He set a bowl of water on the ground for White Dog and told her to stay. She tried to follow him, and three times he had to chase her home.

He went straight to Princess Marina Hospital. He thought if he went early, perhaps he could listen at the windows to know where the babies were. The road was still fairly empty and the light hazy, as though the day was half asleep. When he reached the grounds of the hospital, he walked around the building. At first, all was quiet. He waited. And finally, at the far corner, he heard the sound of crying. It was not Ontibile's voice, but the cries of the child told him where she would be if she was still alive.

Food, he saw, was delivered through a door to the kitchen, and instead of walking in the front, past that Sister who could smell a lie, he decided to walk through the backdoor. If you look as though you know who you are and why you are there, with complete confidence, people usually do not ask you questions. He remembered what his grandfather had told him: hold your head high and expose your throat and chest to danger, and people will think you are not afraid. If you hang your head low like an old donkey, people will say, "Hey, what are you doing here? Get out!" He lifted his head and put his chest out, not puffed out like a silly guinea fowl in mating season, but just enough, and entered.

"*Dumela, rra,*" he said to a man stirring a large pot on a stove. "*O kae?*"

"*Ke teng.*" I am well.

"Sister is waiting for me."

"*Ee hee.*" Ah, yes.

He passed out of the kitchen into the hall, and from there, he quickly turned in the direction from where he'd heard the child's cry. There was no one in the hall outside the kitchen, but directly he came to a place where mothers were crouched in the hall with special food for their little ones. Worry lined their faces. He greeted them and said quietly that he was visiting his niece. A young nurse came to him inside the room and still with his head high, he greeted her and said, "Sister at the front desk said that I could find my niece here, Ontibile Thebe."

"She is over there, sir."

"How is she doing?"

"You are . . . ?"

"*Ee, mma,* I am her uncle. I have traveled here from Mochudi." Meanwhile he was searching searching for her, and then he saw her sitting on a little cot in the corner. She was quite still, but her eyes were watching.

"She is ready to be released but we have no family member."

Amen had not been here. Either he was dead, or alive in Angola, or staying somewhere nearby, knowing that he would be picked up if he came for his daughter. "I'm here to take her to her grandmother. I will be returning to Mochudi this evening."

"*Ee hee,*" said the nurse. She was fresh-faced, and young enough not to know the rules. Ontibile put out her hands to him. He picked her up and held her close, and she wrapped her arms around his neck and laid her cheek against his ear.

"She was not wounded," said the nurse. "She was found under her mother. The police brought her here because they didn't know where else to take her. She has been asking for her mother. I am very sorry for your loss."

His eyes filled.

"Where did you say her granny is?"

"*Ee, mma.* She is in Mochudi." He was lying and lying. He knew nothing about the granny except that Kagiso went to see her now and then.

The nurse brought a discharge paper, and he signed it, using a name that he thought up while he was writing. The nurse gathered up Ontibile's blanket and gave it to him along with a bottle of milk and some biscuits, and he walked out the side door, which was locked from the outside but open on the inside.

When they were out under the open sky, he felt Ontibile's body relax into his. She could not understand anything. She thought he was taking her to Kagiso. He wished with all his heart that his breasts could pour out milk for her. He didn't know what to do, where he would go. His legs took him to the post office to mail the letters he had written, and then toward Naledi. Ontibile seemed to sense that she was headed toward home. Her throat made a little humming sound, and by and by her head fell onto his shoulder, and she slept as they walked. He took her on a route around the shebeen so the loud music wouldn't wake her. By then, the sun was already hot. He put his hand over the top of her head to give her shade, but still, little beads of sweat formed along her hairline and on her upper lip, and her springy hair felt moist in the palm of his hand.

A policeman was standing guard outside Amen's house, and a few people were watching to see what would happen. Nothing was happening. It felt like a cursed place. He asked an old woman staring at the house if she knew Ditsego, a friend of Kagiso's who had a baby about the same age as Ontibile. The woman shook her head and moved away from him. He was sure that Ditsego lived not too far distant. From what he remembered Kagiso saying, she had known her friend before coming to Naledi.

He went next door. "No, *rra*," the woman there said, "I do not know Ditsego, but you could ask Grace Moatihaping who lives just there." She pointed to a shack made of tin. "She knows everyone."

Grace was not home, and he sat on her stoop to wait. Ontibile was still sleeping and growing heavier in his arms. He looked into her face, so peaceful in her dreaming. Grace did not come. Ontibile woke and was hungry. He fed her the biscuits the nurse had given him and gave her the bottle of milk to suck. He asked other people whether they knew Ditsego, and he asked them when Grace would be coming. By then it was afternoon. No one knew anything, or perhaps because of the shooting, they were afraid of him, a stranger.

At the end of the afternoon, Grace returned. She was a large woman who smiled easily. Her complexion was ash colored like the side of a cooking pot, and her teeth were very white. He told her the story, all of it. She had known Kagiso. She reached for Ontibile and took her onto her lap.

"You know Ditsego?"

"I will take you there," she said. But first she offered him tea and bread, which he refused. They set off toward Ditsego's house as the sun was setting. Dust from the day's labors had risen all over Gaborone and caused the sun to glow huge and orange. And then the day's furnace was gone in a blur, and the sky turned a fury of red. Ditsego's house was not far distant from Grace's but it was difficult to get there, the paths twisting this way and that. They found her sitting outside with her baby, who was nursing drowsily. The baby's mouth moved a little, and then it was still for some time until she remembered the breast and sucked once or twice more.

Ditsego listened and wept, her tears falling into her baby's hair. She rose, took the baby inside, and came out without her. When she lifted Ontibile from Isaac's arms, it was as though she'd been born for that moment. She sat back down on the stoop and offered her breast, and Ontibile took it and sucked eagerly.

It became dark before she took Ontibile inside and laid her down on the mat beside the other baby. As the half moon rose with its ragged edge, Isaac talked with Grace and Ditsego about what to do. Yes,

Ditsego knew Kagiso's family in Mochudi. She did not know whether they yet knew about their daughter's death. But she said she would take Ontibile there by bus tomorrow or the next day. Isaac offered to go with her, but she said her husband would be returning from Francistown on the morning train and he would come.

She said she would offer to the family to nurse Ontibile until she was not needing the breast any longer, and then Ontibile could live with her granny in Mochudi. Or if living with her granny was not possible, Ditsego would raise her as her own child.

"Go," she told Isaac. "Don't worry." Isaac went inside and watched Ontibile sleeping. He went down on his hands and knees and kissed her cheek and whispered, "*Sala sentle, ngwanyana.*" Stay well, little one.

He walked a little way with Grace and asked her the way back to Amen's house; he was turned around and had no idea where he was. He felt sick from hunger, and his head swam with sorrow. When at last he knew where he was, he thanked Grace, and they parted ways.

Later, he understood that he should have returned to the Old Village. He might have considered that the house would not be guarded forever. In a week or two weeks, he could have walked in. Because what was there to guard? No one would want anything there: the blood-stained sleeping mats, the few clothes, the cooking pots filled with ghosts. But he imagined the bulldozers coming. The more his head swam, the less he could forget the money that was sitting under the chunk of concrete in the floor of that house.

He found his way to the main path and doubled back. His thought was to wait until the guard left, or at least to wait until he went to sleep. He had never met any all-night guard who did not sleep. While he slept, he would slip into the house, take the money, and be on his way.

22

He stood at a distance and watched. The guard was sitting in such a way that Isaac could see only one side of his face. He was a large, serious man, about Isaac's age, with clear skin and bushy eyebrows. From the way he held his chin, from the way his eyes moved, Isaac thought he was not a mild man. And he thought further that he would have no chance if it came to a physical contest between them.

While he waited, he looked at the place where he'd been standing when he first met Kagiso, the spot where he'd sat on the front stoop with White Dog. He thought Kagiso's breasts would have been plump with milk when she died. This made him so sad he could hardly see or hear or think.

He walked away so he wouldn't arouse suspicion and then returned when the darkness was deeper. All the time, his legs would hardly move because of the hunger in them. Although he had not gone to the shebeen, he was drunk on an idea that wouldn't let him go. When Isaac came back, the guard walked behind the house to relieve himself. When he returned to his post, he ate some jerky that he took from his back pocket. Inside the neighboring lean-to shacks, oil lamps were going out. People had become quiet, although the dogs had not. Isaac thought of White Dog waiting for him in the dark. When he returned, she'd be in the same place where he'd left her.

He walked away and came back. He sat on his haunches just out of sight and waited several hours more. When the guard finally slept, it was fortunate that he did not go to sleep across the threshold. He slept a little to one side. So when Isaac saw that he was snoring soundly, he came from his hiding place and made his way to the door. He knew the place well even in the dark, but it was one thing to know a place, and it was another to feel, crawling on your skin, the evil that lingered there.

As fear crept up the back of his neck, he thought, if you run from things that frighten you, you will never do anything. And very quietly, with his heart pounding into his eye sockets, he crossed the threshold into the house. He felt his way to the room where he had put the money, went down on his knees, and lifted the chunk of concrete. All the time, the hair on the back of his neck was shouting, *Run!* But the money was still there, and when his fingers closed around it, he felt triumphant. What he did not realize was that someone had moved the only chair, a metal chair, to a different place. Where it had been against a wall it was now in the middle of the room. In his haste to leave, he ran into it, and it scraped across the floor with a loud noise. Before he could get out the door into the night, the guard was blocking his way.

The light of a torch flew into his face. "*O mang?!*" the guard shouted loudly.

Isaac gave him his name.

"*O tswa kae?*" He sounded almost as frightened as Isaac.

It didn't seem wise to say where he came from, and he remained silent.

"*O tswa kae?*" the guard repeated, louder still, and Isaac told him he was from the Old Village.

"What is in your hand?"

He showed him the money.

"Where did you get it?"

"There," Isaac said, pointing.

He grabbed Isaac's wrist and said, "Show me." He had not put the concrete back for fear of making noise, and it was clear, once they were inside the room, where he had found it. "You knew it was here."

"Yes."

"Give me the money." Isaac put it in his hand. "You are with the ANC."

"No. I am not with them."

"Then how did you know the money was here?"

"I lived in this place."

"Then you are with the ANC."

"No, *rra*, I am not with them."

"Your speech is South African. You are not from Botswana."

"No, *rra*, I am not from here. May I explain to you?"

"You may explain to my superior. We will wait here until morning when I will be relieved, and then I will take you to the station. Do not try to escape. Do you understand?"

"Yes, *rra*, I do understand. But please let me tell you. I was living here . . ."

"*Rola ditlhako.*"

"My shoes?"

"Take them off."

"But they are my brother's shoes." He was crazy with hunger and fear, or he would not have said such a thing.

"I don't care if they are your grandmother's shoes. Take them off." He had the fiery zeal of a young man doing his first work.

Isaac took them off, and the guard closed the door of the house, with himself and Nthusi's shoes on the outside and Isaac on the inside. It was suddenly very quiet. Isaac felt the man's presence just outside the door, alert. Sitting on the floor in the darkness, terror entered his bones and traveled the river of his blood and beat in his head. He imagined his friends waking to the explosion of guns. He wished to be out of that place, but he also wished that dawn would never come. He was like a monkey cornered by a lion. He had always been told how clever he was. He had begun to believe that his life was charmed. But he thought, sitting on the concrete floor in utter darkness, that he had been stupider than stupid.

After the sun rose, he heard voices speaking outside, and then the door opened. There was the young policeman and an older policeman who'd come to relieve the young one. They looked him up and down. The older man's eyes were puffy and full of sleep. His skin was slack, and his tummy large.

"What is your name?" he asked.

Isaac told him.

"You are South African?"

"*Ee, rra.*"

"What are you doing here?"

"I am a refugee."

"You are with the ANC?"

"No, *rra,* I am not."

"Where are you working?"

"I am a gardener in the Old Village."

"What were you doing in this house?"

"I was getting some money I had saved. I was living here with an old school chum and his family."

"Your friend was with the ANC?"

"I cannot say, *rra.*"

"If you cannot say, he was. Then it is likely that you also are with the ANC."

"I am not with the ANC."

The two men held a conversation at a distance from where Isaac was standing. He could hear the younger one saying that Isaac was lying and the older one neither agreeing nor disputing. In the end, they decided Isaac would be taken to the chief of police. He hoped the old one would take him. He thought he could persuade him on the way to let him go. But it was not to be. He was too fat and tired and didn't wish to walk to town.

"Come," said the younger one. He handed Isaac Nthusi's shoes, which he put on. He had no handcuffs, so he tied a rope tightly around both Isaac's wrists and held it in his hand. Isaac followed him like a goat on a tether. The guard did not wish to walk side by side. All the same, Isaac tried to talk to him. He asked if he was from Gaborone.

"Francistown," he muttered.

"You grew up there?"

He was not wishing to talk further.

When they were almost to town, Isaac tripped over a rock in the road. It would not have made him fall down if he'd eaten and slept.

The policeman was angry, thinking that he had fallen on purpose. "Get up!" he shouted. "Why do you do this?"

The chief of police had not yet arrived when they reached the station. The young policeman and Isaac sat down to wait. Isaac asked for water, but he did not dare to ask for anything else.

When the chief arrived, his secretary brought him a cup of milk tea, and various subordinates went in and out of his office. Finally, Isaac was taken to see him. The policeman who caught him began his story by saying that Isaac was with the ANC and had been found stealing at the house. By telling it this way, Isaac knew he was trying to make himself important, as though he'd caught a big fish, but anyone with any brains could see that he, Isaac, was nothing like a big fish.

The chief looked at him steadily. His eyes seemed large, a little bulging, and between his eyebrows was a deep line. He had short cropped hair and a long face. He didn't give anything away with his face. It was not a bad person's face, but it was closed. He waved the young policeman quiet when he tried to tell the story. "Take off that rope," he said. "You may go now."

The young policeman left the room. Isaac felt that he must be disappointed because he had been trying hard to make a good impression. He relaxed a little after the guard left, his wrists free, but when the chief began asking him questions, the same questions that the older guard had asked him back at the house, he became full of fear. He answered him honestly, and his heart beat in the back of his eyes until he could no longer see properly.

After he'd answered all the questions about the money, about why he was living in Naledi, the chief took a new tack. "If you were living in Naledi, why were you not there on the night of the shootings?"

Isaac told him that he was staying in the house in the Old Village while the madam was on a trip.

"Where was her husband?"

"He was not there." He didn't want to say they were living separately in case madam wished to keep that information private.

"You were staying in the servant's quarters?"

"No, *rra,* I was sleeping in the main house."

"Why is this, when you are an employee?"

This man was an expert rat catcher, good at sniffing things out. "The servants' quarter is occupied."

"Then why was the servant not watching the house instead of you?"

"She was away visiting her mother."

"Then the servant's quarters were empty so you could have stayed there."

His hunger and tiredness pulled him down. He would be found guilty of something, it didn't matter what. "The servant did not wish me to be there."

"Because she did not trust you?"

"No, *rra,* she does not care for men." The ghost of a smile crossed the chief's lips. "Or, rather, she cares for men, but . . ." It was too complicated to explain.

"So you were staying in the main house. I see." Isaac thought maybe it would be all right then, but the chief was waiting to strike.

He dropped his voice. "Your timing was perfect," he said.

"I beg your pardon, *rra?*"

"Who is your mistress? Is she also with the ANC?"

"I am not with the ANC, *rra.*"

"Who are you working for?"

"Her name is Mrs. A. Mendelssohn."

"She is South African?"

"No, *rra,* she is from the United States."

"Her husband is South African?"

"I do not know, *rra.*"

"Does he visit South Africa regularly?"

"I do not know this, *rra.*"

"I thought you said you worked for them."

"*Ee, rra,* but I do not know where he goes."

"So he does go away on a regular basis." Isaac could see that the chief thought he was getting somewhere. He also saw, with a blur of surprise, that he had only one eye. The other eye was made of glass and roamed around. Sometimes it looked where the good eye looked.

Sometimes it went somewhere else. It made Isaac unsteady, as though he might need to vomit.

"He has been away for some time," Isaac said.

The vertical line between his eyebrows deepened. "In South Africa?"

"I do not know this, *rra*."

"Has he taken you on any of his trips?"

"No, *rra*."

"Has he spoken with you about his work?"

"No, *rra*. I do not know him well."

"But you know the missus well? You know her quite well?"

Isaac saw what the chief was getting at and felt himself grow angry. "She is not involved," he said, the heat rising into his face. "She is not involved at all."

"Then you are involved," he said.

"Involved in what?"

"What you were speaking of."

"No, *rra,* I too am not involved."

"How long have you been in Botswana?"

"Eight months."

"Long enough to get the lay of the land."

"Excuse me, *rra*?"

"You were living with ANC people, but conveniently you were not there on the night when you knew there would be a raid by the South African Defense Force. You are a clever man, anyone can see that. You have been playing one side against the other."

"No, *rra,* I am only a gardener."

"You are working with the South African Defense Force, isn't that it? You are a double agent."

"No, *rra.*"

"You are telling me that you are not a double agent?"

"I don't know what this is, double agent."

"Then how do you know enough to say you are not when you did not know what it was?"

"I only work for the madam in the Old Village. No one else."

"Your story is too simple. Where is your passport?"

"I have no passport."

"How did you get into Botswana?"

"I traveled by car."

"Why were you not stopped at the border?"

"I was hiding."

"Where?"

"It's best if I don't say, *rra*."

"You are protecting someone. Who would that be?"

"I cannot say, *rra*." Thinking better of it, he said, "I traveled in a hearse, hidden under the body of a Botswana government official who became late before I left South Africa."

"You are not a good liar. That is impossible. You were in the casket?"

"No, *rra*. Please, sir, I only wish to live my life. I am harming no one." He thought of White Dog waiting for him at the gate. And the cats hungry. "Please let me go now. I am supposed to be looking after the garden and the house in the Old Village. There is no one there to do these things."

The chief looked at him with his good eye while the glass eye looked at the floor. His cheeks were hanging, as though he had not slept well. Isaac could see he didn't know what to do with him. "I need to make a phone call," he said.

He left the room. Perhaps Isaac could have escaped but it seemed that the chief trusted him not to. Besides, where could he have gone? To run was to admit guilt, and he could not fulfill his duties if he was in hiding. His fate was in this chief's hands. They were small hands, he'd noticed. He was a man who wielded power, but he did not look like a bold man to Isaac. More like someone who tried to stay out of trouble, however he might do that. In this, Isaac saw little hope. In that he had one eye and knew what it was to suffer, he saw a grain of hope.

He was gone a long time. Isaac's eyes became heavy and his heart fell into despair. He expected he would go to the prison where the old man with the sunken garden had been. Perhaps he would work in the garden and become proficient with plants. He would be an old man when they set him free, his whole life wasted.

The chief returned. He sat down as though he weighed twice as much as a man of his size. He looked at Isaac. "I believe that you are not telling the truth. I believe that you are a double agent. Botswana is a peace-loving country. We cannot harbor people such as your-self. You are a danger to us. I am sending you back across the border." His good eye twitched once as he said this.

Isaac was stunned, without words for a moment. Then he said, "Please, *rra,* they will kill me there. Let me stay here. I risked my life to come here."

The chief was not a man who changed his mind, although Isaac thought he saw a small flicker of misgiving in his face.

As two policemen led him away, Isaac wondered whether there was any point at which he might have saved himself. If Kopano and he had not stood on that train platform. If he had not met Amen on the path. If he had not fallen a little in love with Amen's wife. If he had eaten and slept the day after the shooting and not become small brained like that bird who fell down the chimney into the jaws of a cat.

They told him to wait. They were searching for a car to take him across the border. He sat on a bench wearing handcuffs, beyond hun-ger. His head hung low. He counted on his fingers the days before madam would be back. Five days. White Dog and Horse and Mr. Ma-goo would die. The young tomato plants and pepper plants would wither and die. She would think that her trust had been misplaced. He imagined her returning, finding the animals dead, the vegetables dead, the kitchen untidy, his bed unmade. He would have made everything nice before she returned. He thought of his mother and Nthusi and his younger brothers and sister. Of Boitumelo whom he was to marry. He thought of his mother's employers who had been so kind to him. He would disappear the way his father had disappeared.

And he thought of Kagiso. His heart was full of grief. Kagiso had woken in terror and known enough to cover Ontibile's body with her own.

23

Alice's trip was over. She was next to the window, looking out. Her frustration was electric, like the spikes of an aloe. As the group scrambled for vehicles, Ian found his way into the middle seat of the Chevy beside her. A small part of him was amused, but the larger part wanted to be driving her wherever she wanted to go.

As Sam climbed into the driver's seat and the truck got under way, Ian said to her, "I thought you were going to throw a wobbler back there."

"I don't know what a wobbler is." Her voice was curt.

"I thought you might deck Haddock."

"He's just a frightened old has-been."

He looked at her. "You feel sorry for him?"

"Imagine living your whole life like that. It would be like living a prison sentence. Did you see his shoes? They're so slippery, he can hardly walk."

"Like a vulture with no toes," said Sam.

It came out of the blue. Ian pictured those lappet-faced vultures with their raw, featherless necks, huge bills, and gimlet eyes. Alice started laughing and couldn't stop. Tears streamed down her cheeks.

"A vulture," said Sam again.

"Oh god, Sam, stop," she said, fighting for air. She settled down, but then she started up again.

"Are you okay?" Ian asked.

"No, I can't stop."

His asking seemed to sober her up enough to speak. She grabbed his hand furtively and said, "I had a roommate once. She had the loudest laugh in the world. We were in a bar one time. I said something she thought was funny, and her head went back and she stopped breathing. I'd never seen anyone do anything like that before. I thought she was choking. She opened her mouth, and this explosion came out. And then on the intake, she snorted almost as loud. I was young. So mortified, I thought I'd just crawl out the door."

"I knew someone who sneezed like that. The first *AHH!* was like a scream. And then she said *Choo.*"

"Was she a romantic interest?"

Her question startled him. "Why do you ask?"

"I just wondered."

"Yes, as a matter of fact, I was bonkers over her. But we had huge rows. We were sloshed a lot of the time. When I stopped drinking, which wasn't for long back then, I saw the light."

"Her sneeze stopped being so cute?"

"It never really was cute." He wasn't thinking about that woman. He needed to say something. They'd soon be in Maun. The next day, they'd be in Nata. She'd be going back to Gaborone. He'd pick up his Land Rover and drive back the way they'd just come, up to the Tsodilo Hills. *Don't go*, he wanted to say. *Come with me.* But he'd be a right bastard to put that proposition to her, especially with her not knowing his whole story.

The road was rough, and Ian's head bounced against the roof of the truck. The convoy got stuck in the sand twice on the way to Maun. The radiator of the Land Rover needed filling up a dozen times before they returned, but it held until the vehicle was able to limp into town.

The group stayed that night at Crocodile Camp on the banks of the Thamalakane River, and everyone but Arthur Haddock gathered on the veranda, drinking bad beer, watching the river turn into a ribbon of blackness. The hippo voices sounded like the bellow of a huge cow. Before the dark swallowed everything, there were their two enormous heads, their eyes and rounded ears and great wide-spaced nostrils just above the water in the shadows of the bank, followed by their hulking broad backs.

Will asked Alice, "Are you glad you came?"

"God, yes."

"Do you think we accomplished anything?"

"I don't know. People can surprise you." Ian watched her. When she wasn't saying everything she felt, he noticed she pushed her tongue into her right cheek, which created an almost imperceptible bulge, like a bubble of tiny words straining to get out.

"Arthur's not the only bloke in the Ministry of Agriculture."

"But he was the one who came, unfortunately."

"You know," said Will, "someday, after millions of animals have piled up against fences, someone's going to say the fences didn't do any good, and they'll come down. The bloody ignorance, it staggers one. You wonder how the human race got this far."

A sudden hissing expulsion of air from the river surprised him. Crocodiles. No one else seemed to have heard it. Ian felt sadness sweep over him, partly at Will's words, partly at what felt suddenly like the waste of his own life. Somehow, things had become fractured. He looked at Alice, thought of the freshness of her laughter, her anger, her grief, how they seemed to pour straight out of some living cauldron in her.

He stood up, holding half a bottle of beer, and left the circle, muttering something about needing to go have a piss. He felt her eyes on him, felt them burrow into the curve of his lower back, almost as though she'd laid a hand there.

He needed to get away from her. A point of no return would soon be reached. He wasn't far from it now. You're on a river. You hear the sound of a waterfall in your ears. You haven't navigated this particular river before, but you've navigated others like it. You're paddling along at the same rate as the river, hardly noticing how fast the trees are whizzing by, when the earth suddenly drops away and the water rushes down into boiling mayhem, leaving no time for regrets, second thoughts, resolutions.

There was something ancient about her large, generous face. Her eyes looked right at you. They weren't drifty like the eyes of most people, looking vaguely in your direction, glancing off. They saw you;

it was like looking into the sea on a cloudy day: gray, blue, green. They were wide-set, her mouth also wide, easy with its shy smile. Her face had a calmness in it, the kind you see in wild animals who have no predators. Her hair was almost always a mess. He liked this. And he liked that it was already almost entirely gray, as though some older wisdom had outpaced her age. It was curly with a kind of wild abandon, and he often had to stop his hand, wanting to tuck it behind an ear, out of her eyes. In the heat of the day, she pinned it up, but not successfully. It often fell down.

He was too old for her. Down the road, it would be miserable for her to be saddled with an old codger shuffling about in bedroom slippers needing his tea, when she was still in the prime of life. Fifteen years is almost a generation. And age aside, he wasn't exactly the catch of a lifetime. He'd pretty much lost whatever looks he had. His grant awards were hit or miss. When necessity called, he taught. When he didn't have to, he wandered about in the hills, discovering what he could. He'd be hard pressed to say where home was, or even that it mattered. That had been a problem with any woman who'd ever wanted him in her life. It would be a problem again.

He felt protective of her. She was a bit of a mug. He needed to get the hell out. Crack of dawn tomorrow. Give her a wide berth tonight. Say a quick good-bye when they reached Nata: it's been dandy, see you someday. Get over whatever hit him, get back to work. Head for the hills. Literally. He hadn't been with a woman in a while. That was part of the problem. A man needs a woman. But Alice didn't need him making a shambles of her life.

As he circled around the side of the lodge, he heard the eerie call of a Pel's fishing owl, the song rising and falling, falling some more. He stood still, not breathing. It reminded him of departing souls. And then he thought, not wanting the thought, of the thousands of animals hung up on fences, perishing for water. Last night, he'd woken himself, crying out in his sleep. He couldn't remember the dream, but he remembered the feel of it. Something important. Running across an empty tundra, arriving too late.

He went around to the road, away from the river, and sat on a stone. He imagined an impala arriving at a water hole, its slenderness mirrored in the surface, spreading its front legs wide before drinking. One animal. You could look at it forever. Something like wonder was what had first drawn him to rock paintings. As a boy, while sitting in the cold pews of a church (out of which he'd bolted the day he was old enough to outrun his mother), he'd seen people going through the motions of awe. A silver chalice lifted at an altar. A passionless hymn. It was fine for those who were there, he supposed, but for him, it was beyond bearing.

Ancient Bushmen pounded hematite for red paint, bound it with blood serum, shaped quills, feathers, or bones for brushes, and found the stillness in themselves to capture life as they'd felt it. You could see it in the paintings: they'd watched, they'd listened, they'd understood their own place in the universe, no greater and no lesser than the animals they painted. You could feel in these paintings how time whirled through them, how the infinite opened before them when they knocked at its door, spilling out its terrible glories.

Any fool would be happy poking around in the hills, he thought, making copies of paintings in a notebook, trying to puzzle out the lives behind the images. But only a handful of San people were now left in Botswana, whose very existence was threatened by these cursed fences. He imagined returning to the place he'd first gone with Alice, carrying proper tools this time, cutting the fence section by section. It wasn't something he wanted to do. You're not born to pull down things other men have erected. Nor did he look forward to the rotting carcasses he'd find on the boundary. But you know when something feels right by the way it sweeps through you. It's no longer an idea but something that inhabits you.

He stood up, as though tonight was already too late. He thought he'd go find her, then he thought he'd leave it, then he thought he'd walk along the road and think a bit. He'd settled on a walk and was half a kilometer down the road when a battered Toyota pickup stopped. The dust settled, and a man got out. His gait was familiar. All at once, Ian recognized Roger, an old friend he'd met on his first trip to

Botswana. It was Roger who'd taken him up to the Tsodilo Hills for the first time.

"Imagine meeting you here!" Roger yelled. Ian thumped him on the back. It had been a couple of years since he'd seen him. Although Ian wasn't a small man himself, Roger was half a head taller, a huge, slow-moving ox, deliberate in every way. His parents were Rhodesian. He'd grown up in Maun, one of four brothers, and was the only one still left in Botswana.

"Where are you coming from?" asked Ian.

"Ghanzi. Had to see a fur trader."

"Shaw?"

Roger nodded. "And you?"

"I've been on a trip," said Ian. "Not alone. We got as far as Sehitwa, a little beyond."

"Who were you with?"

"A guy from agriculture sliding around in city shoes, another guy from Ministry of Local Government and Lands, Will, the wildlife chap—you know him—a woman working on San policy, a few others."

"What were you doing with that lot? Here, jump in." He opened the passenger door, and Ian climbed in.

"Glorified sightseeing. The idea was to talk to people, try to under-stand the needs of all parties, and come up with a reasonable land-use policy, something that won't screw wildlife and the San."

"Good luck with *that*." He drove up the road and stopped in front of Crocodile Camp.

"I've got a favor to ask," Ian said. "You wouldn't be heading toward Nata by any chance?"

"I'm leaving in an hour or so. Just have to grab a bite to eat and fill up with petrol."

"I'd like to hitch a ride."

"No problem. You want dinner first?"

"I've eaten."

"About that woman you mentioned. Is she spoken for?"

"God's sake, Roger. You never quit."

"What does she look like?" They got out of the truck and went up the steps onto the porch. They lingered there a moment, looking in the direction of the truck cooling in the evening shadows.

"Let up, would you?" He felt disloyal going on, but he did. "The woman's American, recently divorced. Alice is her name. She works in Local Government and Lands with C.T. what's his name. She's prematurely gray, nice body. Big bones. Not your type though. You go for the slim, frail sort."

Roger laughed.

Something made Ian turn, and his eyes went hollow. Alice was standing there. And then she was gone.

"Bloody hell," he said.

"You're right," said Roger. "Not my type."

"Put a sock in it, man."

"It's her you're running from, isn't it?"

He didn't answer. But then he said, "You know, forget about Nata. I need to stay the night in Maun after all, head to Nata with the rest of them in the morning."

Roger laughed. "They'll do that to you—you don't know whether you're coming or going."

Fuck you, he wanted to say. But it was his own damn fault. "See you before long, old man. Maybe when I get to Nata, if you're still about."

He stumbled away toward his room, no idea how to make it better. Splashed water on his face and dried it with a towel. Changed his shirt, as though he were starting the day again, then looked in the mirror with a hard eye and said, "You stupid cock up." He turned on his heel without saying another word to that sorry bastard in the mirror and headed down the steps.

He saw her from a distance, sitting with Will on the porch overlooking the river. Neither was speaking, just watching the night. If he joined them, she'd find the earliest opportunity to escape, and that would be that. He waited in the shadows of the building. And waited some more. He'd already made up his mind to clear out, and as those silly nits were fond of saying, God had provided. She'd never want to see him again. As it should be.

But still he waited. As his legs cramped, he treated the pain as a form of penance. His mind chattered. He wanted it to be still a moment, but his thoughts scooted out from beneath him. Something dark flew overhead. He'd never particularly liked Maun, as beautiful as the river was. Depressing expatriate community. A lot of heavy drinkers. Wives in various stages of desperation. People went bonkers in places like this.

Alice stood up just then. Will got to his feet too, waited until she'd gone a few steps, and sat down again, his feet propped back up on the railing.

It turned out it wasn't in him to run her down. It wasn't right. He'd scare her out here in the dark for one thing. For another, she'd know he'd been watching. So he left it and went to his room and thrashed under mosquito netting until the night was used up and its scraps had smudged into dark shadows under his eyes. By morning, he looked and felt like hell.

Alice was up early, still furious with him—the insolence of the man. She felt humiliated, angry with herself for being taken in. She stood on the veranda of the old hotel, trembling with something more than anger, something more vulnerable that she'd just as soon not admit to herself. The morning breeze came off the river. She'd intended to head down there, but the hotel owner's little toy terrier had latched on to her, his front paws wrapped around one of her ankles, pumping away, his ears slapping against his eyes with his violent exertions. She shook her leg. "Get away, Ralph."

She'd always been susceptible to fleas and had noticed the night before that welts appeared on her ankles when Ralph was near. She dragged her canine ball and chain forward, and when she got to the stairs, she thought of bumping him down, but he became satiated and let go. Still, he trailed her with his self-involved little snout. How did people ever love an animal like this?

"Go home, Ralph," she said. "I'm going to the river. There are crocodiles down there who love little dogs." His whole back end wagged. She headed instead for the road, hoping he'd peel off and cling to someone else. The wooden steps creaked, and Ralph trotted in front of her, his scraggly tail held high.

Nothing seemed to move or breathe. Her feet raised small clouds of dust as she walked away from the hotel toward town. She had no destination, but her feet walked faster, as though she did. *He,* that man, was back there somewhere, feeling what she hoped was remorse, but perhaps that was too much to ask for.

Ralph suddenly took off into the undergrowth. "Ralph!" she called. "Ralph! Come here, damn it."

She heard him crashing around, breaking twigs. For a small animal, he made a huge racket. And then the sound of his high-pitched terror. She beat her way down a narrow footpath and found a pack of feral dogs surrounding him. "Get away!" she yelled running toward the pack, waving her arms. She picked up a couple of stones and hurled them. One of them found its mark on the flank of a dog that looked more like a hyena. It slunk off, but it turned and began creeping back.

Ralph whimpered and snarled. Alice hurled several more stones, picked up a stick and brandished it. The pack didn't seem to realize how puny she was, and they turned tail and ran.

Ralph held up a quivering paw. She picked him up and felt his heart beating in the tiny cave of his ribs. He shook all over and buried his nose in her neck. She felt something like love for him then, her disdain swept away by the force of his desire to just be happy and safe. She walked back up the road, imagining Ralph's fleas climbing into her hair, roistering about under her shirt, and delivered him back to Estelle, the owner of the hotel.

She headed back out to the veranda and descended the steps to the river where she'd intended to go in the first place. She imagined Ian standing on the veranda looking out, but when she turned to look, it was empty. And then something odd stirred in her, unbidden, a feeling like what a river might experience if it were a sentient being: the willingness to erase what's gone before, to find a channel through.

They were to leave at seven, but Shakespeare and Sam hadn't turned up, not by seven, not by seven thirty.

They were down to two vehicles. One Land Rover would stay in Maun to get its radiator repaired, and they'd cram into the other two. They were all there waiting, except Alice.

"I'll be down by the river," Ian told Will. He went inside and got a cup of coffee, really wanting a shot of whiskey, and went out the door to the porch and stood near where he'd seen her last night. She wasn't there, of course. The coffee was bad. Probably warmed over from yesterday.

A pair of fish eagles called back and forth to each other: *weeeee-ah,* shrill, repetitive. He felt a sense of doom, and of his own shoddiness. He had another sip of coffee and watched a turquoise kingfisher. He should have left Maun last night. He thought about what he'd do when he reached Nata. Find or borrow some heavy-duty bolt cutters. Outfit himself for two or three weeks away, spend a night in Nata, and be off the next day. He'd drive to the Kuke fence, see if he could cut through that blasted wire, and head for Sepopa and the Tsodilo Hills a few days later. He wanted to get a paper out, which meant finishing the mapping in the hills he'd contracted to do through the grant. The plan gave him little pleasure this morning, and he tossed the remains of the coffee off the porch.

It occurred to him that double-decker buses were roaring down roads in London at this moment, people crowded on streets, greengrocers arranging apples, lions in repose at Trafalgar Square, the Tube with its arteries and veins underneath it all. It might as well be the moon. He suddenly longed for it: life whizzing by, none of it anything to do with him. Too many people knew him here, knew his business. Where do you go to get away? The Gaborone mall? The Tip Top Bazaar, the South Ring Butchery? A movie theater with its films run through the gristmill of South Africa's enlightened censors? He felt constricted, wanted to shout and pound his chest like a mountain gorilla.

His heart sped even before he saw her come around the corner. "Morning," he croaked. "There's a malachite kingfisher out there."

"I don't care if it's a flying moose," she said, turning on her heel.

"Please don't go. I'm sorry about last night."

Her eyes flashed. "You might have been describing a cow heading for the Meat Commission. I thought you were a different sort of man. If I'd known that's how you felt, I wouldn't have wasted a minute with you."

"That's not how I feel. Roger wanted to know what you looked like."

"And how would Roger even know I existed if Roger hadn't been told?"

"He wouldn't have. You were on my mind."

Something crossed her face, swiftly replaced by rage. Her voice shook. "You said it like an auctioneer. 'The woman's American, recently divorced.' *The woman.* As though you don't even know me. Gray hair. Already over the hill. Oh, nice body. But big bones. A lady wrestler. Or maybe an orangutan. And then your old boy laughter. You and Roger, whoever the hell that was, yucking it up at my expense. You're a royal prick, you know that?"

She'd already turned to leave when he said, "I know that. Worse than that. I'm an insensitive lout, a cad, a muttonhead, a piss poor specimen of a man, a foul-mouthed and calumnious knave. If I were a dog, I'd have me put down."

"Good. Now leave me alone." He thought a hint of a smile had flitted over her lips. Her footsteps departed, and he watched her climb into the Land Rover. A male voice from around the side of the building asked, "Where is he?"

"Back there," she said, as though she were talking about a warthog.

"Ian?" Will called. "Bus is leaving. You're in the Land Rover." The gods were laughing, he thought, when they left the last seat next to her in front. Even though he jammed himself over by the door so no part of him was touching her, the road had worsened, and he kept being thrown onto her. Shakespeare drove, and Arthur Haddock and C.T. occupied the backseat. The day was hot and airless, and they ate dust from the vehicle traveling in front of them.

This cockamamie trip: a group of white men and a woman, most of them from outside the country, ushered about by Batswana drivers and cooks. A ship of fools. Mostly well-meaning fools, but lunkheads all the same, himself included. He knew it from the start, before he'd agreed.

He'd had work to do, pressing on him. It puzzled him what had driven him to say yes. You come to trust these instincts, but in this case, beyond stupid.

As they passed north of the Ntwetwe Pan, he thought of her face as they'd crossed. On an impulse, he dug into his shirt pocket, brought out a small pad of paper and a pencil, and wrote. *You said you'd like to camp on the Ntwetwe Pan and wake up there someday. Will you come with me?*

He slid it across his lap toward her.

Her eyes took in the words, and she grabbed the pencil. *You must be mad.*

He took the pencil . . . *about you.* It sounded like a schmaltzy Valentine card. *Please forgive my stupidity. Stay with me tonight in Nata.*

Who do you think I am? She sat for a while with the pad in her lap, her hands covering it, then passed it back.

We can drive to the Pan tomorrow, camp overnight, head for the veterinary fence and make it right this time, and then, if you agree, I'd like to show you the Tsodilo Hills. Come with me. You can have your own tent.

She sat for a long time looking through the windshield. A guinea fowl flew up into a cluster of *mopane* scrub. She breathed in, held her breath, finally let it out.

You smoke. You're crazy. I don't forgive you. She dropped the pad under the seat.

He picked it up. *Please,* he wrote.

24

One Motswana was black, the other white. They passed him off at the border in shackles. Not lingering, Isaac noticed. You don't hand a black man over to the white South African Security Police without a twinge of something that makes you want to put the wretch behind you as soon as you can, bury him in road dust before he'll disturb your dreams at night.

"Get in," the two South Africans said in Afrikaans. They chained him to an iron ring riveted to the floor of the van, rolled up the windows, slammed the doors, laughed with the border guard for a bit while the sun baked Isaac senseless inside the van. When they returned, the meatier of the two began cussing him out. Isaac understood every second or third word, enough to know that they believed he was pocketing money from both sides of the border, all set up to be a rich black bastard, a right clever chap, well we'll see who's clever now.

He tasted the malice, felt it swimming through his blood like a leach looking for a place to lay its mouth hooks. The shaking began in his belly and radiated out to his legs and feet, out to his hands.

The men got in, the van rolled south.

It didn't take long to understand. They want to break your mind— and your heart if they can get at it. But your body is the only thing within their power to shatter. The only thing, unless you go ahead and give them the rest.

He pictured himself on the train platform, groveling. *Please, baas, please help, I beg of you*. Down on his knees, holding the conductor's pant cuff. That's where most people go. And by god, he wouldn't go there again. Not if they poured acid in his eyes.

He thought a moment. It was all very well to say what he would do and what he would not do. Now he was sitting in the back of a van, safe for the moment, the veldt stretching out on all sides. But where he was going was another country altogether, a country that ate souls. All at once, he believed that he would not survive. He saw them throwing his broken body out a tenth-story window. He saw the fabric of his shirt flutter in the wind, his head flopped to one side, his legs splayed. He could not see himself land, only his body in midair. He thought of Nthusi, how he'd once wanted to walk on air, high, like the Flying Wallendas. He thought of the shoes he would never buy his brother. He saw his money in the office of the chief of police. It had been lying on his desk in a pouch when he'd left. The man had not looked dishonest, but where would that money go now? If it had been less, he wondered if they would have let him go. The extra sixty rand given to him in kindness might be the root of his misfortune now. No, stupidity, his own, was the root.

Halfway to Johannesburg, they stopped at a roadside café. The men got out. This time they left a window partway open and locked the doors. He watched them as they leaned against the side wall of a dirty cinderblock building, boisterous as rugby players, eating two large sandwiches, slabs of red meat flapping at the edges of white bread. They returned with a paper cup of water and gave it to Isaac. He would not ask for food, as hungry as he was. To ask would be to go down on his knees holding the pant cuff.

25

When they reached Nata late that morning, Alice told her boss that she'd like a week's leave. She reminded him that she had two weeks' vacation coming to her, none of which she'd taken. "I'm sorry for the short notice," she told him. "It's just that I'm already up here, and Ian has offered to take me to the Tsodilo Hills." She told him she'd write a summary of the trip they'd just taken and have it for him the day she returned.

C.T. looked at her. "There's something you may not know about him," he said.

Something cold went through her. She'd worked with C.T. for two years, and she'd never heard him say anything remotely like this. "I don't mean you're in physical danger. I mean . . . well, it's none of my business really. But hadn't you better come back with us?"

"I'd like to stay."

"How will you get back?"

"I don't know yet."

"Righto. What about the position paper?"

"It's three quarters done. I'll finish it without fail by the end of the month."

"Anything else I need to know?"

"I can try to call you midweek if I'm anywhere near a phone."

"No bother."

"C.T.? Thank you. And thank you for the privilege of this trip."

He told her to take care of herself and moved toward the vehicles. She found Will, explained that she was going to the Tsodilo Hills with

Ian, and asked if he'd mind stopping by her place to check on things and let Isaac know she'd be another week.

His eyebrows went up. "You know what you're about, lass?"

"Will, please."

He smiled. "But you've not asked my opinion, have you?" He scuffed one foot across the dirt as though rubbing something out. "He's fifteen years your senior."

"Maybe not that many."

"Close to, anyway."

"I'll call my neighbor if you'd rather not go by my place."

"That's not what I'm fussing about."

"I know, Will."

"Of course I can check your place."

"Thanks so much." She gave him a hug.

"And if you're not back in a fortnight, I'll send out a search party."

"Say hi to Greta and the kids for me?"

She didn't want to be seen as she removed her things from the back of the Land Rover. Something about it felt ungainly, vaguely humiliating, as though she'd agreed to go off with the first man who'd ever asked her anywhere. Tears weren't far beneath the surface, and just under them lurked a faint nausea. If she hadn't already told C.T. and Will, she'd be tempted to change her mind. She found Sam, Motsumi, Shakespeare, and Ole Olsen, and said good-bye. To Arthur Haddock, she waved as he was getting back into the Land Rover. He looked puzzled, then she saw C.T. say something to him. Arthur didn't look at her after that, as though she'd fallen from the face of the Earth, where the bad women go.

As she stood beside the road, raising one arm, she felt an impulse to run after them. Old Faithful, the truck, drove in front, with the Land Rover behind, carrying Sam, Arthur, C.T., and Will. She'd become fond of them all, even poor old Arthur Haddock with his little fusses and fears and ridiculous shoes. She watched until they took the turn in the road, and then saw their dust rising into the air, and then there was nothing.

Standing in the street alone, the sun felt too bright, the sky too large. She felt that old deep pull toward dark and safety. C.T. and Will seemed to have been saying similar things: you don't know what you're doing, or what men are capable of. It was insulting, but she recognized some possible truth there.

She saw Ian at a distance, recognized his easy gait, half bear, half antelope. "You stayed!" he cried.

"You thought I wouldn't?"

"I wanted to give you space to change your mind."

"I'm here," she said.

"I found you a room. Normally I sleep in a friend's storeroom when I come this way, but I didn't think you'd want to sleep amid the rubble." He pushed a bit of hair out of her face and held her by the shoulders. The light was in her eyes, and he turned so she'd not have to squint. "You look uncertain."

"I don't know what I've done."

"You've done nothing except not go back today. Nothing's irrevocable. You can still take the evening train if you want."

"I don't want to."

"Are you hungry?"

"Yes."

"You'll feel better after you've eaten lunch."

He took her to the old hotel, and they climbed up the creaky wooden steps into the dining room. A few regulars were there, tables already littered with beer bottles. The place felt slovenly, enervated. The waitress, an older white woman with about five watts of energy, hobbled here and there on bad legs, clattering cutlery, swearing under her breath.

Ian introduced Alice when she straggled over. "Bet, Alice. Alice, Bet."

"Charmed," said Bet, whipping out a greasy pad of paper and the stub of a pencil from her apron pocket. "We're out of the hunter's stew, and there's one more bowl of the soup."

"I'll have the tripe and trotters," said Ian.

"I'd like the stewed chicken."

Bet paused. "I wouldn't if I were you."

Alice laughed.

"It's been around the barn and back again."

"A cheese omelet then."

"To drink?"

"Whatever you've got for beer."

"The same," Alice said.

Bet stumped off.

"Nice of her to warn me."

"She's a trouper." He picked up her hand and held it. "What made you stay?"

She thought a moment, then smiled. "When you said you were a foul-mouthed and calumnious knave. If I were a dog, I'd have me put down. And my own tent . . . You know, I never wanted to see you again."

"That was clear enough."

"I'll probably live to regret it."

"Do you mean that?"

"No." She looked at him hard. "No, I won't regret it."

They ate lunch, and the place emptied out. They paid, and Bet clattered dishes and set tables around them. "You mind if we stay?" Ian asked.

"Be my guest," said Bet. "Just as long as you don't ask for anything." She got out the broom, gave the floor an indifferent swipe, and left.

"I want you to see something before we go," he said. He opened his pack. There were a half dozen notebooks there, all the same size, thin, square, bound with thick unlined pages, battered around the edges and numbered in consecutive order. He passed her number one, written in his neat hand, and she read, *The place is called The Rock That Whispers. People have lived in these hills for over one hundred thousand years. There are over four thousand rock paintings here, some of them twenty thousand years old. The San people say this is where the world began. Near the top of the male hill, the spirit who created the world knelt to pray when the rocks were molten. The imprint of his knees is still there. What they call the female hill is nearby, and the child hill not far from that. The fourth hill is unnamed but said to be the male hill's first wife.*

She looked up to find him watching her. Many of the pages in the notebook contained likenesses of rock paintings, neatly copied with a fine black pen. Most were of animals. Some were stylized human figures, and the rest geometric shapes, either rectangles with appendages that seemed to represent arms, legs and penises, or circles which enclosed grids.

"Every one of these paintings has a place in the cosmology of the San. It's likely that the majority represent visions of shamans in trance states."

"Like what you experienced."

"No. I experienced pain and visual distortions, but nothing like ... It's entirely different. When *!kia*—that's their word for an altered state—is very deep, healers cross what they believe is the threshold between the living and the dead. They travel to the dwelling place of the gods to plead for the health of a member of the community, or the community as a whole. The danger is great. Their souls may be taken away by the spirits forever. They wail, they howl, they pull that terrifying sickness into their hands and throw it into the darkness, back to the spirits."

"When you enter *!kia,* your body becomes light, the base of your spine tingles, you feel as though your belly is on fire, as though you have no bones, you tremble all over and lose control of your legs. You can walk on coals without being burned."

She pointed to the geometric designs. "So what's the connection with these?"

"They probably represent trance-induced entopic phenomenon. Images that come from oddities within the fluid of the eye itself—you know, like when you look up at the sky and see floaters.

"At the first stages of trance people see zigzags, grids, wandering lines, dots. Then they hallucinate animals. Deeper still, they *become* animals. On rock paintings, you often see animals fused with human beings.

"Until recently, people thought the art was a literal representation of everyday life. For instance, there's an eastern Cape rock painting of a dying eland with blood falling from its mouth. You could see this just as a dying animal, but in its larger context, eland are animals of the gods, and when they die, they release their supernatural potency to shamans.

"What makes you care the way you do?"

He looked pensive for a moment. "I suppose it's because these paintings go right down to the nub of what we are: powerful testaments to the way humans connect to a larger universe. Whether you believe in God or not, the artists understood that they weren't at the center of the universe, that humans are a small part, surrounded by the power and beauty of the whole. And the fact that the rain each year is rubbing these paintings out, in the same way that the forces of civilization are rubbing out the culture itself, it makes me half crazy."

He stopped suddenly and looked at her as though he'd forgotten her in his torrent of words. "I'm glad you stayed. It was brave of you." He took her hand. "I had a strong impulse to save you from me, to get away from Maun, not even to say good-bye, but I couldn't do it."

"It turned out I didn't want to be saved."

26

They took him to the prison in Johannesburg called Number Four, the place his heart feared most. He had known of many black men dying here—and women dying nearby in the Old Fort near the Constitutional Court. Suffocated, beaten beyond recognition, hung, burned, flayed, electrocuted.

A large door opened under the slab of building, the van entered, and the door closed behind them. The meaty security officer unchained him from the floor of the van and yanked him out by his shirt collar. "You'll be taking off your *broekies* here," said the other one. Women's underwear.

They delivered him to Starkers, a short man with a blunt tool of a head and a smile to make one's flesh crawl. They gave him a stinking pair of rubber sandals and took his brother's leather shoes. He would never see Nthusi's shoes again. Modimo was nowhere on the premises, nowhere on Earth for that matter, the God who'd once caused the noise of a great rushing, the noise of wings and of wheels whirling in air. The God who'd made the tree of life, the heavens and the Earth and all therein. There was only silence now. *Yea, though I walk through the valley of the shadow of death* . . . If he was anywhere, He was the God of suffering. The God of injustice, of fruitless hope. *He maketh me to lie down in green pastures* . . . A white man's God.

Starkers took his name, mashed his fingers into ink and then onto paper, told him to strip, pulled him roughly here and there, made him bend over so his cavernous eyes could inspect. Starkers wrote "communist threat" on a sheet of paper and sent him to be hosed down.

From there it was *emakhulakhuthu,* the dark hole. Tiny concrete isolation cells lined up one after the other off a filthy corridor roofed in barbed wire, each a dunghill of human squalor and suffering. If he didn't die from malnutrition, or at the hands of a man like Starkers, he'd die of typhoid fever. He was given a blanket that smelled of piss, and the door swung shut behind him.

27

After Will returned to Gaborone, he drove to Alice's house. The first thing he noticed was White Dog just inside the gate, lying half upright, half on her side, barely able to lift her head. He thought he'd seen this dog with Isaac, and it gave him a bad feeling, hair-sticking-up-on-the-back-of-his-neck bad. He returned to his house, picked up a cricket bat and an open can of dog food from the refrigerator. He didn't tell Greta why he was making a second trip, or what he was taking with him.

The dog was in the same place when he came back. Will parked his truck just inside the gate, held out his hand and called. "Here, girl." She was too weak to rise.

Greta had said there'd been a short rain since he'd been away, and the evidence was still here—a bowl half filled with water, branches down from the wind, a bucket under a tree with water in the bottom, a drowned mouse floating. He tipped out the water, threw the mouse into the underbrush, and upended the dog food into the bowl. "Good girl," he said. "I won't hurt you." Her nose twitched with the smell of meat, and she tried to get up. "Don't worry, don't worry, I'll just set it down here for you." He brought it close and placed it in front of her. She leaned forward and ate, sitting with her paws flat on the ground. Will crouched nearby and watched her. She was scoured down to bone, hunger pouches under her eyes. It tore his heart to see.

The light was fading, and he wished it had been morning. He didn't want to face what he thought he might be facing, as dark was beginning to push down from the sky. "I'll be back," he said to the dog.

He grabbed the bat and carried it toward the house. "*Koko?*" he said at the door. "Anybody home?" He wasn't a fretful, fearful man, but it took a gathering of courage to make himself enter. "Isaac?" he called. "Isaac! Are you there?" When he'd met him that once, he'd thought him a decent, reliable sort. Not one to go clattering off. He felt the cold creeps traveling along his spine as he entered the kitchen and found the spoiled porridge on the big wooden table, as though someone had left in haste. Something rubbed against his leg, and he jumped a foot sideways. "Christ!" Mr. Magoo swished through his legs, doing a figure eight in and out. "You've taken twenty years off me! Where's the other one?"

He went into the spare bedroom near the outside door and found Isaac's bed unmade, his few clothes in a pile on a chair. His shoes weren't there. The house was darkening, and he made a quick tour through it, heart pounding, finding nothing amiss, before he returned to the kitchen. Magoo trailed him, and he opened a tin of sardines and tipped the whole thing into a bowl. The cat ate in a frenzy. A bag of cat food was ripped open, its contents gone. The milk in the refrigerator was sour, but he filled another bowl with water and left it on the floor, with the door open to the outside.

He carried out another bowl of canned food, along with a bucket of water, to where White Dog sat. When she'd finished the second bowl of food, she lapped a little water and lay down again on her side with a small groan. "Do you want to come with me?" he asked. The tip of her tail lifted and fell. He thought of his five young savages at home. "On second thought, you'll be better off here. Best not to eat any more tonight. Your stomach won't handle it. I'll be by with more in the morning . . . You're waiting for him, aren't you. For Isaac."

At the sound of his name she lifted her head. She watched Will open the door to his truck and get in. Through the rearview mirror, he saw her following him with her eyes until he was out of sight.

Will returned the following morning and found White Dog sitting in the same place where she'd been lying before. The water beside her was nearly gone. He gave her two cans of food and more water, and she stood to eat, her tail wagging softly. When she'd finished, he said, "I'm going to see if I can find Isaac. In the meantime, I'll be by every day. You'll stay here, all right?"

He fed Mr. Magoo and went through the house again for signs of anything out of order. Among Isaac's things was a letter postmarked from South Africa, but he didn't feel right checking the contents. Out in the garden, he found the lettuces pretty well dead. The tomatoes had hung on, along with some low plants, still alive. He touched the skin of a tiny pepper and placed his finger on his tongue. Hot. He turned on the hose and gave them all water, then returned home and talked to Greta.

They agreed he should stop in at the police station on the way to work, see Roland, one of Greta's countrymen who worked there. Not the sharpest tool in the shed but decent enough. Will was out the door when he thought he should try to ring up a wildlife assistant in Sepopa to see if he could get a message to Alice. He came back in, and his youngest son rushed him and grabbed his knees. Will hobbled over to the phone and placed the call, but it didn't go through. Just as well. There was nothing she could do from there. Leave her in peace. He threw his son up in the air, caught him, set him down outside the kitchen door, and was off.

It turned out that Roland was in Francistown helping to orient three new officers and wouldn't be back for a week. Will asked a middle-aged officer at the front desk if he could see the deputy chief. "His mother is ill, *rra*. He has gone to Mochudi."

"Do you know when he'll return?"

"No, *rra,* I have not been told."

"Is there someone else I can speak with? It concerns a missing person."

"You can speak with me, *rra*. I am the officer on duty." M. Molosi, his nametag said, pinned to a well-nourished chest. Will told him the story. When he was finished, M. Molosi said, "This is quite common, *rra*, for a gardener to disappear. Perhaps he was dissatisfied with the madam."

"That was not the case," said Will, who wanted to tell him he'd been in the country for twenty years and didn't need to be told the kind of thing that made gardeners disappear. "He left all of his personal effects, as well as his dog. He was very devoted to his dog and would not have left her behind."

"I see, *rra*. Then perhaps it was a matter of thinking that she was eating more than he could afford. He might have left her with a sad heart. There have been cases like this."

"This is true," said Will, mastering his impatience. "But why would he have left everything else behind, including a clean shirt and a clean pair of pants? Not only that, he left *mabele* on the table, untouched."

This made an impression. "Where is the house?"

"In the Old Village."

"When I am free, you will take me there."

They agreed that M. Molosi would call him at work when another officer could relieve him.

Later, Will accompanied him to Alice's house, showed him through it room by room, introduced Isaac's dog, but he could find no explanation for the disappearance. When he learned that Isaac had been put in charge while madam was away, he hypothesized that he might have fled with something valuable, but this would not explain the porridge.

28

The metal door had a small peephole and a slot for food. Above it were four metal slats, the only source of air or light. In the dimness, the scuttle of insects. A filthy bucket for slops. One blanket. A concrete floor.

A door clanged up the row from his cell. The smells around him were raw, animal. The brute stink of suffering. He felt along the floor with his feet, where to sleep, where to defecate.

The walls were rough, sticky with the respiration of caged men. He listened for the sound of breath on either side of him, heard nothing to his left and thought he could hear a rhythmic scraping to his right.

Before dark, a guard went down the row, clanking as he shoved a bowl of mealie porridge in each slot. Fear rose as the footsteps approached. The slot opened. He took the bowl and spoon, followed by a cup of water. He drank the water quickly—as likely as not to contain a death sentence. Typhoid, gastroenteritis. The porridge was a weak slurry.

After dark fell, he thought he heard a snatch of song somewhere at a distance.

A light bounced against the wall as footsteps came closer. They stopped outside his door, and the beam of a flashlight sliced through the peephole and hit him in the face. The feet shuffled, the light moved away for a second and went back into his eyes.

"What do you want?" His heart pounded.

The footsteps receded, the light faded into blackness.

He lay his head on the floor farthest from the door and wrapped himself in the blanket. Three times during the night, the beam of light hit him. He knew what it meant. There are thousands of ways to break a man.

When do you stop being human?

When the body is so befouled, when you have groveled so deeply, when bitterness eats your bones?

There was a room located at the end of the row of cells where they took people. Every day, and often into the night, he heard moaning, sometimes worse, far worse. He knew that one day, they would take him there.

I will fear no evil: for thou art with me. Thy rod and thy staff, they comfort me. He no longer believed in that kind of rod or staff. Or that he could master fear. God had forsaken that man crying out, asking for mercy. If there was a God, he was indifferent to whether his people lived or died, callous to the manner of their deaths.

If anything were to save him, it would be the strength of his heart and mind, what had been given him in this life. The face of his mother and granny, his father, his sister and brothers. All that he'd seen and understood. They could erase his dreams, they could erase his belief that goodness and mercy shall follow me all the days of my life. They were greedy for every part of a man they could swallow. But unless they bashed his head senseless, they couldn't take the memories that dwelt in him, they couldn't take what he knew. What remains after those precious things are gone is a wild dog chasing in circles, jaws clamped to its tail, a monument to defilement.

Once he'd dreamt of marrying Boitumelo. Don't wait for me, he told Nthusi to tell her. Her warm breath against his neck. Her teeth nipped his flesh, here, here. Her lovely mouth. Her black eyes. Her rump jutting out proudly. How she moved! Like a young giraffe.

That night, he whispered to the person in the cell next to him. He listened for footsteps, whispered again. The man's voice was ruined. Isaac could understand only half his words. He had been kicked in the throat. He could no longer keep food down. He said he had three children. "They are two boys and a girl. The girl's name is Neo, the boys Tebo . . ." The guard was coming. The light shone into Isaac's cell, blinded him, disappeared. The voice next door went silent.

He was grateful he did not have children. He thought about his brother Moses. The game of *mpha,* when Moses was a small boy. He would give Moses a sweet, then say *mpha* and hold out his hand. *Mpha. Give it to me.* To teach that nothing belonged to Moses and Moses alone, all was to be given, to be shared. The sweet would go back into his brother's hand. And again, *mpha. Give it to me.*

Perhaps it had been his fate to return to that house. The money, while important, had not been what mattered. It was going back and facing what had happened.

He had been put on Earth to be of use to others. It had gone wrong from the moment he met Amen. There had been danger there, and he hadn't faced it squarely, had only half stood up to Amen to say that violence was not his way. He had felt the uneasiness in that house from the beginning. White Dog had felt it too.

The chief of police had sent him back across the border because the shootings had scared him. He would not have been sent otherwise. He thought about the land of his birth, here all around him, denied to him now. In the dry season, the land was like an old man, skin of leather, eyes crinkled against sun. After the rains, like a young woman, with curves and silks of green. Would he ever see it again?

29

Behind the old hotel, Alice and Ian sat at a small table, looking out at the moon, one night away from full.

"You look far away," he said.

"I feel worried about home, as though I'd forgotten to turn off the stove."

"There's someone looking after things, right?"

"Yes, but he didn't know I'd be gone this long."

"Will it matter to him?"

"I don't think so. Will is checking on things."

He searched her face. "If you've changed your mind, it's all right."

"Don't keep urging me to go. I would have gone back with the group if I'd wanted to. Have *you* changed your mind?"

"No." He took hold of her hand. "But I need to tell you something. I nearly told you when we met, but I didn't. Then there didn't seem to be an opportunity, and then there was no point because I was never going to see you again.

"I'm married. Gwyneth lives in Gaborone. We were students in Bristol when we met years ago."

"You haven't been living together?"

"No. The marriage is over."

"Does she think it's over?"

"She says she does."

"What's she doing in Gaborone?"

"Working as a secretary for De Beers. She's seeing another bloke— Alec . . ."

She looked at Ian. His glasses were askew, rising on one side, which gave him a disorganized, imploring look. "It's not Gwyneth L'Angley."

"You know her?"

"I met her at a dinner party. I have to admit . . ."

"What?"

"She struck me as not all that curious about anything beyond herself. She drank too much."

"She fights depression. I was never really there for her the way she needed me to be."

"Could anyone have been there in that way?"

"I don't know, but I still don't feel that I've been fair to her."

"She could see who you were from the beginning."

"Maybe she couldn't." His hands were shaking. "Are you shocked?"

"A little. You might have told me sooner. But from what you're saying, it's over. You're married, but not really."

"Do you feel I've lied to you?"

"You didn't tell me the whole story, but I can see why you didn't."

"Heedless" was the word that came to her later. But at that moment, the decision to love him seemed already to have been made. The waiter turned up with coffee, poured two cups, and left. Ian took a swig. "Tastes like weasel piss."

She laughed. Underneath the laughter, though, was a small whiff of uneasiness, even fear. By now, she knew better than to give her life over to a man. It had been a kind of recurring illness, brief respites from her own uncertainties, tethering herself to this one and that one. "I don't doubt you," she said. "I doubt me. I've made little out of my life so far. You've probably never had a day in yours when you've doubted yourself."

"What gave you that daft notion?"

"You seem to know what you're doing, why you're doing it, happy with your work, supremely confident."

"I look like that to you?"

"Of course you do. In contrast, I think why would I be respected for anything I've ever done? I never finished my PhD. I missed a chance to do research in the plateau area of central-northern Nigeria. And then I missed a second chance to study the Romani people in southern Europe. I got married to Lawrence and came out here. There are so many things I'd have been interested in doing. Now I'm a paper pusher."

"You're worthy of respect because of who you are, Alice Mendelssohn. I can't imagine not respecting you. You've lived your life honorably."

Hasse flashed through her head, his pink cock lying contentedly on the surface of the bath water. "Not entirely."

"And you won't be a paper pusher for the rest of your life. You can finish your PhD if that's what you want. Or you can do something else." He looked straight at her. "You can do whatever you want. And of course I have doubts, like anyone. Doubts about how I've chosen to live. I've hurt people. Not just Gwyneth. I'm beginning to want things I never thought I wanted before. I'm not saying I'd ever have these things—roots, a home—or be able to stand them if I did. I'm saying I see them differently."

"What's changed?"

"You, for one."

"You hardly know me."

He picked up her hand, turned it over the way a palm reader might. "It doesn't matter that I hardly know you . . . You looked like a girl just then. Did you have a nickname as a kid?"

"Quackers." She laughed. "I loved ducks."

"My mum called me Nummy. I don't know where the name came from. She's the only one in the world who ever called me that."

"Were you close?"

"Yes. To both my parents. I remember when I figured out they'd die someday and leave me behind. I sat under the stairs mourning like a pope. It took me a bit longer to figure out I was going to die too. I worry about the San the way I used to worry about my mum and dad."

The wind was up, the Southern Cross tilted, shining halfway up the sky. "It'll be a full moon tomorrow on the Pan," he said. He took her hand and walked her back to her room. He kissed her and left quickly.

After he was gone, she came back outdoors and stood in the shadows. In the wind, the story of everything could be heard: time stretching in all directions, singing through the river of souls who'd carried breath over thousands of years.

That night, she dreamt of a dog running down an empty thruway. She'd never seen a dog run so fast. Golden and streaking. It kept veering into the lane, and she was scared she'd hit it with her car. At one point, it disappeared. She looked through the rearview mirror, and it was on the ground, thrashing. She stopped, opened the door of the car, and it got up, a golden retriever with no collar and no tag. She wanted to bring it with her but she wasn't able to. Her life wasn't right. She left the golden dog in the middle of the road. He sat there, not running, just watching as she drove away.

30

Ian had already loaded the Land Rover with tents and food and tools and supplies before Alice was up. They left for the Ntwetwe Pan at five in the morning. The moon was gone, but a couple of stars still shone overhead.

"You look wonderful," he said, taking her hand and touching the back of it to his cheek.

"Last night," she said, "I bathed from stem to stern."

"That makes two of us. You should have seen the drain. Like a mud bath. In about an hour, we'll be as grubby as before." He sounded happy at the prospect.

He climbed into the vehicle after her. "I thought we'd go to Kube Island and camp there, if you agree," he said. "It's between Ntwetwe and Sowa, on the southern end. We'll drive across the pan as we did before, but we'll go farther in. I think there's still a track from near the island to Mopipi and Lake Xau. I brought two tents—the bigger one's for you."

As they drove west, the *mopane* scrub opened out to clumps of palm, and then closed in again. They passed a few springbok, a small herd of zebra. A lone male ostrich crossed the road in front of them. A few kilometers later, she asked him to stop so she could pee, and she stumbled away from the road over parched earth, swishing through yellow grass.

As they stood together at the northernmost edge of the pan looking south, the desolation seemed even more unnerving than before.

He said, "I've brought a high-lift jack."

"Do you think we'll need it?"

"Don't know."

As they proceeded across the pan, they were baking inside an oven on wheels. Islands were dotted here and there, almost perfectly round and covered with grass, some of them tiny, one large enough to host a small herd of gemsbok. They bumped over a gravel bed. She thought of the fish who'd swum here, small and great. The flamingos in such numbers they would have turned the sky the color of sunrise. *Surely goodness and mercy shall follow me all the days of my life.* The words came to her suddenly, ones she hadn't spoken since Sunday school. Right behind them, she felt another force biding its time: something utterly without mercy. It waited in the heat and stillness, the light that blinded. The forces were one and the same, as though the whiteness had wiped clear every distinction on Earth.

Ian stopped the Land Rover. "Need to rest my eyes."

"Know where we are?"

"The moon." He turned to her and brushed the hair from her face. "Okay?" The place tore words from her mouth and replaced them with silence. She squeezed his hand and offered him an orange. He peeled it and held out half to her. By early afternoon, they'd reached Kube. Stunted baobabs dotted the surface of granite outcroppings. Yellow grasses blew in the west wind, rippling, as though a hand were being drawn across them.

They pitched the two tents side by side in the grass by the shore of the lake that once was. Ian rummaged around in the back of the vehicle and brought out a tall aluminum billy can that he filled with water. Alice had never seen anything like it. It had a hole in the center, all the way up. He put twigs in the space under and inside the elongated doughnut hole, and lit a small fire. The water boiled fast in this contraption, and a few minutes later, they sat in the shade of the Land Rover in two folding chairs, looking west, drinking tea from tin cups.

"When I was a girl," she said, "I used to look at a picture book with my mom. There was a page with thousands of pink flamingos on a salt lake somewhere in Africa. Every time we came to that page, my mother would say how she longed to be in a place like that."

"Do you long for places?"

"Not really. Melancholy is more my thing. But that's different."

"Is it?"

"The way it floats. Without an object."

He touched her hand. "My longings have been of a different sort. How to be alone with Alice and away from Arthur Haddock."

She smiled. "Here we are."

"I thought you were going to hit me when I called you 'lovey.'"

"I thought I was going to hit you too."

"This one's got some spunk, I said to myself."

"Oh you did, did you?"

The wind sounded thin through the baobab trees, a kind of high, stretched-out sound. "I was thinking," she said, "about what Ngwaga said about you."

"Do you mean, will I ever be different?"

"I don't want you to be anyone but you, Ian Henry."

"Are you asking, how would it ever work if we were together?"

"Yes, I guess that's what I'm asking."

"I don't know. It's never worked before."

She looked at him and dashed the dregs of her tea onto the ground. "I don't believe the past controls the future."

"Fair enough."

"And the wind does get tired and have to stop blowing every so often."

He stood up, leaned over, and kissed her. When she stood and pressed her body to his, her legs were weak from the wanting of him. She pulled him toward the large tent. It was like entering a mouth, with the heat of the sun gathered there. He left the large flap open to the wind and slipped off his shoes. She hugged him toward her and lifted his T-shirt up over his shoulders and head. He kissed her ear and her hair and her lips. She undid his belt buckle and fumbled him out of his shorts. She brushed her lips against his nipple. He shuddered, ripped off her shirt, unhooked her bra with one hand, arching her up against him as he unclasped her pants. His mouth touched her neck. His body was no longer young. Hands on damp skin. Here. And here. A scar rimpled the skin of his shoulder. What she felt was something like a hard rain: violence and brightness and beauty.

The wind sighed through the trees, but neither of them heard it.

They lay back against the sleeping bag, his arm under her head, her hair disheveled. His eyes were closed, his breath even. She watched him, his chest rising and falling. Wrinkles creased his earlobes. His age made him dearer to her. In some irrational part of her, she still thought she'd live forever, but she could see that he would not. She closed her eyes and slept until the heat made her stir. He woke and laid his palm against her hair. "Do you know the story of Lynx and Morning Star?"

"Tell me," she said.

He stopped and looked at her, ran his hand forward through her hair.

"Morning Star wanted a bride, and out of all the animals, he chose Lynx. He'd seen her walking alone at night and fallen in love as he watched her move. Liquid, like a river.

"They were happy together, but no sooner had their union taken place than a shadow entered their lives. With hulking shoulders and hunger and jealousy, Hyena set out to break apart the marriage with her dark magic. She transformed the food of Lynx into poison that would rob her of her will to live. Lynx's fur lost its shine. Her eyes grew dull. She no longer groomed herself or cared for anything.

"Hyena threw Lynx out of her hut and moved in. Lynx's sister hastened to Morning Star and told him that the light of his life was in danger. Morning Star's rage was unbounded. He flew to Earth with his spear in hand. Hyena saw him coming and rushed from the hut in terror. As Hyena dodged to protect herself from his spear, her hind leg caught on the coals of the cooking fire. She was burned so badly that from that day forward, she walked lopsided.

"Lynx grew strong again. Morning Star shone brightly between night and day, brighter than before because he knew he had to stay vigilant against the forces of darkness in the universe."

"Vigilant against the forces of darkness," she said. She lay with her back next to the tent wall, one hand under a bunched-up pillow, facing him. She could smell old rainy seasons, sun, and wind in the canvas. His elbow was bent, his hand holding up his head. She caught his index finger in her fist. "Are you afraid of anything?"

"Me?"

This amused her. As though someone else were in the tent with them. "Yes, you."

He kissed her hair. "When I was a kid, I was terrified of great naked mole rats."

She laughed.

"My father showed me a picture once in a book. I used to dream about them and wake up screaming. My mum would come rushing in, 'What's the matter, what's the matter?' and I'd say, 'The Great Naked Mole Rats!'"

"What do they look like?"

"Tiny piggy eyes, so small they can hardly see." He sat up in agitation. "Their skin is a pinky yellowish gray and all wrinkly, ending with a ratty tail; they have four huge yellowish buck teeth that dominate their face. I was obsessed with them. I did research at the local library, hoping to get to the bottom of it. It turns out their skin doesn't have a neurotransmitter responsible for pain, so you can paint them with acid and they feel nothing. Their social life is like bees or termites. They have one queen and only a couple of select males who can reproduce. The rest are workers, functioning in a kind of caste system. Some are tunnelers, some are soldiers, protecting the colony. They tell who's friend or foe by smell. They roll around in their shit to update their smell. When they're cold, they huddle together in a disgusting hairless mass of flesh. When they're hot, they head into the nether reaches of their tunnels. They live up to twenty years, longer sometimes, but a lot of that living is sleep. They're like some great jaundice-skinned Uncle Harry who came to Christmas dinner and went to sleep on the couch and never left."

"Do you have an Uncle Harry?"

"No. But if I did . . . You really wouldn't believe how disgusting these naked mole rats are. I'll have to find you a picture. In my young dreams, they were enormous. In fact they're only a few centimeters long."

She laughed again.

"Why? What's so funny?"

She didn't answer. "What about now? Are you afraid of anything now? You ducked my question."

"Did I?" He held her palm and spread her fingers out one by one. He nibbled the webbed skin between her thumb and first finger. "I'll tell you what I'm afraid of. I'm afraid of bad people. But right now, at this moment, I'm afraid I won't prove good enough for you."

"Why would you say such a thing?"

"You don't know me all that well."

"I know enough."

He grew serious. "What do you know?"

"I know you're not easily domesticated. That you have unusual passions. That you have little patience for bureaucrats."

"What you don't know is that I'm stubborn to the point of intractable. And underneath the nice guy, I'm really a bit of a selfish bastard."

She ran a finger around and over his nipple. "I'll take you the way you are, all of you."

That night, they lay side by side in the tent, exhausted. His hand was palm down on her belly, his eyes closed. By moonlight, she watched his face as he went from light to heavier sleep, the laugh lines around his eyes etched deep and then smoothing as he let go of the day. Heat radiated from his palm and dampened her belly. She felt gratefulness for him beside her and an odd dread. She didn't trust that dread, knew its roots came from her mother. As a child, when she'd ridden her bicycle down her street, her mother's voice echoed in her head, "Be careful!" while the wind blew free through her hair, singing a different song. Ian's breath deepened beside her, and he began to snore softly, a gentle rasping sound.

Who could blame her mother? To say good-bye to a young husband one night, to watch him climb into his police cruiser, to be woken in the middle of the night with the news. It had been an exciting story to tell in school. Sometimes she said her father's police cruiser had exploded. All they found was his badge. When she was older, she no longer told the story to anyone. She imagined her father in his car, a quarter moon in a dark sky. Venus and Jupiter oddly aligned near the moon, Venus so bright, it nearly outshone the moon. And that moment when her father leaped, believing he would land on solid bridge and finding only air beneath him, he would have felt astonishment, perhaps not even fear.

What she wanted to keep alive were the bright eyes of a father she'd seen in photographs, smiling next to her mother. And if she was honest with herself, she wanted to share a piece of that awe, that largeness as he fell through the night sky, a small comet, streaking down as most fathers do not. She had known him only briefly. There were no particular memories to miss, only that moment when he'd been almost as bright as a planet.

She turned and put her arm over Ian's waist. His eyes flickered as though he were still driving in deep sand, and then his breath settled.

She first saw it as a red scratch the next day, laying down a delicate path from her foot toward her ankle. She thought it was made by a thorn. But later, her head throbbed and a fever began to rampage through her blood, roaring into her ears, singeing bones, hollowing her eye sockets into dry craters. She told Ian she was frightened. "I don't know what's the matter." Her vision blurred and scrambled—the tent roof turned in a slow circle she thought was the sky. She threw the pillow away from her, as Ian tucked it under her head again. His voice was magnified beyond bearing. When he spoke, tears came to her eyes. His face pressed close to hers. "Tell me where you hurt." The thought of answering him—like vomiting up the center of the Earth. She was out of her head. She scrambled out of the tent which enclosed her like a body bag. He brought out a mat for her to lie on and laid wet towels over her chest. When darkness swept over them, she had no idea where she was. The stars fell, growing brighter as they neared the campfire, hovering briefly, then growing larger still, swirling in fiery reds and yellows and blues. She turned in space, lifted from the ground, somersaulted and twirled like an astronaut without an umbilical cord.

Ian said, "Did you get bitten?"

"Where?" she screamed.

He held a flashlight, pointing at her feet first. He was trying to vaporize them. She fought him with all her strength.

"Bloody hell!" he cried. "Do I have to belt you one?!" He sat on her chest and held her arms. She didn't remember what happened next. Maybe he knocked her out. Later, he told her that in the light of his flashlight, he'd found the red streak, all the way to her thigh by then. And he dosed her with the antibiotics he always carried—wrestling her to get them down.

She found herself in an endless dream, trying to get a nest of snakes to a hospital. They were in a Pyrex custard cup, writhing and spilling and shooting out over the lobby of a hotel. She kept gathering them, and they'd shrink and pulse, then shoot out again. The dream went round and round, and she began to cry, out of frustration and helplessness.

And then her skin began to cool. Her eyes opened and fell onto Ian. No disintegrating heavens, just the two of them camped under a couple of dwarf baobab trees, the sun coming up warm and bright over the pan, doves making their mournful sound in the trees. His face was deeply lined, dark bags under his eyes.

"You're back," he said, holding her.

"What do you think it was?"

"Tick bite fever."

"How do you know?"

"Between your toes. I found the evidence last night. There's a streak of red running up your leg."

"If it had reached my heart, would I have died?"

"No. No, you wouldn't have. I was going to pack you straight into the Land Rover, but I didn't know if I could find my way in the dark."

"What did I say to you last night?"

"Best goes unrepeated. You were a wild animal . . ."

"I'm sorry."

"You're all right, my love, that's what matters. What do you want for breakfast? I'm thinking we should eat and then go get a proper antibiotic for you."

"What did you give me?"

"Erythromycin, I think."

"You're not sure?"

"Sometimes I switch the bottles."

"Well, it's working . . . and I don't want to go. Why should we?"

"It seems like a good idea."

"I don't want to go anywhere."

"All right, but what do you want for breakfast?"

"A cup of tea?"

"And what else?"

"Some porridge?"

"And what else?"

"That's it." She held out her hand to him.

He grabbed it and grew quiet. "Don't ever do that . . . I couldn't bear it, Alice . . ."

He turned to go, but she hung onto his hand. "It goes both ways."

They stayed there that day and another night. He made stew, and they sat in the shade on the camp chairs, watching the birds come and go, the light shift over the pan. "If that tick hadn't gotten me," she said, "we would have left this morning and we would have missed all this."

Toward nightfall, she said, "I've been thinking that I'm not going to be able to come with you after all. My legs are weak as noodles. There'll be another time. I'd like you to drive me back to Francistown tomorrow and put me on an overnight train."

"I'd carry you up those hills if you want."

She touched his lips.

"Or I can drive you back to Gaborone."

"The conductor will bring a blanket roll. I'll be rocked all night. I'll call my neighbor and ask her to pick me up on the other end."

"I want to drive you."

"I want you to be doing what you were planning to do. You'll tell me about it. Maybe we can meet halfway in a couple of weeks when you come back."

"It's what you want?"

"It's what I want."

That night, they lay together in the big tent. She was still feverish, and when he came into her, she felt his coolness against her heat. She would have liked him to stay there forever. They moved together gently, peacefully, stopping, beginning again, her fever knocking down the borders between them.

They slept, and woke early. Morning Star was brighter than ever, hope on the horizon, the howl of the hyena banished. Ian drove across the pan, then northward, back to Gweta and east to Francistown. They ate dinner together, and he walked her to the platform where the southbound passenger train waited. "Stay here tonight," he said, "and let me drive you in the morning."

"No," she said, kissing him. She let him go, and he put his arms around her again and kissed her harder. She climbed up the steps into the train. When she opened the window of the compartment to wave, he was already walking down the platform. He didn't turn.

31

In his mind's eye, he saw her face flushed with fever, her hair stuck to her cheek with sweat, her eyes swimming. Driving her back out to the main road, he'd wanted to keep harm from her forever. But that feeling was mixed with something stronger that had nothing to do with keeping her safe. Once he'd seen pictures of the living bridges of Cherrapunji in northeastern India, made from the roots of rubber trees. Some of them were a hundred feet long and could hold the weight of fifty villagers. The bridges were grown from secondary roots, using betel nut trunks sliced down the middle and hollowed out, to create root pathways. This was how it felt with Alice: a living bridge between them.

He'd planned to leave Francistown that night but realized his spare tire was in bad shape. God would be unlikely to provide. By the time he'd be able to find a new tire and get himself organized, he thought he might as well stay for the night. But it turned out to be a night that would have been better spent elsewhere.

An hour after dropping off Alice, he bumped into Gwyneth at the hotel. She was up from Gaborone doing business for De Beers. Her old demon, depression, had caught up with her. She'd cut off all her hair. She was into her second whiskey sour, standing disconsolately with her back to a window.

"What are you doing here?"

"Work. What about you?"

"I just dropped someone off at the train."

"A woman."

"How did you know?"

"I can see her on your face."

"Have you had dinner?" he asked.

"No."

"Want to join me?"

"You wouldn't rather be alone with your amorous thoughts?" That was the beginning. The weeping in his arms and her regrets about her life followed. He preferred not to think about what happened next. The odd thing was how good it still was with her, after all they'd been through. How many times had he cursed the day he'd met her, and yet this, these blindly loving bodies . . . this remained.

The following morning he was out before dawn, heading west. He drove fast, trying to outrun the night that clung to him. If Gwyneth had been a manipulator, he would have known what to do, but she lived at the mercy of inner hellions that threatened to erase her. He told himself that he'd been a lifeline last night, nothing more. And even as he had the thought, he knew the "nothing more" wasn't quite true. He imagined telling Alice, then he imagined not telling her, and neither seemed right.

He planned to turn south on a track between Bushman Pits and Maun, and head toward the southeast corner of the Kuke fence, working his way west as he cut fence cable. His hope was that animals trapped both to the east and south might find their way toward the Okavango through at first a narrow opening and then a gradually widening one. There was no predicting when the rains would come to this part of the country, or even if they'd come at all.

Etched into the map in his mind, Ian pictured the northern wilderness of Botswana as a wire prison. The Kuke veterinary fence, running from the Namibian border across the northern boundary of the Central Kgalagadi had been constructed in 1958. A similar cordon fence, running along the international border between Namibia and Botswana, enclosed three and a half sides of a box. It made him nearly crazy to think about it. It was no different from penning wild animals, withholding food and water, and watching them die.

His hands, which rattled on the steering wheel of the Land Rover most of the day, still shook after he climbed out that evening. South of the main road under a small clump of trees, he pitched a tent, laid out his sleeping bag, and built a fire. Dust kicked up by a herd of cattle that'd passed through, choked the air, and the sun blazed down to Earth, huge and white with a dark streak across it. He made a supper of beans and a bit of goat meat he'd bought in Francistown, and ate meditatively, listening to the night sounds. The sky was dead clear. The cry of a spotted hyena, rising quickly, ended with an exclamation point. He thought he heard thunder, and then realized it was wishful thinking.

He opened a packet of Marie biscuits and munched one after another. Without asking to, Alice had called his life into question, his long held assumptions about what mattered, his independence elevated to a quasi religion. He was still traveling forward on the momentum of his former life, but the ground underneath was rifting.

By early afternoon of the next day, he reached the intersection of the Kuke fence and the Makalamabedi portion. He drove across the veldt, searching for wildlife and found a mixed herd of wildebeest and zebra at a distance of several kilometers west, moving slowly in the direction of the fence. Carcasses littered the landscape, beasts dead from thirst and famine. Among the living were very few young ones. He parked the Land Rover near the section of fence where he planned to start, unbolted his license plate, and hid it under a blanket in the back.

Five strands of thick wire were strung between wooden standards. He tested the tension on the cable to see whether it was likely to snap out when it was cut. Probably not. From the backseat, he lifted out an industrial-sized bolt cutter with solid pipe handles and black rubber grips that his friend Leonard had lent him. Leonard said it would cut through anything—something like an eighteen-hundred-kilogram cutting force for a twenty-five-kilogram force on the handles.

Ian opened the jaw of the thing, positioned it around the bottom wire and pushed the handles together. *Snap.* The wire coiled back on itself in two directions. He moved up to the next cable and did the same. All the way up through the five cables. Would the ends of the wires injure animals? He thought it best to cut through close to the standard and coil the loose ends of wire around the adjoining post as best he could.

He moved to the next post. He told himself he'd do five standards, or twenty-five cables, and rest. Twenty-five more cables, rest. After a hundred cables, he'd drink some water. He made it through only seventy-five before needing water. He paused and went back to wrap the wires around the posts. By the end of the day, he'd averaged something like eight posts an hour. Nothing brilliant, but the pace was manageable. Close to fifty standards by six P.M. About 150 meters. It wasn't a large enough opening to make a real difference, but if a herd traveled along the fence looking for a way through, they'd find it here.

On the third day, he came back at six in the morning and found evidence that a small herd had passed through to the other side—hoof prints of wildebeest and zebra, possibly steenbok. As he moved west, he found more carcasses of wildebeest, and farther along, part of the carcass of a giraffe that must have died or been killed in the night. Three cape vultures circled, their white bodies glowing in the sun, dark tails spread and black wing feathers stretched out like fingers, feet dangling oddly, like something dead. Their wingspan was at least three meters wide. As they descended, their bodies tensed; their feet became suddenly poised and muscular. They landed, and two of them hopped, hissing and cackling to the carcass, naked throats extended, their black beaks lethal as the bolt cutters Ian held in his hand. At the outskirts, slightly away from the carcass, one waited, its neck S shaped. After a time, they took off, trailing death, climbing on warm thermals.

He set to work again, still moving west. The bolt cutter was doing a number on his arms and shoulders after only a couple of days' work. The pain disgusted him. In his twenties, he could have worked three times this fast and not felt a thing.

He opened another forty-five standards before noon, dropped the bolt cutters where he stopped, and walked to the Land Rover to get the billy can for tea. The work made him ravenous; he'd be running short of food within a day or two and needing to return to Maun. He lit a fire and boiled water, opened a tin of sardines, and made a sandwich of fish and bread. A few wildebeest, with a young one trailing, moved along away from the opening he'd cut. They looked weak enough to push over. Ian put down the sandwich and tea, ran around behind them, and waved his arms, until they turned around and walked in the other direction toward the opening in the fence. He urged them along until they went through. Water was eighty kilometers away.

On the fourth day, he was clipping and sweating and didn't hear a Land Rover come up behind him until it was almost on him. A red-faced man leaned out the window. "What the hell you think you're doing, mate?"

"Cutting wire."

"I've got eyes. What the bloody hell for?"

"Notice the animal carcasses? They can't get to water."

"Well, see those cattle over there? Those are part of my herd. That's my living. Hoof-and-mouth will wipe me out in a matter of weeks."

"No one's studied whether the fence prevents the spread of hoof-and-mouth."

"Study? What the hell did they put it up for if it didn't help? Look, mate, this isn't a conversation. I'm telling you. Get out." He lifted a shotgun. "You're destroying government property."

"If you want to look at it like that, it's been good chatting. What's your name anyway?"

"You think you're pretty smart, don't you? You won't get it from me."

Ian picked up his bolt cutter and billy can. "Well, I'll be off." Without turning, he walked the few yards to his Land Rover, picturing the back of his head in crosshairs. He heard the sound of the other vehicle leaving and rubbed his hand over the back of his neck.

On the way back to the main road, he thought, that guy was trying to make a living, so why didn't he give a damn? But some wildebeest and its calf trying to stay alive, he'd risk his life for. He bumped over the veldt, avoiding an anthill. He knew the greed, the small-mindedness of a man, that was why, but animals, they don't take more than they need. He stopped, replaced the license plate, and bumped down the rough track.

He guessed he was finished here. He'd head south of Sehitwa, west of the Mabele a Pudi Hills, where the fence was about the same distance to water.

32

For two days now, there'd been no porridge. The footsteps brought only water to his door. Isaac tried to speak to the man in the cell next to his, but there was no answer.

His belly had stopped crying out. There is a point when the body relinquishes its pain and waits dumbly. He was growing unable to stand with any steadiness. He noticed that his mind had blurred like his body, his thoughts increasingly muddled, his fear wilder. He imagined there would come a time when fear too would go the way of hunger: the savage animal eating his heart would someday grow weary.

The wall beside him had once been whitewashed, but was now gray and smeared. Before darkness descended, a dim light fell through the transom slats, and he peered at what looked like scratchings. A series of lines. Sixty-seven of them. What had happened on the sixty-eighth day? He wanted to believe the man who'd made those scratches was alive, but he'd never heard of anyone being released from Number Four. Nelson Mandela, yes, but they'd taken him to Robben Island and would never let him go.

He laid a finger on the sixty-seventh line. His eyes strayed around the wall as the cell grew dark. He believed he could see marks farther above his head, perhaps a word. He rose to his knees to see it better, but the light was too dim.

From an early age, Isaac had been taught to believe he'd been chosen for a life above the ordinary. He saw now that hubris had crept into his soul, inhabited his thoughts. Perhaps he had been chosen not for the extraordinary, but for this.

As dark overtook him, he heard a group of prisoners singing in a distant cell block.

Hamba khale umkhonto
Wemkhonto
Mkhonto wesizwe
Thina Bantu bomkhonto siz'misele
Ukuwabulala
Wona lamabhulu.

They were singing of Umkhonto, the spear of the nation. Singing to bring death and destruction down upon the heads of the Boers. Around him, down the block of the isolation wing, a voice joined them, here, there, and his own lifted into the darkness.

At dawn, he heard the footsteps of two guards. His heart pounded. The door of the cell next to his clanged open.

There were rough voices, a scuffling sound.

"*Eish,* that gave me a fright."

"*Fokken klank.*"

"*Jou dronkie!*" You drunkard. "*Ag man, get his legs.*"

This is how he'd go, with bickering and swearing and a heave ho into a hole in the ground.

His sense of time was gone. How much time passed before another door clanged down the row? And then the moans began: that terrible labor. The screams would be coming. He knew this particular voice now and believed this man would die. Afterward, they would come for him. *Amandla!* he whispered. *Ngawethu! Power! The power is ours!* Not today, not tomorrow, but . . . it had almost ceased to matter whether he was here to see a world transformed.

33

"You look terrible," Lillian said. "Here, give me that." Alice dropped her bag. Her head swam, and her knees shook. To her dazed eyes, the old Gaborone train station looked like a daguerreotype, its surface painted in silver halide. People moving about hauling boxes and trunks looked oddly still. "I tried to call you earlier," she said.

"Gerald and I went away, a spur of the moment thing. While you were gone, he came home and said he wanted to take me to Victoria Falls for our thirtieth anniversary."

"How was it?"

"The best holiday we've ever taken." She put Alice's bag in the truck and opened the door for her. "You poor thing. You look like hell warmed over."

"Thanks, Lillian. Has there been any rain?"

"I heard there was a shower while we were gone. Nothing much."

"It's a dust bowl up north."

"Some bloke has been around your place. A European."

"I asked Will to let Isaac know I'd be a few days late . . . Do you know if Itumeleng's back?"

"I saw her hanging out laundry."

As Lillian drove toward the Old Village, Alice recognized a woman she'd seen before, knitting as she walked, carrying a baby on her back. The bush stretched out on the left, a tangle of footpaths and low scrub; on the right were houses thrown up so fast, she thought some of them hadn't been there when she left. Lillian turned right off the main road, then pulled into the driveway, maneuvering around White Dog. "You leave that bag. You have no business carrying anything."

Itumeleng greeted Alice as she stroked White Dog.

"Take good care of her, okay?" said Lillian. "She's sick." She handed the bag to Itumeleng and hugged Alice good-bye. "I'll bring by some food later. You go have a good sit on the veranda, and a nap."

"Thanks, Lillian." She watched her go and turned to Itumeleng. "Where's Isaac?"

"*Ga ke itse, mma.* Only the dog is here."

"He wasn't here when you got back?"

"No, *mma.* I think he has gone. Or maybe he is late."

"Why would you say such a thing?"

"If he is staying at the place where there is the shooting, he is dead, *mma.* They come and kill the ANC people. Only one little baby is still alive."

"I don't understand."

"While you were away, *mma.* The South African police come over the border."

"When was this?"

"After you leave, *mma.*"

"The South African police crossed the border?"

"*Ee, mma.*"

". . . But Isaac is not with the ANC."

"Then maybe he go home to see his mother in South Africa."

"He couldn't go back even if he wanted to. He left illegally."

"I don't know, *mma.* I don't know where he is gone. One cat, the Horse, is also missing."

Alice went inside and slumped down in a chair in the living room. A few minutes later Itumeleng brought her sweet tea. A pile of mail sat next to her, and she picked up a couple of envelopes and set them back down without opening them. Two were from home, one from her mother. A heap of soot sat at the base of the hearth, gleaming in a ray of sun that sliced down the chimney. She wondered where it had come from. And wondered how she could have lived in this house as long as she had without noticing the way the sun fell through the darkness of brick and dust and reappeared on the hearth.

The tea was lukewarm, and she drank it fast. And then sat with the cup shaking in her lap, her legs still weak. She got to her feet and tried to call Will, but the phone lines were down. Half an hour later, she tried again and finally drove around to his and Greta's house.

One of Will's young sons had made a bow and arrow and was shooting a stick into the air and running toward the falling trajectory, trying to get the stick to hit him on the head. One of the family's large dogs walked out of the shade and came toward her with the end of her tail wagging.

"Hey, beautiful," said Alice, leaning over to pat her head.

"You're back!" Greta yelled, yanking a pair of child's socks off the line. What couldn't Greta do? Corral squirming boys for bath time, whip up dinner for a small village at the drop of a hat. She stopped suddenly and studied Alice. "What's wrong with you?"

"I came down with tick bite fever." Alice bit her lip.

"Come here," said Greta, folding her into her arms.

Tears came, and Greta said, "Oh, poppet, you're exhausted. When was the last decent meal you had?"

"I'm all right. I came by to see if Will had seen Isaac."

"No. We have no idea where he went. Will went round to the police station. One of the officers came down to your house. There's no trace of him."

"He wouldn't have left his dog."

"That's what we thought."

"I don't know what to do."

Greta grabbed a few more clothes off the line and threw them over her shoulder. "I'd go back to the police. Come on in, I'll give you a cuppa."

"I just had one."

"Well, stay for dinner then. We'll eat in an hour or so."

"Thanks, sweetie, not today."

At home, Itumeleng heated up a beef stew and gave Alice a bowlful.

Alice looked at her fondly, thinking she was one of the homeliest people she'd ever met. A thin scar began at the round of her cheek and plunged toward her jaw. Her face was huge, her eyes large, her eyebrows a jumble. One gold and one white front tooth sat side by side. The few times Alice had seen her go out at night, a stain of pink lipstick blazed across the white and gold.

"I've decided to go to the police," Alice said.

"No, madam, you must not. It will make trouble."

"Are you afraid it will make trouble for you?" Alice stood up and set her empty plate in the sink.

Itumeleng sloshed water into a dented pot. "No, I am not afraid of them. I am not afraid of anyone." The back of her neck was moist with sweat. She wore a pink uniform, stained under the arms. Alice had not wanted her to wear a uniform, but Itumeleng had wanted one. She had this pink one and a green one.

"He would not have left his dog unless something had happened to him."

"Leave it, madam." Itumeleng banged the pot. "Last year you did not know him."

"But I know him now."

"Next year, again you will not know him."

"I hope to know him next year."

"If you have a child, then you are not asking for trouble like this," Itumeleng said. She kept her eyes on the ground and walked out the backdoor.

Alice picked up the pot Itumeleng had set down and slammed it against the table.

The deputy chief of police did not look well. Mr. Tebape's skin was tired and pitted, his shoulders sagged. The chief of police was out of town. Mr. Tebape hadn't wanted to see her, and his secretary had tried to pawn her off on someone else. She sat in an uncomfortable wooden chair on the opposite side of his desk. She explained that Will had seen another member of the police force when Mr. Tebape was out of town.

"My mother was ill," he said, as though she'd accused him of something.

"I hope she's better now."

"She is not better, she is late," he said with a slight quaver.

"I'm very sorry."

"*Ke a leboga, mma*," he thanked her. He moved a cup from one place on his desk to another place and looked at her for the first time.

She explained the circumstances surrounding Isaac's disappearance.

"Which town is he from?"

She hesitated. "He is from South Africa. Pretoria."

"Legal or illegal?"

"Will I get him in trouble if I say illegal?"

A small twitch of a smile passed over his lips. "No, madam."

"Illegal. His name is Isaac Muthethe."

Mr. Tebape shifted in his seat. "I do not know anything about this man," he said.

"Is it possible that anyone on your force would know anything?"

"I will make inquiries," he said. "Tell me his name again."

She spelled it for him while he wrote it down. "He was . . . is a very responsible, peace-loving person. He had been a medical student before coming here. He needed to flee for political reasons."

Mr. Tebape nodded. "I will let you know, madam, if I have discovered anything. If Mr. Muthethe returns, he must apply for political asylum at that time."

"Yes, of course."

He stood. The interview was over. The heat smacked her as she stood to leave.

She'd been deep into a dream when the phone rang after midnight. She jumped up and ran from the bedroom in a panic, stubbing her toe on a corner of the couch.

"Did I wake you?" he said.

"Yes. Where are you?"

"Maun. I'm sorry to call so late. I just got in. No place to phone you from."

"How are you?" she asked.

"I've missed you. Are you all right?"

"Almost better, but a strange thing's happened. Isaac's missing. He left his dog. I went to the deputy chief of police today and got nowhere."

"Maybe he took off."

"He's not that sort of person."

"Do you have an address for his family?"

"No."

"I don't know what to suggest."

"I don't know what to do, either."

"I'm sorry. I wish I were there with you." His voice sounded husky.

"Oh, god, that makes two of us. What have you been doing?"

"Cutting fence. First at the southeast corner of the Kuke fence, not far from where we were. I borrowed a wire cutter. I was making fine progress but a red-necked rancher threw a spanner in the works. Had a bit of a row, and he told me to get out—from the other end of a shotgun."

"Jesus."

"I thought of telling him to piss off but it didn't seem a good plan. He was a dodgy sort of fellow. So I moved on, drove to another section of fence south of Sehitwa."

She was quiet a moment. "It's hopeless, you know."

"I know it."

"Dangerous too. That rancher could have blown you off the face of the Earth. Don't do it anymore, darling. Write a letter."

"I've talked to them already."

"Talk to someone higher up."

"And why would anyone listen to me?"

"Write a letter to the minister, go see the president."

"It's not how I operate." She pictured him sitting in Maun, the river beyond, a glass of beer nearby.

"You could learn a new trick."

"What you see is what you get." He went quiet. "Listen, if things don't change . . . I can't work in a country where animals are dying like this. You and I could live in England for a bit, then perhaps I can get a grant to do some work in East Africa."

"I can't leave right now."

"I love you, Alice."

It made the breath go out of her. She said nothing for a moment. "I can't go, at least not now, with Isaac missing."

"Can you still come to Mahalapye this weekend? We can talk about it."

"You remember I'm supposed to be at that government do after work on Friday?"

"I'll be in Mahalapye Friday night. Maybe you'll manage to get away early."

She whispered good-bye and set the phone down. Back in bed, she lay awake in the dark. It was tempting to leave here, start a life together elsewhere. She liked England, could imagine living there. And she could imagine, almost, a life with Ian.

But Isaac would not have abandoned her, and she wouldn't abandon him. She thought how, at the end of each day, he and White Dog headed up the road together, the dust in the air turning the contours of things shimmery. It was possible he led a double life, but somehow, she didn't think so. She knew nothing, though, about him or the family he'd left behind. They were shadows, the kind of caricatures that white people carry in their heads when they think about Africa: no shoes, no school, no future.

34

Alice looked up from her desk on Friday afternoon onto a blank concrete wall. She'd finished the position paper on land use that she'd promised her boss, and delivered it. She pictured herself at the cocktail party after work, holding a glass of wine, making small talk with people she never wanted to see in the first place. The hell with it, she thought. She returned a couple of phone calls, wrote a memo, and went out to her truck. A restless wind blew, and before long, she was driving in rain so violent, it felt mythic. She made her way north half as fast as normal, nearly blinded, through rivers of mud. By the time she arrived it was nearly dark. She was drenched getting inside. The Dew Drop Inn felt damp and deserted. She called out a hello. Ian appeared from the back and wrapped her in his arms. He placed a small parcel in her hands and moved a strand of her streaming hair behind her ear.

"What's this?"

"I hope you like it."

She unwrapped the package and found a wooden object, a little bigger than the palm of her hand. She raised her eyebrows.

"A Bushman piano," he said. "Hold it like this and pluck the keys with your thumb." It made a clanking sound, accompanied by the rattle of ostrich egg beads strung onto a metal wire.

"I adore it."

"An old man gave it to me. It's made from stolen fence wire. The wood was blackened over a fire."

She kissed him on the mouth. She was about to tell him it was the nicest present anyone had ever given her when Berndt, the owner, appeared from behind a faded curtain, looking rumpled, as though he'd been napping. He was sixty something, with a smell of cigarettes clinging to him. Alice's hand rested furtively on Ian's ass, his on hers.

"Right, then," Ian said quickly, crisply, "time for us to get settled in." He turned to Alice. "Berndt has given us a *rondavel,* separate from the house, out back." She could tell he'd engineered this separate dwelling.

But Berndt wouldn't hear of it. "Dinner is served," he said. "There's no point going out in that rain and then coming in again." There'd be beef. That went without saying. Potatoes. A mushy veg. And some kind of inedible pudding with custard sauce. That was optimistic. She'd eaten here a couple of times before. She didn't want dinner, she wanted this man beside her.

Berndt led the way to a large room in the central part of the inn, facing out to the darkness. Ian and Alice were the only guests.

Then Boom Boom entered, an Australian woman who'd taken over the kitchen at some point during the past year. Who knew how she'd come to be here? She was large, loud, and wore a pink satin stole tipped with fur, a long, flowing sequined skirt, and little yellow pumps that she'd poured her feet into. Her lipstick, bright crimson, was applied in a great pointed *M* on her upper lip.

She'd hired five Batswana—boys she called them—as helpers and cooks. Two of the boys stood out in the dining room, hands clasped over their crotches, looking cowed, waiting to bring out the food.

They served tiny Korean pancakes with a ginger sauce for appetizers, fresh bream for the main course. Boom Boom drank steadily—tumblers of Irish whiskey—and played Strauss waltzes and orchestral potboilers on an old reel-to-reel tape recorder.

The door opened, and a man blew in whose eyes were wild and dazed. Berndt invited him to sit down and have some dinner and asked where he'd come from.

"Francistown." He'd had some work up there.

There was a silence. Francistown lay to the north, and the only road between Francistown and Mahalapye crossed a single-lane bridge with no guard rails. Even on the sunniest day, the bridge was a horror to cross, with its long drop to the river. But tonight, with the river rising to flood level, the bridge would have been hidden, indistinguishable from water.

"How in the name of bloody hell did you get over the bridge?" asked Berndt.

The man, a stranger to these roads, said, "What bridge?"

They looked at him.

"You never saw the bridge?" asked Ian. "You've got a bloody angel sitting on your shoulder."

"I never saw anything," the man said.

"You need to thank your God," said Berndt, pouring him a Scotch.

The man downed it, his hands shaking. "I have children," he said, "six of them."

Alice felt death's cold breath on the back of her neck. She thought of that rushing water, a man passing over a one lane bridge through a gift of pure grace. He had a small mustache on a large, florid face. His eyes kept saying, Why me, why was I allowed to live?

"You never know how you'll die," said Berndt, "or when. I read once that more people are kicked to death by mules . . ."

"Our friend here is thinking of his children," Ian interrupted.

There was an awkward silence. "It's all right," said the man. "I didn't die."

"Thank God," said Alice.

"You live a charmed life," said Ian, standing. "Good luck to you. And to your family." He shook the man's hand. "I think we'll be heading off to bed. First-rate dinner. Our compliments to Boom Boom and her staff."

They refused Berndt's offer of an umbrella—it would only have shredded in the wind. Holding hands in the darkness, they tottered forward while the rain poured down their necks and streamed off their feet. Ian caught her as she fell over the stone threshold in front of the door. She opened it and pushed it shut behind them, and they grabbed for each other.

"I'll light the lamp," he whispered.

"No." Her body shook. She tugged at his trousers and pulled his wet shirt off, her teeth chattering. He wrapped her in a blanket, but it wasn't cold she was feeling. She felt the mane of his hair, wet around her face as he leaned over her on the bed, the smell of him, earth.

Was the world still here? Dark penetrated every corner of the room. She stroked his hair and ran her finger over the outside of his ear. His hand anchored her, held squarely in the center of her back.

"You're amazingly lovely," he said.

"You can't see me."

"I can feel you."

She burrowed her head lower until it lay against his chest. The sheets held the smell of them, and under that, the remnants of sun when they'd hung on the line to dry.

"I wonder what that poor bastard is thinking right now."

"That more people die from being kicked by mules . . ."

He laughed. "It almost makes me believe in some madman up there pulling the strings."

She stroked his shoulder. "Did you ever believe in a madman in the sky?"

"I had a devout period early on. But then I broke our neighbor's parlor window by mistake. My dad gave me a thrashing, and I understood there was no God. The smashed window was an accident, and I thought God should have known that and made my father forgive me."

Smiling into his chest, she said, "Maybe you were being tested."

"I failed the test." He got up and lit the kerosene lamp. It sputtered and flickered and threw crazy shadows around the room as the rain slashed at the window.

"You know the odd thing?" he asked.

"What?"

"I believe in the gods who aren't my own more than I ever believed in the God I was supposed to believe in." He stroked her hair the way you'd stroke a cat. "Did you ever see *The Seventh Seal*?"

She nodded.

"That guy blowing in tonight reminded me of the scene—remember? That little family of actors fleeing in the covered wagon through the forest in the storm, death at their heels?"

"I remember."

"I saw that film at least five times. You remember the knight?"

"Yes."

"*My life has been a futile pursuit, a wandering, a great deal of talk without meaning.* And then he says he'll use his temporary reprieve from Death for one meaningful deed."

"What would you do for a reprieve?"

"I don't believe in good deeds. As soon as you call them good, they stop being good. I'd do what I'm doing now. My whole life is a temporary reprieve, running out every day."

"Don't say that."

"I'm not young."

"Well, you can't leave before I do."

"There's an excellent chance I will."

"If you keep having showdowns with ranchers, yes. Promise me you'll stop."

"I'll think about stopping when I've done one more section of the Kuke fence."

"Please."

"This matters to me," he said.

"I know. Those animals matter to me too. But you matter more."

They were quiet together a moment before he said, "I've never before felt the way I feel about you. Not when I was with Gwyneth, not with anyone ever before."

She kissed him. "Do you still talk to her?"

"To Gwyneth?" His eyes shifted away from hers, and he sat up in bed. "Actually, I happened to run into her a few weeks ago. She was up in Francistown on business. It wasn't planned. It was the day you left." He hesitated. "I won't lie to you, Alice. We spent the night together."

She felt hard slapped. "That very night?"

"She was in bad shape."

"So you thought you'd cheer her up."

"Alice."

"You said it was over."

"It *is* over."

"How could you say what you just said to me after spending the night with her?"

"What I said to you is true, true as anything I've ever spoken."

"I won't be 'the other woman' around the edges of your marriage."

"Alice, please, you're not listening."

"That very night you put me on the train?"

"Darling, you're being foolish."

"I'm not foolish." She crawled out of bed, threw on a shirt and a pair of shorts and headed into the rain. She'd forgotten her shoes, and she wasn't going back for them. The path was a stream, and she was crying hard now. The lights of the main house were still on, and she made her way toward them, over rough stones, and then beyond them, into her truck. She sat behind the steering wheel and thought of driving home, but she wouldn't make it in this weather, and she'd left her purse and keys behind. Her body was still warm from his, and then it wasn't warm anymore. The water on her body and clothes evaporated, and she began to shiver.

She thought of Ian sitting on the bed alone in that little *rondavel*, and her heart went halfway out to him. After she and Lawrence had split, hadn't she told Muriel that the final straw wasn't Erika, but his dishonesty? Was that a crock, or had she meant it? Ian told her the truth. So he lost his head one night. Was that a crime?

But the very night he'd put her on the train? It felt as though their time on the pan had meant nothing to him. But that wasn't true, and she knew it.

He was sitting on the floor when she came in, his back against the bed, his feet stretched straight out in front of him, his hair every which way.

"Darling, you're soaked," he said. He tried to wrap her in a blanket, but she shrugged him off, still crying, and sat on the bed against the headboard. He sat back down on the floor. "Look, at least let me tell you. Gwyneth and I haven't lived together for four years. She's with another bloke. But she's been depressed. She needed to talk. Yes, I was trying to cheer her up, and one thing led to another. It was a one-for-old-time's-sake kind of thing. It just happened."

She looked at him. "It didn't just happen. You weren't exactly a by-stander."

"I know that."

"And how come you're not divorced if you haven't been together in four years?"

"We haven't gotten around to it."

"How could you not get around to it?"

"It hasn't been a priority. The marriage is over. There were no worldly goods to divide, no children. I don't need a magistrate or a piece of paper to tell me it's finished."

"Are you planning to keep on fucking each other?"

Angry now, he said, "I'm fond of her, she's fond of me. But it was a mistake . . . Maybe somewhere in me, I knew how serious it was with you. Maybe I was a bit scared."

"Do you want to be free? Because if you do, you are."

"Look, I'm sorry, my love. What more can I say?" His tone soft-ened. "I've gone raving bonkers over you. If that's not enough, then I'll be off."

She regarded him coolly. "It feels sloppy to still be married. Sloppier still to spend the night with her."

"I'm sloppy."

There was an edge in his voice, something she hadn't heard before. Impatience, a touch of *if this isn't good enough for you, well, then fuck it.*

There didn't seem to be anything more to say. But it also didn't seem possible to go on. A door slammed inside her head, but it wasn't she who'd slammed it. Something in him. Some hard indifference: *Don't try to change me, or there'll be trouble.* Registering it, she backed off.

She lay back against the pillow, wrapped in misery. She loved this man, and there he was sitting on the floor. Take him, warts and all, or leave him was what he was saying.

She patted the bed. "Come on up here," she said. "What are you do-ing down there?"

They slept late the next day. The rain and wind had stopped by the time he opened his eyes. The sun traced its way from the right side of a red lacquer chest and made its way toward a hideous umbrella stand made from an elephant foot. Ian peered into Alice's face as she slept. She'd kicked off the covers and wore only a white T-shirt. He loved her small breasts, the androgynous appeal of her body.

He shifted quietly in bed, saw the striations of light coming in the window, and thought of snow, the long shadows of trees out his win-dow when he'd lived in Norway with Gwyneth years ago. He'd wake in the middle of the night and look out a small window by their loft bed. Sometimes the moon would be there, sometimes the wind, some-times utter silence. He missed the cold, the way it narrowed thought down to the pinch of survival. But he didn't miss the crowding, the small rooms, the two of them huddled in front of a double bar electric fire.

He regretted the night in Francistown for Alice's sake, but it had also felt right at the time. He hadn't tried to explain this to Alice, but he didn't believe in the sharp edges of endings. That's really why he hadn't bothered with the divorce. Gwyneth had needed him that night. They still understood each other, and it had happened. They'd still be to-gether if they hadn't fought so much. She was a good sort underneath all that mess of depression and self-delusion and self-involvement, but he couldn't take the fighting and the continual mood shifts.

Alice stirred and opened her eyes. She smiled when she saw him. And then folded her arms over her breasts.

"Why'd you do that?" he asked softly.

"I don't know."

He watched while she got out of bed, pulled off the T-shirt and pulled on a different shirt and shorts, and splashed water on her face. "Are you okay?" he asked.

"Why?"

"You look far away."

"I'm still half in a dream."

He searched her face for signs of trouble. "Tell me."

"I don't know. Other people's dreams are boring."

"Come on, tell me."

"I was standing at the bottom of a ravine looking up at the lights of a vehicle, way up high at the lip of a cliff. Suddenly the lights plunged over the top, bounced down the first incline. The truck careened over the next lip and picked up speed. I thought at first it was a man alone in the driver's seat. But a young woman sat beside him, slid over on the seat all the way next to him. Her mouth was partway open, as though she was too terrified to scream.

"I don't remember the truck turning over until it was upside down in water. Their heads were underwater, upside down."

"God," said Ian. "What was all that about?"

"I don't know."

"Are you and I all right?"

She looked at him as though she was trying to make up her mind. "Yes." The air after the rain felt newly scrubbed, a faint smell of wet dog.

He kissed her on the mouth. "I'm sorry to upset you."

She touched the top of his arm with two fingers, tentatively, down, up, down. They got back under the sheet together. Her body felt familiar and kind to him, then ravishing, an eloquence of heat, strange and lovely.

Afterward, they lay together, sweaty. He asked, "Remember Ginsberg?"

"Hmmm?" Her eyes were closed.

He crooned in her ear. "*The world is holy! The skin is holy!*"

"People don't use that word anymore."

"Holy?"

"It's a good word."

Later, they ate what Berndt called "a proper English breakfast." Fried tomatoes, fried sausages, fried bread, eggs over lightly, toast with jam. Boom Boom was nowhere in sight. After breakfast, they went for a walk; then Ian worked on a paper he was writing on geometrics for the Center for World Indigenous Studies. Alice read a trashy novel that she'd found lying in a corner of the room. Late in the afternoon, they crept into bed again.

She'd planned to leave that afternoon—she'd asked to meet with Gaborone's chief of police the next morning at eight—but she decided to get up early to give them one more night together. She told Ian she was anxious about the meeting with the police chief.

That evening, she wasn't hungry when the food came. Ian ate pork chops and mashed potatoes and half of her dinner. She poked at a pile of glazed carrots, garnished with parsley. Ian drank a Castle Lager and before he'd finished one glass, asked for another. Vaguely, she wondered if he was an alcoholic. Two glasses didn't add up to anything, but then he had a third, and finished up half of hers before they stood up and made their way back to the room. Drink had made him garrulous. His noisy intelligence spilled out, his large, affectionate hand swept around her waist. She felt vaguely irritated.

He was large in every way. It wasn't out of ego that he took up so much space, she thought, although sometimes it felt that way. It was out of enthusiasm, his own commotion and curiosity about life. She wouldn't wish that away, not for a moment. In bed, he asked how did a seer know the whereabouts of a herd of game? In traditional cultures, he said, people recognized the importance of those liminal, in-between states. But the more "civilized" a culture became, the less reverence people had for strangeness and ambiguity. The time he'd gone through to the other side, he'd seen his grandfather coming toward him. So strange, so beautiful, he murmured. He was practically weeping, telling her.

She put her arms around him and held him. His heart beat fast, as though he was in the grip of some urgency. He went to sleep all at once, as though someone had hit him over the head with a rock. She lay beside him and watched him for a while, exhausted, as though she'd been half consumed. In that fire, though, something had taken hold of her, a love she couldn't really account for. She thought of the world he loved: where the wind harbored words that foretold danger; footsteps disappeared in storms of sand; animals and people changed shape;

mirages appeared and flickered into nothing; invisible stars sang. What she knew was that with him, the world was large, chaotic, and generous; without him, small and starved and, somehow, wrong.

She woke at three thirty without the alarm and propped herself up on one elbow. Ian was lying on his back, his mouth partway open. His face, for the first time, looked old to her. His hair was thrown around the pillow. One hand was fisted near his cheek, the other open at his groin. Her heart went out to him. Be safe, she whispered, before she rolled softly from the bed.

35

Three hundred seventy kilometers to the south, deep-voiced thunder rumbled outside the prison. It was his twenty-seventh day of solitary confinement. Any day, he expected they would come for him. His mind was wooly, exhausted, fragmented, his heart full of sorrow. A few hours ago, he'd vomited up something that smelled like it had once been fish. His bowels had turned liquid. His body smelled as rancid as bad meat.

Earlier that night, a guard had stood outside his cell. Isaac heard him shuffling around and then Afrikaans muttered through the food hole. "I'll make things easier for you. Get you real food. A shower." What the man wanted was sex. With his bad skin and rotten teeth and bald head and white skin.

He heard footsteps leaving.

Not far away, the sound of the man they were breaking. Through the slit in the door where they passed him food, he'd seen this young man being led away. Now he heard him crying for his mother, crying out to God. When the man went still, Isaac stood in his cell, his back against the damp cement, and prayed. Some night, that man would be still for good, and they'd come for him.

He thought of Botswana, the journey under the hearse, the choking dust. Waking up to White Dog and the woman, her kindness, the way she threw water over him and laughed. Setting out down the path, the bad luck of meeting Amen. He pictured White Dog, the way she crossed her paws when she waited, the single black dot on her muzzle, how she seemed to gaze into the sky as though her planet was up there. He saw the madam's hair, like the wild hair of an African woman who's never braided it. He remembered her anger at her husband, that time when the water was shooting up, and he understood that she was not a person who would forgive or forget easily. But there was something else in her, a certain patience, slow to come to the boil. Her eyes looked at you, straight at you, unlike the eyes of most people.

He imagined her disappointment with him. She would have found another gardener by now. Maybe she would have gone back to her country. It was possible. She had nothing to hold her.

If White Dog were alive, she'd be waiting. Mostly bad things fell from the sky, but this small one with the black dot on her muzzle and the faraway look in her eyes was here on Earth for some good reason. And in that truth was a kind of hopefulness.

He heard breathing outside his cell. He lifted his head and could smell that guard once more. It made him sick that a man like that would be looking for him. *Go away, rubbish man.*

"*Wat is u naam?*" the guard whispered.

He gave his prisoner number, not his name. "*Vyf sewe twee vier een.*" 57341.

"*U naam,*" the voice said, impatient. There was no further sound, only constricted adenoidal breathing. He could imagine the mouth open, expectant. Then, "They're coming for you tomorrow. I can save you."

"No one can save me."

"I can make things better for you."

You touch me, and I'll kill you.

The voice was low now, saying what he wanted to do.

Isaac's innards turned over. He thought of the last meal he'd eaten, the small chunks of rancid meat floating in mealie meal, and vomited again before he was over the pail.

"Go away," he said. "I'm sick." The mess on his feet, stench of rot. A blessing. The man moved on.

Isaac heard the whisper several cells down, felt himself want to retch again. With a blast of will, he kept it down. A cell door creaked open. He wondered if the guard had told the truth, if they'd come for him tomorrow. He considered how he might die, not by their hands, but by his own when it got to that. It might be the only thing he'd trade for sex, a length of rope.

36

The road was empty when Alice set out that morning, darkness with a hint of light in the east but not enough to see by. The rain had gouged huge gullies into the surface of the road. In the shadow caused by her headlights, she hardly saw the holes until she was on top of them. Normally, she'd be traveling eighty or ninety kilometers an hour, but not this morning. She hated this road. Dozens of people died on it every year. If it wasn't erosion, it was sliding sand that turned you over before you knew what happened, trucks barreling out of nowhere, passing and leaving a thick fog of dust behind them.

Behind her, through the rearview mirror, she saw a light coming toward her. She thought of Ingmar Bergman's *The Seventh Seal*, the little family of actors with death at their heels, their caravan rattling and swaying pell-mell through the forest. The lights were gaining on her. Her heart beat into her eye sockets. The wide lights of a truck.

It was breathing down her neck now. She wanted to pull off to the side, but the road was like a riverbed with high banks. There was no stopping or getting away. Her little Toyota swayed in the sand, and she held her breath as the monster behind her swung out, skimmed past, and swallowed the road in front of her. The sun had risen. The morning sky was smeared with haze. A hornbill lumbered through the air across the road, looking as though it was more pterodactyl than bird.

She thought about the courage it had taken Ian to go to that place where he went. She doubted she could have done it. As a child, she'd been terrified of hypnotism. It seemed to come down to trust. How much, she wondered, had she ever trusted another person—body, mind, and soul? How could she know that what she felt for Ian was not, somehow, shot through with illusion? She could give her life to him and find suddenly that she'd been mistaken. Or, their love could erode until one day she'd wake up and realize she no longer loved him.

It seemed utterly impossible that this could happen, but hadn't it seemed equally impossible with Lawrence? Not exactly. She and Lawrence had slid into each other's lives in simple, naive faith. She knew now how love could vanish, and she believed with all her heart it would not happen again. She'd felt something last night she'd never felt with anyone on Earth. She had only the crudest words for it. It was connected to a depth of intensity and to something as ancient as the fossilized knee prints of the spirit who'd knelt to create the universe.

Ian was far from perfect, anyone could see that. He talked too much, drank too much, was helpless in the face of his appetites. He was immoderate in his opinions and enthusiasms, at times outrageous. But there was courage in him to spare, and integrity. He wasn't the sort to slip things under the carpet. She could count on his imperfections, and she thought she could even count on loving them, or at least loving him in spite of them, maybe even because of them. Life with him would be surprising, changeable as wind. They would be unlikely to have a child, unlikely to ever live in the United States. There would be stretches when he'd be away from her. She'd be pushed to make something equally large of her own life.

She passed through Debeeti as the acacia trees began to be lit by sun. Then Mosomane and Mochudi. It was a marvel how this landscape, so brown, had entered her. How she'd grown accustomed to the taste of dust in her mouth from June to December. It was hard to imagine the woods in Ohio anymore, home to green moss, deep layers of fallen leaves, robins. When had she last heard a robin sing? Or a white-throated sparrow? Or seen a field of green grass combed by wind? Could she bear it if she never again lived in her own country? She hadn't missed her mother when she'd first come out here, but she did now. And she missed the ring of spring: peepers singing in the swamp. And the trudging sound of a city bus. And oddly, Walter Cronkite. She missed snowy Sunday afternoons, newspapers with editorial pages, grocery stores with well-stocked shelves.

She missed how the swing that hung from a maple tree in her mother's yard could flood her with recollections, the way one memory led to another: the feel of her girl-thin body as she pumped her way into the sky, the toes of her Buster Brown shoes— scuffed, blunt-toed, homely as moles—straining to touch one high leaf of that tree.

Here, she lived only in the present and the future. At times, it was a relief to escape the past. But forever? How bad the margarine tasted here, like rendered fat. And the smell of butchered beef everywhere, tough, overripe. But then there was beauty: women carrying square cans of water on their heads, the way their bodies moved under the weight of the water. The wild thorns bursting into blossom when the land around them was dry as dung. On Sundays, a scattering of men walking to church with dusty, beaten black hats held in their hands. Women wearing the uniform of the Congregationalists: dark skirts and white blouses, with bright blue sashes and white turbans around their heads. And their singing, voices swooping slow and deep.

She passed through Phakalane and Mogoditshane. A boy herded five goats across the road in front of her. His shirt was dust colored, his young body looked dazed with sleep. She was supposed to go to dinner at Muriel's tonight, but she'd need to beg off. It would be a triumph just to make it through the day.

When she drove in, exhausted, White Dog was there at the end of the driveway. The tip of her tail moved slightly in recognition. As far as she knew, White Dog hadn't left her post since Isaac had disappeared. Alice brought her breakfast and fresh water and set it next to her. She went back into the house and stood in front of her closet and stared at the clothes hanging there. She felt vaguely off center—it was no longer possible to imagine a life without Ian. And yet a life with him did not include even the barest prospect of calm domesticity. What *was* their life together? Islands of ravenous love surrounded by oceans of separateness.

She went into the bathroom and couldn't get the the toilet to flush. The tank was high up, and she pulled the chain, *klunk*, waited, pulled the chain three more times, and still nothing happened. It infuriated her. She yanked the chain four more times, and on the fifth pull, the water rushed down the pipe. She filled the bathtub until the water no longer ran hot from the faucet, turned it off, and climbed in. There was no time to sink into the pleasure of it. She lay back a moment, then lathered up and rinsed off. Toweling herself dry, she felt unaccountably close to tears. She grabbed a blue gray, short-sleeved dress, close-fitting, cut fairly high at the neck.

She had no hair dryer. She combed her damp hair, pinned it back, fed Magoo (still no sign of Horse), grabbed a piece of bread, stuffed a few work papers into a canvas bag, put on her sandals, and went out to the truck. It occurred to her as she slammed the door that the chief of police might like to see some tangible piece of evidence that Isaac existed. She ran back inside to the room where he'd slept, and picked up a letter written by his mother.

As she backed out the driveway, White Dog got to her feet. "Yes, I'm going to see about him," she said.

"Please, madam," he said, indicating a chair on the far side of a battered desk. He was drinking tea but didn't offer to get her a cup. He had a long, weary face, as though the collective misdeeds of his fellow men had made his jowls heavy. She felt herself in the presence of someone who would believe the worst about you and ask questions later.

"What can I do for you?" he asked, his question obligatory rather than encouraging.

"My gardener is missing."

"Yes?"

"He's not the sort of person to disappear."

"People can surprise you," he said.

"I was away on a trip up north, and he was minding the house and garden. When I returned, he was gone."

"Did you find anything missing?"

"No. And his dog was still there. He loved that dog. He would never have left her."

"What makes you so sure, madam?"

"I know."

She could see this was insufficient.

"He is a Motswana?"

"A South African."

"Here illegally?"

"*Ee, rra,* I believe so."

"Name?"

"Isaac Muthethe."

He stopped a moment. She noticed with a start that he had a glass eye. Between the real eye and the glass eye was a deep worry line. The glass eye didn't look in her direction. Floor, wall, anywhere but where the other eye looked. "And your name?"

She told him.

"Excuse me a moment, madam." He went to his filing cabinet and opened a drawer. He brought a manila folder to his desk and pored over it for a few moments.

"I recall the case now. I am sorry to say, madam, your gardener was a double agent, working both for the ANC and the South African Defense Force. I interviewed him myself. He pretended that he did not know what a double agent was. He is a clever chap."

"He is an intelligent man," she said, "but he is no double agent. He was in medical school in South Africa before coming to Botswana. He is a good, decent man."

"Then why was he here?"

"I don't know. I assumed his life was in danger back home."

"So you see?"

"See what?"

"You see that you do not know. When I asked him how he had entered Botswana, he said he had come by car. When I pressed him further, he said that he had traveled under a casket. Madam, people do not enter this country traveling under a corpse." He laughed, a small, dry laugh that sounded as though it had been living in a dark closet.

"Where is he?"

"He is not in Botswana." The chief's eye slid away from her. "He is in South Africa. I signed the deportation order with my own hand."

"You deported him? You *deported* him?"

"Individuals such as this one, madam, are a danger to our country. We have no army. We have only our brains and common sense."

"What evidence did you have?"

"One of my officers found him at the scene of the shooting, one day following, taking money from the floor of the house. He himself had been living in that ANC house."

"Where was this house?"

"In Naledi, madam. An officer found him in this very house in the middle of the night and brought him in. After interviewing him, I was convinced of his guilt and deported him. He was not at the house when the shooting occurred. Do you know why? Because he knew it would happen. He saved himself and let the women and children die.

"I wondered whether you and your husband were involved. I did some background checks on you and found nothing."

"At least you checked before accusing us. But your hasty speculations about Isaac Muthethe couldn't have been further from the truth. He wasn't there because I'd asked him to stay at my house in the Old Village while I was away." A flicker of doubt crossed the chief's features.

"Where is he now?"

"I don't know, madam. My men delivered him into the hands of the South African Defense Force."

"Oh, dear God." She stood up abruptly. "What have you done?"

"I did my duty, madam. That is all I have done. Is there anything else I can do for you?"

"Do you know the names of the South Africans who took him away?"

"No, madam."

"You've made a serious mistake," she said, her voice shaking with anger.

"No, madam. You don't understand. He will be in no danger there. He has a good relationship with the police."

"With all due respect, *rra*, you have no idea what you're talking about. There's a good chance you've condemned an innocent man to death."

She picked up her bag and left. Her whole body trembled with rage. Modimo, *nthusa,* she heard those women's voices sing, slow and deep like wind. *Help me, God.* She had never, not since she was eleven or twelve, believed in a Being of that sort, with fingers in every human pie, but she wanted Him now.

She put the truck in gear and exploded out of the parking lot. She drove out of town, yelling, "Bastard!" Her voice reverberated through the truck cab, puny, impotent. The sky was blue and cloudless, and its complacency inflamed her further.

She turned right at the road to the dam, not trusting herself to drive safely, and pulled over to the side. She pictured Isaac puttering about the garden, his hands cupped around a plant. She saw him drag thorn bushes around the base of the half-dead tree to protect the crested barbets from the cats. When she compared Isaac to just about anyone she knew, herself included, he came out a notch above. Humility in spades, a natural dignity, the sort of person you'd trust in the hardest times, the sort of human being who ought to be peopling the Earth. But he was smaller than small now. If he'd been accused of double dealings . . . no one likes a liar and a cheat. And where he'd gone, he sure as hell wouldn't be innocent until proven guilty. She remembered the day when he'd killed the black mamba. That quick ferocity. So what if he *had* been with the ANC. Who could blame him? But she'd bet her two feet he wasn't a double agent.

She turned the truck around, sick at heart, and drove back to her office. Her boss was on the phone when she went to find him. He indicated a chair. A picture of his three children and his wife, Susan, smiled from a bookcase on one wall. Susan was grinning bravely, but underneath the smile was something else. Alice had been to their house a couple of times, a tidy, well-run home, bursting with kid energy, barely contained. Susan had the look of a woman whose life was permanently on hold. Alice imagined her catching up with herself around sixty, when there'd be hell to pay. And C.T., a kindly, nonassertive man, a little over his head in every sphere, would hardly be equal to it.

He got off the phone and greeted Alice warmly. "Haven't seen much of you since you returned. Are you better now?"

"Yes, thanks for asking."

"Tick bite fever's no joke."

"No. But I'm sorry I was a few days late with the position paper."

"It couldn't be helped." However, his eyes said it could have been helped if she hadn't gotten it into her head to run off with that fellow who was still married. "I've got a few changes to suggest," he said. He dug around in a tower of documents and handed the paper to her. "But you've done an excellent job. Just those few corrections and we'll ship it off to the permanent secretary and minister." Coming from him, this was high praise.

"C.T., I'm afraid I've got to go home."

"You're not well?"

"My gardener has been apprehended and deported to South Africa. The chief of police seemed to think he was a double agent."

"And *is* he?"

"Definitely not."

"I'm sorry to hear it. But at this point I'm afraid there's not much to be done."

Anger throbbed behind her eyes. A wildness overtook her. "If this were Susan, would you say there was nothing to be done?"

"No."

"I'm sorry, I didn't mean to attack you."

"I just want to caution you not to do anything you'll regret."

She thought of asking him to quit the avuncularity. It annoyed her that he seemed to have pegged her as a hotheaded nitwit. "I'm going to try to locate his family, that's all. I think they need to know. I've got to go through his papers, see if I can find an address."

"I understand."

"I'll have those changes done for you by tomorrow."

"No worries."

She greeted White Dog and patted her on the head. The bed in Isaac's room was made in rumpled fashion. Under it, in a cardboard box, were a few clothes, most of which she'd passed on to him from Lawrence. At the bottom of the box were four letters, three in the same hand, one in a different hand, all from Pretoria. She opened one of the three. It was written in Setswana, but she recognized a few words, piecing together the news from his mother that Isaac had told her earlier: his brothers unable to attend school because they had no shoes. There was no return address on the envelope, but there was a post office box address inside, at the top of the letter. Alice opened a second letter, and the same address appeared inside. She jotted it down, replaced the letter in the envelope, and put both letters back at the bottom of the box under his clothes.

She wrote to his mother in English, expecting she'd be able to find a translator. In it, she explained what had happened and asked where Isaac was likely to have been taken. On her way back to work, she dropped the letter in a mailbox and prepared herself to wait a couple of weeks for a reply.

That evening, she drove to Naledi, the air so hot it knocked the breath out of her. Heat oozed from every blade of grass, from every parched, shriveled, hapless leaf. She parked and walked into a rabbit warren of paths. In front of a cardboard house, a young boy pushed a little wire car with tin can wheels. Goat droppings littered the way. She passed a man going the other way. She greeted him, and he stood long enough for her to ask directions to the house the South Africans had targeted.

"That way, *mma*."

She thanked him and turned left at the tree he'd indicated, but almost immediately, there was a choice of paths, one leading beside a house made from a car chassis, the other to the right. She stopped and turned around and stopped again. Her head hurt. Something dark pulled at her. Not fear, something worse.

"Hello, madam," a soft voice said behind her.

She turned and found a young boy. "How are you?" He laughed, hearing himself speak English.

"I'm fine," she said, smiling. "How are you?"

He laughed again, his eyes snapping bright. "I am fine. How are you?"

"Fine," she said again. She put out her hand in greeting, and he took it, his hand smooth in hers. "Do you understand English?" she asked.

His eyes clouded. "*Ga ke itse, mma.*"

She loved that she was not strange to this boy. As she walked along the path, he danced backward, facing her. He accompanied her like this a few steps, then turned and charged away, jet-propelled.

She was lost in a maze of paths. The shimmer of sun cast a strange glow over the landscape. A little girl in a red dress walked away from her, down a path. The mother carried a white parasol. Two older girls came in her direction, hand in hand, the taller one wearing a short blue dress faded on the shoulders and sleeves, still bright under her arms where the sun hadn't touched it. "Where are you from, madam?" the tall one asked in school-stiff English.

"From America."

"New York?" asked the younger girl.

Alice laughed. "No."

"Empire State Building?" said the taller one.

She pictured herself in the fist of King Kong. "No," she laughed again. "From Cincinnati."

"Cin-cin-naa-ti! Cin-cin-naa-ti!"

"Where are you going, madam?"

"I want to find the house where the shooting happened."

The girls looked puzzled. Alice mimed holding a gun, and they understood. The taller one took Alice by the hand and pulled her down the path, turned right, left, and left again, skirted a shebeen, walked a little farther, and pointed to a house. The girls disappeared, and she walked toward it. The sun was low in the sky, shining on a naked tree; a woman at a distance scrubbed a cooking pot with sand.

The house felt wounded, contaminated. She peeked in the door and saw a room stripped nearly bare except for a whitewashed wall splotched with something dark. A few pages from a glossy magazine were stuck to the wall with nails. Her eyes returned to the spray of darkness on the wall. She stepped inside, searching for something to identify its inhabitants. As she crossed the room, she tripped over a loose chunk of concrete on the floor, which skittered away from her. The second room contained a mattress and a battered cooking pot. The mattress was spattered with the same darkness as the walls in the first room. She'd expected the house would tell her something, but it gave up nothing but its wounds. She covered her mouth with her hand and stumbled out.

In her head, a phrase played behind her eyes. *Blank and pitiless as the sun.* Yeats, that ferocious old man, lover of women, singer of woes. *The falcon cannot hear the falconer* . . . Was there a place in the world, had there ever been a place on Earth, where the strong didn't victimize the weak? Outside were Caterpillar tracks that stopped just short of the side wall, as though someone had intended to bulldoze the house and then backed away. Perspiration trickled between her breasts. She followed the retreating tracks, thinking they'd lead her back to the main road. Under her sandals, she felt the undulations of earth churned up by the teeth of the bulldozer.

In the distance, she heard an odd *plink, plinking.* She walked toward it, not sure what it was. As she came closer, she heard music, and then saw him. The old man's face was deeply gouged and furrowed, his eyes tight shut, his forehead pressed into ridges of concentration, his mouth open, singing. His hair was a dusty gray; the stubble on his cheeks and chin and upper lip also gray. His hands were huge, like those of a man seated with an anvil rather than a one-stringed guitar. A single wire stretched from one end of a long, flat fingerboard to the other. The lower end of the fingerboard was positioned between his knees. The other end rested on his shoulder, topped off with a crumpled five-gallon drum, which added a twangy resonance. With his left hand, he created the pitch on the string; with a curved stick held in his right hand, he stroked the wire. As Alice stood and listened, it seemed in those small strummings lay the hope of a small universe, a universe with no place for a white woman, but still, hope is hope. It was only when he stopped playing and opened his eyes that she saw he was blind.

Lying in bed that night, she thought again of Isaac. She didn't believe the South Africans would have set him free when he crossed the border. She knew what they did to people in those prisons. Tortured, thrown from high windows. Suicide they called it. He was bright enough and educated enough that a couple of ruffians would be only too happy to humiliate him, beat him down, punish him to the very limits of what one man can do to another. She got out of bed and went into the kitchen for a glass of water.

Standing by the sink, she recalled a place she and her mother had once been in Hawaii, the only long trip the two of them had ever taken together. They'd been told about the ruins of a temple, located near the birthplace of King Kamehameha. The road there was heavily gullied and impassable, and they set out on foot as the wind roared down a twenty-five-mile-wide corridor between Maui and the Big Island. They had no idea what they were looking for, and then they saw it, Pu'ukoholā Heiau, on a bare hillside. A wild desolation. You could feel the power of the place even from a distance, fierce and implacable as a god.

They climbed the hill and entered a rock enclosure. Inside was a great stone, cupped to hold a human body, a channel cut at heart level for the letting of blood. Above, the sky was blue, without end.

She stood next to her mother, seeing the high priests waiting with their knives, a young man or woman being led there, bound at the wrists. Was it her imagination, or was the brutality of the world deepening, growing more rapacious, the means of torture more elaborate than those ancient times when they'd killed one man to save many? Isaac's death, if they killed him, would go unnoticed and save no one.

37

Near the Kuke veterinary fence on the boundary of Ngamiland and the Ghanzi District, an old woman from the /Xai/Xai community was out alone digging *hu'uru* tubers from the ground. It was early morning, just after sunrise. Over her shoulder was slung a rough bag, made from the hide of a duiker. The bag held two small tubers and a hollow shell of an ostrich egg. In her left hand was a digging stick. Her feet were bare, her belly wrinkled with age. As she dug, her small breasts swung in rhythm with her stick. Her skin was deep bronze, her hair a rusty black, shot through with gray. If she'd been with her family at night sitting around a fire, she would have smiled easily. Now, her face was without expression except for a taut intensity around the mouth.

It was February, and no rain had fallen. Perhaps there would be none this year. Food would soon become scarce, and water more hidden. Next to a shrub she began to dig with her stick until she was crouched next to a hole as deep as the length of her arm. At the end of a reed, she wrapped grass and placed it upright in the hole. She pushed the sand back into the hole and pressed it down around the edges of the standing reed. She sat patiently. When she sucked the reed, a vacuum was created, and the water was forced up into her mouth. She swallowed a small amount and dribbled the rest into the ostrich egg shell. When there was no more water coming up the reed, she plugged the hole of the ostrich egg with grass and placed it back in her traveling sack. The wind was coming up. She moved to another shrub and repeated the process, although this time she took no water for herself.

. . .

Nearby, but out of sight and earshot, Ian worked. The day had not yet heated up. Wisps of mist rose from the earth. A dove called from a tree with its mournful, repetitive song. He'd walked about half a kilometer from his vehicle and was making his way back, cutting cable as he went. It went faster than it had at the beginning, but he was also seeing fewer live animals. As he wielded the huge wire cutter in the heat, he thought that rarely in his life had he been able to answer what exactly he was doing or why. In spite of what Alice had said, it often felt to him that his life's purpose was unsteady. You could easily spend your whole life scattering your energies across the landscape. "Keep your eye on the ball," his father used to say, not meaning cricket or rugby. But which ball was the question.

Snap, went another cable.

The rock paintings waited. He was aware of falling into what one of his anthropology professors warned against—mistaking social action for research. Still, unless you had a heart of gunmetal, how could you come to know a people without also coming to know their needs and desperations? A small group of buffalo rummaged in the brush behind him. One rubbed on an anthill, trying to rid itself of parasites. An oxpecker bird sat on its back. There were no young ones among them.

He moved along the fence meditatively, snapping wire as he went. He thought of Alice, her anger, her body, her blue gray eyes like the sea on an overcast day. Was it so terrible to spend one night with a former wife? Well, technically still a wife. She was right—he was sloppy, untidy. He couldn't really blame her for flipping out. But if she'd known his heart, she would have seen Morning Star and Lynx clear enough.

He snapped another cable, which twisted back and nearly struck him in the face.

He hadn't told Alice the whole story of their night in Francistown. Gwyneth had said she still loved him, that her life would never be right again. He'd replied that she'd forgotten all their troubles. She'd sat in bed, not speaking, shaking her head, her short hair sticking up in spikes. She looked like a patient in Bedlam. He hadn't meant to say it: "You chopped off all your beautiful hair."

"I was done with it," she said. Once upon a time she'd said the same about him. He wished he'd never met her, that he'd had the sense to run. But she'd intrigued him with her wintry aspect, her dark hair falling over her white face like a shelf. She frightened him too, and in that fright lay some dark, sexual energy that he couldn't put his arms around. He knew now what a sitting duck he'd been. He knew nothing about depression, had never felt that hopeless, subbasement mildew of spirit. She reminded him of a child whose knees are drawn up to her chin, who thinks there will be no end to it. How do you walk away from that kind of despair without feeling like a complete bastard?

Snap, went another cable, and another.

In the rhythm of destruction, he felt a confirmation of purpose. But thirst was catching up with him. He had only a small amount of water left in his plastic bottle, and he was a long way from his vehicle.

Xixae dug again for water and placed her reed upright. This time, only a few drops came to her lips.

Long ago, when she was a young woman, she had taken her eyes off her young daughter and walked behind her shelter to talk with a friend. Her little girl had taken a burning stick from the fire and thrown it onto the dry bedding grass. There had been no rain. The shelter exploded in flames. By the time they were able to get to her, her skin was flayed, her hair smelled like a veldt fire. A powerful healer had done his best, but after two days, the ancestors came for her.

Her small band of people buried her daughter near the campsite and moved to another site. Xixae thought that she too would die. But they didn't want her yet in the realm of Kauha. Her womb went as dry as the earth around her. Her husband would no longer lie with her. He told her that she had become an old woman overnight. Time passed. She could laugh again now, but the laughter was wrapped around tears.

A puff of dust spread out over the dry savannah and then a distant rumble, softer and longer lived than thunder, floated into the air. Ian thought little of it, until he saw them at a distance, running, closing the distance between him and them.

The buffalo he'd seen rummaging behind him were the advance guard of a large herd. Had they felt in some part of their beast brains the uncoiling of the wire? They were coming this way in a fast-kindled, heedless frenzy. Closer now, he made out their small, cranky eyes, low ears, and shelf of horn laid flat across their foreheads, parted down the middle, and swept up like a handlebar mustache.

The front beasts were close now. Impossible to outrun them along the fence. The herd stretched too wide. The big ones, he knew, weighed close to a ton. He had no gun with him. Nothing to scare them but his wildly waving arms and puny man voice.

Dumb as hell, they seemed to be following a large male that ran in zigzag fashion, as though dodging bullets. *FUCK OFF!* he heard his tiny voice yell. *BUGGER OFF!* And then he knew he'd die. He'd watched buffalo charge lions, elephants even. They'd run him over without even seeing him. The dust was in his nostrils now. All thought ceased. He was aware of the sky, the socks riding down his ankles into his shoes, the heavy tool in his hand. Fifteen meters from him, the wrinkled forehead of the lead buffalo bulged. It was coming straight for him. At the last moment, Ian lunged sideways as the brute swerved in the other direction. It rammed his left side with its shoulder, not intent on injuring him, just oblivious to everything but its own urgency. Ian was thrown backward toward the fence. He scrambled from the ground toward a fence post, and hung on.

The pain running through him was dark and hot. He was engulfed in dust. His mind said, smoke. He thought he heard the grinding gears of large trucks laboring up hills. He tried to let the wooden post protect him, but it was thin and the beasts struck him clumsily as they went past on both sides. With each blow, he was knocked off his feet and tried to scramble away but there was no protection. Their breath was grassy and overripe, their hides raked with nicks and scars. He had not hated them before, but he did now, their witless thundering, their low, ragged ears and hard skulls. They would have trampled their own young. They were that blind, their necessity that great.

It was a dumb way to die. He protected his head with his arms and curled up tight. The ground under him shook. He crawled toward the post and tried to pull himself partway up, but too much was broken. He clung to it with his right arm, like a child around the leg of its mother. At last, the noise around him dimmed. In time, the herd thinned out. A few stragglers followed at a distance, but finally, they too were gone, blundering across the savannah.

The fence cutting tool lay near the opening, broken by their trampling.

He slipped all the way to the ground and lay still. His breathing was rough, his tongue and brain could not form words. His legs were big silent rooms, without feeling. His mind was a shrug, his body a tiny village without water or hope.

He saw everything clearly now. It was a shame he'd only learned now. *You were going to save the world.* He wanted to laugh but he hurt too much. The world does not wish to be saved. It carries us a short distance and drops us when it's done with us.

The sun went down. Deep purple swept over blue, followed by purple charcoal, then black. The night grew cold. The Southern Cross hung in the sky, and near it Alpha Centauri and Omega Centauri, containing more than a million stars, the coal sack, a dark nebula in the Milky Way. He lost consciousness; his dreams were black and muddled. Off and on, he woke to searing pain and went under again.

Day broke with a new ferocity, as though the sun had burst raging from the dark night. He opened one crusty eye. He had a memory of wet nostrils sniffing him in the night. Was it a dream? It occurred to him that he was alive. He felt neither disappointment nor relief, only a dull feeling that he ought to move. He tested one leg. It had no feeling. His mind bumped toward Alice. He called to her. His throat made a rasping sound, sand against sand.

He realized he hadn't been able to imagine their future. Numbly, he thought he'd been too slow, too stupid. *Love,* that's what they say matters—those with near misses whose bodies stop and start back up again, people who've seen that white light, who've turned around and found their way back to Earth. Without love, there's nothing. Those people who've been dead and come back talk nonstop about love, something large and interconnected and overarching. He could sense it in the tiny dried bit of grass moving back and forth in the dust in front of his nose. He had once loved the sound of wind. He had loved the wide feet of the women in the market and their dark-eyed children hiding behind them.

When he came to again, a voice inside him said, *You're fucked, mate.* The sun blazed. The day was young, still tender, but already beyond hot. His flesh was iron in the forge. He squinted at his water bottle on the ground several yards away. No sense trying to reach it; the beasts had flattened it. He figured his vehicle was somewhere between a quarter and a half kilometer away. He tried moving his body over the ground, lying on his back, bending the good leg and pushing with one foot until the leg straightened. Three pushes, and he drifted out of consciousness. When he opened his eyes, he'd hardly moved. If he worked all day, he might make ten feet.

When there was nothing more to be done, when they sent his mother home from the hospital for the last time, she'd said to him, "Never mind. We all die sometime, Nummy." Damn it, Mum, he'd wanted to say, where's the fight in you? Now in blinding sun, he saw black wings. His mother had loved crows, dusky wings whistling after her crusts of bread and bacon rind.

The sun caused spectral rays to shine around objects, as though each blade of grass, shrub, post had become a miniature sun animated with its own source of radiance. He closed his eyes and opened them. It took the rays a moment to appear again. He felt nauseated. His breathing was fast, shallow, like a young bird.

Keep your head, he thought, shutting his eyes. Once an old Bushman had told him of a time he'd wandered too far after game and misjudged the distance back to camp. It was the dry season. He sat on the ground, dying of thirst. But before lying down for the last time, he threw dirt into the air. The dust flying upward said, *Help me.* Back where his people were, they saw the plume of dust and came for him.

With his right hand, he reached out for a handful of dirt and cast it upward. And again.

38

Xixae and her niece, Nxuka, were out early, searching for *mongongos*. The young woman was pregnant with her first child. Occasionally, she touched her belly as she walked. The morning was fresh, and mist rose from the dried grasses as the sun climbed away from the horizon. As they walked, Nxuka told a story. The old woman's laughter floated through the air. They were not in a hurry. Their bags were empty, but they had all day.

They stopped to dig a Herero cucumber, taking part and leaving a portion to bear fruit for the next season. They walked on, and Xixae led them to a place where she remembered a few berries of *n/ang* might still be hanging, but the bush was empty. The sky was deep blue and the air still. They saw three duiker in the distance. Across the sky was a thin blue cloud, high up, like someone had run a stick across the sky. It was the sort of odd, unnatural cloud that the great flashing birds leave when they fly high. Xixae wondered how these birds had come into the world. A person who often smoked *dagga* told her that men flew inside the glittering birds, but she thought the man's brain had grown confused. She too liked *dagga* every now and then, but lately, her chest was filled with coughing and she did not feel like smoking.

The old woman took note of a small puff of dust in the direction of the fence, thinking it strange that there should be this disturbance without wind. She imagined it might have been caused by a bush squirrel, or a guinea fowl. She watched, and there it was again. Perhaps it was an animal or bird that could be taken easily. Nxuka had not eaten meat in many days, and the baby would be crying for it. She pointed, but Nxuka had not seen what she'd seen.

As they walked toward the fence, there was no further sign of anything. In the dust at their feet were the tracks of many buffalo. Their spoor was several hours old, perhaps as much as a day. They had been running. In the dry season, she had seen buffalo, wildebeest, zebra, giraffe piled up at the fence, vultures feasting. But these buffalo did not seem to have been stopped by the fence, and there were no vultures in the sky. She considered that perhaps they had been buffalo spirits, who had passed through the earthly fence without hindrance. And perhaps it was the heel of one of the spirits that had thrown up the two puffs of dust. Perhaps they were telling her that her time had come.

She told Nxuka to wait under a small tree while she walked toward the fence. As she drew closer, she saw a heap of dusty blue and gray on the ground. Near it was a tool of some sort. She crept toward the heap on the ground and saw it was a man. He was lying on his back, his eyes closed, the sun beating on his face. One of his legs was bent at an odd angle. By the shallow rising and falling of his chest, she saw that he was alive. She looked into his face and realized that she had seen this man before. He had visited their campfire once, the only white man she'd ever heard speaking their language.

All around him, the strands of the fence were cut. She saw now. He had let the beasts through to water, and they had broken his body. She called to Nxuka. The young woman lifted the man's head and wet his lips with water. When he tasted it, his eyes opened. He groaned a little when they set his head down on the ground. The old woman said she would stay with him to shield his head from the sun while her brother's daughter went for help.

In his dream, there were two women, a young one with a belly as round as a melon, and an old grandmother whose skin had fallen into a thousand wrinkles. The old woman stood between him and the sun. She stood and stood like a tree.

He heard the knight's voice speaking. *My life has been a futile pursuit, a wandering*. In his dream, the old woman changed into Alice. He wanted to tell her something lingering at the outer reaches of his mind, dark, the way a shadow falls on the edge of a roof. He wanted to tell her . . . He tried to shift his hip. He imagined a hyena already there, tearing at his flesh. He was impaled on the pain, unable to move. His mind lifted a moment. He needed to tell her . . .

Xixae bent over to listen to his words, but she couldn't understand. In her heart, she did not believe this man who lay on the ground could be helped. He was too badly broken. Komtsa Xau, however, was a great healer, his mind made of lightning.

The sun was hot on her head. She sat on her heels to rest, moving closer to the man to give him shade. Her feet were planted wide, the space between her toes filled with fine dust. With both hands, she held a staff in front of her for balance.

When she closed her eyes and half drowsed, she heard the voice of her grandmother telling her a story she'd told long ago. When the sun was at its zenith, she heard the others coming, and then she saw them: her brother's daughter with her husband, Rraditshipi, and Komtsa Xau, the healer.

The old woman moved out of the way, and Komtsa Xau knelt down at the man's side. He laid his hands on his chest and closed his eyes, listening. When he opened his eyes, he said they must carry the man back to camp with them. They had brought poles and a kaross with them, and they laid the man on the kaross. When they carried him over rough ground, he groaned and lost consciousness.

Back at their campfire, they moistened his forehead with water and rubbed his body with herbs. The old woman made a broth from the skin of a francolin and spooned the liquid into his mouth, but he could not swallow. That night, they laid him by a campfire they'd built.

The women sang low, voices breaking like wind. Their hands clapped in a complicated rhythm, bodies swaying against each other, faces lit with fire. The sound floated into the night, intermingled with other night sounds: of hyenas, slow snakes moving across sand. The coals of the fire glowed; sparks leaped upward.

A few men tied rattles to their ankles and began to dance in a circle around the fire, slow at first, then heating up. The women's voices grew more urgent. Sweat poured from the dancer's bodies. Komtsa's legs went weak, and he fell down. He crawled to the white man. He saw where the bones were shattered, where the blood had become obstructed. The man's breath was unsteady. He noted the broken man's spirit, how it fluttered and couldn't make up its mind between this world and the next. He laid himself alongside the man's body, pressing the heat of his healing into him. He told the ancestors that this man still had work to do on Earth. They did not reply to him. He left them and returned to the man, trying again to press his healing into his heart and broken places.

Afterward, Komtsa lay motionless beside the fire, cold and spent. His brother's son could not revive him for a long time. He rubbed and rubbed his skin to warm him.

Ian smelled ash and smoke. There was intention in the hands against his chest, and great heat, pushing him toward life. *Let me be,* his mind said, but his throat was closed. He felt warmth the entire length of him, and something like hope. He heard his father's voice. In front of his eyes was the sparkle of a lake without shores. Birds drank. Animals gathered. It was a time before humans. For a moment, the pain left him. When it returned, he cried out, but his throat made no sound. He drifted on that lake, in and out of consciousness. The moon was close to full, the stars dimmed around its brightness. He'd never seen it so bright. It dropped down, closer. His chest rasped; his breathing was shallow and filled with pain. They brought karosses and banked the fire to keep him warm, and then all was still.

His hands and feet grew colder. He shivered uncontrollably. By morning, he was gone.

39

Before the sun rose, the old woman beside him opened her eyes and turned to him. His eyes were open, looking upward toward the dimming stars. She tried to close his eyes with her fingers, but he was no longer warm. She sat down next to him and took his hand. It felt as though she and this man now spoke the same language, when before she could not understand him. Like all creatures on Earth, his footprints would be erased by wind. We live like birds, her mind whispered. The birds move from one tree to the next, building nests. This is how we live. The wind erases our footprints as we move, season by season. And then one day, we are no longer alive on Earth, and our footsteps are gone forever. The land is our blood, the clouds our hair.

The fire was out beside her, only gray ash remaining. She sat up and stuck her feet straight out in front of her. She looked into his face, which had become peaceful. She did not wish the others to wake. She would like to keep him company for the whole of the day and into the following night as he journeyed away. A small cloud appeared above the horizon where the rising sun was shining upward. The cloud became lit inside and the edges turned gold and then bronze. As the sun rose, the cloud disappeared.

She heard a few people stirring, cracking kindling; cooking fires came to life.

Others came and sat near his body. No one spoke. They felt the wind heave itself against their living bodies, saw it stir the dead man's hair and fold over the collar of his shirt.

The old woman, Xixae, let go of his hand. She asked whether they should bury him as one of their own, or drive his body to Maun. Dixhao, her brother's son, had found Ian's Land Rover along the fence line. Some of the people said they must take him to Maun, or there would be trouble. Some said no, it would be better to bury him here.

The old woman thought of her daughter whose life had been lost. She remembered digging her grave, how the earth was difficult to turn over. She'd thought back then that she too would die. And now she was an old woman, and this man, like her daughter, was gone. One cannot know why things happen as they do. "He must be buried here," she said. "He is a white man, but he is a San white man."

The others agreed. And they decided that Nxuka's husband, Rraditshipi, who knew driving, would take the vehicle to Maun. And Nxuka, who had four years of school and knew a little Setswana (and even a small amount of English) would try to find some person who might know this man. Her baby was not coming until the following moon, and she would go with her husband. Xixae searched Ian's pockets and handed the keys to Nxuka's husband and the wallet to Nxuka.

Later that morning, they wrapped Ian in a wildebeest skin and buried him near a shepherd tree. The tree was misshapen, blasted from wind and sand. Its bark was pale gray with white patches, pitted and folded in places, the lower branches heavily grazed.

That afternoon, the small group of San moved camp so that no one would accidentally walk over the grave. They moved west, in the direction of Tsao, carrying everything on their backs. The only signature of their presence was the brief, lingering footprints, and the two sticks that Xixae placed in the ground so that her husband, who was out tracking a wounded steenbok, would know in which direction they had gone.

To the north, the flood plains of the Okavango were beginning to fill with water and spread south like great fingers of life. Months before, the rains had fallen in Angola. Water had flooded the Benguela Plateau and flowed southeast across the Caprivi Strip, poured through the Popa Falls rapids, and crossed into Botswana at Mohembo. Now, it gradually traveled south over the flood plains. It would take several more months for the 11 trillion liters of water to cover the delta and still more months to find its way around islands of papyrus, through wandering channels and on to Maun.

The herd of buffalo that had thundered through the cut fence was halfway to the open channels of the Okavango. Some of the weakest among them had perished. The grass was parched and sparse. But the others kept on, oblivious to everything but the promise of green grass and water.

40

Nxuka and Rraditshipi slept next to the Land Rover that night, folded together on the ground near the front tires. The windows of the vehicle were open, and the vinyl of the seats, cooling from the day's heat, gave off a strange smell. Nxuka's dreams were uneasy, and her baby stirred in her belly. Near midnight, one small foot pushed outward with such vigor that if Nxuka had woken and looked down in the moonlight, she could have seen a tiny heel and five toes.

The next morning, Nxuka found a stash of tobacco in the glove compartment. They rolled a cigarette each, smoked it, and sat in the morning light while the birds woke. On the floor of the Land Rover, they found a copy of the *Rand Daily Mail*. They could not read the words, but there were pictures of a white man shaking the hand of another white man, and on another page, a white man running with a soccer ball. "Only white men in this paper," Nxuka said, clicking the words with tongue and lips.

She climbed into the passenger seat, her husband turned the key in the ignition, and they started down the track. It was rough and pitted, and Nxuka held her arms under her belly to shield the baby. Several hours later, where a small track joined a larger one, her water broke, and she went into labor.

By the time they reached Maun, Rraditshipi was driving fast, erratically; the emergency brake, which he'd forgotten to release, was smoking. Nxuka had believed it would be another moon before the baby would come. The thought of a hospital frightened her, but it frightened her more to think of her husband delivering their child on the seat of the Land Rover, which smelled farther from sweet grass and wind than anything she had ever smelled.

Three hours later, their baby was born, the first San baby delivered at the Maun General Hospital in seven years. The baby was premature and weighed less than four pounds. His head was hardly bigger than an apple; his eyes were calm and wise. A nurse asked Nxuka what the name should be. Nxuka could see that the nurse didn't believe her baby would survive and hardly cared to name it. She reached for Ian's wallet on the bedside table, and asked the nurse to read the name to her. "Ian Thorne Henry," the nurse said, and Nxuka told her, "That is the baby's name." She believed that this name, IanThorneHenry, would protect her child. Two people with the same name would not die within days of each other.

All day, a procession of nurses came to see the Bushman baby. Whenever one of them asked the name, Nxuka gave her the wallet and said, "This is his name." One young nurse in training, a Seventh-Day Adventist from Iowa City, came on night duty, and asked, "Where did you get this wallet?"

"He is late," said Nxuka.

She looked at Nxuka more closely. "Did you steal this man's wallet?"

"He is late," repeated Nxuka, more loudly. Her baby sucked weakly at her breast.

"You'd better give me that wallet."

Nxuka put it between her legs and began to cry. "I want Rradit-shipi."

The young nurse went to fetch the night charge nurse. "We have a theft on our hands."

Nurse Mooletse entered the room and put her hand on the tiny baby's head. "He is drinking your milk well?"

"Yes," said Nxuka.

"He's a beautiful boy."

"She has a wallet that doesn't belong to her."

"What is the baby's name?"

"IanThorneHenry," said Nxuka, passing her the wallet.

"Where did you get this?"

"That man is late."

"I see."

"The buffalo step on him. We carry him to our camp but he is too sick."

"Where did you bury him?"

"At old camp. Then we move to a new camp."

"I understand."

"His Land Rover is there." She pointed out the window. "Rraditshipi is finding someone to give."

"Your husband doesn't need to worry about the vehicle. Tell him to bring me the keys. I'll look for someone who knew this man." She took fifty rand out of the wallet. "This is for your baby. And do not wrap him in blankets. It is too hot, understand?" She stroked the small head once more and left.

She came back a moment later. "How will you and your husband get home?"

"We are used to walking. Sometimes we will find a lift."

The following night, her only night off, Nurse Mooletse made her way to the hotel in Maun and found a Britisher who knew a man named Roger who knew Ian Henry. The bartender said Roger was at Crocodile Camp, a twelve-kilometer drive from Maun. "Tell him he must come to the hotel in Maun immediately," she told him. And no, she could not talk about this matter over the telephone. She sat on a chair on the porch waiting, while all around her, men drank whiskey and beer. The moon was an odd color. When she looked back at it a couple of minutes later, it had changed shape.

In the Old Village, Alice sat at a sprawling dinner table with Will and Greta. Will had made chicken curry, and the table was littered with bits of rice, a few chicken bones, napkins stained with curry sauce. The kids had been sent to bed for the night. But they kept popping up, running into the room. One was thirsty. Another thought he heard a monster under the bed. Greta went to their room. "If I hear one more peep out of any of you," she said, "you *will* see a monster, and it won't

be pretty. Now shut your eyes and go to sleep. We're going outdoors."
She came back, grabbed a bottle of wine, and headed for the patio. She
handed the bottle to Will and went back inside for a small packet she
had stashed in a drawer.

"Black Magic African," she said to Alice. The contents of the plastic
bag looked like rotted black leaf.

She passed it over to Alice for a sniff. "Where'd you come by this?"

"Will got it off someone at work."

They climbed a cinder-block wall that separated their garden from
the neighbors' and dangled their legs while Will rolled a thin joint.
The weed produced thick white smoke and turned out to be ruin-
ously strong, slightly harsh at the back of the throat, with a deep,
satisfying taste. It wasn't long before they were howling with laughter.
At some point Alice looked at the moon and said, "Look at that. It's a
different shape."

"Get out," Will said.

"No really. There's a bite out of it."

Will squinted toward it. "It hasn't changed."

"I swear it has."

They talked about the cosmos for a while, feeling grand, wise, happy.
"Look, there it goes again," she said.

Greta peered up. "She's right."

"What's happening?" Alice was laughing now, with a touch of fear
licking around the edges.

"I don't know." Will's hand waved vaguely in front of his face. "One
of those primitive things."

Greta and Alice nearly fell off the wall. It was the funniest thing
they'd ever heard.

"Wait," said Greta. "It's a whatchamacallit. An eclipse. We're in the
middle of an eclipse of the moon. If we were on the moon where the
bite's out of it, we would have fallen through space."

41

The news from Nurse Mooletse brought Roger to his knees. That night, he set out for Gaborone in Ian's Land Rover, feeling that what he had to tell couldn't be told any way but eye to eye. He thought the woman's name was Alice. He was pretty sure Ian had said she worked in Local Government and Lands.

Never had he felt such sudden grief and strangeness. To steady himself, he'd had another beer before leaving, and now he didn't trust his mind or his eyes. The sand was deep, and he hadn't passed another vehicle since leaving the outskirts of Maun. He remembered the last night he'd seen Ian, how his friend had been in such dreadful love, his mind dashing in circles, his heart jumping the track, burdened with the force of its commotion.

He'd met a guy on his last trip to Nata who'd said Ian had borrowed a bolt cutter to cut sections of agricultural fencing. It was a daft thing to do, but it didn't surprise him. Ian would have landed in jail if he'd been caught, and the chances were good of that. But jail at least would have saved him ending up under the sands of the Kalahari.

He couldn't believe he was gone. But here were the four wheels of Ian's vehicle under him and the rattling roof cage above him and Ian's wallet beside him. The nurse said they'd buried him somewhere in the Kalahari. Not many died as Ian had, but few saw the world as he did, either. He passed through Bushman Pits with a long, dark stretch of road in front of him. What worried him were animals crossing. By the time you saw their eyes in the headlights, it was already too late. He figured if he didn't fall asleep and flip the vehicle, he could be in Francistown by eight or nine in the morning. Another five or six hours to Gaborone driving full speed. He wanted to reach her before she left work.

He made it to Francistown for a quick breakfast and coffee, added petrol to the tank, and started down the road toward Gaborone, 430 kilometers of hard driving ahead. Seruli, then Dikabi, and on to Palapye. The sleepless night was catching up with him. In Palapye, he stopped for another coffee and set off again. North of Mahalapye, he remembered the one-lane bridge over the river and pulled off the road for a quick nap. Punch drunk, he couldn't trust himself to get the fucking wheels onto the center of that bridge. He felt sad and sick and soul weary when he woke. He got out of the Land Rover, peed into a bush, and drove on. The dust from the few cars and trucks he passed could be seen a long way off, and the blur of their passing remained with him long after they'd gone. By the time he reached the Dew Drop Inn, he couldn't drive any longer. He pulled into the parking lot, took another twenty-minute nap, and went on, promising himself no more stops until he arrived at the Ministry of Local Government and Lands. Probably three hours away. He finally pulled in at half past three. It took him less than fifteen minutes to find out where she was. Someone pointed the way to her office, but he stopped, having to face how he'd tell her.

He found a men's room, splashed water on his face, and dried his face with the front of his shirt. He lingered in the hallway near her office and heard her voice speaking with someone on the phone. It occurred to him that she would never again in her life be clear of what he was about to say. He walked past her office and looked in. He recognized her immediately, the curly hair, partly gray, big bones. He didn't see the blue gray eyes until she put down the phone and looked up. She recognized him, and he saw in the what-the-hell look she gave him, that she remembered where she'd last seen him.

"I've got to tell you something," he said.

She froze, as though she already knew.

And then, "You're lying! Get out."

"Hold on. You'll want to know. It happened the day before yesterday. Or maybe on Sunday. They buried him in the Kalahari, near the Kuke fence."

She stared at him.

"I'm so sorry." He gave her Ian's wallet. She opened it and saw his picture.

He told her as much as he knew. And he told her the name of the baby that had been born.

Her eyes slipped from his face, and tears ran down her cheeks. She pounded her fist against the cinder-block wall, over and over. She made no sound except that rhythmic beating. She climbed into the knee hole under her desk and curled up, knees to forehead. He stood at a distance and waited. He went away and came back with a cup of milk tea. "Drink this," he said, setting it near her foot. Her hand swept it to one side.

He sat on the floor near the door, and still she didn't move. When it grew dark, he lay down on his side and put his head on his arm. His eyes were open. He pictured the road he'd traveled in the dark last night, the strangeness of the light falling from the moon, the 430 kilometers south, the endless dust. He felt her love for Ian like something alive. She cried fitfully, was quiet a while and then he heard her again. Finally he slept.

He woke in the dark to the sound of her shuffling free of the desk. She brushed past him into the hall. When she returned from the bathroom, he said, "I'm here. Don't be frightened." She sat on the floor, knees drawn up, her arms hugging them. Her hair had fallen partway over her face. The night was very hot. He saw from her face that she knew the truth of what he'd told her, all the way down to the bottom of it. He could just see one eye, like the glow of an animal crossing a road. "I'm sorry," he said again.

She cried softly, the sound muffled by her knees. "Do you know where they buried him?" she asked.

"No, I'm sorry. I don't know."

At dawn, he left her sleeping. He laid the keys of Ian's Land Rover on her desk with the license plate number and a note saying it was hers now, that he'd parked it at the side of the ministry building. He walked to the train station, drank a whiskey, bought breakfast, and waited for the next train to Francistown.

She woke with a start out of a dream and found herself on the concrete floor of her office. Her limbs felt numb, dead. She pictured Ian as she'd seen him that last night in Mahalapye. He'd drunk too much. He couldn't stop talking. He talked about strangeness, about how "civilized" people had the appetite for it educated out of them. He'd thrown his arm around her waist, bearlike. She'd been irritated without knowing exactly why.

She got up off the floor, disembodied. The San people had buried him. She'd never know where. It could be anywhere in that endless sand.

Her mind raced. That night, they hadn't made love. He'd talked about how he'd slipped between two worlds. He'd seen his grandfather coming toward him, walking down a column of light.

That last morning, he was sleeping on his back, his hair thrown around the pillow. His left hand was fisted near his face, his right hand open at his groin. She'd decided not to wake him. She looked at him, whispered for him to be safe before she rolled from the bed. Later, he would have woken alone, wondered for a moment where she was, and then remembered she was gone.

Loss swallowed her. She heard people moving around out in the corridor, arriving for work. At some point Thabo would be bringing the tea cart around.

She called her boss, but he didn't answer his phone. She called again and again. She held the telephone away from her ear and let it keep ringing. She pushed her hair away from her eyes with the palm of her hand while she waited for a voice to answer and was struck by the ordinariness of the gesture. People lived ordinary lives.

"Hello?" she heard on the other end of the phone.

Her words would not come.

"Hello?" he said once more.

"Is that you, C.T.?"

"Alice?"

"Ian died." To say it was to believe it.

"Where are you?"

"My office." She set the phone down in its cradle.

Her boss found her there, standing with the tips of her fingers on the phone as though it connected her to something.

"When did it happen?" he asked.

She shook her head. She saw the pity in his eyes and how he paused before he came and put an awkward arm around her.

"I left Mahalapye without saying a proper good-bye. They say he was in a buffalo stampede. The San buried him. His friend left this." She picked up the wallet to show him, she held the keys to his Land Rover in her hand. She thought, some of his molecules have passed from his wallet to my hand.

"Have you been here all night?"

"Yes."

"Can I take you home?"

"I was going. I wanted to tell you."

"I think I'd better drive you."

She heard the sound of the tea cart rattling down the hall toward her office. "I don't want to see anyone."

"Yes, I understand." He stepped out into the hall and the tea cart rattled past the door.

"Let me take you."

"What will I do?"

"Alice. Let me drive you."

"What will I do?"

"Want me to call someone for you?"

"I don't know. You better take me home."

They drove down the road in C.T.'s car. She was aware of his discomfort. He was a shy man. She was sorry to put him in this position.

White Dog was there at the entrance to the driveway, waiting, her paws crossed over each other. "I'm okay now," she said to C.T. Before he could wonder what to do, she got out of the car. "Thank you so much," she said. "I'll try to come to work tomorrow if I can."

He got out of the car and came around to her side. "You take whatever time you need." He put his arms around her. She didn't want to sob into his shirt, but she couldn't help herself. Finally she pulled away and told him she was all right, that he should go back to work. He got into his car and started to back out, then stopped and leaned out the passenger side window. "I could stay a while. Make you a cup of tea."

"Thank you, C.T. Itumeleng will be here. Thank you."

"I'm very sorry," he said, sliding back toward the driver's seat. She watched him back out and disappear down the road. She sat down in the dirt next to White Dog and put her head on her fur. She heard White Dog's breath going in and out next to her ear. In her mind's eye she saw the sand swept by wind across the floor of the desert where he lay, grains lifting and falling. She saw Ian's shaggy head, his large warm hand, the rain pounding outside, felt the pulse of his love inside her. She saw the three hills where they'd never go now: the male, female and child, the dent in the rock where the first soul had knelt.

The broad back of Ian receding, his head set at an expectant angle, the creak of oars, the boat crossing the river and coming back empty. The key to his Land Rover in her hand. Don't go, my darling. Where are you now? Where in all the vast places have you gone?

42

Itumeleng had already finished for the day, and Alice called no one. She'd spoken the words once to C.T., and she couldn't speak them again. When she fell into bed that night, White Dog followed and sat in the doorway of a house she'd never before entered. At some point, Alice woke in the dark to find a moist snout on her arm. And then a fist to the throat when she remembered. She turned on a small lamp and made her way to the bathroom. The moon shone through the windows, and she turned on no more lights. As she came into the bathroom, she caught a glimpse of something in the mirror. Not herself. The afterimage of something. She looked more closely, but the mirror was empty.

She walked back through the darkened living room into the bedroom and lay down. White Dog, unsure of her welcome, climbed onto the bed one foot at a time, slowly, keeping herself as flat as possible. "It's okay," Alice said, smoothing her neck. Her voice was strange to her. Everything was filled with strangeness, the air as though quivering, the stars as though singing backward songs, their light flowing back into their own immensity.

In the morning, Itumeleng came into the kitchen and Alice told her. She called Will and Greta after that, and had hardly put down the phone when Greta was there beside her. "Oh, poppet." She put her arms around her. "I'm so very sorry. You'd found someone to love, to love with everything in you, the rarest thing . . ."

"Please don't," she said. "If I start crying, I'll never stop."

"Those beasts were desperate for water, I suppose."

"Ian was cutting the fence."

"You knew this?"

She nodded. "He couldn't bear it . . . their thirst."

"I only want to say one thing, which may make you cry. Will and I were wrong about him."

"I know."

"What can I do?"

"I'm not sure. Take me to work this morning when you get the kids off to school? I need to retrieve his Land Rover. It's at the ministry. His friend Roger brought it down."

"Where's your truck?"

"Also there. C.T. drove me home yesterday."

"Do you want me to bring your truck home for you? I can leave ours for Will. I dropped him off this morning."

"If you would." She dug Ian's keys out of her purse. "I'm going to Maun." She'd only just realized it.

"When are you going?"

"Today."

"You wouldn't be better off waiting?"

"I have to go." She pictured Ian buried somewhere in that vast land south of Maun, sand blowing sideways, covering up all traces of where he lay. Her ears rang with a crazy urgency. She imagined her hands, digging.

"Shall I come with you?"

"Thank you, no. I'll take White Dog to keep me company."

"Shall I feed the cats for you?"

"There's only one cat now. Horse went missing again. I'll ask Itumeleng."

There was no earthly point to it, she knew. But she packed a bag for herself, dog food for White Dog, talked to Itumeleng, and left from the ministry after Greta dropped her and White Dog off. The cars and trucks on the north-south road pushed her to drive faster than she wanted to. A percussive rhythm between the wheels and the road corrugations intensified, and the Land Rover slid sideways as she fought with the wheel and brought it back into line. White Dog's nose inched out the window as she grew more confident. A slow-moving hornbill passed in front of the windshield.

Inside his Land Rover, Ian was everywhere. The leather case for his sunglasses. A gauge for checking tire pressure. A can opener. His long-sleeved bush shirt. A cap, darkened from sweat. On the floor, a rumpled copy of *Botswana Notes and Records*, a couple of water bottles, a discarded paper bag. In the far back, a large container of water, canned goods, the two tents he'd put up on the Ntwetwe Pan, a rock he'd picked up from there. His notebooks.

North of Mochudi, she got stuck behind a bush drag. She saw it from a distance, like a beast on the horizon. Underneath that crazy cathedral-high swirl of dust, there would be a lone man, with a kerchief over his mouth and nose, bouncing along on a tractor that pulled a mountain of thorn bushes weighted down with old tires. When Ian had taken her to the train in Francistown, they'd gotten held up behind a similar bush drag. An old man was driving the tractor. His hair was white, his back and shoulders lean. Ian had called him "a one-man commotion." He liked that word, commotion. He'd used it when he'd told her about knocking down Mrs. Cratchley's flower beds as a kid. Her eyes filled to hear the sound of his words in her ear. She suddenly wished to die on this road. The thought shocked her. She could feel the desire already risen inside her like an exotic flower blooming in dust. She turned the wheel and pulled out into that brown cloud to pass the bush drag, more than half expecting to meet someone head on. Something like disappointment passed through her as she pulled back safely in front of the tractor. And then anger at herself. Kill yourself, but don't take other people with you. Or an innocent dog either, for that matter.

White Dog sat straight up on the seat. For a moment, Alice envied her ability to live in an eternal today. But no, that wasn't true. Why else would she have sat for weeks at the end of the driveway? She thought, I'd sit at the end of the driveway too if it would bring him back. Her eyes swam again, and the road disappeared. She pulled off onto a small track. *Where are you?* she asked into the dusty air. Her belly hurt from crying. White Dog thrust her nose under her elbow and pushed up, and she reached out and patted the top of her head. It felt as though part of her had gone with him, some chasm yawning between the here and the beyond. She looked out onto the landscape with its parched grass and flat-topped acacias with their thirsty gray green leaves. A single cloud floated in the sky. She thought of a Bushman story she'd once read about how the wind takes away our footsteps when we die. And then she thought about what Ngwaga had said about Ian. He could blow anywhere now. Maybe some part of him was still on Earth. Maybe he'd gone elsewhere. Maybe he'd just returned to matter, spent, nothing more than that.

But I'm alive, she thought. You've left me here. Her mother had run after a dead man all those years, wearing away a deep gully of grief under her feet. She shuddered. There was no point driving to Maun. She sat a moment longer, turned the Land Rover around, and headed back the way she'd come. She was clear-eyed now. Where there'd been tears was now emptiness.

She pulled in the driveway and shut off the engine. Itumeleng greeted her, brought her a cup of tea, and understood that she wanted to be left alone. Alice went out into the garden and sat on the rock by the huge aloes, where she'd seen Isaac sitting. It was quiet and wild and the aloes with their big fleshy gray green spikes bulged with living moisture they'd gathered and stored to carry them through the dry seasons. Out of their centers, crazy stalks of orange flowers rose to a height of twelve or fifteen feet.

She heard something behind her, turned, and saw White Dog sitting at the base of the rock. And when Alice got up to return to the house, she trailed her, taking up her position outside the door.

43

That night, a letter addressed to Isaac sat in one of three bulging canvas mail bags in the Mafeking train station. The bags were slumped, secured with heavy metal buckles at the top, each with a hole for a tag, sitting beneath a painted tin sign:

VIR GEBRUIK DEUR BLANKES
FOR USE BY WHITE PERSONS
THESE PUBLIC PREMISES AND THE AMENITIES
THEREOF HAVE BEEN RESERVED FOR THE
EXCLUSIVE USE OF WHITE PERSONS.
By Order Provincial Secretary

Inside the bags, letters from white and nonwhite persons were jumbled together, pressed against each other. Words from courts of law, lovers, mothers, car dealers, ministers, swindlers. Outside on the train platform, three lightbulbs shone at a distance from one another. The air was moist, the lights ringed with fog.

Nowhere can he find the man he once knew inside him. He's nothing now, less than a bug. His lips are cracked, they've broken his thumbs. When he eats the food they slop into a bowl, he must hold his spoon between two fingers. Often it is too dark to see. He thinks, there is nothing that a man will not do to another man. Every moment, he is afraid. It is what they've wanted all along.

Fear is the mystery. If he can conquer that, he is no longer theirs. But he is unable to make his mind bend away from the place where a small animal inside him is cornered and terrified.

Sometimes he remembers his brothers and sisters. He remembers caring for them when his mother was taken away for the passbook violations, how he looked for food day and night, until he had turned into a sniffing dog-boy, food-hunting machine.

He has nearly forgotten the letter he wrote to his mother and her employers before he was deported, saying that he would care for his sister and two brothers. Those he loves have all but disappeared, squashed thin and hard and cold as glass in the small place he has managed to keep alive inside. It will not be possible much longer. Soon the hyena men will have all of him.

Something in his head hums ceaselessly, low in pitch. He feels the terror like a pit inside him. He forces his mind to crawl out of it.

He turns the pages of his medical textbook over in his mind, reviewing the bones of the hand. The wrist: scaphoid, lunate, triquetrum, pisiform, trapezium, trapezoid, capitate, hamate, arrayed in two rows of four, nestled in a bowl created by the hollow between the ulna and the radius. The five metacarpals of the palm. The fourteen digital bones, or phalanges, three on each finger (digitus secundus manus, digitus tertius, digitus annularis, digitus minimus manus), two on each thumb.

A small shaft of light comes in through the slit in the door. He looks at his right hand in the dimness. His thumb is swollen and blue. His other fingers also are swollen. He looks away.

Then the intrinsic muscle groups: the hypothenar and thenar muscles, the interossei muscles, and the lumbricals. The abductor pollicis brevis, opponens pollicis, flexor pollicis brevis, adductor pollicis brevis and opponens digiti minimi brevis, flexor digiti minimi brevis, abductor digiti minimi . . .

He hears footsteps, a metallic click. "Get up," a voice says. "They want you."

44

To the north, apartheid sympathizers had poisoned five hundred Umkhonto we Sizwe trainees at the Novo Catengue camp in Angola. Amen, who'd escaped the bombing in Gaborone, had been away at a meeting the night the tainted beans and porridge were served. He couldn't help notice that it was a pattern for harm to pass him by while it struck those he loved.

Tonight, he sat alone on a hill overlooking the camp. Below him, figures straggled in and out of tents. The camp looked like a wounded organism. Many of his friends were in the hospital. Without thinking, the palm of his right hand stroked the dusty ground beside him, as it once stroked the shoulder of his wife. For the first time since he'd undertaken this work, he doubted his strength to continue. His joy, his life, were gone. There was no way to find Ontibile without risking arrest.

He had heard no news of Isaac and assumed that he too was dead. It was one more regret, piled on a sea of regrets. He should have been there, as he should have been beside his sister in Soweto when they opened fire.

That night, Alice slept fitfully.

She was crawling over a trestle bridge made of sticks, north of Mahalapye. She felt a train approaching through the vibrations in her feet. She climbed to one side of the trestle and pushed her body over the edge. A river was rushing below. She counted to herself as she hung on: seven, eight, nine. A light rain began to fall. She watched as it settled on the backs of her hands, the fine hairs glistening with drops of water.

She woke into a land of grief, a ship adrift. Ian's death had opened channels into decades of remembered and forgotten sorrows. The sky lightened along the horizon. She sat up in bed and then lay back down.

Wildly, she thought perhaps Roger had been lying. For reasons of his own, he'd stolen Ian's wallet. Ian was poking among the rocks in the Tsodilo Hills, just setting out this morning with the dew still held in the shadows of the hills. This was the weekend they would meet in Mahalapye. They'd worked it out the night before they'd parted last time. She'd drive up on Friday, leave work a little early, probably get there before him. She could feel the gladness of his hands on her back, pulling her close.

But how had Roger gotten his Land Rover?

If she could reverse time, she'd go back to the day they'd set out for Moremi, just the two of them. She remembered that predawn light, their stealth. She'd offered him a cup of coffee. He'd asked how her marriage had come apart. She'd told him that Lawrence was a decent man but she'd felt dead around him.

I understand that kind of dead, he'd said. *It's better to be all the way dead.*

From the moment his eyes rested on those thirsty animals and he'd said, *Poor bastards,* he was doomed. A lesser man—no, a different man—would have said there was nothing that could be done. He wasn't that sort of person. He never could have been. It's one of the things she loved in him, and it's what killed him. Not the stampede, but his desire to do what was right, not in the eyes of the law but in the eyes of something bigger than himself.

An arrow dropped to Earth, stuck fast. Its shaft quivered.

She imagined what he might have done had he lived. On their way back to Francistown when she was still feverish, he'd spoken to her about his wish to find something in those hills that was big enough to wake the world up to the significance of the San people. He believed there were caves in the Tsodilo Hills where one could find evidence of the world's first religion. She imagined he'd been right about what was there, but it would be too late by the time someone stumbled upon it.

What she and her boss were doing was puny in the face of the forces arrayed against the San: cattle, drought, poachers, the encroachment of farmers and western culture, the disillusionment of San teenagers, tuberculosis, the loss of language, tourism, the list went on.

White Dog buried her snout in Alice's bent elbow and urged her up and out of bed.

Itumeleng was in the kitchen already, scrubbing a pot with salt. She'd burned beans in it a couple of days before. Magoo was waiting for breakfast.

Today she would call Muriel. And her mother. Tell them. The words came to her. *It's a fearful thing to love what death can touch.* Her mother would understand with her whole being. Muriel would understand less.

45

Her mother's voice came to her distantly, as though an ocean current were flowing through the phone line. Only a couple of weeks before, Alice had written her mother that she'd fallen in love with someone she felt she could love forever. Today, she told her that Ian was dead. Across oceans, she cried. Her mother offered to get on the next plane, and Alice told her no.

"I'll quit my job, take a leave of absence."

"No, Mom."

They went back and forth. She heard her mother's stifled crying. "You're so far away."

"I'll find my feet again."

"Come home."

"I can't, Mom. Not now, not yet."

The connection went dead. She tried calling back but couldn't get through. She didn't want to return to Cincinnati. Out the window she saw White Dog sitting by the driveway. She thought of Checkers, the black and white dog of her childhood who used to sit beside her bed all night.

Her bedroom had been on the second floor of an old house. A huge silver maple grew in her neighbor's yard, its limbs stretched toward her window. When the night was still, the leaves whispered, and when the wind was shrill, the branches tossed and banged against the house, like a raging old man. *Let me in, let me in!* A squirrel built a nest she could see from her window, lined with shredded bark and grass. Baby squirrels were born hairless, their eyes closed. Their parents rushed around all day and brought them sumac fuzz to eat. The nest turned fuzzy pink. The babies grew and ran about on the limbs. New people bought the house next door, and they had the tree cut down. The great limbs lay on the ground like fallen elephants. By the end of the week, only sawdust and a stump remained.

That kind of sorrow was what waited for her in Cincinnati. What would they do all day? Cry? Every morning she'd wake up to the memory of a loss. One loss would give way to another, the way a fire travels underground after lightning strikes a tree, the roots of one tree igniting the next.

She tried calling her mother again without success. There was something she needed to say.

She remembered as a teenager thinking, *It's easy enough to love a dead man.* They require no understanding. They aren't unreasonable or moody or demanding. They want nothing but loyalty. Well, your daughter's alive. She's living under your nose. Try loving her, why don't you?

She'd been unfair back then. Her mother had loved her and still loved her. What more could she ask for? She'd like to tell her that she'd been as good a mother as she knew how to be. But she still didn't want to be in Cincinnati.

Her mother called back the following day and asked her once again to come home.

"I can't leave right now, Mom. I need to ride this out here."

"Because he's buried there?"

"That's part of it."

"I understand."

"You're the best mother anyone could have. I just need to be here. And I want you to be living your life there."

"I'll worry about you every moment."

"Mom, I've got to get to work. Please don't worry. I'm going to be all right. I have friends here who care. Will and Greta. Muriel. My neighbor, Lillian."

"I miss you, darling. You're too far away."

"I know, Mom. I'm sorry. I love you."

They said good-bye, and Alice sat for a moment by the phone. One of her earliest memories was sitting in a kitchen sink, her mother holding a bar of Sweetheart soap and running her hands over the bones of her shoulders. Never again would the love between them be that uncomplicated.

A letter arrived that day, addressed to Isaac, postmarked Pretoria. She hesitated to open it but then did. It was written in Afrikaans. *Hoe gaan dit met jou?* How are you? Beyond that, she had no idea what it said. There were numbers in the text, which was all she could decipher. It was signed Hendrik Pretorius. She walked back to her truck, trying to think of someone who knew Afrikaans.

Lillian had a friend. She'd been over for dinner on a night Lawrence and Alice had been there. She tried to recall the name. Like a mosquito repellent. Petronella, that was it. Pet for short. Pet Steyn. She couldn't remember Pet's husband's name, but he treated her as though she didn't have a brain in her head. Maybe she didn't, but she could probably translate the letter. On the other hand, what if it contained information that shouldn't be shared? But no one with any sense would send incendiary information across the South African border. Pet lived off the Outer Ring Road, and Alice drove straight there. She didn't want a "no" over the phone.

Pet answered her knock wearing a lime green leisure suit. She was thin, nearly anorexic, the top of her arms corded. Her face was heavily made up, giving her fine features a certain coarseness.

Alice explained about Isaac's disappearance.

"So you want this translated."

Alice nodded. Pet went into the kitchen and brought back a tray with two glasses of iced tea and set it down on a low table in the living room. "I'm not very literary," she said, sipping from her glass.

"It doesn't matter, don't worry." The house was cool, still, empty. Alice couldn't imagine what Pet did all day while her husband was at work. A blank, clean, crushing life. She took a gulp of tea. "Don't worry," said Alice again.

Pet put on her reading glasses, looked over the first page, and began. "The items you requested will be on the northbound passenger train, arriving 9:02 A.M., May 26 in Mafeking station. Gaborone, at 3:42 P.M. The items are unaccompanied. For obvious reasons, it is important that you meet this train."

"What items are those?" asked Pet, laying the letter down in her lap.

"I don't know," said Alice.

"Who *are* these people?"

"I don't know that either. They know Isaac."

"Who's Isaac?"

"My gardener. The man who disappeared. Is there more there?"

Pet picked up the letter again. "Please inform us immediately that the pickup has been successful." She turned the page over. "Then they give their phone number. It's signed Hendrik Pretorius." She looked at Alice. "How well do you know Isaac?"

"As I said, he was my gardener."

"Was he involved with the ANC?"

"He may have been. I don't know."

"If I were you, I'd throw this letter away and have nothing more to do with it."

You're not me, thought Alice. She always hated it when people said "if I were you."

"It sounds to me like an arms shipment. I'm telling you, I'd have nothing whatsoever to do with this. The ANC is full of desperate individuals."

And why are they desperate? thought Alice. Because they've been fucked over all their lives. And they haven't a goddamned thing to lose. "It's not necessarily arms," she said. "And if it is, I'll leave them there." She stood up. "I really appreciate your time and your help."

"To tell you the truth," said Pet, "I regret helping you." She handed over the letter. "Promise me that you won't meet that train."

Alice said nothing.

"Listen," said Pet, "I hardly know you. But I know South Africa. To be perfectly blunt, you wouldn't know squat about what goes on there."

"I appreciate your help. I'm sorry if I've upset you."

The shipment was three days away. She damn well would meet that train. She went home and found that the electricity had gone off all over the Old Village. Itumeleng had left dinner on the table for her, covered with a dish towel, but she wasn't hungry. She got up to call the phone number in the letter, but there was no dial tone. That was nothing new.

The next day she kept trying. On the evening of March 25, hours before she was to meet the train, she dialed again, and this time the call went through. A man's voice answered in Afrikaans, the voice shaded, deep, elderly. "I don't speak Afrikaans," Alice said. "Do you speak English?"

"Of course."

She explained where she was calling from and that Isaac had worked for her as a gardener until he'd disappeared. And she apologized for opening his mail.

"Where's Isaac?"

"He's been deported. The police believed he was a double agent."

For a moment, Alice thought the phone had gone dead. When Hendrik spoke again, his voice was raspy. "I've known Isaac since he was a young boy. He's never been anything but exemplary. This couldn't be worse. God help him ... What did you say your name was?"

"Alice Mendelssohn."

"Alice, what are your circumstances?"

"I'm an American. I work for the Botswana government."

"Are you married?"

"No."

"Are you strong?"

The question took her by surprise. "Physically?"

"No, I mean strong."

"Yes, I suppose I am."

"I must ask my wife ... no, there's nothing to be done. The shipment is already on its way. I can't give you the details. My phone may be compromised. All I can tell you is that this is extremely problematic. Isaac's mother has worked for us for years. She and my wife and I deliberated about what was the right thing to do. We had no idea he wouldn't be there. Can you meet the train?"

"Yes, but what do I look for?"

"I think it will be apparent once the train has unloaded and the platform has emptied. And please call." The conversation felt wooly, dreamlike.

"When?"

"As soon as possible. Whatever happens."

"Yes, I'll be there. I'll let you know." She rang off.

After dinner, she walked over to Will and Greta's house, carrying a flashlight, needing to be surrounded by the chaos of a prospering family. It was Friday night and the kids were still up, the littlest one in tears over a broken arrow. "Never mind," Will said. "I'll make you a new one."

"But it won't be the same. There won't ever be one like this one." His son cradled the broken bits in his arms.

"You're right, there will never be one just the same. But listen Bronco-roo, it's past your bedtime, and your mother and I want to talk to Alice."

"Why can't I talk to her?"

"You wouldn't be talking. You'd be shouting. Now get your pajamas on. Now. I mean it."

He went off.

Greta poured a glass of Stellenbosch for each of them and sat down and put her feet up on a stool. Then the little one was back, staggering with fatigue. "Come on, tiger," Greta said. "Bedtime."

He began to cry. "I'm not tired, not a bit tired."

Greta laughed. "I've never seen such a tired boy. C'mon now, I'll read to you about the mouse dentist who tricked the fox who had the sore tooth."

"And he was going to eat the mouse after the mouse fixed his tooth." He stumbled after her.

The two bigger boys were still outside, up a tree. Will called them in. They stood in the middle of the living room like wild animals, cornered, having to be polite. Soon, they disappeared into their room.

"Just watching you makes me tired," Alice said.

"You find your groove. They're good kids. The problem is they have ten times the energy we do. Did you never want kids of your own?"

"It never happened. Probably a good thing considering how things have turned out."

"The only good thing about no kids is that you're not stuck having to be nice to Lawrence the rest of your life." She thought of what a child of Ian's and hers would have been like. Fierce, curious, lively. Don't go there, she told herself. She took a gulp of wine. "So. Something's happened. A letter came for Isaac."

Greta came back into the room. "He's conked. We didn't get three pages into the story." Will handed over her glass of wine and she sank into a chair.

"A letter came for Isaac," Will said.

"I had Petronella translate it. It was in Afrikaans."

"Who?"

"Pet. I think you'd know her, at least by sight. That tidy, uptight South African woman? She was very unhappy with the contents. I just spoke to the man from Pretoria who sent the letter. A shipment is coming tomorrow by train, but he couldn't tell me what was in it. He thought his phone might be tapped."

"It sounds like arms."

"I don't know. I'm meeting the train tomorrow."

"Is that wise?"

"I promised."

"Do you want me to come?" Will asked.

"Thanks, but I don't want to get you into trouble. I'll leave it on the platform and call the police if it looks dangerous."

"You won't do anything foolish," said Greta.

Alice laughed. "Spoken like a true mother."

"And you'll let us know?"

"Of course."

"How *are* you?" Greta asked.

She had another swallow of wine and set down her glass, unable to speak for a moment. "I'm managing. When I think about him, sometimes I almost can't breathe. Like trying to get my breath underwater."

She really meant like trying to breathe under sand. Too often, she imagined his body, the sand clogging his nose, his mouth. The thought of him suffocating took her to a place beyond bearing, as insane as she knew it was. She rubbed her face with her open palms.

"My mother called. She wants me to come home."

"And?"

"I told her no."

46

She'd been standing on the platform since half past three. The train was already over an hour late. The heat rose up through the soles of her sandals, and her stomach turned over. She felt that whatever was coming down the tracks would change her life irrevocably. She thought of Ian, ready for anything, heart wide open. Next to him, she felt cautious, slow to trust. It was one of the things she'd loved about him—how he'd made her unafraid.

All at once, it seemed the activity around her increased. Porters appeared, an old man with a large metal container of milk tea shuffled onto the platform. She felt the train's presence at a distance before she saw it. Then the single light far down the tracks. She stood up a little straighter and took a step back. It was closer, and then very close. People crowded the platform, and the noise of the steam engine and huge pistons engulfed the crowd. The brakes screeched, the steam spread out over them like a vision from hell. As the steam cleared, passengers began to pour down the steps of the train carrying suitcases, paper bags, boxes wrapped with string, chickens in crates. She peered into faces, searching for a person with a question mark to match hers. A pair of lovers embraced, weeping, and Alice's eyes pooled to see their happiness.

The platform began to clear. She walked up and down searching for Isaac's name among the parcels that railway workers had loaded into the large-wheeled iron carts. The hubbub subsided. A couple of skinny boys came and pushed the iron carts toward the freight office, and she was left standing on the quiet platform. She was thirsty, exhausted. There was nothing here. She'd go home and call Hendrik Pretorius.

Just then, she caught sight of a boy and girl huddled together beside a wooden coal bin. The boy, who appeared to be about seven or eight, had an arm protectively around the girl. His legs were spindly and looked dusted with ash; his eyes were bright as a bird's. The girl's hair was neatly plaited in a dozen or more sticking-out braids, each one finished off with a different colored plastic barrette. She looked a year or two younger than the boy. Her blue dress was faded almost to white at the shoulders, too small for her, so the fabric was rucked across her chest. She'd lost a shoe and stood on one foot, her bare instep resting on the top of a white plastic sandal.

As Alice approached them, she saw that the girl was trembling.

"Isaac?" she asked them. "Isaac? *A o itse* Isaac?" Do you know Isaac?

"Isaac *o kae?*" the boy asked eagerly. Where is he?

"*Ga ke itse,*" Alice said. I don't know.

The girl began to cry.

"Isaac," Alice repeated. "Come with me. *Tla kwano.* Come.

"Come," she said again.

The boy took the girl's hand and pulled her along.

The girl nearly refused to get into the truck, and she whimpered all the way down the road to the Old Village. Alice sat them both down at the big wooden table in the kitchen and scrambled four eggs, thinking that might be a familiar food. They ate it. And toast with butter and jam. Then she made mealie meal porridge, and they ate that and drank two glasses of milk each.

When they'd finished, Alice pointed to herself. "Alice. *Leina la gago ke mang?*"

"Moses," said the boy.

"Moses," she repeated. "Moses." He smiled.

She asked the girl her name. There was no reply.

"Lulu," said the boy.

"That's a nice name," said Alice. "Lulu."

"Isaac *o kae?*" asked Moses. Where is Isaac?

"*Ga ke itse.*"

"Isaac *o kae?*" Moses asked again.

"Wait a moment." Alice walked out behind the house to Itumeleng's servant's quarters. "Itumeleng?!" she called. "Can you come?"

Lulu would not close her eyes. The chair felt hard on her bottom, and her heart beat wildly. She felt she might be sick. It would have been better not to eat that white woman's food. She had gone outside calling to someone, but what would she come back carrying? Back home she had heard stories of enchantresses who lure children to their homes and put them in the stove and eat them. They fatten children with food that cannot be resisted, and when they are fat . . . zoop! The enchantresses are sweet, like the food. They find children wandering in the desert without their mothers, in trouble, and they are kind and smile like this white woman.

Moses was not clever. If something glittered, he took it in his hand without thinking, but there are things that glitter that you must never take in your hand. She would not eat any more food in this place.

She understood now that her mother had lied to them. She told them that Isaac was not far away, that he was working in a place near where they would go to school. They would not have to speak Afrikaans at this school, and the teachers would be kind and not beat them. They would live with Isaac during the week, and they would come to their granny on the weekends. The place was not far away, she said. They would like it there. The night before they were to leave, Lulu heard her mother weeping. She had come from Pretoria to see them in Bophuthatswana. "Never mind," she said when Lulu asked her why she was crying. "You will get a good education."

"How will we get home?"

"You will come by train. Don't worry. It is not far. Isaac will put you on the train."

"But why have you given me a knapsack? The children who go to school have only small sacks."

"You are going to a special school. Now be quiet and listen to me. These are the papers that you must give to the conductor when you are going on the train ... Moses! *Tla kwano!* ... I am giving these papers to Lulu not to lose them. If the conductor asks where you are going, say you are going to stay with your brother in Gaborone. If the conductor asks if you are from South Africa, you must say, 'No, I am from Botswana, I have only been visiting my granny in South Africa.' Can you remember this?"

Lulu nodded her head.

"Moses, where are you from?"

He grinned. "From Bophutatswana."

She cuffed him on the side of his head. "It's not a funny joke. You are not from Bophuthatswana."

"Lulu, where are you from?"

"I am from Botswana," she said.

"Do you know where in Botswana you are from?"

"No."

"You are from Gaborone. This is where you must get off the train."

"Where are you from?" she asked Moses.

"I am from Botswana in Gaborone."

"No, you are from Gaborone in Botswana. Lulu, where do you come from?"

"I am from Gaborone in Botswana."

Moses asked her why they must say these things, and their mother told him to stop with his questions, that he must only remember what to say. "Otherwise they will throw you off the train." Lulu imagined the two of them sailing through the air while the train laughed down the tracks with its white smoke. Her mother had told her that they must get off the train in Mafeking and find a Motswana to ask the way to the train that left for Gaborone. "Do you understand? Tell me it back." Lulu told her. Moses was a year older than she, but her mother knew that she wouldn't forget. She had given her the papers because she had more sense.

But she knew now that they'd been tricked. She didn't understand why her mother would send them to this white woman. And where was Isaac? She turned in the chair and looked at the stove behind her. The door was large enough to shove her in. Their mother had put them on the train, and it was only when they had been traveling from the time the sun rose until it was high in the sky that she knew that Gaborone in Botswana was at such a distance that they would not be traveling home on the weekend to see their granny and that maybe they would never see her again. She didn't want to cry because crying makes the spirit come out of you her mother said, but the tears rolled down her cheeks. She wiped her nose with the back of her arm, and the snot dried in a streak like the trails the snails left on the wild spinach her grandmother gathered after the rains.

The white woman came back and with her came a black woman with a little child holding her mother's skirts. The black woman asked in Setswana, "Where are you from?" And before Lulu could warn him, Moses said, "Bophuthatswana."

Lulu said, "Gaborone in Botswana."

"That is where you are now," the black woman said in Setswana. "You are in Gaborone. *Lo tswa kae?*" Where are you from?

"Gaborone in Botswana," Lulu said again.

"Isaac *o kae?*" Moses asked. Where is he?

"He's not here," Itumeleng said in Setswana. "We don't know where he is. He has disappeared."

Lulu began to whimper.

"You must sleep," the black woman said. "It's late now. Isaac will come back."

"*Ke batla* Isaac!" I want Isaac! She was wailing now, her spirit pouring out where it could be scooped up, but she couldn't stop herself. Itumeleng picked her up in her arms, and Lulu felt the hands of Itumeleng's little girl rubbing her bare leg where it dangled. That little girl had not yet been eaten. Even though Lulu was a big girl and old enough to carry important papers, Itumeleng jostled her in her arms the way a mother does a young child, and Lulu felt herself giving in to the deep crooning that came from the stranger's throat.

Alice woke before six, tiptoed to the room where the children slept, and paused at the door. Lulu was invisible, under the sheet. Moses slept on his back, arms flung out to the side as though he'd fallen backward into tall grass.

Outside, the crested barbet sang in the tree. Small bits of white paper floated in the air, lit in the tree, fluttered on in the breeze. Her eyes were still full of sleep, and it took her a moment to realize that the white butterflies were migrating. She'd asked Will about them once and learned that one of their host plants was the shepherd tree. They traveled up Africa toward Madagascar, maybe as far as India. Here were a few dozen forerunners, but there would be more coming, and more behind them. Their wings were edged with a soft brown, but she remembered the effect when they traveled in the tens of thousands: a sea of white, the air alive, wind made manifest.

White Dog stretched out her front paws, shook herself awake, and pressed her snout into Alice's hand. Alice brought out food and water and set it down for her. It was nearly an hour before the children woke. Moses found her in the kitchen, and Lulu trailed behind.

"*Dumela, rra,*" Alice said. "*A o bolawa ke tlala?* Are you hungry?"

"*Ee, mma.*"

Lulu ran away and hid under the covers. It annoyed Alice, and then she was annoyed with herself for being annoyed. Had Lulu ever talked to a white woman? She filled a bowl with porridge and added milk. Moses ate what she'd given him, and a second bowl.

"Lulu *o kae?*" she asked Moses. He shrugged and put a napkin over his head to communicate to Alice that his sister was shy.

"Take her this, please?" She said it in English, and he began to eat the porridge she'd dished up for Lulu.

"For Lulu." He laughed and disappeared with the bowl. And came back.

"You'd like more?"

"*Ee, mma.*" He ate with enormous concentration. When he'd finished, he said, "Isaac *o kae?*"

"*Ga ke itse.*" He asked again, as though she hadn't understood. "*Ga ke itse.* I'm sorry. I don't know." She sat down at the table next to him and they were quiet for a while. His smile melted her heart. She walked into the small bedroom, Moses following.

"*Dumela, mma,*" said Alice to the sheet. "Lulu, come out, I want to see you."

"Lulu, come out, I want to see you," Moses repeated.

Alice tugged at the sheet gently. "Lulu, please come out."

"Lulu, please come out," the echo said.

A small hand held fiercely to the sheet.

That night, she called Hendrik Pretorius after the children were asleep. "I'll call you back," he said. Fifteen minutes later, the phone rang.

"I tried calling you last night but couldn't get through," she said. "I found the children. They're here, asleep in the other room."

"Thank god."

It sounded as though the phone had gone dead. ". . . Hello, are you there?"

"Yes, yes, I'm here. First let me say I'm sorry. It wasn't meant to happen this way. Isaac wrote to his mother asking that we send the children to Botswana. He said it was a good place, a safe place, and he wanted them to have a chance at a different life. He mentioned you in the letter and said he was working as a gardener at your house. I was in favor of them going. His mother was reluctant. It would mean losing them, maybe forever. What tipped the scales was Nthusi's death."

"Nthusi?"

"Isaac's older brother. He worked in the mines. There was a collapse. He died last month. Isaac's mother said if that was the fate awaiting her children, then they should go. Tshepiso, another one of Isaac's brothers, couldn't be persuaded to go. He's still with the grandmother in Bophuthatswana."

"Isaac never said anything . . ."

"Perhaps he thought you wouldn't agree."

"I don't know what he thought, and I don't know what's to be done now. Lulu won't speak, won't look at me. She's very unhappy and wants to go home. Moses keeps asking where is Isaac, where is Isaac?"

"I don't know what to say."

"Can their mother call? She works for you? During the day, could she call?"

"Yes, of course."

"I could drive them back home."

"Where?"

"To their mother."

"That's impossible. They can't live there."

"To their grandmother?"

"You wouldn't be allowed there."

"What about putting them back on a train?"

"How would they explain themselves at the border? It's one thing getting into Botswana. The children said they were going to visit their brother. It appears there was no problem. Going the other direction, I can't imagine what would happen."

"Perhaps Isaac will be back."

"He won't be back. I made some inquiries today. He's in prison."

"Oh, dear god."

"They've taken him to Number Four in Jo'burg. The place is unspeakable. My wife and I are completely torn up over it. Many don't get out alive . . . we're devastated."

She was stunned, appalled. "You're a lawyer?"

"In a country where the laws of the land are rotten to the core. I would move heaven and earth to help this young man. If you could keep the children until . . . Hello? Is that possible?"

She couldn't imagine how it was possible. "Yes, of course I will."

"I'll call again in a few days. I think it's best that I call you, not the other way around."

She hung up and went outside. Her throat was dry, her hands shaking. Out in the pool of light spilling from the kitchen, she felt a flash of anger. What was Isaac thinking? Would he even have told her before they arrived? But it didn't matter now. Nothing mattered except getting him out. She could hardly bear to think about what they'd do to him, what they might have already done. Out of the corner of her eye, she saw a flash of white. The moon was bright. More butterflies had come.

47

"I want you to tell them what's happened to their brother," Alice said.

"*Nnyaa, mma.*"

"It's better for them to know."

"*Nnyaa, mma*, it is not better," said Itumeleng. "They are thinking, this is what happens to people who come to Botswana. They are thinking, oh, they will send me to prison too."

Alice shrugged with impatience. "Well, can you tell them I want to take them to school to register them today? Can you at least tell them that?"

"*Ee, mma* . . . Moses! Lulu! *Tla kwano!* Come!" She set her daughter down at the table with a bowl of porridge in front of her.

"You're going to school," Itumeleng said to Moses in Setswana. "Lulu *o kae?* Go fetch Lulu." He ran out of the room and came back a few minutes later without her. Itumeleng stood with her hands on her hips. "Do you want to go to school?"

"*Ee, mma.*"

"You are not going unless Lulu comes."

He disappeared again and came back dragging his crying sister. Her knees looked dry and dusty even though Itumeleng had given them a bath just last night. Her one shoe dangled in her hand.

"Forget it," said Alice. "It's not going to happen today. Tell them no school. I must find Lulu new shoes. And they'll need school uniforms."

She felt a wave of grief coming on and fled out onto the veranda. She said his name out loud, and her knees buckled. It was so hot her dress clung to her back. She squinted into the sun and drew her hand over her eyes. "Come back, damn it." She had an impulse to look for him—to go to all the places they'd ever been together.

Get real, a voice said in her head. *Pull yourself together.* She shuddered as though a cold wind had blown through her. When she opened her eyes, a flash of aqua, almost iridescent, caught her eye. A lilac-breasted roller sailed between two tall stalks of aloe, near the rock where Isaac had liked to sit. She remembered him in this quiet place. What came to her was a Bible verse her grandmother had given her to learn: "Naked came I out of my mother's womb, and naked shall I return thither: the Lord gave, and the Lord hath taken away; blessed be the name of the Lord." Job had lost his seven thousand sheep, his three thousand camels, his five hundred yoke of oxen, his five hundred she asses. A wind had come and smote the four corners of a house where his seven sons and three daughters were eating and drinking wine. The house had fallen, killing them all. And still Job said, ". . . blessed be the name of the Lord." It was a story of God's unbearable cruelty, a story of testing a man to the outer limits to see what he was made of. What kind of a God would do that to a faithful man?

The lilac-breasted roller flew again. She thought it must be the most beautiful bird ever created, with its shining wings, aqua tipped with deeper blue, its lilac throat and breast, white feathered forehead, and perfect dark eye. She thought of God speaking out of the whirlwind, how He reminded Job (as though he needed reminding by then) who had caused the morning stars to sing, who shut up the sea with doors and commanded the proud waves to come only this far, no farther. If He could harness the stars and the ocean, why could He not harness cruelty? Was it more powerful than all the stars and oceans?

She turned back toward the house. In the children's room, Alice found Lulu back under the sheet. "Isaac wants you to go to school," she said to the lump. She had no words but English. "Goddamn it, I can't make you understand, but you'll have to get used to being here." She sat on the foot of the bed. The sheet quivered. "Isaac wants you to go to school." Every time she said "Isaac," the sheet grew still. "Your brother Isaac loves you. That's why you're here. But Isaac is in trouble.

This is what you can do to help your brother. You can go to school. This is what he wanted for you. Do you understand?" The lump in the sheet moved away, closer to the wall.

Hendrik called just after two in the afternoon and put the children's mother on the line. Alice said a few words to her in Setswana and heard a few soft words back. When she'd exhausted her Setswana, she said in English how sorry she was about Nthusi and Isaac. And added that she'd do everything in her power to take care of the children. Their mother said, "*Ee, mma. Ee, mma,*" over and over and thanked her, although Alice had no idea how much she'd understood. She called Lulu and Moses to the phone and left the room while they spoke. Later, Itumeleng told her that the children now knew where Isaac was. They also knew that their oldest brother had died in the mines.

By day, Ian was like the stars, there but not there. At night was when the beasts of grief came for her. Grief was like a pig that had once scared her as a child. It ate everything in sight, and as she sat on a fence looking down on it, tried to pull her into its pen by her shoelaces, drawing her toward the smelly slop of itself.

She wondered whether Ian had time to know he was leaving the Earth, or had he died instantly? She wanted him to have had time to make peace with himself. She woke with the moon shining outside the window thinking, He cared more for his principles than he cared for love. His passion reminded her of those early explorers, a Shackleton at the South Pole, a Livingstone searching for the source of the Nile, a doomed Mallory on Everest. How many men had lost their lives trying to be heroes?

On the other side of the house, Lulu opened her eyes to darkness. What came to her was the time Nthusi tried to walk the tightrope. A rope tied to the bumper of an old car, the smell of sweat. "Like this," said Nthusi. "Hold the rope high, straight." She and Isaac held on to their end and Nthusi put one foot on the rope and then the other. Lulu and Isaac slid toward the bumper. "Flying Wallenda!" Nthusi shouted, falling to the ground. The smell of the rope was dusty, sharp, like ants.

Today on the telephone, her mother had told her. She'd said the words to her daughter, her voice shaking. A wall of the mine had collapsed. Nthusi was buried and dead. Dirt filling his nostrils. Laughing Nthusi. And Isaac in prison, Oh. Her mother said she must have courage now more than ever. She was a clever girl. She and Moses must learn everything they could learn, and one day they'd be able to go home, when things were better, because they would get better, things could not stay this way forever.

But that was not true. They could stay this way forever. She'd heard in her mother's voice that she missed her children. She'd thought about asking her mother why she'd lied to her, but there were bigger things to be said.

Lulu put her arms around Moses. "Wake up," she whispered. "We must go back. Wake up."

Moses opened his eyes, grumbled, and closed them again.

When Nthusi left for the mines, he told Lulu that she would go to school with the money he sent to their mother. She would go to college like Isaac. She was a good girl. She mustn't cry for him. He was to meet a truck that would take him to the mines. She watched him walk down the road carrying his clothes in a plastic sack and imagined him standing in the back of the truck as it roared away, his hands hanging onto the wooden slats. The dust of the road would have swirled up, and he would have smiled as though he were going on holiday, but inside he would not have been smiling.

What was she doing in this place? This foreign place without her mother, without her granny, with Tshepiso far away, with Nthusi dead, with no Isaac.

She got out of bed. The concrete floor, polished with red wax, looked black in the moonlight. It was cool on her feet. She opened the door to the outside and nearly fell over White Dog. Her bare feet took her out toward the road. The trees made a canopy over her head. The stars twinkled between the branches, cold and far away. They did not look friendly, those stars. She turned when she saw White Dog following her. "Go home," she told her. She knew the way to the train tracks. Straight up the road, then she wasn't sure, but her feet would take her.

White Dog followed close behind. She took hold of Lulu's shirt and yanked. She barked and ran around her in circles, barked and barked. Lulu kicked out. The dog ran ahead, faced her and refused to move. Lulu stepped around her and continued on. When she'd walked halfway to town, she heard footsteps behind her. She ran away from them as fast as she could. The footsteps behind her pounded the soft shoulder, closer, and then her brother's voice called out her name.

She stopped. "*Dikgopo tsame di botlhoko,*" she said. My ribs hurt.

"What were you going to do?" he said in Setswana. "Walk back to Granny's? *Gaetsho re fa.*" This is our home now.

"*Tsamaya,*" she said. Go away. She sat on the ground.

He told her that she'd scared him, that she must not ever leave him like that again."

Lulu looked at her feet.

"*A o bolailwe ke letsatsi?*" Are you thirsty?

"*Ee.*"

"*A re tsamayeng.*" Let's go.

White Dog led the way, her tail high. It was still dark when they reached the house and crept through the door and into bed.

The moon reflected off the whitewashed wall in the room. Her eyes were wide open. Her family had fallen to pieces. Only Moses and his snoring were left. Her mother had said that her father had found another woman, that he was never coming back, but Lulu didn't believe this, not when she'd felt the strength of her father's love. She didn't remember him well, but she remembered that he had love in his eyes for her mother. They had fought and sometimes the fighting was loud, but at the end of it, there was the look in his eyes, still there.

But now that was finished, and he was gone. And Nthusi was dead. And her baby sister gone. And Isaac in prison. And Tshepiso would not come on the train with her and Moses. Her mother said Lulu was the smartest one, after Isaac, although she did not feel smart. If she was so smart, what was she doing here? And why had she not seen that her mother was lying? She said that Isaac would be there to meet them, that the school was not far distant from Boputhatswana, that they could come home and see their granny every week. But once she was on the train and sitting on a hard seat, her feet dangling in air, with the grass blurry out the window they were leaving things behind so fast—houses and dogs and people and the very sky itself—she knew how much she had left behind and how impossible it would be to return.

Her mother had lied. She must have known they would never go if they knew the truth. Something in her knew it was for the best, but what was for the best? Her mother had not wanted her to go to a school where she must speak Afrikaans. And Lulu had not wanted to go where the teachers beat you if your head dropped down on the desk when the heat of the afternoon sun pounded on the tin roof. Your head did it without asking your permission and you could not help yourself. Her mother had not known about the beatings, but she knew about Afrikaans, and she had said, "That is *their* language, not ours."

But this place where she and Moses were now, this was not their place, in the same way that Afrikaans was not their language. Surely it was better to be in a place where you belonged, speaking a language that was not yours, than it was to be in a place where you didn't belong and speaking the right language. Her mother said the homeland where they lived with their granny was not their home. But it was the only home Lulu had, so was that not home?

If Isaac were here, it would be different. She did not know what it meant to be in prison. Was it like the mines, where the roof collapses on certain people so they die, those who are unlucky? She thought it was worse than that. She believed more people died in prison than in the mines. No one sent money home from prison. To be in prison was like a chicken trapped in a cage. The only reason chickens are put in cages is to go to market to be sold and then their heads are chopped off. Certain people who were in prison stayed alive. She had held the hand of her mother in a crowd to hear the words of someone who had once been in prison. But this man was later killed. She had also heard that people are beaten so badly that even when they live, they are like broken eggs. Isaac was to be a doctor. Only a few black people had the chance to go to university and then to medical school. But he had left school and South Africa and given up his one chance. She had asked Granny why he had done this, but her granny had not answered. She had only said that it was not safe for him to stay in South Africa.

So he had come to Gaborone in Botswana to be safe, but now he was in the most dangerous place of all, in a cage like a chicken. Is this what happened when you went to school for many years, through university and to medical school, nonwhite section? Everyone said that she must go to school: her mother, Nthusi, Isaac, her granny. Her granny had cried when she and Moses and Tshepiso had needed to stop going because they had no money. Still, she did not want to go to school here. Perhaps they beat children here too. Perhaps they spoke the language that the missus spoke. She only knew the words hello howareyou iamfine. If they spoke that language, Lulu would be lost, like a bird blown in the wind.

Tomorrow the missus would take them to school to be registered. Behind her eyes, there was a pounding. Itumeleng said she must wear her new shoes and not cry. She must take Moses by the hand and watch over him because even though he was the older one, she was the more reliable one. Her mother had told her this before she left, but she no longer believed everything her mother told her. She did believe that Nthusi was dead though, because she heard the truth in her mother's tears. And she believed that Isaac was in prison because she could hear her mother's fear.

Her throat missed her mother; it was hard to swallow. And her cheek missed her granny's cheek against it.

But she would go with Moses and the missus to school because it was too far to get back home, and even if she found the train station and the train to take her across the border going the other way, she wouldn't know what to say to the conductor. Her mother had only told her what to say going in one direction but not what she must say going home. And Lulu had not thought to ask because Isaac would be there to meet them. Now she was only a small girl who didn't know how to get home.

Itumeleng had a daughter, and she did not need another one. The white missus had no children, but Lulu had never heard of a white woman having a black child. In South Africa she thought you would go to prison for this. Her mother had told her that Gaborone in Botswana was a different kind of country, that black people and white people lived together differently. This white woman whose name was Alice had gray hair like an old woman, but she was not old. Her hair was curly like the hair of an African woman, but she did not wear it in plaits. It was all over her head like something wild. If a child had hair like that, people would say her mother was not caring for her properly. This Alice was not unkind. She had bought Lulu new shoes. Very nice shoes that were not too large like some shoes she had worn that went flap, flap when she walked, or shoes that Moses had already worn so hard before they were passed on to her that her toes came out of the holes. Never before had she had new shoes in a pink color for a girl. And in the mornings this Alice missus greeted Moses and Lulu in their own language even though she could not speak it well. She tried to speak it for Lulu and Moses so that they would not feel sad and lonely. But when she spoke Setswana, it made Lulu feel more lonely. She would never say this to Alice the white woman because she could see that would hurt her feelings but nevertheless it was true. It would always be true no matter how many words of Setswana she learned because her skin was *blank* and Lulu's was *nie blank*.

She closed her eyes and went to sleep, and when Itumeleng got them up in the morning, she noticed right away. "Your feet are dirty," she said. "Where you been last night?"

"Don't tell missus," said Moses.

"Did White Dog go with you?"

"*Ee, mma,*" said Lulu.

"*Tlhapa dinao.*" Wash your feet. "Hurry."

48

White Dog lay outside the school under a thorn tree waiting for Moses and Lulu, eyes closed against the sun, dreaming. Her legs twitched, and her toenails made a rattling noise against the metal water bowl that Alice had left for her. Down a path she ran in her dream, across an open, dusty patch of ground. Something was at her heels. Her whiskers trembled in small spasms as she bared her teeth. Her heart pounded. Her hackles stood up like a small brush fire. She couldn't see her pursuers, but she could hear them, yapping, snarling, gaining on her. Their feet thundered; she smelled the dust of their pursuit. Closer, closer came the leader of the pack, and she woke suddenly, confused. What world was she in? She raised her head and sniffed the air.

Children spilled out the door of the school, yelling into the hot sun. There was someone she was waiting for. The boy came to her, touched her back. The girl knelt down and put her hands over White Dog's ears until the sound was like a river rushing to the sea, a river she'd never seen or heard, a sea a dog cannot imagine.

Lulu and Moses had been placed in the same classroom. Heavenly Mosepe, the wife of the minister of education, was their teacher. She moved like a great ship; she was both stern and loving, managing a classroom of thirty-seven children as effortlessly as she would have managed the World Bank.

Each morning, Moses and Lulu dressed in their school uniforms— Lulu in a blue pinafore, Moses in a blue shirt with a collar, and dark blue shorts. They rode with Alice and White Dog up the Old Village

Road, past the fire station and library and into the dusty school yard with its single-story cinder-block building and tin roof that popped and muttered with the changing sun and clouds. A week after they began school, Alice got a call from the school nurse. "The children have lice," she said.

"Oh," said Alice, her voice noncommittal.

"You must come now, madam."

"Can I pick them up at the end of the day?" She was preparing for a pan-African conference on indigenous populations, to be held in Gaborone the following week. Twenty-seven representatives from thirteen Commonwealth African countries would be attending.

"No, *mma*, you must come immediately. Otherwise, the lice will jump onto the heads of other children."

She grabbed a bunch of papers, stuffed them into her bag, and left the office. She found White Dog sitting under her favorite tree outside the school. Alice called her, picked up the children, and drove to the pharmacy, where Ari Schwartz stood behind the counter. He was a Canadian who'd come out to Botswana after his wife died. He had no children and no other family and had wanted to do something useful with his life. He studied Setswana every night at home; there were few words he didn't know, but because he was tone deaf and Setswana was a tonal language, nothing prevented him from saying *kubu*, the word for hippopotamus, when he meant *khubu*, the word for belly button.

"Yes, Alice, what can I do for you?"

"The children have been sent home from school."

"Let me guess. Lice?" He leaned over the counter and looked over the tops of his glasses at Moses and Lulu. His eyes were bright, and he had big pendulous ears and a rich tenor voice.

He tried Setswana. "Lice, is it?"

Moses grinned as though he'd won a prize.

"Is your head itching, eh? Back of your neck, around your ears?"

Lulu spread out her palms and held them over her hair as though containing the lice.

"This will take care of those little buggers." He passed a glass bottle filled with a vile-looking brown liquid over the counter to Alice.

"Every other day for a week, shampoo their heads. And you'll need to comb out the nits with this." He held up a metal comb. "Plastic works for European hair, but not their hair . . .

"Your servant's children?" he asked confidentially.

"No," said Alice. She didn't know what to call them. "I'm looking after them."

They got back in the truck, and Alice's scalp began to itch. It itched all the way home, just where Ari had suggested: at the back of her neck, around her ears.

"Into the bathtub," she said to the children, helping them out of the truck.

Itumeleng was washing clothes in the tub, her daughter sitting on the floor next to her, playing with clothespins. She looked up from her sloshing. "Why are you here, *mma*?"

"Lice," said Alice.

"What is this lice?"

"Little bugs in the hair." Alice scratched her head.

Itumeleng picked up her daughter, and ran to the servant's quarters.

"For Christ's sake," muttered Alice. "It's not bubonic plague." She scooped the wet clothes out of the tub into a large bucket and filled the tub with warm water. She slammed down the toilet seat and sat on it. "Get in," she said to Lulu and Moses.

They shed their clothes. Moses banged his knee on the lip of the tub as he climbed in. "Ha!" he said, sitting down. Lulu joined him. Her ribs jutted out against her skin. She folded her arms over her brown chest.

After their shampoo, Alice sat Moses down in a chair in the kitchen and shone the brightest light in the house on his head. She pulled the metal comb through his short, curly hair. He fidgeted and whined while Lulu watched. The comb was useless. The nits clung to each hair, and she needed to pull off each one between two fingernails, like a mama baboon.

Lulu's hair was thick and plaited. Alice undid the plaits and sectioned off the hair. "*A o lapile?*" she asked after an hour, pulling out another hard-clinging nit. Are you tired? Lulu nodded gravely. After two hours Lulu had hardly moved. My god, she thought, this child has a will of iron. Afterward, she gathered sheets and towels and clothes, filled the bathtub, and washed everything in sight.

She drove the children to school the following day and worked non-stop on the conference. That was Wednesday. On Thursday, she got a call from the nurse. "There is an egg on Lulu's head." Alice pictured a raw egg sitting on top, the yolk a big raised polka dot. The nurse's voice was disapproving.

"Yes, I'm coming."

She picked up White Dog and both children. The shampooing and nit picking and scrubbing of every piece of fabric in the house continued, off and on, until the day before the conference.

Will stopped by after work. "What am I going to do if the lice cop calls tomorrow? Tell twenty-seven delegates from thirteen Common-wealth African countries that I have to go home to deal with lice?"

"You have them too?" He took a step backward.

"No. But I'll throw those urchins out on the street if they've given them to me."

"You seem to have developed some passion around this topic."

"I wouldn't wish this on my worst enemy."

"The boys got them last year. It took us three months . . ."

"Don't tell me. Please."

"How is Lulu doing?"

"The other day, I finished going through her hair. She jumped off the chair and put her arms around my legs. I was so surprised, you could have knocked me over." On her lips she could still feel Lulu's damp hair, the smell of coal tar shampoo, when she bent and kissed the top of her head.

"And Isaac?"

"Hendrik has an appointment with a deputy minister of correctional services later in the week. He told me this guy owes him a favor. Otherwise, no news."

"What about you?"

"Don't ask. And please don't say anything sympathetic. I can't handle it."

The conference lasted five days, with the delegates housed at the university dormitory. About a quarter of them were members of indigenous populations. Two of the delegates were Seventh-Day Adventists, who couldn't drink tea or coffee during breaks. "Starch water"—cow's milk mixed with hot water—was what they preferred. One woman from Seychelles was nursing a baby. Each country was responsible for a two-hour presentation, a few with longer slots. In addition, there were anthropologists and sociologists from Cape Town, Lusaka, Nairobi, and abroad, experts on land use, economists holding forth about traditional economies, and one of Ian's colleagues talking about indigenous art. Ian would have been there.

Four nights into the conference, Alice got a call from her boss. A Kenyan, a big vulnerable, blustery guy, had gotten drunk and was threatening to throw himself out a third-floor window. Alice asked Itumeleng to keep an eye on the kids and rushed to the university. C.T. was standing outside the dorm room with about a dozen people. One moment the Kenyan was raving angry and the next moment weeping. "Don't go near him," said C.T., as Alice made a move to enter the room. "He's violent."

"Get them away from me!" the man was shouting. "Stop staring!"

"Go back to your rooms, please," said Alice. People drifted away. C.T. went away to call campus security while Alice stood watch.

After everyone had left, she stood at the threshold and asked, "May I come in?" The man made a movement with his head. She came and sat on the bed next to him. The window was open behind them. "What's going on?"

"She won't pick up the phone."

"Your wife?"

"No."

"Someone important to you."

He nodded. "I hoped she would be my wife. My friend told me he saw her with another man."

"How long have you known her?"

"All my life. She's the love of my life."

"I'm so sorry," she said. "Perhaps she will still remember how much you love her."

"No. She says she doesn't respect me."

"Then you must find someone who loves and respects you as you deserve to be loved. And when you get home, you must stop drinking so much."

He talked some more, and she listened. Finally without thinking, she told him about Ian. And then she was crying. It surprised the Kenyan, but she didn't care. The weeks of holding back poured out of her. She closed the window behind them. In his tender, slobbery way, he comforted her. By the time C.T. and campus security arrived, it was all over.

The following day, the conference ended. She fell into bed, too wound up to sleep, and lay in the dark, eyes wide open. Once she'd seen a chart of the universe, from small to large. On one end was the tiny neutrino. Moving up in size was the core of an electron, protons, an atom's nucleus, a hydrogen atom. Getting larger, a virus, a red blood cell, a grain of pollen, a poppy seed, a fly, a hen's egg, an ostrich egg, a human being. A lion, an elephant, a baobab tree, the Victoria Falls, Mt. Everest, the moon, Mercury, Mars, Earth, the sun. Then Sirius, Regulus, Pollux. Betelgeuse. The Helix Nebula. The Crab Nebula. The whole of our local galactic group, 150,000,000 light-years across. Out to the entire observable universe. And everything beyond that. In the middle of all that, there she was. What is one person? Nothing. Ian had said something like this, that night they were talking by the fire. You get the proportions wrong and think your life is all that matters. It helped to remember, this small dot that she was.

49

Hendrik called to say that he'd tried to get clearance to see Isaac without success, but he was planning to be in touch with a few more people he thought might help. At the very least, he hoped his inquiries might afford Isaac a measure of protection. Alice asked what she could do.

"Nothing," said Hendrik. "Pray."

It turned out he was more than a lawyer. He'd served under Vorster's government after the assassination of Prime Minister Verwoerd. Much of his life, he told her, he'd believed it was possible to create change from within if you were smarter than the next guy and willing to play the game, at least part of the time. His job had involved trying to integrate South Africa into the international community. He'd been instrumental in winning the repeal of legislation that prohibited multiracial sports. But finally his role sickened him, literally. He had a heart attack, which flattened him for six months. When he got back on his feet, he quit the government, but he still knew many people in the halls of power, some of them friends.

"Would it help if I came down?"

"Definitely not. We feel judged by your country. If I can be blunt, you'd be an impediment, not a help. Pray. That's all you can do." When she got off the phone, she went out to Isaac's garden. She'd thrown water on his vegetables when she thought of it, but too often she hadn't thought of it, and the sun had baked them into the ground.

The next night over supper, Alice told Moses and Lulu that they would light a candle every evening for Isaac. She lit a match and said,

"For Isaac." She shushed them for a moment and closed her eyes. When she opened them, Lulu's were closed too.

"Isaac *o kae?*" asked Moses for the thousandth time.

"Isaac is in prison." Alice crouched down with her wrists together, as though shackled.

"*A o lwala?*" Is he sick? Lulu asked.

"*Ga ke itse.*" I don't know. "Hendrik Pretorius, you know him? Mister Pretorius? Your mother is working there?" Their faces were blank. "Pretorius. Your mother. *Mma wa gago.*" She picked up a broom and swept the floor. "Your mother is working for Mr. and Mrs. Pretorius."

Moses laughed and took the broom.

"Pretoria?" Lulu asked.

"Not Pretoria. Pretorius."

"*Ke eng?*" Lulu pointed to the candle. What is it called?

"Candle."

"Candle. *Molelo.*"

Moses pointed to his plate. "*Nama.*"

"Meat," said Alice.

Lulu to her glass. "*Masi.*"

"Milk."

After she'd put them to bed, Alice turned off all the lights in the house and went into the living room and sat on the couch in the dark. She and Lawrence had found the wooden couch frame discarded at the dump, a lovely carved hardwood that was scarred and dinged. She'd sanded it down, an act of faith for their lives together; they'd had the cushions made at the prison. The bright green fabric felt cool now in the dark. All the creatures outdoors were asleep like this green, waiting for the light of day. She felt her way in the darkness, footstep by footstep, to the bedroom. There were no curtains on the windows. She pressed her face to the screen and saw a few stars held in the boughs of the syringa trees.

Isaac o kae? She saw in her mind's eye a dozen more questions on Moses's face. *Why is he not here? When will he come? What will happen to me? When will I see my mother? Why did she send us here? Who are you? What are you to us?*

50

For a couple of days now, they've stopped taking him out of his cell. His head throbs without end, his vision has blurred. Each breath he takes pushes his broken ribs toward pain.

He runs a hand over his head. It is no longer his head. There is no hair on it. And the shape is wrong. They shaved his hair when he came to this place, and they've shaved it again. Lice, they said. *Dirty kaffir lice. They all have lice.* But it's not true. He has never had lice. Not in all his born days. His head is now the head of a skinny man. Lumps where there were none.

He is an old man now. They have broken his ribs, five or six, maybe more. He is older than that old sick man who dug the sunken garden and gave him the hot pepper seeds. He is broken in more places than he can count. His nose, pushed to one side, blood clotted underneath. Traveling under the hearse, he thought he would die. He knows now he was not even close to death then. He can feel the line between life and death in this place, has prayed to cross it, to be granted peace.

Amen. Meeting Amen was where it began. If he'd walked down that footpath a quarter of an hour earlier, a quarter of an hour later, he would have slept somewhere else that night. Who knows where he would have ended up? But it would not have been with Amen and Kagiso. It would not all have unfolded.

Why are they not coming for him now? It has been a day, perhaps two. How often has he prayed to God to let him die, a God who has proven to be deaf, blind, criminally indifferent.

How is it that a small voice, even now, is saying, *live!* Some stubborn, reptilian creaking urgency wants to draw one more breath. And after that, one more. And again and again.

Surely death will be like water merging with water.

They have not been coming for him for several days now. He believes his usefulness to them has ended. *What is the chaff to the wheat? saith the Lord.* They will come with their sharp threshing instruments and beat him small and blow him away as chaff.

Surely death will be like the earth dissolving in the rains, running before the deluge, merging with the moving waters. Or like letting your hands go from the branch of a tall tree and dropping, falling through space, the fall never ending, black nothingness forever.

51

Workmen had been banging on the roof of the Ministry of Local Government and Lands all morning when the phone rang. "Hello!" Alice yelled into receiver.

It was Heavenly Mosepe. The nurse had found an egg on Moses. "You must come get the children."

There was silence on Alice's end.

"Hello?"

"Yes, hello."

"You must wash everything made of cloth in the house, then they will stop."

"They will never stop."

"They will stop, madam."

She slammed out of work and picked up the children. "Still?" asked Ari Schwartz. He pulled out another bottle of vile brown liquid. One of his eyes wept easily. When Alice first knew him, she thought he was grieving for his wife. He held out the bottle, dabbed at the corner of his eye, and shoved his handkerchief back in his pocket.

"Don't you have anything else? That stuff doesn't work."

"I have one more thing. Surefire, but you must use it very carefully. Not a drop in the children's eyes." He went behind a curtain and came back with a cork-stoppered bottle filled with black liquid. "The instructions are written on the back. Follow them closely."

"It won't hurt them?"

"No, just keep it out of their eyes. Use it every day for three days. By the end of that time, the lice will be dispatched."

"I'll make you a cake if it's true."

"Chocolate is my favorite," he said, pulling out his handkerchief again. "Looks like rain."

"Let's hope." Alice paid him, and he wished her luck.

The wind was blowing low and steady, sweeping dust across the length of the mall. The title of the movie at the cinema was obscured by brown haze. The dust clung to everything: windshields, foreheads, shoes, the umbrellas under which the Mbukush women sat in their stalls. They were folding them now, gathering their wares, taking cover. The wind seemed to increase in ferocity as they walked back to the truck. It tossed hats. A can rolled across a flat expanse between the electrical shop and the road. White Dog put her ears back, and Lulu covered them with her hands.

"*Pula e kae?*" said Alice. Where's the rain? There'd been so little, and soon winter would come, with no possibility of more.

"She is coming," said Moses, practicing his English.

Alice drove home while the wind nudged the truck sideways. In the driveway, a few drops fell. "Hurry!" she said, gathering her papers. A lightning bolt rent the sky, followed by a jolt of thunder. She took Lulu's hand and ran toward the house. Moses had already ducked inside.

White Dog refused to cross the threshold. "Come!" but she planted herself outside, her body shaking. "Come on!" yelled Alice, but she was too frightened to move. Another burst of thunder shook the air. Never had Alice in her childhood been afraid of thunderstorms, but here people actually died from lightning strikes. Often. Alice tried to pick White Dog up to bring her in, but she ran away, then came creeping back toward the threshold. "Don't then."

Alice felt the storm enter her. She ran from room to room, furious, gathering sheets and towels and hurling them onto a mounting pile on the living room floor. Pillows, dish towels, every stitch of clothing in the house. The rain pelted down now, lightning blanched the sky, and the wind screamed and shrieked and shook branches loose and threw them to the ground. The children watched wide-eyed as she grabbed things and threw them onto the pile. After a time, she sat down on the mound, spent. Outside it was just rain now.

"*Ke batla borotho,*" Lulu said suddenly.

"We have no bread. Do you want to make it?" She mimed stirring.

"*Ee, mma.*"

"You know how to make it?"

"*Ee, mma.*"

Alice got out yeast and mixed it with water, set a five-kilo bag of flour, a large bowl, and a bread pan on the wooden table.

"Do you want me to help?" Alice pointed to her, and then to Lulu.

Lulu pointed to herself.

Alice went to the living room and carried a huge load of clothes to the bathtub, turned on the hot water, added soap, and filled the tub half full. She took off her sandals and climbed into the tub and pounded the clothes with her feet. She pulled out the plug and let the soapy water drain, replaced the plug, and filled up the bathtub again. She rinsed the clothes, let out the water, and wrung each item with her hands.

She went to the kitchen to find buckets for the clothes and put on her brakes at the doorway. The large bag of flour had fallen to the floor. Lulu and Moses were rolling in it and laughing. Flour had drifted around the front legs of the table and the stool. Lulu's hair snowed onto the red concrete floor. Where Moses was wet from the rain, his skin had turned to a white paste. The two of them looked up suddenly, and stopped. Alice laughed, threw a little flour onto their heads, and left them to it. She grabbed a couple of buckets, thinking, If I were a real mother, I'd stop them. But when in their lives will they ever get to do this again?

The rain ended. She hung clothes and sheets and towels on the line out by the crested barbet's tree, and draped clothes over aloe plants and bushes all over the yard while Moses and Lulu swept and scrubbed the kitchen floor. Alice hosed them off by the backdoor, the two of them screaming and running over the muddy ground.

That night the phone rang. "I've spoken to him." Hendrik's voice sounded deeply exhausted, old. It took her a moment to understand he meant the deputy minister of correctional services. "He said he'll look into it and get back to me. If he frees him, Isaac will be permanently expelled from South Africa. You would need to find a way to secure political asylum in Botswana. That could be tricky, considering why he was thrown out."

"Is he safe?"

"No one's safe where he is."

"You sound tired."

"I'm an old man." He paused. "My wife's been ill. I haven't told you. She has lung cancer. Never smoked a day in her life."

"I'm very sorry."

"We've been married fifty-three years."

"I'm sorry, Hendrik."

"She went into the hospital yesterday for treatment. I'm going there overnight. I'll sleep on a cot in her room."

She was quiet a moment and then told him she'd pray for them.

The children were in bed. Itumeleng's little house in back was dark. She went into the bathroom and brushed her teeth. Perhaps Isaac was alive, perhaps not. The deputy minister wouldn't have known, either way. He would have reassured Hendrik, told him what he wanted to hear. Or maybe he'd only said he'd look into it but was lying. Someone in that role would not be trustworthy. A superthug with blood on his hands, a great deal of blood.

52

A week passed, and another week. She heard from Hendrik only once. His wife was home from the hospital, but not doing well. He'd tried contacting the deputy minister, but the man had not returned his calls.

The lice were vanquished, and the three of them delivered a chocolate cake to Mr. Schwartz, who wept real tears.

Three days later, Hendrik called to say that the deputy minister had called. Isaac would be freed and expelled from South Africa if Botswana would permit him entry. Until that time, he would remain in prison.

"We're only partway there," he said. "We don't know what's happened to him. The important thing now is getting an entry permit and asylum on your end. Every day counts."

She realized she should have been working on this all along, but it had seemed useless while he was in prison. "Please call me tomorrow or the day after," she said. "I'll do everything I can."

She considered going back to the chief of police, but he didn't seem to be a man who could be swayed, except by a higher authority. Directly after school, she went to speak with Heavenly Mosepe, who knew every permanent secretary and minister in government.

"Quett Masire is the person who can help," Heavenly said. The vice president. "Do you know him?"

"His wife is teaching me Setswana, but I don't know him." She'd met him once at a reception. She remembered thinking at the time that this man had been loved as a child. It was an odd thing to have thought, but now, it gave her hope.

"I will speak with him," said Heavenly. "I have known him many years. Can you say without a doubt that this man is not a danger to anyone here?"

"I would swear it on my father's grave."

Quett Masire was out of town attending a conference in Tanzania, and there was no way to contact him. When he returned, four days later, Heavenly did what she'd promised. Several days after that, she received a communication that Vice President Masire had spoken with the chief of police and after reading the file on Isaac determined that there'd been insufficient evidence to warrant a deportation. The office of the vice president would send an official all-clear to the South African government and ask immigration authorities to grant Isaac political asylum. Alice knew she wasn't supposed to call Hendrik, but she did anyway. She was beyond herself with joy, and he was cautiously optimistic.

But there ensued a holdup on the South African side. The deputy minister of correctional services needed to confer with the minister, who had gone on vacation. No one could say when he'd return. Another week went by.

"Tell me this is a bad dream," Alice said when Hendrik told her the news. "Isaac could die because some fat minister is sunning himself in Zanzibar."

"I'll make another inquiry tomorrow," Hendrik said. "It's all I can do."

Three nights later, he called. "I have good news. He says he'll free Isaac. I'm told he's to be driven to the border next Tuesday. I'm not allowed to see him. That probably means he's in bad shape. They don't like showing their handiwork. You should probably arrange a hospital bed.

"Things could still go wrong. You could wait all day at the border and go back home without him. He might not even be alive."

"Why do you say that?"

"This sort of thing happens. Officials clear a person, and he dies before he's released. They blame it on mental instability. I'll be sending you duplicate documents. I want you to have a copy, just in case. Normally, the guards carry only the one set, but I don't want to take any chances. I bribed an office clerk. He could lose his job." He left it unsaid that something equally bad, or worse, could happen to him.

"I've found someone traveling up to Gaborone the day after tomorrow. He'll carry the papers. He's quite high ranking, so he shouldn't get stopped. Where can he find you?"

"At the Ministry of Local Government and Lands."

"His name is Diederik Devalk."

"D-e-v-a-l-k?"

"Correct. He has a meeting at eleven at the Ministry of Finance. I don't know when to tell you to expect him, before or after that."

She told him she'd be in her office all day. "How is your wife, Hendrik?"

"A little better today. The news has brightened us both."

Devalk turned up at quarter past ten. He was charming: an impeccably fitted gray suit, head held high, dark eyes, pale skin, longish dark hair, combed back, long fingers that grasped hers in a cool handshake. He passed her a large envelope, which she slid into her desk. The state of her cinder-block office embarrassed her. She found him a cup of tea and a biscuit.

His accent was South African, but it had a touch of British in it. She was fascinated by a small stain on the sleeve of his gray suit. It so much didn't belong there. He asked her nothing about her involvement with Isaac. She was grateful. She asked him about his journey, whether he lived in Johannesburg, what his work involved. Yes, Jo'burg was his home. He worked for the government, and also closely with the diamond industry, principally De Beers.

His face bore the ravages of his powerbroking role between the diamond industry and the South African government, but still, she liked him, the boy in him close enough to the surface to be seen. She imagined him getting out of bed in the morning, mussed from sleep, grumpy, before he donned his public self. When he took his leave, their eyes met, and hers unaccountably welled up. He held her hand a little longer than necessary. Since Ian had died, she'd felt nothing for any man and hardly recognized the brief flicker Devalk inspired. After he'd gone, she opened the envelope he'd left. Foolscap-sized sheets of paper, government seals, densely written Afrikaans. The only thing she recognized was the name, Isaac Muthethe. All afternoon, she kept opening the drawer and sliding it closed again, making sure the envelope was there. She skipped lunch. She hardly dared go to the bathroom.

When she picked up Moses and Lulu after school, she thought of telling them where she'd be going Tuesday, but she couldn't bear to disappoint them. She turned to look at them sitting side by side on the seat of the truck. Lulu had ripped her uniform and scraped her knee. A white gauze pad, already dusty, covered the scrape. Moses said in broken English that someone had pushed her and he'd pushed that someone. Alice turned to Lulu. "I'm sorry someone was mean to you."

She smiled crookedly. "*Mma?*" She didn't understand.

Tuesday morning, Alice drove the children to school and started south toward the Ramatlabama border gate. There was almost no traffic, and no dust. Every rock on Kgale Hill stood out. She saw a boy out early with two goats, and two schoolgirls with bows in their hair. Her hands on the wheel shook with the deep corrugations in the road. By sunset, it would be all over, one way or the other, when the border gate closed for the night.

She passed through Lobatse, and on toward the border. From a distance, she could smell the Botswana Meat Commission's abattoir, stinking of blood and fire. Some of those poor beasts trekked hundreds of kilometers to get here, with no idea where they were going.

She made her way south of Lobatse, and far away, she saw the border. At the Botswana gate, she told the guard that she would not be passing through to South Africa, that she was waiting for a South African who'd been granted political asylum. She pulled the documents out of the envelope, together with a copy of a document from Quett Masire's office. The guard looked over the pages and passed them back to her. "*Go siame, mma.*" Okay.

Driving toward the South African side, she spotted two white guards standing sentinel in the shade of an ugly building, one just inside, one outside. They wore khaki uniforms—shorts and kneesocks, crisp, short-sleeved shirts. Both had guns in shoulder holsters. A third man, a black African, worked at a distance from them, washing an official car with a rag and a bucket. He was in the open, the sun so hot it was shouting now, moving his rag slowly over the bumper, and back again, then over the curve of the fender.

Alice parked the truck and walked toward the two guards. The one closest to her watched her, shifting uneasily. He reminded her of an animal in the wild. Approach them in a truck, and they're calm enough, but out of your vehicle, you're to be feared. She carried her purse over one shoulder, the large envelope between her elbow and side. Instinctively, she put her palms out so they'd see she was unarmed and harmless.

She greeted them in English. "Good morning to you," and got an unenthusiastic greeting back. "Do you know English?" she asked. One nodded. "I won't be crossing the border. I'm waiting for someone who has received political asylum." She gave them Isaac's name. "I have some documents." She held out the envelope to them. The tall guard looked at the contents briefly and asked, "When's he coming?"

"I don't know."

"You'll have to wait over there." The tall man pointed to a patch of open ground near where the man was washing the truck. Bastards. There was shade elsewhere but not a scrap of shade where he'd indicated. A pickup traveling fast from the South African side approached the gate. It stopped, and the shorter guard left the shade of the building to talk to the driver. There was a brief conversation, and the gate lifted. Alice went to move her truck, facing it toward the South African gate. It was too hot in the cab of the truck, even with both doors open. She got out, and a tiny, almost imperceptible breeze stirred her blue dress as she stood. A dove sat on the roof of the fortresslike building where the guards stood. Alice loved the song of nearly every bird in the world, including the sarcastic go-away bird. But not this dove. From the moment she'd first heard it, she'd found its call depressing and oddly claustrophobic. Hearing it was like being on a long bus ride, sitting next to someone who complained incessantly. She thought, I can ignore it, just pay no attention. But before long, she wanted to hurl stones at it. *Shut up! Shut up!* It went on and on.

She'd told Will and Greta where she was going and asked if they'd pick up the children if she wasn't back by three. Will had offered to drive down with her, but she said she thought it best to go on her own, there was no telling whether Isaac would even make it. Her stomach turned over. She felt the evil smell from here, through those gates, felt it in the starched complacence of the guard's khaki uniforms, in the short-cropped hair, in the pathetic eagerness of the black man washing the car in the sun. She took a swig of water from a gallon jug she'd brought with her.

A large truck roared up to the gate from the Botswana side, sounding like a bull in rut, something wrong with its gear-shifting mechanism. She began to count vehicles. Four from the South African side. Seven from the Botswana side, six more from South Africa, three more from Botswana.

Isaac heard the key in the metal door and the creak of the hinge. Light poured in, and his hand went over his eyes. It was a different guard. Never before had he seen this person. He had a neck as big as a bull's, bulging out of his collar.

"Get up," the man said.

Isaac got slowly to his feet.

"*Fok, kaffir,* you stink."

He could no longer smell himself.

The guard attached shackles to his ankles. As though he could run.

"Get going."

He clambered to his feet and shuffled out the door. He was too numb to feel the sun on his face. It was the first time he'd been outdoors since they'd brought him in; he could now see that his cell was part of a long tunnel of cells that stretched along a desolate scrape of ground.

"Where am I going?"

In Afrikaans, "You'll find out soon enough."

"Please tell me where you're taking me."

"*Hou jou bek.*" Shut your mouth

He felt a stick prod him from behind. He slowed his steps. He would, damn it all, die in dignity, not prodded like a fucking ox. One of his knees no longer bent. He rounded the corner and limped along a path leading to a road. A car waited there, its motor idling. He imagined they would take him to police headquarters where they'd push him out a high window and call it suicide. He thought of his mother. It grieved him terribly to think of her. He stumbled, felt the stick in his back.

The bitter heart eats its owner, she'd told him. To be bitter, he knew now, one must feel something personal in the hatred that comes at you. He didn't feel anything like that. The ugliness around him flailed like a goat drowning in a flooded river. If a leg of that goat happened to strike you, it has just struck, that's all. The Earth had a habit of begetting monsters, hatched from ignorance and greed. They had schooled him in hatred these months, and it now lived in him, like a fact you can't forget. Perhaps it was as well for him to die. The world did not need more hate. He thought of Boitumelo—her beauty, her goodness, her skin so perfect you could lap it like milk. Tears came to his eyes, the first he'd felt in weeks.

"Get in," the guard told him.

His legs wanted to run, but they had no running in them. He climbed into the back of the car. There was a man behind the steering wheel. The first guard opened the front door on the passenger's side and sat down as heavily as a sack of mealie meal. The car started. He felt his bowels loosen, prayed not to shit his pants. "Where are you taking me?"

"Keep quiet, *jou lae donner.*" Dirty bastard.

"*Fok,*" the driver said, "it'll be past nightfall before we're back."

The guard grunted. Instead of winding through city streets toward police headquarters, the car headed out of town. Soon they were on open roads. Isaac saw signs to Krugersdorp. "Let me out," he said. "I need to shit."

"You'll shit when we say shit," said the driver.

The sun was so bright his eyes watered. He felt a numbness in his soul. He remembered in school his teacher telling him about Socrates drinking the cup of poison hemlock. At first the poison went to his ankles, then his calves. As the numbness reached his waist, Socrates said to his friend, "We owe a cock to Asclepius. Don't forget to pay it." That was a true man, to remember even as he was dying what was owed.

Isaac's body heaved. "I'll have to shit in the car if you don't stop." He no longer cared. He'd shit in their damned car. The two men spoke to each other. The driver slammed on the brakes. "Get out," he said.

Isaac limped out of the car, hurried behind a low shrub, and let fly all the noxious poison in him. He was disgusted to the marrow of his bones. He didn't care how they killed him. He would never eat another morsel of food from the hands of men like these. He pulled up his trousers and got back into the car. His hatred was pure, flowing through him cleanly.

They passed through the outskirts of Krugersdorp. On the other side of the city, he shaded his eyes and saw a small sign to Olifants Nek and behind it, small *rondavel*s like his grandmother's. A rooster, three hens, children crouched in the dust. He thought of his younger brothers and sister. The eagerness in Moses's eyes, his small body in sleep.

He nodded into a stupor and woke as the car was pulling to a stop. Terror flooded his legs and arms. Halfway inside a dream, he suddenly pictured a snub-nosed revolver, arms dragging him out to a desolate spot filled with low *mopane* scrub and the droppings of wild goats, the last sweet, pure sound of a bush shrike before he was reduced to nothing. But the car had stopped at a shack for food. He could smell the fat popping out of the *boerewors,* the rancid smell of oil. His guts churned. He was starving, and he would eat nothing at the hands of these men. Not that he'd be offered anything. The fat-necked guard ate two sausage sandwiches, stuffing them into his mouth. They swilled a beer each, the fat man farted, and they got back into the car.

"Where are you taking me?" Isaac asked.

"We told you, shut your trap." The driver slowed down and speeded up again. For a few heady moments, he thought they might dump him out on the side of the road. But why would they go to all the trouble of driving so far? They skirted Rustenberg, Swartruggens, Groot Marico. The rains had greened the landscape. He remembered once feeling gladness at this sight, but that old feeling was frozen inside him, like a postcard sent long ago, faded beyond recognition.

She was terrified for him. Say he made it out alive. How would they have broken him? *Coo, coo, ca-koo, cu-coo*, went the dove. *Coo, coo, ca-koo, cu-coo*.

Last night her mother had called and asked Alice where she saw herself next year. Alice had snapped back, "You sound like a job interviewer, Mom. I don't know. I don't know about next week." Her mother had gone quiet. Alice imagined her standing in the hallway, gripping the phone in her left hand, a shaft of light from the window halfway up the stairs striking her hair. She pictured the slight stoop of her shoulders, her vulnerability and love.

I'm sorry, she wanted to tell her now. She'd been hunting for the electric bill just before the phone rang. She'd opened a dresser drawer, thinking she might have stuck it in there for safekeeping, and found the Bushman piano Ian had given her. She'd picked it up, plucked a few tinny notes, and found herself kneeling on the floor, her knees buckled under her.

Coo, coo, ca-koo, cu-coo. She counted forty iterations before it stopped. She stared down the road on the South African side. The heat shimmered on its surface. Any car coming that way would look as though it were swimming toward the border. The sun was directly overhead now. She searched the ground for a stone, picked it up, and weighted down one end of a towel on the roof of the truck and draped it over the open doorway to create shade. Her eyes burned and her thoughts melted and ran here and there.

Her heart went out to Isaac's mother. One by one, she'd lost her children. Isaac, Nthusi, Moses, Lulu. If they ever let him out of prison, he'd never again be allowed back over the border to visit her. And she'd never legally make it to Botswana.

The two men in the front of the vehicle were holding a conversation in Afrikaans that Isaac couldn't understand. He gathered that it had to do with him, but he felt nothing but a vast indifference. "This side of Zeerust," the one with the thick neck said.

He had seen a signpost not far back: 27 kilometers to Zeerust. Whatever was going to happen to him would happen within twenty-seven kilometers. Something fluttered inside him, a bird trying to rise, and sank back down. About fifteen kilometers out of Zeerust, the driver said, "This will do." The car turned off the main road, took another side road, until they were alone on a stretch of track so sparsely traveled as to hardly be a track. Low, rounded hills overlapped at a distance. A small herd of cattle and goats grazed in the middle distance.

"Get out," said the driver.

The large-necked man held a gun.

Isaac tried to take a deep breath to steady himself, but his broken ribs stopped him. "Please," he said, "I need to take another shit."

They seemed to consider this for a moment, and the driver said, "Go on then," not unkindly. And then, "Don't try anything."

He staggered behind a thorn bush, his stomach roiling. He thought of running, but it was useless. They'd overtake him in two strides. He squatted and let loose, too scared to be disgusted. He checked the ground for a rock, anything that might serve as a weapon, and found nothing.

He stood.

"Get over here," the driver said. The thick-necked man tied his hands behind his back and put a canvas bag over his head. It smelled of dust and the unpleasant sweetness of nitrogen fertilizer. They led him a short way from the road and told him to kneel. He felt the muzzle of the gun pressed to the side of his head and shut his eyes under the darkness of the bag.

He stopped breathing and waited.

Instead of an explosion, he heard laughter. They left him kneeling while they laughed and laughed. He heard them slapping their thighs, imagined them elbowing each other, their necks swollen with laughter. The driver ripped off the bag and untied his hands. *Hahahaha*, guffawed the large-necked man. The man couldn't get hold of himself. He took a piss behind a shrub and came back, still laughing.

"Let's get moving," said the driver, finished with the joke.

Isaac climbed back into the car. The fat-necked man chuckled and muttered to himself: ". . . like a scared bloody rock rabbit."

Dully, he understood that what they'd done was as cruel as anything a man can do to another man, but he knew it only through a great numbness, as though his rage was unhinged from his heart, perched on a hillside. He was neither relieved to be alive nor wishing to be dead. An Earth he had once loved floated before him like an inert picture of an Earth. He looked out the window and saw nothing.

He closed his eyes as the car moved. The road became more rutted and bumpy. He heard traffic passing, large trucks and a few cars, but he didn't open his eyes until the car slowed. Instinctively, he hunkered down low in the seat. In front of them was a large metal gate, and on either side of it, barbed wire stretching as far as the eye could see. Inside, an ugly concrete building stood like a stockade on a narrow stretch of ground. Beyond it lay another gate and more barbed wire. He'd not heard of a prison north of Zeerust. Something woke in him. He'd fight with everything he had before they got him in there, die before they put him in another rathole.

"End of the road," said the driver, opening the rear door.

"I'm not going in there."

"Where do you think you're going then?"

"Kill me first."

A man in uniform came to the window and looked in on Isaac. He seemed shocked at what he saw. A conversation took place between him and the driver. A woman was standing beyond the stockade-type building, at least he thought it was a woman. Her dress was blue. It moved slightly in the breeze.

53

She'd seen the car from a long way down the road. Something about it made her pay attention. It was black, low slung. It pulled up to the gate, and the shorter of the two border guards let it through.

Two white men got out wearing uniforms. The border guard bent down and looked into the backseat of the car. Someone was back there, but the sun glared through the windshield and she couldn't make out a face. One of the two men in uniform, the thicker one, passed some papers to the shorter guard. The border guard studied them. He passed the papers to the other guard, who looked them over. The shorter guard turned in Alice's direction. She might have been a tree, or a goat, by the way he gestured toward her.

She froze, and her stomach flipped over. She walked toward them. One of the men in uniform opened the backdoor of the black car. A figure got out, a black man. He stood, swaying slightly. She came closer. It wasn't Isaac's face or his body she recognized, both altered beyond recognition, but some shred of dignity.

"My god," she whispered, "what have they done to you?"

A light entered his eyes briefly and went out. She couldn't tell if he knew who she was. She wanted to take his hand, but she thought there must be a rule against it.

"Is this the man?" said the taller of the two border guards. His face said, *How could anyone want him?*

"Yes. Isaac Muthethe."

"He's free to go," said the border guard.

"Now?" she asked.

"Take him," the thick-necked one from the black car said. "That's what he said."

Leering at her, his companion asked, "So where's your husband?"

She ignored him. "Isaac, my truck is over there." She turned away, and Isaac stumbled after her, barely able to walk. She felt the back of her neck crawl, thinking of their eyes watching. She opened the passenger's side for Isaac, and he ducked his head. She saw his body shake with the effort of getting in. Her throat constricted, her vision swam. She got into the driver's side and drove toward the other gate. The truck filled with an unspeakable smell.

"*Dumela, rra,*" she said, greeting the guard on the Botswana side for the second time that day. She held out the papers for him to check once more. He peered in at Isaac and flinched. "*Go siame, mma,*" he said, waving her through.

The gate lifted, and they headed up the dusty road toward Lobatse. Out of the corner of her eye, she saw Isaac sitting stiffly, one hand clasped over the other. His hands were thin, so thin they seemed hollowed out, his thumbs swollen and dark purple.

"*A o batla metsi?*" she asked, pointing to the jug of water.

"*Ee, mma,*" he said, but he didn't reach for it, as though they'd stripped him of volition. She drove north until she spotted a small turnoff. "Please," she said, reaching for the water and handing it to him.

He uncapped the jug and poured water from above so his lips never touched the mouth of the container. He drank deeply, with his eyes closed. He looked shattered, the bones of his face skeletal. She handed him half a cheese sandwich and took the other half. The cheese had melted in the heat and lay limply inside the bread. He took the sandwich carefully, ate a bite slowly and ate the rest quickly.

"White Dog is dead, yes?" he said, his words barely audible.

"No, she's alive. She waited for you. Also, Moses and Lulu are with me now."

"I don't understand."

"Your brother and sister. You sent a letter to your mother, do you remember?"

"They've come?"

"Your mother didn't know you'd been deported. I met them at the train station. They sleep in the room where you were sleeping."

"In Naledi?"

"No, no. At my house."

"At your house," he repeated.

"They are going to school now." It was like talking to a thick curtain with a man behind it. "Lulu and Moses came to Gaborone by train. Hendrik Pretorius arranged it."

"Hendrik Pretorius?"

"He is the one who got you released from prison."

"Are we going to see him now?"

"We're going to Gaborone. You're back in Botswana now."

"And my mother? Is she alive?"

"Yes."

"And my father?"

"I don't know."

"And Nthusi?"

She stopped. "Your brother?"

"Yes."

"I heard from Hendrik that your brother died in the mines. There was a collapse. It happened several months ago. I'm very sorry."

She glanced at him. He'd closed his eyes. In his face, it seemed she could map the world's history of sorrow. He coughed again, a sound that seemed to pull up everything in him.

"Isaac," she said, "I'm going to be taking you to the hospital."

"Yes," he said. She'd expected an argument. They drove a short distance, and he said, "Please, *mma,* I need to get out."

She found a place to stop, and he opened the door. "Do you need help?" He didn't answer, and she averted her eyes while he staggered behind a bush.

When he returned, he said, "I'm sorry, *mma.* I've caused so much trouble." She waved his words away and started up the truck. "While you were away," he said, "I made a very bad mistake." It seemed to hurt him to speak.

"Don't worry, you can tell me later."

"I need to tell you now. I hid the money under a stone for my family back home. I was staying in the house with my friend and his wife and baby and some others. My friend, Amen, and his comrades were with the ANC. I wasn't working for the ANC, only staying there. I came to Botswana wanting peace. Perhaps this was selfish of me, but I only wanted peace." A large truck passed them going in the same direction, kicking up a storm of dust. She slowed, straining to see through the windshield.

"They attacked Amen's house. His wife died. The baby lived. I don't know whether Amen is alive or dead. I wanted the money under the stone to send back home, the money you gave me together with what I had saved. I thought they would bulldoze the house. I went like a thief while the guard was sleeping. He woke and took me to the police. The chief of police said I was a double agent and deported me.

"Another thing I must tell you," he said. "Amen sold your bicycle without my permission. He needed the money. I was very angry, but the bicycle is gone. When I'm able to work again, I'll pay you back a little bit this month, a little bit next month, until I have paid for it all."

"Please, don't worry. All you need to think about is getting back on your feet. No one can harm you now. Do you understand? They've given you political asylum here. You're a legal resident."

"*Ee, mma.*" He coughed again, a terrible sound, and grew quiet. She drove more slowly than usual, as though he could break if she hit too many potholes. She gripped the steering wheel as another dust storm arose from a passing vehicle. She glanced up at the hot blue sky and hoped the men who'd done this would suffer the flames of hell for all eternity.

54

The Sister who'd months ago refused Isaac entrance was the first person to meet them at the front doors of Princess Marina Hospital. Her mouth pursed when she saw him, and her nose twitched with distaste. Alice explained that Isaac had been in a South African prison and needed immediate care. The Sister looked him up and down quickly and said, "All right then, come."

Alice started to follow them, but the nurse turned to her and said, "You must go now, madam. You will return tomorrow."

"I won't get in the way, I promise."

"Madam, it is not possible."

Alice touched Isaac's hand and murmured something he couldn't understand. It startled him. It was the first kind touch he'd felt in longer than he could remember. He watched her turn and leave, then followed the Sister down the hallway. Halfway to the ward, he collapsed. He couldn't recall how he'd ended up on the floor, only that things had gone dark.

The Sister put him in an isolation room with green walls and a small, high window. Another Sister came and offered him water. He drank a little and fell back onto the pillow. One moment he shivered, and the next moment he was on fire. "Forty point two degrees Celsius," he heard the nurse say.

"Typhoid," he thought dully. Every joint in his body ached. His head was a large bass drum that some maniac was pounding. The first Sister returned. He began to shake uncontrollably. Her pale lips reminded him of Number Four.

"Have you been in a place where hygiene might have been compromised?" she asked.

He laughed bleakly. "An . . . an understatement."

"We will begin treating you with antibiotics, and then see what else."

"An invasion of the mesenteric lymph nodes. Chloromycetin?"

She covered her surprise. "Yes, that's the antibiotic of choice. Who are you?"

"An undesirable." He didn't want to give her any information.

She put a cold hand on his forehead. The Hand of Death.

"Ah!" He pulled away.

"Tomorrow we will move you to the ward. Tonight you will stay here. You must have a bath. You're filthy." She went away. When the other Sister returned, she urged him to drink more water. She bathed his head and neck and arms in cool water and made him swallow the first dose of the antibiotic. He recognized the beginnings of a feverish terror he'd had several times as a child. His head seemed to grow large and hard, and the room slowly revolved. He fought the horror. And then it erupted like lava flowing down a hillside, fiery, engulfing. He tried to get out.

The lights of the room flickered and went dark. When the generator kicked in, the light was duller. He had no idea whether it was day or night, or what country he was in.

Across town, the lights gave notice before they finally went out. Moses and Lulu were in the bathtub. The last of the bird songs were gone from the air. Lulu had wet a washcloth and laid it over her tummy. Moses pushed a plastic truck up the sides of the tub and down, *brmm brmmming* underwater and then up and out again. The lights flicked off, then on for thirty seconds, then off for good.

The sky had the smallest remnants of light in it, enough for Alice to find her way to the kitchen, where she felt with her hands across the big wooden table to the kerosene lamp. The glass sides of the lamp were slick with spilled kerosene, and the fragile shade clattered lightly against its restraining metal cup as she pulled it toward her. The matchbox should have been next to the lamp, but it wasn't. She felt her way into the living room, pawed along the mantel, and found the box. All was quiet in the bathroom. A small stab of worry crossed her mind, and then she heard a splash. She made her way back toward the lamp, and at the kitchen threshold, slid the matchbox open and took out a match. She heard laughter, the darkness full of children.

Lulu laughed again. Her voice was strange for a child's. Deep, gravelly, like sand thrown against a windowpane. Alice struck the match, and the kitchen sprang to life. She lifted the lamp chimney, lit the wick, and adjusted the flame, dark at its center, bright at the edges.

"I'm coming," she called to the children, replacing the chimney. Her knee knocked against the wall as she turned, and her mind bumped against Isaac. The Sister in charge had seemed neither kind nor unkind. Full of business she was, with her capable hands and long, stern backbone. Healing was her job, her face said, like any other. But it was not like any other job. It dealt with the mysteries of the human soul. Isaac could come back to the world, or he might not, and who on Earth knew why one person returned and another didn't?

She moved toward the bathroom with the lamp, momentarily blinded by the flame. At the doorway, she paused. Lulu was sprawled back against the tub and Moses sat between her legs leaning into her, the back of his head on her chest; his little willy floated placidly on the surface of the water. She wanted to tell them that Isaac was in the hospital, very near, but it felt too cruel. They wouldn't be allowed to see him. She set the lamp on a shelf above the sink and grabbed a towel. "Come," she said, and Moses scrambled up and let himself be wrapped up and dried. Then Lulu. Alice helped them brush their teeth and find their nighttime T-shirts. They climbed into bed together, and she sat next to them.

"Story," said Moses.

She sat on the bed, where she usually read to them, but she didn't pick up a book. "Isaac is in Botswana," she said, feeling suddenly that she couldn't keep this from them after all. "Isaac is in Gaborone. He's very sick. *O a lwala thata*. You can see him when he's better." The lamp flickered.

"Where is Isaac?" asked Moses in English.

"He's in the hospital," she said. "*Sepatela. O ile ngakeng*. He had to see the doctor. *O a lwala*. He is not well. The nurses are helping him get better. *Baamusi*. You understand?"

She felt something in her hair, a hand stroking from the top of her head down her neck. And then there were two hands stroking. First one, then the other. She held one small wrist lightly, followed the arm up to Lulu's shoulder and began to cry. "Isaac is in Botswana, my darlings."

"See him?" asked Moses.

Alice scrubbed away the tears with the back of her hand. "Not now. Isaac, *o a lwala*. Itumeleng will explain more tomorrow. Lie down now and go to sleep." Their eyes were wide. She tucked a sheet around them and kissed them both. "*Robala sentle,* Moses." Sleep well. "*Robala sentle,* Lulu."

She walked back to the kitchen with the lamp, set it on the table, and blew out the flame. As she headed outdoors, her hair still felt the imprint of Lulu's hands. The door was open, no boundary between dark and dark. White Dog was there, sitting on the threshold. "You haven't had dinner, have you?" She stumbled around in the dark and brought out dog food. White Dog's tail wagged. "Isaac is back." Was it her imagination, or did the tail stop a moment, her stance become more alert? Alice set the dog food down, and White Dog's head bowed to her dish, her tail still wagging. She heard Isaac's voice telling her never to walk in the garden at night, and she moved only a few steps away from the house, enough to see the Southern Cross.

In her head, she spoke to her mother across continents. If you could see these children, she told her, you'd understand. I've told you nothing about Isaac. I didn't want to worry you. But there's Isaac too, who may come back and may not come back to the world.

And there's Ian who will never return, but this is where I can find him. He would never come to Cincinnati. It's not his sort of place. You would say the dead can find you anywhere, but it's not true. She felt his presence there in the dark, but tonight it seemed dimmer, as though he were slipping away. There was a shattering inside her like the chimney of a lantern, the flame freed, and then darkness.

55

A day later, lying in bed next to a whitewashed wall, he couldn't remember the details of when he'd come here. He recalled Alice's blue dress blowing in the wind at the border, but nothing after that. The wall near his bed had a crack that ran from the top of the window to the ceiling. Halfway up the crack, a mosquito was squashed, desiccated, stuck to the wall. His mind went back to the first day he'd worked for her. He'd dug a square garden. Almost angrily, she'd asked him why he'd made it square. She'd intimidated him. Now he saw who she really was.

X-rays revealed a shattered left kneecap, broken nose, seven broken ribs, and the remnants of a concussion. He needed no one to tell him he had typhoid or that his thumbs were broken. His hunch about TB was confirmed. The wonder was that he'd survived, but he felt no joy at the prospect of life continuing. His heart was filled with emptiness.

Unable to sit in a bath, he was taken into a shower by the only male nurse on the staff. The nurse, Wes, built low and squat, was from the United States. "God, man, you stink," were his first words. He wheeled Isaac down the hall in a wheelchair, stopped near the shower, and said, "I've got to get in there with you."

"You don't want to do that," said Isaac.

"You'll fall down and hit your head, and then I'll be in trouble." He undressed him, and Isaac could see him trying not to gag. He turned on the shower and helped Isaac step in, gripping his shoulder. He took off his own shoes and followed him into the stall.

"You didn't take off your clothes," said Isaac.

"I need something between you and me. You've got scabies. Move over. When was the last time you bathed?"

"Before I was deported. Early May. What is it now?"

"Christ, man. August. Over three months."

"It feels longer." Isaac thought of a time when he'd been stripped, struck with a rubber hose, nearly drowned, and left all night on a concrete floor. "I don't count that as bathing, though."

"What don't you count?"

He realized he'd been talking to himself. "No matter." The water fell hard onto his shaved head, onto his back and the bandage covering a wound on his shoulder, stinging as it fell. He could smell his own rank odor rising. The water running off him was gray, the color of long-dead meat. Wes shampooed his naked head, and Isaac made his mind go numb as the soap entered the welts.

"Where have you come from?"

"A prison in Jo'burg."

Wes said nothing, just ran his hand over Isaac's neck, his one shoulder without the wound, his arms, his back, his chest, his privates, while he held him upright with the other hand. He moved the soap over his thighs, over the knee without the brace, down his calves, his feet. When he'd finished, he started at the top again.

"Again?"

"You're still filthy."

Halfway through, Isaac told him he had to go to the toilet.

"Can't it wait?"

"Sorry. No."

They dripped across the floor. His body revolted him. It felt as though he'd never be rid of the beastliness inside him. His mind disgusted him more. All the places he'd gone for comfort within himself were spoiled and rotten.

As he wobbled back to the shower, Wes asked, "What the hell did they feed you?"

"Soup. Porridge." He laughed and then wondered what the laughter was for. Floating maggots. It wasn't all that funny.

Wes gripped his shoulder tighter. "I've got you," he said. "Go ahead. Step in." He finished washing him, toweled him off, and gave him a clean hospital gown. Isaac's legs barely carried him back to bed, where Wes dressed his wounds. "Want anything else?" he heard through layers of oblivion. He slept seventeen hours, through dinner and breakfast and a visit from Alice, who sat beside him for half an hour, watching him sleep, and then left quietly.

They transferred him to a TB ward with seven other men, all of them old. The man in the bed beside him looked like someone he'd once known. The man slept all day, and when he woke, he coughed into a towel spotted with blood.

At night, Isaac could just see stars out a window. In a book Hendrik Pretorius had once given him, he'd read that our bodies are made of dust and matter from stars. Where had he gone, the part of him that was no longer here? The numbness inside, he thought, was something like what happens to a rat after a dog catches it. At first, the animal screams in pain. Then something causes its body to go numb, and as it goes from life to death, it feels little pain. The rat-numbness started the day they broke his nose and dislocated his shoulder. After the hot pain came nothing, a sense of watching himself from a distance. They dragged him back to his cell, and he lay there. When he came to, he realized a guard was watching him through the slit. He crawled into a corner. The eye disappeared.

He'd kept passing out from the pain in the shoulder. He tried to clear his head enough to remember the directions for how to relocate an anterior dislocation: Keep the upper arm perpendicular to the ground, elbow bent at a ninety-degree angle. Rotate the arm inward toward the chest. Make a fist with the hand on the injured side and slowly rotate the arm and shoulder outward. He pushed outward with the good arm as tears rolled down his cheeks. After several tries he heard a pop, and leaned into the wall.

When he came to again, he thought of his mother, how she'd once taken him to an open-air tent where a pastor was speaking. The man said, "Be grateful. There is not one moment in life when it is not possible to be grateful." He was not grateful. He wished to die. He'd watched open heart surgery, had been astonished at how much abuse a human body can bear and still go on living. The only thing he felt through the curtain of pain was fear that his body would hang on.

And now, was he grateful? He was swept with numbness.

On the second day in the hospital, the old man next to him muttered under his breath, "*Nosa tshingwana yotlhe.*" Water the whole garden. "*Dilo tse di swabile.*" These things are dried up.

It came to him then. "*Monna mogolo,*" he said. "I know you."

The man turned his head and squinted at him. "I don't know you."

"You gave me seeds. Hot pepper seeds. I met you in the garden. I dug a big hole like yours. I hit the water main."

The old man's face crinkled into a smile. "*Ke gakologelwa,*" he whispered. I remember. And then he laughed, setting off a chain of coughing. Isaac reached for the towel between their two beds, and handed it to him. The man gathered his breath and closed his eyes. His face looked as though he'd seen two hundred dry seasons. He breathed hard for a few minutes, then turned to Isaac. "Why are you here?"

"I was in prison in South Africa."

"You lived."

I am dead, Isaac thought. As empty as that sack they put over my head. He felt the old man looking at him.

"Are you sleeping at night?" Isaac asked him.

"*Dikgopo tsa me.*" My ribs.

"Do you have night sweats?"

"*Ee, rra.*" He caught his breath. "But no matter. Soon it will be finished."

"You have somebody visiting you?"

"*Nnyaa, rra.* There is no one left."

She brought soup with her, and a book she thought he might like, Peter Matthiessen's *The Tree Where Man Was Born.* The Sister met her at the door. "You are not allowed in the TB ward," she said.

"Can Mr. Muthethe come out?"

"You must wait two weeks after treatment begins."

"If I wear a face mask?"

"No exceptions."

"I see." She shifted to her other foot. "But I've already visited him."

"On the TB ward?"

She realized she shouldn't have spoken. "The room where he was in isolation."

"You should not have been allowed."

"So the answer is no?"

"The answer is no. I will see that these things are taken to him."

A young nurse in training brought him a parcel containing a tin of beef and tomato soup. And a large book. He was not hungry for anything but the book. He propped it on his belly and turned to the first page. There was a picture of a baobab tree, its trunk dark against golden grass standing as though nothing could ever move it. And on the second and third pages, a large blue mountain with two tops. The left side and the right side were like two brothers, rising equally, and the tops so high they turned to cloud. On the next page was a cheetah sitting on its haunches, looking to one side. Its coat was golden white, covered with dark spots. Running from its eye to its mouth was a dark line, like a trail of tears. He turned to the next page, and then he returned to the cheetah's face. He studied its neck fur sticking up as though a breeze ruffled it, the long tufts in its ears.

On the page following, he found an old Dinka song from the South Sudan.

In the time when Dendid created all things,
He created the sun,
And the sun is born, and dies, and comes again.
He created the moon,
And the moon is born, and dies, and comes again;
He created the stars,
And the stars are born, and die, and come again;
He created man,
And man is born, and dies, and does not come again.

They had put his thumbs in casts, and they stuck up as he held the book. He read the words again. He heard the old gardener straining next to him, his breath creaking in and out, his eyes closed, as though his lungs were saying, *and does not come again, and does not come again.* He would be fighting for air until his heart stopped beating, and then he would be finished with this world.

Wes came to his bedside and told Isaac that he must walk. He got him up and grasped him firmly by the elbow. Isaac shuffled like an old man. When they reached the door, the sun was so bright, he needed to close his eyes until they were nothing more than slits. The pain in his knee made his mind go numb. They walked out onto the grounds, where the dirt had been swept clean with stick brooms. He thought of the people inside: the old man laboring for breath, women laboring for babies. Wes told him he must come out every day. His mind said, Why? Why bother? A shadow passed overhead, and Isaac looked into the sky. Thousands of quelea birds were migrating, in huge flocks. They landed here and there with their red bills, red feet, dun-colored bodies, black masks, and flew on, black against the sky, surging and turning like paper chains.

56

In the middle of the night, Alice woke to Lulu crying herself out of a bad dream. Alice picked her up and held her in her arms and sat on the bed next to Moses, who was curled into a small ball. Lulu's body was warm from sleep, and her cheeks where she'd been crying, left a wetness at Alice's breast. If this had been her own child, she would have asked what had frightened her. But all she could offer was her own warm body. "*Ke batla* Isaac," Lulu said over and over. I want Isaac. Where is he? "*O kae?*"

Alice rocked her and crooned, "I know, I know. I'm sorry. He's coming soon." She had no words to tell the children why Isaac was close but they couldn't see him. She'd asked Itumeleng to explain, but they still didn't understand. Sitting on the edge of the bed with this sobbing child, she decided that she must ask their teacher to talk to them. Lulu was as sensitive as a seismograph to tremors. Life would not be easy for her. She couldn't escape anything through oblivion, unlike Moses, whose life force could blast through rock. In time, Lulu's breath evened out, and her body relaxed. Alice laid her gently down beside Moses and tucked the sheet around them both.

She was wide awake now. Someday she'd get to the Tsodilo Hills, where she and Ian had planned to go. If anyplace had been home for him, it was the hill where the First Spirit had left the imprint of his knees. Where was home for her? She didn't know. And she realized in the asking that she wanted a home as much as she'd ever wanted anything. She had heard it said, *We live by hope, but a reed never becomes a mosetlha tree by dreaming.* You make what you want, not dream it. A home with Ian would have been a restless, nomadic place, like the tents the Bedouins carry on their backs. He'd said it to her more than once. "I'm no good for you, love."

"Who are you to say that?" she'd shot back. He was a wild creature in the shape of a man. She'd loved this wildness in him. Somehow they would have made a life together.

Lulu and Moses were now the center of a small, uncertain thing. She guessed she could call it a home: a roof without walls, a hearth with two glowing coals. Not fragile exactly, but unsteady on its feet. She heard a clattering in the kitchen and got up. Moses was standing in a puddle of water in the middle of the floor in his T-shirt holding the aluminum kettle, dented where he'd dropped it.

"*Ke tsoga makuku*." I wake up very early. "Tea?" he asked brightly, practicing his English.

"*Ee, ke batla,*" she said, laughing. "But the sun isn't shining yet."

"No problem. The sun she comes."

57

All that day and into the night, the old gardener strained for breath. His extremities were cold to the touch. The light faded from the sky, and Isaac sat next to him on the bed. "I'm here, old man," he whispered in Setswana.

"*O mang?*" the old man whispered. Who are you? His hands reached toward the ceiling, opening and shutting, their veins large and swollen. He muttered incomprehensible things. His breathing became noisy. Isaac turned the man's head to one side to keep him from choking.

He remembered the day they'd met, the pride the old man took in the sunken garden. It was his garden, although that man with the red face who'd yelled at Isaac would have said he owned everything and the old man nothing. Soon this old man would be gone: bones and skin and all that was inside his head: the names of things, the woman he'd once loved, the secrets of his heart, the disappointments and bitterness, the sweetness of his garden.

He thought of his own father, alive or not alive, and his mother's anger. She would believe she'd been betrayed to her dying day. When he was better, when they let him out of here, he would try to call her. It made him dizzy to think of hearing her voice again.

Hours passed. The old man's hand twitched in his, and his breathing stopped a moment, then started again. It was quiet now on the ward. All the men around him were sleeping, and he imagined the nurses were asleep too, in their chairs. A dull light reflected off the linoleum in the hall. All he could see was the old man's profile, and his chest trying to rise and fall.

He thought of Kopano, shoved under the train. And the man in the cell next to his, who'd never again see his children. And the young man who'd cried out for his mother, pleaded to God. After their voices had gone still, Isaac had not grieved for them. There was no grieving in that place. For there to be grief, there must be love, but hate had consumed it all.

The old man tried to sit up. He got his elbows halfway under him and collapsed. Isaac put his arm under his shoulders and lifted him until he was half sitting. He could not hold him because of the weakness in his arms. He laid him gently down and reached for the pillow off his bed, lifted the man again, and laid him down on the two pillows. The old man began to breathe rapidly through his mouth. His breath stopped abruptly, and then he began again. His lips were becoming blue, and his eyes were closed. Isaac laid his hand lightly on the man's chest.

Several times more his breath started up rapidly, then stopped. Each pause lasted longer, and each time it stopped, Isaac thought he was gone. He waited and held his own breath. And then the old man breathed no more.

Isaac closed his mouth for him. He felt he had been witness to something beyond reckoning, that he was not worthy of what he'd seen. He did not know how to pray for the dead, but he whispered, "Modimo, I beg you to have mercy on this soul, passing from Earth to the great beyond. Forgive him, and let him find perfect love and rest in peace." The old man's jaw dropped open again. Isaac closed it gently. He was exhausted and returned to his own bed. He thought of calling a nurse but the old man's soul could take its leave more peacefully if his body was not disturbed until morning. Lying beside him with his eyes open, he realized he had never learned the old man's name. To him, he would always be simply the old man.

The next morning, on the slope of the old man's sunken garden, a flower bloomed, opening into five white petals and three white curling stamens. The old man had planted the flower, *wahlenbergia caledonica*, from seed. He'd been waiting to see the white petals unfold, tinted, as he knew they'd be, with the lightest shade of purple. One by one, the birds in the cages began to sing. First a pair of yellow canaries, then a lovebird, the glossy starlings and bulbuls, then the tiny zebra finches with their orange beaks and feet. A light dew lifted from a blue spur-flower and a Chinese ground orchid, from the gray green leaves of a mound of widow's tears, and from a clump of blue-eyed grass. The red-faced man who'd shouted at Isaac stood in the doorway of his house, listening.

58

Two weeks after starting his medication for tuberculosis and typhoid, they moved Isaac out of the TB ward into a general medical ward. He was still very weak and had little appetite. Alice brought him a drawing from Lulu and another from Moses. Lulu's was of their school and their teacher, with White Dog sitting outside under a tree. Moses had drawn Alice's house, the outside on one half of the page, their bed with the two of them in it on the other half.

Alice sat on Isaac's bed. There was no other place to sit. Her hair, which was usually gathered into a messy knot at the nape of her neck, was down around her face. Her eyes were very blue and she looked at him intently.

"How are you?" she asked. It overwhelmed him. He felt a ridiculous and dangerous urge to touch her hair where it had fallen around her chin, to push it back around her ear.

"I am going better," he said, as though he were a truck with an engine.

"Have they said when you can leave?"

"My lungs must be clear, and also I must be strong enough to walk around the building three times without stopping."

"And how many times can you walk now?"

His face clouded. "I am not in a hurry to go."

"Because you have nowhere to stay?"

"Yes, madam."

"You can stay with me. But don't call me madam."

He stopped. He could feel his ears ring, and then he said it. "I cannot live under the same roof as you, Alice." To call her by her name, he felt that the sky would tumble to Earth.

She didn't seem to notice. "Because you're African and I'm European? Because you're a man and I'm a woman?"

"Yes."

"Because people would talk?"

"That also."

"Do you care what people would say?"

He thought a moment. "No, I don't care what people think or what they say. I care about going to prison. I will never go back to prison. I would kill myself first. And I care about hurting you."

She glanced at his face and bowed her head. Out the window, the mourning doves on the roof called. "Do you think you'd go to prison for living in the same house? Even with Moses and Lulu there?"

"In my mind, I think no. In my heart, I think yes."

She saw how easy it was for her. She could say, *Don't be ridiculous, you know it's different here,* but she'd be playing with him, with a soul so wounded.

"How are Moses and Lulu?"

"They ask after you every day. Shall I bring them to visit?"

"Not here, no. I'll see them before long . . . And White Dog?"

"She's waiting for you."

"And you?" he asked.

Unaccountably, her eyes filled with tears. She waited a moment before she spoke. "A man I loved was killed while you were in prison. He was caught in a buffalo stampede up near Maun." It felt unseemly to cry in front of him after what he'd suffered. She covered her eyes and turned away. He sat quietly, and when she turned back, his eyes looked pained.

"I'm sorry," he said.

They were quiet together for a while.

Finally she said, "If you can't live under the same roof, you can build a *rondavel* for yourself in the garden."

"The land belongs to the government. It's not possible."

"Perhaps it is possible." The hospital gown hung from his thin frame.

"Would you like me to bring some clothes for you from home? I think there's a pair of pants there and a shirt."

"Yes."

"Have you thought about later when you're better, what you might want to do? Do you want to go back to school?"

He looked at her as though she were mad. "I will never be able to return there."

"I'm not talking about South Africa. You could get a scholarship to study somewhere else. Zambia. Europe. The United States. I can help you."

He didn't answer, and she saw that she should shut up. He was ashen-faced, the wound on his shoulder still suppurated. His dreams had vanished. He looked like a man waiting to die. She stood up. "I'll be back tomorrow," she said. She walked out the front door of the hospital, past a row of women in kerchiefs sitting on the low concrete wall, with their little metal bowls of food for their loved ones.

On her way home, she thought of Mogoditshane, a small village outside Gaborone. She'd only been there once or twice but she loved the shade trees and chickens scratching about, the *rondavels* with their tight thatching, the neat mud walls with decorative patterns of contrasting mud. She could have two *rondavels* built, one for her, and one for Isaac and the children. Or she could stay where she was, have a house built for them in Mogoditshane, and leave them to it. Or she could do her own washing and cleaning, find another job for Itumeleng, and give Isaac the servant's quarters. Whatever occurred to her, she bumped up against his haunted face, his eyes without a future. She had never seen a face like that.

She drove into the driveway and found the children playing in Ian's Land Rover, Lulu in the driver's seat, Itumeleng beside her, and Moses and Itumleleng's daughter in the backseat. It gave her a start to see all this life in that dead thing.

Alice asked Itumeleng if she would mind watching the children a little longer. "*Ee, mma,*" she said, but her face said, I'm tired, the day is over. *I'm sorry,* Alice mouthed as she turned around and drove back to the hospital.

She sat down on Isaac's bed and was quiet a moment before saying, "Help me understand what it's like for you now."

He shut his eyes and said, "It is impossible to understand."

"I might understand a little. I too have lost something."

He opened his eyes, studied her face a moment, and seemed to make a decision. "I never knew from moment to moment," he said quietly, "if they would come or when they would come. And when they came, I never knew what part of my body they would break, whether I would survive to see another day." His words grew more halting. "What they did was ... how can I say? Without purpose. At first I tried to discover what made them do this, what made them do that. If I was quiet, did that make things better or worse? What if I spoke? But never was there ... what is the word? Never was any one thing connected to another. One day they were using their fists and their boots. Another day they were drowning me. Another day, electric cattle prod on the tongue. I taught myself to stop trying to understand anything. I made my mind and body ..." He turned one hand palm upward and swept the other hand over it as though erasing it. "I became blank inside. I was an animal, nothing more."

She remembered the snake in the garden, the way it had tried to strike and strike, and in its dying had coiled.

"When they drove me toward the border, they pretended they were going to kill me. They had a gun. They tied my hands behind my back. They put a sack over my head. They took me out into the bush. And then they laughed."

She closed her eyes and shrank from the image of him standing there with a sack over his head. The laughter in his ears.

"After that, I didn't care. Shoot me. When I saw you I thought it was a dream. Even then I didn't know whether I cared to live. Now there is a blank space inside. I tell you truly. If I knew I would be like this forever, I would wish to die. When I was young, I was full of plans. Now, there is nothing." He stopped and put one hand over the other.

"Until my dying day," she said, "I will hate those people who did this to you." He sat very still and turned his head to the wall. "They took everything they could take from you," she went on, "and now you're empty. It was the only way you could survive. No one knows what part of you will come back. Maybe what was there is gone forever. Maybe it will return. Perhaps when you see the children, you will begin to know ..."

He closed his eyes at the mention of them.

"Whatever happens, you have a place to come to. I have a tent. If you don't feel comfortable sleeping inside the house, maybe you would feel all right sleeping in the tent in the garden. You can think about it."

She stood up. "Do you need anything?" He seemed to not want her to leave.

"No, nothing." He was quiet awhile, and then said, "I would like to stay in the tent, not in the house. I want to be near Moses and Lulu. When they tell me I am ready to leave here, I wish to walk to the Old Village, the same as I walked the first time. When I came here, I knew nothing and my feet showed me where to go. Again, perhaps they will show me."

She took his hand before she left. She had no more words, and then she was gone.

59

Out of scraps of two-by-fours and plywood, Will built a ten-by-ten-foot tent platform by the flat rock in the garden. With wild enthusiasm, Lulu and Moses and Will's youngest son helped him pound nails. Late in the afternoon the day before Isaac expected to be discharged, the five of them raised an old canvas tent that Alice had bought a year earlier at a government sale. It covered nearly the whole platform and smelled of kerosene lamps and night and the wax coating that would keep the rain out.

Will transported a frame and bed from town in his pickup, and the children tripped all over themselves carrying a corner of the mattress, flopping down on it inside the tent.

Itumeleng stood in the garden, shaking her head. "A tent is for the bush," she muttered. But in some sudden desire to have the garden restored by the time Isaac returned, she filled a bucket with water and flung it over the ravaged plants. The tomatoes were dead, the chili peppers had disappeared as though they'd never been, and the cabbages were husks. The only vegetable still alive was one Alice detested—the woody rape with its indigestible spines and indefatigable, bitter, twisted leaves.

Alice brought out sheets and a pillow and made the bed. The children went off with Will to return a power saw he'd borrowed to build the tent platform. The three of them sat in the open bed of the truck, their backs to the cab, leaning into each other, Lulu in the center. Will said they could come for dinner, and invited Alice.

"Just the kids, if that's okay with you," she said. "I could use a bit of quiet."

White Dog moved from her station at the end of the driveway and came to sit next to her on the stone stoop. The air had begun to cool. The moon rose copper beyond the colonial style mansion across the way that was due to be knocked down to make way for houses made from concrete blocks. She reached out with the tip of her finger, and the moon went out of the sky. Sitting there, she remembered the smell of Ian's skin after the rain in Mahalapye, dust rising from him the way dust rises from earth.

During her childhood, her mother had at times felt her father's presence in the house, in a creak of a door hinge, footsteps on the attic stairs, once in a light turning on in a room when no one had flipped a switch. She couldn't say whether her mother's apparitions had been in any sense real or not, but she thought Ian's presence had passed near her several times, never indoors, often in the flight of birds. Earlier today, she'd looked into the sky and seen a flock of quelea, migrating, turning in the sky almost as one bird, moving like the shadow of a cloud, and she'd felt him in the spaces between those thousands of wings, in that churning, determined, mysterious flight. She thought of the millions of migrating creatures and humans throughout the history of the world. Small boats setting sail in the Pacific Ocean with a handful of Polynesians, steadied by nothing more than wind and stars. A young man on the coast of Ireland waving from a ship to a family he'd never lay eyes on again. Her mind struck Ian again. She heard a sudden earthquake of hooves, imagined his last moments. The silhouette of his Land Rover stood in the yard. It would become Isaac's if he wished. He could learn to drive, get a decent-paying government job until he figured out what he wanted to do.

"Isaac is coming tomorrow," she said to White Dog. Her tail thumped.

What had struck her the last couple of times she'd visited the hospital was Isaac's stillness. It was not the stillness of a tree, or a mountain, or a monk. She had not seen this kind of stillness in anyone before. It was a stillness that must be utterly respected and left to itself to heal.

His belongings had been stored in a box on the porch. She'd washed his pants and shirt a couple of days before. Dirt was still ground into the knees of his trousers where he'd knelt in the garden. The sleeve of his shirt was torn. She remembered the rip in the fabric and left White Dog's side. By the light of a lamp near the sofa, she began to sew. A passage by Whitman came to her. He'd described the moon shining over a Civil War battlefield and the scene below: the clang of metal against metal, the dying horses, the woods on fire, the dead and maimed. Those who hadn't perished from musket wounds lay waiting for help for two days and nights. The moon's soft light, unlike the sun that parched their lips, had transported them beyond the hell they endured.

The pain of the world still caught her by surprise—the ignorance, the need to diminish, mock, obliterate a man. She placed Isaac's pants and mended shirt in a paper bag, along with another set of clothes and a pair of shoes and socks that Will had given her. She felt low tonight, right down to the soles of her feet. She hated knowing that Moses and Lulu would soon be hanging onto a scarecrow-man who might return to them and might not.

When she arrived at Princess Marina Hospital the next morning, Isaac was sitting up in his hospital gown, his thin legs dangling off the bed. His skin had a gray pallor, and his eyes were without sparkle. He looked as though he couldn't walk twenty feet. "I'm ready," he said.

"Have they given you breakfast?"

"The same porridge I made the last morning at your house. I left it that morning without eating, and now I have eaten it." He smiled.

She passed him the paper bag. "Your old trousers and shirt are in there, and some new clothes from my friend Will. I think you remember him. Whichever you want to wear . . . I'll be waiting for you outside."

It took him a long time. She sat on the concrete wall where relatives waited for their loved ones. An old woman in a yellow kerchief sat near her. After some time, an old man in pajamas shuffled out to join her. Although neither of them spoke, their bodies made a complete circle.

When Isaac came out, he was wearing his own clothes and Will's shoes and socks. Two nurses were with him, one on each side. In their faces, she could see their fondness for him. Wes passed him his bag of belongings and a cane, and both he and the young Motswana nurse kissed him good-bye.

When they'd turned to go inside, he said, "My shirt is mended. Did Itumeleng sew it?"

"No." She felt shy to tell him. He tottered a little on his feet. "Here, sit down," she said. "I'll trade you." She passed him food and water, and he passed her the bag the nurse had given him, along with the rest of the clothes. It felt as though he were setting out across the continent of Africa.

"I may not come until sunset."

"However long it takes."

Finally, they stood. He touched her arm and said, "You can leave me now. Thank you, Alice Mendelssohn."

He started down the road. One knee bent normally, the other was still splinted. Even in the time he'd been gone, new houses had been built and new roads carved out of the wilderness. It surprised him how much had changed. The town felt like a living organism, its feelers moving out and out, consuming bush as it went. His limp, and the cane the nurses had given him, made his footsteps sound foreign. He walked as far as he might have walked to make one circle around the hospital and stopped. He'd covered hardly any distance at all. He told himself that he had made it three times around the hospital, and if he could do that, he could make the equivalent three times again. And then again.

A donkey cart creaked past, made out of a car sliced in half, driven by a white-haired man. People walking along the road seemed to move faster than he'd remembered. The sun felt brighter, crueler. He heard loud footsteps behind him. His heart sped. He kept walking and didn't turn.

A young man passed him, carrying a sack of oranges over one shoulder, sweat darkening his shirt between his shoulder blades. A pickup truck roared by, loaded with people. Isaac's first thought was that they were being transported to prison. But when he looked again, they were laughing, some of them singing.

He stopped to catch his breath. There was no shade on the road, and he stepped off into the bush and down a path that had been scoured clean by the feet of people and goats. He found a small bit of shade under an acacia tree. He felt calm there and drank a little water from the bottle Alice had given him and reached into the pocket of his trousers for a handkerchief to mop his forehead.

He checked the front pockets and then the back, but found only a small piece of paper folded into itself. When he opened it, there was a pale, flat seed, the eighth chili pepper he'd saved for Kagiso and misplaced. He folded the seed back in the paper and replaced it carefully in his back pocket. He walked back into the sun and started again toward the Old Village.

The sun was growing higher in the sky now. Fewer people were on the road. He'd walked perhaps a quarter of the way. He walked and stopped, walked some more, and rested. He traveled to that place in himself where his mind was blank to pain. She'd put cashews and bread in the bag. He ate half a piece of bread, drank some water, and started down the road once more. First the leg that couldn't bend, then the other.

He walked another fifty yards and stopped to rest, lifting his arm to wipe his forehead on the sleeve of his shirt. His fingers touched the place Alice had mended. He pulled the sleeve out from his arm and studied the tiny stitches.

A police car came toward him with its hazard lights flashing. A long dark car followed it. Terror seized him, and his feet headed off the road into the bush. He would have crouched low if his knee had permitted it. *No one can harm you now,* Alice had told him. He didn't believe this. But he made himself stop and stand his ground, thinking he wouldn't live a flinching sort of life. He'd rather be dead. As he stood, he noticed other people had stopped to look. Cars and trucks pulled over. The police car was traveling at a sedate pace. A small Botswana flag (blue for rain, black and white for racial harmony) flew from the antenna of the dark car that followed. A uniformed driver sat in front.

Behind the driver in the backseat, he recognized Sir Seretse Khama and his wife, Lady Khama. He'd stared at their picture in the *Botswana Daily News* when he'd first arrived in the country. In the photo, they'd held scissors together to cut the ribbon at the opening of an agricultural fair. Their hands had touched, and he'd thought, Surely not. His brain said the same words again, but here they were, driving past. The sound of cheering was in his ears. He could practically touch Lady Khama's white gloved hand as she waved it out the window. He held his hand out toward her, and for a moment, a fraction of a second, their eyes met. Then she was gone.

He wished with all his heart that Nthusi could have been here. What he'd just seen—a black president sitting next to his white wife— was an even greater miracle than the Flying Wallendas.

Toward the middle of the afternoon, he saw in the far distance the large shade trees that marked the Old Village. At one time, he knew he would have felt joy. He stopped under a rag of shade and leaned against a spindly tree. All of his bread was gone and most of the water. There were still a few nuts, which he held in the palm of his hand and ate. Because his knee wouldn't let him rise again, he couldn't sit on the ground, but here he could lean and gather his strength. He thought of White Dog. And Lulu, her sturdiness, her laughter. And Moses. He recalled a lifetime ago how his young brother had made a toy car out of wire, lids of tin cans for wheels, a driver's seat out of a margarine tub, and a steering wheel with a long wire attached so he could run along, with the car in front of him.

He'd been a different Isaac then. It was one thing to heal your body. Harder to heal the invisible. He'd meant what he'd said to Alice. If he knew he'd be like this forever, he'd find a way to die. This was not life, what was inside him.

Alice had said in the hospital that no one knew how much of him would come back. He remembered before leaving South Africa, one of his professors in medical school had been researching nerve regeneration. The peripheral nervous system, he'd said, was capable of regrowth. At a wound site, after the debris of damaged tissue is cleared away, Schwann cells form clusters that secrete substances that assist axons in the formation of bridges between the two segments of a severed nerve.

Some core thing in him was still intact, he knew, capable of ghosted feeling. He could feel fear, a sign that his body wanted to live. And he felt something akin to love, for Moses and Lulu and Tshepiso, for his mother and father, for Hendrik and Hester Pretorius, for White Dog, and for Alice too. So he was not dead, he thought, only diminished by something that had severed feeling from the rest of him. He had not yet cleared away the debris. He was at the numbness stage: severed nerves without bridges. But perhaps this wasn't the end. Perhaps there would be something more.

He limped along. What was it that made life? A future, something stretching before you. Moses had built his little car in such a way that it rattled along in front of him as he steered it. He, Isaac, had no car rattling in front of him. His car was behind him.

He remembered his mother long ago telling him about the oceans on Earth. She'd said that the waters were so big, you couldn't see to the land on the other side. The waters, she'd heard, had threads that connected to the moon. When the moon was full, the tides were high. She didn't know where the water came from and went back to. It was a mystery. He remembered her face as she'd talked, lit up with something larger than herself. He'd lost the thread between himself and this mystery. Call it God, call it the tides or the moon, he couldn't feel the wonder of things. Even more than the loss of a future, this emptiness pained him beyond measure.

There was something else he felt, almost but not quite lost. By the end, he didn't care whether they took his life or not, but he wouldn't let them have the memory of the people he loved. Those people were in him still, some of them dead, most of them still alive. He remembered the crested barbet falling down the chimney, his feathers blackened with soot, rescued from the jaws of the cat. It had stood on the curtain rod, so shocked it couldn't move. He'd put it in his hand and taken it outside, and it had stood a moment before flying to the high branch of the tree where its mate waited. There were those on the branch waiting for him.

The sun had reached its peak several hours earlier and was traveling down the sky. His shoulder throbbed, and his leg, but he wanted to keep going now until he reached his destination. Another third of a kilometer, then around the corner where the store stood, then down the road a short distance and another corner, and he would see the house. He wasn't thinking now, just moving ahead in a kind of trance. He passed down the next stretch of road without seeing and came around the last corner. The first thing he noticed was the tent in the garden, standing by the flat rock where he'd gone to read the letter from his mother.

As he limped toward the house, he made out three figures on the stoop, two black heads and a furry white one between them, like a black-and white-photograph. White Dog lifted her nose. All at once, she clambered to her feet and let out a sound halfway between a cry and a howl. She was running, Lulu and Moses behind, a streak of white, paws on his chest. The children were in his arms now, laughing. And then he saw Alice come out of the house, wearing the same blue dress that had been part of a strange dream, blowing in the wind at the border.

Acknowledgments

Heartfelt thanks to my early readers, Rhonda Berg, Nicole d'Entremont, Jeanne Hayman, Kate Kennedy, Robin Lippincott, Nomakhosi Mntuyedwa, Sena Jeter Naslund, Catherine Seager, Susan Williams, and Alisa Wolf, whose honesty and encouragement have made this book what it is.

My gratefulness to Andrew Seager for introducing me to a country that will live in me forever. And to Keletso Ragabane, who welcomed me when I knew nothing.

My love and gratitude to friends who have been like family, and family treasured beyond words: Susan Allen, Edith Allison, Casey Doldissen, Kate Kennedy, Namdol Kalsang, Alan Morse, Dean Morse, Philip Morse, Louise Packness, Alan Seager, Catherine Seager, Xavier Simcock, and Elizabeth Young.

To my agent, the amazing and indefatigable Jane Gelfman; to my editor at Penguin (USA), the incomparable Kathryn Court; and to my editor at Penguin (UK), Juliet Annan, my deepest thanks.

To Carla Bolte, interior designer; Beth Caspar, copy editor; Maddie Philips, production manager; and Jim Tierney, jacket designer, this book is better and more beautiful for your abundant talents. To Tara Singh, assistant editor at Penguin, and Cathy Gleason at Gelfman Schneider Literary Agents, I thank you for your kind and knowledgeable help.

Many thanks to the staff, students, and faculty members at Spalding University's brief residency master of fine arts in writing program, a lively, vigorous, and life-affirming community of writers.

353

Thank you to Priscilla Webster and Rose Ann Walsh at the Peaks Island library for procuring so many fine books. And to the following writers whose research, artwork, and eloquence have deepened my understanding of the long-term effects of torture and of the remarkable culture of the !Kung San people: Paul Augustinus, *Botswana: A Brush with the Wild;* David Coulson and Alec Campbell, *African Rock Art;* James Denbow and Phenyo Thebe, *Culture and Customs of Botswana;* Nicholas England, *Music Among the Ju/'hoansi and Related Peoples of Namibia, Botswana and Angola;* Peter Johnson and Anthony Bannister, *Okavango;* Willemien Le Roux and Alison White, *Voices of the San;* Richard Katz, *Boiling Energy: Community Healing Among the Kalahari Kung;* Bradford Keeney, *Kalahari Bushmen Healers;* Peter Matthiessen, *The Tree Where Man Was Born;* Leanh Nguyen, "The Question of Survival: The Death of Desire and the Weight of Life"; Pippa Skotnes, *Claim to the Country: The Archive of Lucy Lloyd and Wilhelm Bleek.*

Finally, I am grateful to the community of Peaks Island and to its artists, writers, musicians, and oddballs whose presence, along with the birds and ever-changing sky and sea, has been a daily source of inspiration, joy, and nourishment.